PRAIS
INTERFACE: CONNECTIONS

5 stars **Very Pleased with This Book!**

This was an excellent read for me. I usually avoid dystopian fiction, but I'm pleased I got this one. Wonderful character growth can be seen in Emerson, Quinn, and Ana. The most striking realization was how much I related to and cared about their plight. It's obvious that the author places a premium on strong female characters, and these three are no exception. The author's worldbuilding struck me as both intricate and credible. When I finished a book, I found myself wondering about the characters long after I had put it down. The following chapter has my full attention.

5 stars **A Sci-Fi Master Class**

Interface is a master class on how to write a great sci-fi novel. It has great characters, and original story, and a powerful message about our planet and how we are treating her. Interface takes place in the beginnings of a post-apocalyptic world. It is not quite at the point of no return yet, but if the people are not careful, it could be the end of humanity. The warring sides mirror ideas that we see in our own world. This could very much be an allegory for how we operate in our own time. After you are done reading, you will come away with new ideas of what we need to do in our own world to avoid ending up in a world like the one in the book.

5 stars **Challenges Our Trust in Technological Solutions**

Interface, Book One: Connection is a compelling and thought-provoking work. Hillhouse has crafted a universe that is both interesting and entertaining, leaving readers yearning for more. If you're seeking for a book to keep you interested and stimulate your mind, pick this one up.

5 stars **Loads of Fun**

This is a good book, plain and simple. The story grabbed me very quickly and I managed to read it in one sitting at the weekend. Not often that that happens and I think that says it all, no?

5 stars **Sci-fi Grounded in Stewardship**

The writing style is easy to follow, with pros that are engaging with relatable dialogue. Main characters have a sense of heart that is seemingly absent in so many modern sci-fi novels, which was appreciated. Looking forward to future installments

5 stars **Incredible World Build!**

I greatly enjoyed this read, enough to turn around and re-read it again after finishing the first time. If you have a taste for post-apocalyptic stories with one foot planted firmly in speculative fiction and the other in your backyard, you will absolutely enjoy this. Can't wait for the next installment!

5 stars **Very Captivating!**

This book is a captivating tale of a post-apocalyptic world where hope and freedom are scarce commodities. The characters are well-developed, and the story is engrossing, with enough twists and turns to keep the reader engaged. The author skillfully explores themes of power, corruption, and the struggle for independence in a world where those in charge are not always benevolent.

5 stars **Creative!**

A creative use of today's climate crisis and projecting into the future it's aftermath. I enjoyed the science that was based on factual interpolation.

5 stars **Great Book!**

"Interface" is a fascinating and introspective read about the protagonist's fight for freedom from an evil government and the post-apocalyptic world, with well-developed and believable characters and impressive world-building. I strongly recommend it!

5 stars **A Great Adventure!**

I really loved this book! Although I'm not a big fan of dystopian novels, I'm really glad I read this one. The character development of Emerson, Quinn, and Ana is wonderful. More importantly, I found that I really empathized and cared about them. It's clear that the author is invested in strong women, and the three here are exceptional.

I love experiencing the alternative worlds of this kind of writing from the imaginations of the most creative individuals. Interface is exceptional. It ties you to the present with descriptions of life outside the city, and, for better or worse, brings you to the future with the Interface. A fascinating read. The title says, "Book One". I am ready for more.

5 stars **Modern Lit with Classical Depths**

As I began to read, I was pleased by the depths of the story-telling, character building, and thought provoking plot-lines. I glanced at the bio of the author to actually find that the name is a pen name for two people who are well read and educated. This book was definitely well put together.

5 stars **Amazing!**

This story got my attention from the first until the las page. Especially the characters are very interesting.

I am definitely gonna read it again.

5 stars **Fresh and Hopeful**

The main characters are developed and approachable. This take on a post-apocalyptic world steps way beyond your average zombie/mutant genre and goes so far as to educate the reader to environmental issues going on today and how they could play out in the not too distant future. The description and dialog are very rich and layered in a way that while painting visuals never before seen............create a familiarity that makes you want to stay.

5 stars **Great Classic Sci-Fi**

This book reminded me of great sci-fi from the past, Heinlen, Asimov and others. It posits an imaginable dystopian future resulting from known issues currently being ignored or disregarded. The science makes sense. The future makes sense. The triumph of a free thinker unencumbered by the double speak and programming reinforces my understanding that knowledge is the most important thing to hand down to our children.

It was a great read.

5 stars **Get Comfortable**

I think you're going to enjoy this book! I had a hard time putting it down, real page turner. I'd start reading and next thing I know its been 2 hours. Totally worth the lack of sleep this past week. To me, the details and descriptions were incredible. I can't wait to read the next one! I'm already recommending it to my friends.

5 stars **Powerful. Worth the Read!**

I was swept away. The descriptions of food and sex were great. This is a new author to watch. This novel should be a movie or a Netflix series. I can't wait for the next book!

5 stars **Palette Cleanser**

Lovely world building with interesting character dynamics. I greatly enjoyed this read. If you have a preference for post apoc novels you will like this installment

5 stars **Deeply Sympathetic to the Injuries to Our Planet Wrapped in a Very Cool Storyline.**

The author is a good writer. Easy to sink into the story. Reminds me of early Stephen King in his prose and ability to capture the ordinary and mix it with the dramatic.

5 stars **Thoughtful**

A well-imagined yarn of the not-too-distant future. A vision that seems sadly possible, considering the steady creep of climate change and general technological hubris. And an awful end-state for today's digital divide: the wealthy and well-connected can get "Interface" implants that let them control the world's increasingly complex technologies. The poor are left behind.

Loved the characters, both the good ones and the bad ones. Also, the ones who are not technically human. Most of all, I liked the sense of hope that pervades the story, even in its darkest moments. I'm interested to see that story play out in the next installment

5 stars **Good Read**

I highly recommend this book to anyone who enjoys a well-written and engaging story. The author has done an excellent job of creating characters that are both relatable and interesting, and the plot is full of twists and turns that keep you guessing until the very end. If you're looking for a book that you won't be able to put down, this is definitely one to check out.

5 stars **A Story About Image, Power and Truth**
If this book is not about us, the current state of our collective political will, technology that is threatening to spiral out of hand and earth that promises disaster to come, then I don't know what to tell you. Very interesting way of telling the story of the human race and it's probable ending as most think. For transparence, I got the ARC of this book.

5 stars **Great Book**
It is hopeful, realistic and instructive in its reverence for the planet.

5 stars **Grab a Tea or Coffee and Travel Through This Great Read!**
I love this book and can't wait for the next in line. This is a great read, one you will find hard to put down. I don't write spoilers so you will have to enter the journey on your own, but it will be worth every minute!

5 stars **Realistic and Instructive in its Reverence for the Planet.**
Interface: Book One: Connection is a science fiction novel that explores the potential consequences of advanced technologies and their impact on society.
The author's ability to create a believable and compelling world is fantastic. I appreciate the book's fast-paced plot, engaging characters, and thought-provoking themes.
If you enjoy science fiction and are interested in exploring the potential consequences of advanced technologies, Interface: Book One: Connection may be a book worth checking out. I really enjoyed reading this!

5 stars **Beautifully Written with a Deserving Hero.**

The cover hooked me right away, but I stayed because Emerson Lloyd, the main character, felt so real it was as if I knew him. It is a well-paced, quick read that will keep you cheering for Emerson as he finds his way in a post-apocalyptic world filled with both wonderful and terrible people. I loved the tech in the simulation used as Emerson learned to fly. It was just the right amount of sci-fi, believable but not quite realized from what we know now. And the entire book gave me memories of *Ender's Game*, which was one of my all-time favs as a kid.

Really fun read with a powerful message that sounds almost too close to home right now. Bravo. Can't wait for more books from the author.

5 stars **Great Read!**

From the first paragraph you're in; brought into a world that is both simple and complex. Varied societies have sprung up as humans have learned to adapt from the loss of advanced civilization. All depend in some way on artifacts from the past. Nature has adapted too. An intuitive read. There's no need for long-winded character introductions or verbose world descriptions. You effortlessly form a relationship with the characters as you travel through their world with them. This clever story connects its post-apocalyptic world to our present-day mistakes, making clear credible links to our possible future. A compelling story that has as much to say about us today as it does about the world you are transported to.

INTERFACE

BOOK ONE: CONNECTION

R. K. HILLHOUSE

PROLOGUE

The child was sound asleep when they arrived at Chandler's home. He tucked the boy into the spare bed and poured himself a tumbler of whiskey, then set the device to record and settled back into his most comfortable chair, one of the first he'd made, a hand-tanned elk hide seat and back stretched on a simple bowed oak frame. A few short hours before, he'd been told that his daughter and son-in-law were dead and that old friends in the Enforcers had intercepted his grandson before his adoption registration.

Even though he hadn't seen or talked to Deborah Soo in years, her death made a hole in his chest that he wouldn't dare look into for fear he might disappear. Chandler was the sort who planned things. By the time the tumbler was empty, he'd resigned himself to the new truth of things. Emerson's arrival would lead to changes he could hardly imagine. And at seventy-five, Chandler Estes realized if he wanted to remember his thoughts, he'd have to record them. Soon enough, he would need to explain the world the boy inherited. *What better time to begin?* he thought.

Chandler switched on the recorder and spoke.

◆

Nearly halfway through the twenty-first century, the decline of civilization, which had been picking up speed for the past twenty years, culminated in collapse. Few at the time realized what was happening. It was true; the revolution was not televised.

Because it was more akin to a glacier grinding across the continent, scraping up mountains as it crept, the collapse didn't look like the end until after it was over. It was like humans continuously took more and more from the pillars holding up their society, and in what seemed like one day, the whole system just fell on their heads.

And like any complex system failure, no one thing precipitated the collapse. It was a combination of creeping consequences.

Industrial/chemical farming methods had been killing the soil for a century. It was damaged to the point that crops stopped growing. Dead soil could not support life. Besides, the nutritional value of everything had been slipping away for years. If the viruses had not done it, starvation would have.

The climate of the planet began to shift in earnest in the beginning of 2000. By the time of the collapse in the 2030s, it was still shifting, more erratically than ever with no sign that ocean or air currents would ever stabilize. Between sea-level and temperature rise, life on the planet was dying off faster every day. The mega-storms that raged over the continents for most of the past fifty years began with the collapse too. Coastlines became unrecognizable; mapping was a futile act in the face of mega-storms and tidal destruction. No one lived on the oceans anymore except the most insane Outsiders, militiamen, or apocalypse survivor-types.

Strangely, a decade before The Death made everything irrelevant, a breakthrough in neural-net processing created a tool that drastically changed the power balance of all civilization. Unfortunately, it was too late to stop the collapse. That ship set sail at the beginning of the twentieth century. Thank you, John D. Rockefeller.

The breakthrough was called The Interface. It was designed to solve the problem of performing complex processes under the extreme high-gravity pressures of quantum acceleration by connecting the pilot's imagination to physical controls and bypassing all bodily functions. But in the end, the power of The Interface split the whole world into two classes: those who had The Interface and everybody else. In short, The Interface allowed humans to control machines with their minds, even when semi-conscious. Of course, after The Death, no one had any interest in interstellar transport any longer. Eating became most people's highest priority. The world was mired back in the lower levels of Maslow's hierarchy.

When Interface Industries proposed a population-wide integration of all machines with The Interface Technology, the death knell for free society sounded—but few heard it. The nails sealing the coffin of self-government were driven in by The Interface Implementation Act, passed unanimously by both houses of Congress and signed into law by the U.S. president a year later. It funded the use of Interface tech into all machines associated with government business. Ten short years later, it too covered the Earth.

This sort of bill was how the telegraph, railroads, interstate highways, telephones, high-speed Internet, and most military weapons manufacturing industries were originally funded. First, those who stood to make the most put their hand out to the government under the banner of "the public good." Laws that created money for the initial rollout become part of the accepted budget. Next, when the project needed more cash, it was always presented as "critical to the success" of the original law. And since a huge percentage of the market had adopted the technology, it was nearly impossible to shut down. Of course, legislators didn't want to shut the faucet of money they'd signed into law.

It was this way with the all of the technology rollouts of the twentieth century, and it was the hole in the government's armor against complete takeover. Once The Interface was implemented, it spread like a virus and consumed all aspects of human life. The mandates to expand and extend the law came a short two years later. It was lucrative legislation all around. In return for the votes that enabled funding, Interface Industries granted massive contracts to the representatives' home states. The pork flowed! Not to mention record contributions to their political action committees. Other wealthy nations quickly signed on for Interface implementation, and in a very short time, the company had control over most processes globally. Political ideologies became irrelevant as the new, neural implants became ubiquitous.

Within five years, the changes were unmistakable and irrevocable. Lawmakers and dictators alike abdicated their responsibilities to AI-based consensus solutions provided by Interface Technologies. Elected representatives became redundant, and the entire idea of representative government became archaic overnight because of direct, personal-choice voting. The Interface took control of every type of machine. Essentially, Interface Industries became the gatekeeper to any and all processes and professions. If you wanted to drive a car or operate a 100-story crane, you had to be certified to use The Interface. Certification involved costly training, the purchase of a renewable lease on the circuitry carried in a pocket-watchsized disk, and a neural implant. The population quickly divided into the implanted vs. the non-implanted.

Users were sponsored by their employers with Interfaces for family members, a valuable benefit. But less than 10 percent of the population was employed in the kind of jobs that could offer such tasty perks. The rest of the population quickly became non-employable, non-citizens, adding to the already overwhelming millions of disenfranchised, malnourished humans worldwide. Forgotten people. Outsiders. Dreks.

The coup d'état had been complete and bloodless. And then, in 2032, like flushing a toilet, back when water was used to move sewage, the virus arrived and killed most of the world. It made its host braindead within twenty-four hours of infection. Organ shutdown followed less than a week later. A few lucky ones escaped into the confines of The City—a sanctuary built with resources from Interface Industries, to protect the wealthiest and their minions. The City became one of a very few centers of civilization left.

The discovery of a fungi-based protein source and the invention of replication were perfected by Interface Industries after The Death.

Chemicals used to stop the weeds and the others to stop the bugs, mixed with the ones that cleaned the food in storage, were dumped into the sewage systems of the time. Wastewater found its way to the rivers and then the sea. This cocktail of poisons accumulated in people's bones, slowly attacking nervous systems, fascia, connective tissue, hormone production, and enzyme manufacturing. For many years the growing weakness appeared normal. Those who remembered a different time were dead.

By the end, most men were sterile. Most women could not carry to term. Western hegemonic medicine spent billions in the final decades to find a "cure," but it was too little, too late. When it struck, there were rumors about where the virus came from, but that's always what happens after a catastrophe, doesn't it? Blame, shame, advertise, cash in. By the time the disease burned itself out, no one cared if it was a plan or an accident. They were seeking survival and stability. Interface Industries provided both in the new design for civilization at The City.

It's always the same cycle. Except it didn't matter this time. Almost anyone who had been eating mainstream foods and living inside modern society was already sick. The citizens were lied to about it. And when they were dying, they were shocked and confused that such a thing could happen. Hadn't they done everything right?

More than 80 percent of the world was erased in ten months. Only a few people survived, and the ones that could went to The City and pounded on the gates to be let in. The corporate titans who built the wall called themselves Lords and decided who was a person and who was not.

◆ ◆ ◆

INTERFACE

PART ONE

FLYING

He was flying. There was no sound, no sensation of wind. He'd had flying dreams for as long as he could remember, even before he came to live with his grandfather. But the shuttle trip to his new home made the dream reality. The boy sat in his grandfather's lap. He'd been crying but couldn't remember why. His shoulder was sore; maybe that was why he was upset, but everything in his body felt woozy. His eyes felt blurry. The big man smelled good. His clothes were soft, and the curve of his body fit the small boy's back perfectly so that his head fit snugly under Chandler's chin.

When the shuttle rose into the air, the world crystalized. He realized, *I'm flying!* A wide grin ignited his small face. Any other thoughts or feelings were swept away at that moment.

His grandfather never told him the whole story in one piece. What he figured out was cobbled together from things the old man let slip over the years. Apparently, an old Enforcer friend came to Chandler with the news of his mother and father's death. His grandfather flew to The City, picked him up, and brought him home.

He told the old man about the flying dreams. They were always different and always the same: he was alone, flying. There was no sound, no sensation of wind. Sometimes he was naked. It was just him and the sprawling vista, a million different skies. And the feeling was indescribable. He thought of it as happy, but it was more. If the five-year-old boy had been able to articulate it, he might have used words like ecstatic or euphoric, even orgasmic. The dreams were portents, showing him his destiny. But as he grew older, he seldom remembered them, and the memory faded.

When he was five, his grandpa, Chandler Estes, became his only living relative and the center of his world. And the boy, Emerson Lloyde, with his ice-blue eyes and white-blond hair, became the center of his grandfather's. The old man was retired, which for people of his age meant he didn't work for a living anymore. For people of the boy's generation, it was meaningless. No one in The City "worked" at jobs anymore.

The Authority passed for government in The City; as far as they were concerned, the boy died with his parents. If Chandler's friend hadn't helped, Emerson would have been put into the system and paired with some other people's pod. Either that or snatched up by the Lords; that's mainly what they called themselves. Everyone else referred to them as Founders or Elites.

The boy didn't exist in The City world anymore. He lived so far outside its boundaries now, his memories had become dreams. And stories about The City could have been a fantasy novel for as much as they had to do with his new life. Grandpa had lived there too, once. A long time ago. But he came back to the homeplace, as he called it. "Long enough ago so I don't miss it anymore," he'd say. Emmer never understood what there was to miss. By the way his grandpa talked about it, The City was a prison where people were fed goo.

That was one of the few things he'd say about it.

Grandpa only spoke when he needed. He'd say, "Small talk is the noise people fill their heads with so they can't hear the truth." He didn't tolerate Emerson's six-year-old rambling. The boy was a little afraid of him, though he kept it to himself. His grandpa could stop him from talking with a look.

Chandler Estes's "silence is golden" policy was suspended in the event of a good yarn. He showed the boy how it was done, and eventually, Emmer began telling his own. It was the way they shared the time together. In the silence following Chandler's stories, Emmer absorbed as much as he could, as if the boy could tell the opportunity was a limited-time offer and he shouldn't waste a moment.

In the short decade they shared, Emmer and his grandpa lived outdoors as much or more than they lived in the house. It didn't matter what the weather was. Chandler was not an "avid woodsman" or a survivalist. He was a man who believed that he should take care of himself and others. No matter what the situation. He was happiest when demonstrating his competence to himself. Teaching it to Emmer made him feel young, even though he could tell his body was not. The fact of his looming demise didn't detract from sheer joy the act gave him. Chandler Estes, who spent much of his life casting about for purpose, was truly at peace after Emerson arrived.

Chandler sometimes wondered why many of the children he'd known, including his own daughter, were so disconnected from life and the world. A younger Chandler blamed it on electronic distractions and poor values. He avoided those sorts of debates now, not that he debated with anyone any longer. He believed a child needed constant attention until he didn't. And when that time came for Emmer, the boy would let him know, give him a signal. The fact was Emmer had become his *whole* world. He was determined to raise him right. Love snuck up on him.

At his core, Chandler was an engineer. And like every other solution he had ever crafted, he thought long and hard about how he should begin to raise a child at age seventy-five. The first thing he realized was that he might not live to see the boy grow up. Chandler reasoned, "This boy *will* become a man. He will model himself on the only other man in his life. The best I can do for him in the future is to show the boy how to be his best self."

In that way, Chandler Estes designed Emerson Lloyde's character even though his idea of a good parent diverged from his actions along the way. He lost his temper. He yelled. He failed. He tried again. That was the best he could say. But no matter how he acted, he was aware of the fact that he was molding a man, a man he might never know; he apologized quickly

3

and sincerely when he realized he was wrong. This was the course he set his ship upon, though the wind often blew him into unexplored waters.

Emmer didn't know his grandpa's plan, and, like his grandpa, he had a rebellious nature, which would present Chandler with the normal unpredictable potholes on the road to parenting. Chandler was destined to be surprised and confused. He needed to surrender repeatedly. Which was hard for anyone, but especially for an old man who'd professed to having been around the block a few times.

◆

Emerson was an unusually sensitive and respectful child. He was fascinated by the tiny world on the ground and would sit on the floor or in the grass nearby wherever Chandler was working, talking and acting out the voices of the things he imagined. This included whatever six- or eight-legged creatures stumbled into the boy's games. Though the climate change had caused many insects to vanish, others seemed to thrive in the absence of human stressors. Bees recovered quickly when pesticides were no longer used, but insects were never Chandler's favorite subject. He would step on a bug without noticing. Emerson, however, was fascinated with their alien culture and design and included them seamlessly into his play without a thought.

Chandler would pick him up by wrapping his arm around the boy's body under his arms and carry him like a sack of grain, moving him from outdoor to indoors with little thought. He made the six-year-old a vest with a handle on the back so he could simply pick him up like a suitcase.

After fixing a window on the house, he grabbed the boy's handle and hauled him in to wash up for dinner. Though he was normally an ultra-observant man, Chandler was tired, focused on the task of making dinner for the child, and he didn't see that his grandson's arm was completely covered in honeybees. They crawled over each other like a single organism repeatedly folding in on itself. There were easily a hundred.

Chandler acted allergic to venomous insects of all types. When he set the boy down on the kitchen floor and noticed them, he was surprised and backed away. Emerson was smiling, babbling something to the bees in his own private language. A few crawled on his other hand, up his neck, and across his cheek. Chandler was uncharacteristically paralyzed. There were just *too many* of them.

But Emerson was unbothered. He rocked himself to his feet, walked to the open door, and shook his hand. One of the insects, probably the queen, launched and flew a zigzag course into the woods. The others followed in a small swarm. The last bee waited near Emerson's ear as if it were thanking him. He put his finger to his neck, allowing the drone to crawl on. Emerson pointed in the direction the swarm had flown, and the last bee departed.

He watched until they were gone and said, "They were just restin', Grandpa."

◆

When he was eight, Emerson found his grandfather's worn Enforcer coat when he was rummaging around in the storage lockers at the back of the shop. He tried it on, and though it was a little baggy in the shoulders and ended up looking more like a parka with a button front and a fleece collar. Emerson was big for his age. He brought it to Chandler and asked if he could have it.

The old man didn't like the coat; too many bad memories were attached to that time. But he was always one to reenvision the uses of cast-away items and designed a super-insulated liner for the jacket. Emerson wore it whenever the temperature dropped below twenty-one Celsius. Chandler had to repair it repeatedly, but the boy would not give it up.

◆ ◆ ◆

HIDING IN PLAIN SIGHT

They were installing a new solar well pump in the late spring, which used to be a sloppy wet time, but which was now, like most of the other seasons, wildly unpredictable. The day promised to be warm and dry with a light breeze. Grandpa used a portable solar charger to top up the tractor batteries that morning. Since refined diesel was no longer sold at every corner market in the country, he distilled salvaged cooking oil into biodiesel by mixing it with benzine. Pure benzine had to be traded for. Chandler got his from a travelling merchant; ginseng root was popular, as was turmeric and mandrake, all of which he cultivated in the woods.

Emmer and he used the tractor's front hydraulics to pull the pump out of a 200-foot-deep hole. The work was tedious and required Chandler to pull a segment of pipe and wire up as far as the loader could lift, while Emmer attached a block clamp near the ground to keep it from falling back into the hole and then moving the cinch down the pipe again and repeating the whole process. The well took about ten pulls. The pipe was rusted, and the work required the boy to put his whole body into it. His clothes were streaked with mud and rust.

The tractor was old, but still nearly silent due to the pollution laws of the 2020s. The old man was thankful for the fuel-efficiency regulations of that time as well, though that was fifty years ago, and even for the time, they were too little too late and had no virtually no effect on CO_2 levels. One tank of homemade diesel lasted nearly a year.

"Yeah, Emmer. Didn't help at all 'cause you can't close the door after the horse is out of the barn."

Emmer had only seen pictures of horses; it took a moment for him to understand what the archaic saying meant.

His grandpa never slowed down. He continued, "Besides, they never went after the real polluters: big oil, transportation, the fucking military. They were never really trying to save the goddamned planet—they were just turning a quick buck. Whole shitload a good it did 'em. Money ain't worth squat now." His laugh would sometimes turn into a coughing fit that scared young Emmer. But after a rest and *hockin' a greasy goober*, as Chandler called it, he'd always get back up and finish the job.

While they worked, Grandpa told Emmer stories. Sometimes they were about history in general, and sometimes they were specifically about his history. Working outdoors—whether it was hunting, tracking or fixing the well pump—was Emmer's classroom. Through the years, his grandpa told him about the world before and now. And he tried to include every-thing that would make a difference for the boy.

He told him about his time in The City as a soldier in the Enforcers.

"I was young and impatient. Like you, only a little older. I was training with these career guys. Men and women who always wanted to be in the military. Most of them had dreams of glory, except the biggest glory most Enforcers got was by clearing the refugees away from the main gates. That was back when Outsiders still dreamed of getting in, before the way was closed."

Chandler was twenty-five when he was drafted into the Enforcer army. He wanted to be a machinist, but the fledgling Enforcer troop was shorthanded. The Lords closed the gates, having determined that the pop-ulation was sufficient to operate the society they'd designed. The people on the outside of the walls were no different from the ones inside. But in order for the new society to function properly, distinct classes had to be established, and the number of people was critical. The Lords mandated efficiency. It was controlled from the highest levels.

The people on the outside were designated non-human and forgotten. Many were related to the ones on the inside. The ensuing strife caused a crisis of enforcement both for the Insiders and the Outsiders. Being of corporate mentality, the solution was externalized. Even though there was no longer money, the Lords always acted with an eye to the bottom line. For the safety and wellbeing of all, this would be no exception. Attempting to communicate with Outsiders was considered espionage. And with warning, the accused would be modified or removed.

"And I didn't want to be there. I wanted adventure, freedom and…" He looked at Emmer, raised his eyebrows, and said, "women."

Emmer waited for the moral of the story. With Grandpa, there was always a moral. He didn't know for certain what the old goat was referring to by bringing up women in such a way. At eight, his body was still on the innocent side of puberty. But Emmer had seen pictures of women's naked bodies in the huge stores his grandfather had archived. He even had a vague recollection of his mother's round softness and the feelings joined to it. He had an *idea* of what his grandpa was saying.

"But I was stuck. My dad was a newcomer, and I had no pull with The Authority. They needed bodies, and mine was one of the many they took. I was not accustomed to being told what to do. My parents were not authoritarians."

Chandler made exceptions to his silence rule for reasonable questions. Emmer asked, "What's authoritarian mean?"

He said, "Some people think that everybody except them is stupid. They believe it's kind of them, being so smart and wise and all, to keep the rest of us stupid humans safe. They used to call themselves liberals. But those names became meaningless in the end. And they weren't the only authoritarians. There were these other folks who also thought they were smarter than everybody else. Called themselves conservatives. They believed most people were evil, nasty fuckers who would just as soon steal

9

your leg as take your life to keep themselves in power. Of course, they were just describing themselves.

"All these authoritarians believed they could tell you what to do. And for some reason, a whole lotta people let 'em do it. But our people, the people you and are I both descended from? We believe you should think for yourself. Anyway, the career Enforcers lived in an authoritarian world. It wasn't the same world I came from. So, I did and said whatever they wanted while I waited calmly for my chance to escape."

Emmer could tell a moral was coming; there was always a moral. Emerson loved his grandpa even if he hardly ever smiled. He felt safe and never fought with him. But he understood what Chandler meant when he talked about authoritarianism. He was pretty sure that was the way his grandpa treated him. Kindly, usually with some reasoning he might or might not understand, but with a punishing hand for sure. It didn't matter to him at the time. He had already learned to listen and nod when he disagreed with the old man. Emerson had experienced the violent and unforgiving nature of life. It was burned into his brain at an early age, even if he was too young to recognize what he'd seen. And like a lot of smart children, he forced himself to behave in order to survive. He willed the injustice to be invisible, and so it would remain until it was not.

Chandler said, "Never show them what's in your heart, Emerson. Show 'em what they expect to see and wait for your chance."

Emerson thought, *Yes, sir, I always do.*

They had pulled the last few meters of pipe. The well pump, just a silver capsule the size of a fat ferret with fine mesh at the bottom and a connector at the top, dangled from the chain hooked to the tractor's bucket. Chandler let it hang while he disconnected the fittings and laid the pump in the tall grass. He was talking about the connectors, mostly mumbling to himself, punctuated by yelling at Emmer for tools.

The boy let his mind drift, watching a whale-shaped cloud the size of an ocean liner inch across the hazy, late afternoon blue. His grandpa wasn't aware that he was an authoritarian. That was confusing. But Emmer was fine with it. He'd already learned the art of keeping his heart private. His grandpa loved him, yes. But as safe as he felt, Emerson knew to always be on guard. He had already learned by eight years old that the only person he could ever fully trust was himself. His mom and dad were his prime example.

Chandler stopped to look at the boy. His heart sped up a little, warming with strong emotion that spread to his neck and then his cheeks. Emmer felt his look and turned toward him. He said, "What, Grandpa?"

Chandler didn't look away. He was proud of this beautiful boy with his streaked blond hair and his mother's iron jaw. And he wasn't ashamed of his tears. He said, "Aw, nothin', boy. What do you see?"

Emmer pointed. "A whale. See? It's a big one. As big as a container ship."

Chandler's voice trembled. "I see. Yeah." But he wept even harder and had to sit in the grass, cradling his shaggy grey head in his hands. Emerson stood next to him with his small fingertips resting gently on the creases in the old man's sunburned neck, an intimate gesture for a boy. Chandler was grieving; Emerson could feel it. Not a word was ever spoken about it.

There had been no whales on Planet Earth for fifty years. The only whales or container ships the boy ever saw were in picture books that anyone from The City would call antiques.

◆ ◆ ◆

THE HUNTING TRIP

Each winter, before the first snow, Chandler and Emerson would take several weeks to hunt elk and gather roots, herbs, and bark. They would pack light, head west until they hit the Inland Sea, then turn and come back. The trip out was to take note of the changing land and the animals' current habits. The trip back would be for collecting several animals for processing and storage for the rest of the winter. While they traveled, Chandler would tell stories about hunting trips from before Emerson was born.

"Most people think that animals are dumb. Originally, that just meant they couldn't speak, but the settlers were so afraid of the outside world, they made their very existence a competition—man versus nature. And since they thought everything outside themselves was inferior, that's all they could see. But those same settlers didn't know how to survive. They shat where they slept and drank water downstream of the dead. They stole from each other and poisoned the indigenous people who understood how to be nurtured by the planet. And because they were always afraid that some wild boogeyman, a devil of their own invention, was going to come and steal back all they had stolen, they eventually came around to killing everything.

"Those 'animals?' They were far more civilized than the settlers. And the ones who created The City are the direct descendants of them."

He was silent for a few minutes and added, as he often did, "The people out west of the Inland Sea understand that." He'd get a distant look in his eyes when he spoke about the west.

Chandler led, collecting culinary and medicinal herbs, and roots and mushrooms, treasures that Emerson didn't see before they appeared in Chandler's hand. The boy followed close behind him. He would hold back branches and otherwise look out for Emerson, but he expected the boy to go where he went. They came to a stream. It was only three meters across, but the rushing water had eroded the banks, creating a deep spot. There was a submerged rock in the center. Without considering it, Chandler stepped to the rock with a single stride and then to the other side. He turned to make sure Emerson was okay. The boy stood frozen at the edge, staring at the churning water, a look of intense concentration on his face.

Chandler said, "What is it, boy?" It was getting late, and the arthritis in his knees was paining him. There had been a change in the weather, complicating the situation, distracting him further. Emerson didn't speak; he continued to stare.

Chandler lost his patience and yelled, "Goddamnit, boy, c'mon. We're losing the light. Cross the damn stream!"

Emerson didn't shift his gaze, still looking at the rushing stream. He said softly, "I can't, Grandpa." His breathing hitched.

The old man saw Emerson's suffering then and realized even though the boy may have grown into a fit, fifteen-year-old young man, inside him, the fears of a five-year-old child lived on. Chandler softened his tone and said, "I'm coming. Don't worry." He crossed back and gave his grandson a hug. "I'm sorry, son. I wasn't thinking." Emerson inhaled in his grandfather's smell; his breathing slowed. They found an easier crossing a short way downstream.

◆

As they moved through the forest, they would come across ruins of the prior civilization slouching into the dirt as the woods took the land back. Some artifacts lasted longer than others. Though the roads were mostly covered with a few inches of topsoil, only plants with shallow roots would grow there. A paved road, even one that hasn't been used in fifty years, left permanent scars on the skin of the planet.

There were still buildings, but most leaked. Chandler said, "It won't be long before water and cold combine to erase them completely. The people who thrived in this region less than 100 years ago died off faster than their cousins in the cities. Most of the rural land outside the cities was farmland. Industrial agriculture required farmers to conform to the pressures of the market. Because the market forced them to use poisons, endocrine disruptors, estrogen mimickers, which ended up in the placentas of women on distant islands, the birthrates dropped, and the cancer rates climbed.

"It was worse for these rural folk because they lived inside it. The water table, the rivers and streams, the soil, the grasses, the animals that fed on the land and all the food they produced, was loaded with these chemicals. Herbicides, insecticides, fungicides. Specially modified seeds became the only thing that could survive the natural environment." Chandler spat whenever he got onto the subject. And walking through this post-collapse landscape, the evidence was everywhere, reminding him at every turn and making him grouchier than usual.

Chandler had taken this trip every year for decades. He witnessed the pre-collapse and the post. Most of the houses that were here were gone by the time Emerson came around. He showed the boy a concealed block foundation and searched for the hand-pump well that once fed the owners of the house.

He found it in a spot that was probably once the kitchen. There was a stove that had fallen through the rotted floor so all you could see was the top when you looked down into its hole. Chandler raised and lowered the lever a few times and said, "Feels like the seals will hold. Open a bag." He pumped swiftly for a minute. Emmer pulled a collapsible bucket out of his day pack and unsnapped it so it unfolded to a waterproof, three-liter "sink." He noticed the muscles and veins standing out on his grandpa's neck and almost stopped him. He was aware of how old his grandpa was, and though the old man tried to hide it from him, he was always planning how he'd survive if Chandler died unexpectedly. The worry kept him in a near-constant state of anxiety, which he kept to himself. The water gurgled up out of the pipe and into the bag Emerson held.

Chandler took a test strip from a tube in his pack and dipped it into the water. He held the strip up and said, "Nope. Crap. I thought the aquifer would have recovered by now. Fuckers!" He spit on the ground.

Behind the house, they found an area that must have been a parking lot judging from the shape and another building that appeared to be have been a restaurant. Chandler said, "Let's check around back to see if there is a grease dumpster. I can mark our location and come back when we need to make fuel." But the building and the dumpsters had already been picked clean.

There was a red-and-white plastic cooler half buried in the mud and weeds. Emerson crouched down and pried open the lid. He called, "Hey Grandpa. Look at this!"

Inside were several books in plastic library covers in pristine condition. Emerson picked up *Edison: His Life and Inventions*, and thumbed through the pages. Chandler said, "Take what you want to carry."

Emerson closed the cooler. He said, "In case we come back this way," and smiled. He only took the book about Edison. He would read it until the pages fell out.

They left the house and continued west. Chandler explained to Emmer, "On top of folks' weakened state, the virus took most of the population in the first wave. The second, third, fourth, and fifth waves cleaned up the stragglers to the tune of seven and a half billion. That's a lot of damn zeros, boy."

Fifteen-year-old Emmer was deep in the images that his grandpa's words evoked. He asked absently, "How many zeros, Grampa?"

Chandler always stopped walking for dramatic effect when he felt a teachable moment arrive. Already riding on the wave of hormones released by puberty, Emmer found his grandfather's caricature of a HOLD EVERYTHING! moment silly. He already had an ear-to-ear grin before Chandler spoke, but he kept himself from laughing.

"You should know already. But since you obviously don't, we are going to make an illustration."

Emmer stopped smiling and said, "I guess we're camping here."

Chandler said, "Collect some sticks, twenty-five millimeters thick." He held up his thumb and first finger to illustrate the measurement.

The shadows were getting long by the time Emerson had collected the sticks. The light in the forest at that time of year was grey, cold, and somehow sharp-edged. Like it was a razor blade slicing the last tendrils of green life away for winter. As if the light participated in putting the forest to bed.

When Emmer had collected a pile ranging from half a meter to a meter long, Chandler unfolded a serrated titanium tree saw and quickly cut each of them into fifteen-centimeter lengths. When he was done, he had 100 little logs the same length laid out in a line, side by side. He took one, cut a two-millimeter-thick disk off one end, and tossed it to Emerson, who snatched it out of the air like it was a silver dollar.

Chandler pointed at the sticks and said, "Let's say each of these represents 1000 men, women, and children. I would need 100 of them to make 100,000, right? Simple. Imagine if each one was 100,000. Then they would equal a million. If each of them was one million, 100 would be 100 million. You see where this is going, right? If they were each worth 100 million, it would still take 100 of them to get to a billion. There were eight of those billions on Earth before.

"After the collapse, there were only 20 million." He pointed to the disk of wood in Emmer's hand. "Shaving this two-millimeter slice off 100 million sticks represents the number of people left. See all those other sticks there? That's all the dead people."

Emerson looked at the row of ninety-nine small logs and said, "What did you do with all the bodies?"

Chandler pushed them into a pile and used a laser ignitor to start the fire. He said, "Same thing we are going to do with these: burn 'em. It took years. And the flames lit the night sky." Emerson watched the smoke as the sparks rose, swirling into the blackness.

17

◆

The sky was featureless and grey when they left the homeplace on the morning of November twenty. It stayed that way for the first week. Grey and brooding, as though the sky got lower every day, and soon they would be carrying it on their shoulders. Grandpa liked to stop at three to set up camp before dark. Emerson was the designated fire starter; Chandler didn't let him have his lighter and instead made the boy practice using flint and steel or a friction stick and some lint he kept collected in a little tin box.

They had seen some elk sign, but it was mostly old and dried. Chandler blew on his cow call, but no bulls responded. He and the boy were eating protein bars made from mushrooms and seeds with an occasional squirrel or turkey. Game dwindled. The winter hunt used to take two weeks. Last year, they didn't see any elk for four. Chandler hoped it was cyclic but he didn't see any indication of the trend reversing. He told Emmer they might have to change to another sort of game, though he wasn't sure what. The deer were long gone. Elk populations rose following the collapse, but the animals he found got smaller as time went on. Occasionally, they would see dead ones who appeared to have a wasting sickness. Chandler spat and cursed when he discovered them. They were not being hunted out; they were just dying.

The woods had been sick, too and all these years later were only just beginning to grow back. After the pesticides began dissipating, a different kind of forest progression took over. The normal first line after scrubby brush and thick berry fields should have been conifer forests, pines and firs and the like, but what was growing in was hackberry and lotus. What Chandler's grandpa called shit trees. The oaks and maples, chestnut and black walnut, dogwood and gum trees hadn't returned. And the briars grew like steep walls of thorns in the fields where corn and soy had been over planted for generations. There, the soil was near dead. Even after fifty years of decay and buildup, the ground was still dry and crunchy beneath the tangles.

They crossed wide swaths of treeless dead zones where highways ran. But most of the land was flat and tree sparse, like walking above timber line.

The way was nearly impassable outside of the paths animals and Chandler had worn in over the years. The understory was knotted with vines and stickers. When they crested small hills, Emerson could see low mountains in the distance to the northeast behind them. But the sky remained dark, and the air was "full of moist" as Chandler called it.

Emerson saw it first. Chandler thought it was the ruin of a garage. The forest had opened up some. At least the brambles only grew where there was a break in the canopy. The trees were older here, signaling that they were in a place that was forested before the collapse. It was a four- or five-meter-tall shed with a tin roof. When they got close, they recognized the new lock on the titanium panel securing the door. The windows were shuttered. Chandler said, "Probably a trapper from The City, out here every couple days to check his snares. That's an Interface lock. Only a person with the implant can open it. Stay back. He might have an intrusion routine that sprays acid or mace. Besides, you should always respect another man's property. Walk on and leave this as we found it. No telling what sort of surveillance he has."

At the bottom of the hill, west of the shack, they stopped at a small stream to fill their bottles. The water was running quickly and appeared clear, but Chandler tested it anyway, finding it safe. They crossed the stream with one step.

Later that morning, an icy drizzle began. They heard elk bellowing several miles away and decided to move in that direction until the weather got worse. They sheltered under a rock outcropping in a cold mist. Chandler uncovered a nest of termites, and the two had an extra protein snack. The weather cleared, and they walked until Chandler said the sun was two fingers from the horizon. Emerson couldn't even see the sun. He had to trust his grandfather that it was there. He was thankful for his felted boots, the warm, waterproof jacket, fur-lined mittens, and hat. The woods were like an empty cathedral. A stick snapped underfoot and echoed in the distance. The temperature dropped, and the leaf litter became crisp.

There was no game. Emmer sat near their fire and drank bouillon. Chandler taught him how to make it in a slow cooker from whatever meat was left in the freezers. He told Emmer that the first bouillon was made by a French military chef for Napoleon in order to feed his armies as they got farther from supply lines. It sounded reasonable, but Emerson heard something in the story that made him look it up. He found out later that his grandpa's story was a fabrication. Auguste Escoffier made the first bouillon cube in the late 1800s, along with standardizing and cleaning up the modern kitchen of his day. But dehydrated meat stock was common as long ago as the 1700s and was referred to as portable soup, a staple for seamen and explorers in the eighteenth and nineteenth centuries. Emmer never mentioned the truth to Chandler.

Next morning, ice had formed on them and broke off in splinters when they stood. Grandpa never built a morning fire, so they started moving to keep warm. The air was saturated. Walking was like pushing through a frozen slurry. The forest seemingly spread out forever in all directions. Chandler bent to inspect some scat. He said, "This isn't elk. It's big, though. Too big for us."

Though the warming trend on the continent had been moving north, some northern animals were venturing south, probably for food. A few hours later, the temperature seemed to rise a little, though their breath still plumed out ahead of them like steam. A nearby branch fell, and they froze. Chandler unholstered his crossbow and nocked a short, titanium-tipped razor arrow. Something shuffled in the brush just out of sight and around the corner of an evergreen bush. Emerson held his breath. Chandler raised the bow and looked through the telescope sight.

He whispered, "Hold…"

A moose stepped out from behind a bush and reached his impossibly huge head up to pluck the last leaf off a white birch tree. His antlers spanned at least three meters and looked like an alien satellite dish. He didn't look at the old man or the boy but stepped gingerly through the tangles and slowly moved away.

"Way too big."

"I was afraid I'd piss myself, Grandpa. I didn't know animals got that big."

"He shouldn't be this far south. He was big but thin—I think they're starving."

The clouds began to lift as they neared the shore of the Inland Sea. The woods ended a few hundred meters from the edge; scrubby grass and rocks filled the space up to the drop off. The sun wavered, an orange disk in the watery sky. Emmer said, "I envisioned a beach before I came here the first time. It looks like the surf has taken more of the bank."

Chandler said, "I estimate that the land is eroding at a rate of a meter and a half a year. Don't go near it. The underpinning bank is unstable, and you don't want to find yourself in a mudslide slipping three meters down into that."

The water was high and the current fierce. Emerson looked out into the flat vastness of the sea and shivered. "You don't have to worry about that."

Chandler said, "Yeah, we oughta get you over that fear. Maybe this summer we can mess around when the creek is low. I can teach you to swim."

He had said this before. Emerson always refused.

Emerson looked out over blue-grey water. Small white caps of froth dotted the surface as far as he could see. He said, "How far do you think it goes?"

"Could be a mile, could be 100. They say pilots don't carry enough fuel to cross it. Shuttles are designed that way. The Elites in The City aren't interested in exploration. They are too busy brutalizing their people to care about what's out there."

"What do you think is out there?"

"I believe there are people like us out there. The ones who got away. People who value taking care of themselves and the ones they love and aren't obsessed with power or wealth. People who are satisfied with a full belly and a loving family around a warm fire. People who help each other and live in harmony with the bounty of the earth we were given."

Emerson said, "It sounds like a prayer."

"It is a prayer. And this is my church." He stretched his arms out and above his head and laughed, shouting, "My church welcomes everybody!"

◆ ◆ ◆

MULE

The sun never really came out. To Chandler, it felt like a sickroom, curtains drawn down to milky light. When he was a child, he'd had a fever. He remembered faces angry with fear; they were worried and kept him closed up in a dark room. As though the sunlight was somehow evil. He scoffed.

Emmer said, "What?" They had started back, and it was near noon, but it felt like dusk.

Chandler said, "Nothing. Just thinking about how wrong people can be. They used to think that keeping sick people in airless, dimly lit rooms would keep them from getting sicker. Today feels like one of those rooms. They called it a sickroom."

"Sounds like it would make me sick…" A bull elk trumpeted in the hollow ahead. The old man and the boy stopped. A cow answered. Chandler motioned him to be silent.

Chandler blew his cow call and listened. It echoed eerily. Just as Chandler was relaxing, the bull trumpeted again. "He's closer," he whispered, looking around for a natural blind.

"Over there." Emerson pointed at a thicket of hemlock surrounded by elderberry.

Chandler said, "Move slow." They both crept. The bull trumpeted again, still closer.

"It's weird. He's acting confused."

A moment later, the animal stepped out of the brush. Chandler nocked an arrow and sighted. He pulled the trigger, but something moved quickly from the shadows, and the elk bolted. The arrow caught the bull in the right flank. It flopped up and down as the animal bounded away.

Chandler said, "What the fuck was that? Shit! Never mind. We have to track that elk. He's wounded now. It's our obligation to finish him and not leave him out there to suffer."

Emerson said, "I think it was a bobcat or a lynx. It was big."

Chandler said, "I haven't seen either of those in years. Heard a bobcat a few years before you came along. Sounded like the scream of a terrified woman."

They found the place where the bull was feeding. There was blood on a branch. Chandler squatted. His knees snapped. "See this?" He picked up some dark brown droppings and pinched one between his fingers. "This is the look and texture of a fresh one. And see this little pinch at the end? If it was a cow, the scat would have a pinch at both ends. This is from a bull. It has a dimple at one end." He wiped his hand on his pants and put his mitten back on.

"C'mon, he'll be easy to follow, but it may take a while. And if we're lucky, he'll lead us to his herd, and we will have all the meat we need."

They tracked the wounded elk for the rest of the day. Emerson thought he saw movement once, but when he stopped and stared, there was nothing. Near sunset, he said, "Grandpa, shouldn't we stop and make camp? I'm hungry."

"We have to track him until we get him."

"In the dark?"

"Afraid so. There's a moon, though you'd hardly know it. It will be light enough to see. Blood is almost iridescent in moonlight. Eat some jerky. That's what we have it for. Remember to drink more water with it."

They tracked into the night. Sunset was a purple smudge at the edge of the woods. A light snow began as the last light drained away. The old man was right. It wasn't hard to see. But it was getting hard to stay awake. By midnight, Emerson was asleep on his feet, bumping into trees and tripping over roots. The snow was getting thick, and clouds obscured the moon, compounding the difficulty.

Chandler said, "As much as I hate to admit it, we need to seek cover. This storm looks like it's just getting started. You rest here and I'll track a little farther. When I get back, we'll put up the shelter." He ignited a handheld heater. It radiated a globe of heated air three meters wide for several hours per solar charge. His grandpa shuffled off.

Emerson ate a piece of jerky and drank. Remembering what Chandler said about how concentrated the protein was, he drank more, then lay down near the heater. He didn't allow himself to completely surrender to sleep. His grandfather taught him how to rest without losing consciousness. He'd told him, "Back when humans lived outdoors in harmony with the living world, everyone knew how to rest this way." He had trained himself over the years; Emerson was a natural.

As Emmer lay there, he tried to think about the gifts the day had brought but instead wondered what was on the other side of the inland ocean. He drifted in imaginings about The Interface and flying shuttles to the other side. He remembered the pictures of boats he'd seen. There were barges, paddle wheelers, sail boats, and even rowboats. *It didn't make sense that nobody ever tried to cross,* he thought. Suddenly, Emerson realized that he had to pee, desperately.

He got up and looked around. The moon was half full and high, but the cloud cover reduced the light to a milky glow. The sky was hazy with snow flurries, making the diffuse light look milky. Peeing where he or his grandfather might sit or sleep was foolish. He stepped out of the circle of warmth and was shocked by the damp cold assaulting his face. He almost pissed his pants while he walked quickly to a clump of brush and began relieving himself. The urine steamed, and he sighed. Once he'd buttoned up, he turned to go back to the bubble of warmth and took a step. The snare was near the trunk of the rhododendron he'd just peed on. Emerson was flipped up into the air so fast the blood rushed to his head, and he momentarily passed out. He dangled from a wire, slamming repeatedly into a gnarly Bodock tree. Once the world stopped spinning and he caught his breath, blood dripped onto his face. The titanium snare wire cut into his ankle, and a two-inch thorn had punctured his leg.

His globe of warmth was ten meters away. Emerson could see the aura from it shrinking. Soon, it would be out of charge. He thought of calling out for help, but if his grandpa was anywhere near the herd, yelling would spook them. So, he stayed quiet as the globe of heat got smaller and smaller. When it was a half meter wide, the canister clicked, and the glow faded.

He didn't have a watch, and there was no reason to bring his PDA on a hunting trip into the wilderness. When he had tried, his grandfather took it and told him, "Look with your own damn eyes and think with your brain, boy!" There was no way to contact Chandler anyway. He couldn't tell the time. The dawn was a thin blue rumor on the eastern edge of the woods when Chandler returned with the arrow hours later.

When he saw his grandson strung up like a slaughtered animal, he followed the snare cable, found the retractor attached to the tree, and pulled the release pin. Emmer dropped like a stone. Chandler said, "How in fuck's name did you get caught in that?" He didn't wait for an answer while inspecting Emerson's leg.

"That's a titanium cable. I don't have any way to cut it."

Emerson said, "What would the trapper do? How does he get the fox out of the trap?"

"The animal would be dead, Emerson. He'd just cut the leg off."

Emerson wasn't one to panic easily. But the concern on his grandfather's face frightened him. Chandler knew what had to be done and in what order, but he didn't want to panic the child unnecessarily. He smiled and said, "First thing we need is fire. Food next. Once the camp is established, we can go over our options." He was looking directly into Emerson's eyes, holding the boy steady with his words. It was Chandler's habit; he would hold Emerson up until the boy was able to stand on his own again.

Leaving the last handheld heater ignited, he left in search of wood. The weather felt pregnant, overdue, and fed up. A fire was burning within twenty minutes. It was still very early but, as Chandler remarked, "We're up now. Might as well have a warm drink and something to eat while we reason this out."

And later, with mugs of tea and buckwheat cereal warming them from the inside, Emmer and his grandfather talked. Chandler said, "Good news first. We have plenty of wood for heat, food, and water. Bad news is you are caught in a trap that I can't get you out of. But don't panic yet." Emmer smiled; his grandfather had everything under control. "I know where I can find the tools we need. That trapper's shack will have a cutter."

Emmer said, "How are you going to get in there? It's locked with that lock, you said it. You can't open it without the Interface!"

"Don't get all out of breath. I told you I have a plan."

"And it's a day's walk from here. I gotta stay here in the cold for—for—days?"

Chandler sat near Emerson and put his arm on the boy's shoulder. "You will be fine. I'm going to give you a pile of wood. You have provisions. And I'll leave my gun with you."

This made Emmer feel a little better. Chandler never let him fire his pistol. At least he'd have something to keep him busy if he got bored. Chandler went on, "But don't use it unless you must. We don't know who's listening."

The fifteen-year-old frowned, but he knew that after a day, his grandpa would be too far away to hear. And besides, he could always say a wolf or a bear was getting close, even though neither of them had ever seen signs of a wolf or a bear. "I'll go in the morning so we can set up the shelter in the daylight."

The next morning, Chandler unfolded the dome. It was another of his carbon nano-fiber inventions, a paper-thin structure with astounding insulating properties that weighed next to nothing and created a two-man shelter tall enough to stand in, folded into a notepad-sized package.

Over a bowl of cold porridge, a cup of chicory coffee, and some heated jerky, Chandler explained the truth to Emerson. He said, "Nothing in life is certain. We can plan all we like, but life gets in our shit like a stone in your boot. The best we can do is be prepared for what might happen and be willing to change direction if called on. Remember, flexibility is what lets a willow survive a wind storm."

Emerson nodded. He was half listening. Chandler had given this speech before.

"It shouldn't take me more than a day to get to the trapper's shack. I can be on my way back as soon as I get the proper tools. That means I should be back in no more than two days. Got it? So, what if something else gets in my way? To be safe, let's add another day. That seems fair."

Emerson said, "What? What happens after three days?"

Chandler held the boy's shoulders and looked into his eyes. "Nothing is certain. Nothing is sure. Something could happen to me. We don't know. So, if I'm not back after three days, I need you to accept that I'm not coming back."

"What? No. I'm confused."

"What do you have to do if I can't rescue you, Emerson?"

"No, I can't."

"If you don't, you will die too. I know it's terrible, but you must face the truth. If I cannot rescue you, you will have to rescue yourself."

Emerson and Chandler had encountered fur trapper's kills before. One year, when the snow came early, they discovered a tripped snare with a chewed-off rabbit's leg still in it. The blood splatters on the fresh snow were gruesome. The animal's bloody tracks, three dark holes and one red mark, disappeared into the underbrush. Emerson knew exactly what his grandfather was telling him.

Chandler opened his day sack and removed the medical kit. He said, "There is cauterizing powder and a stainless-steel wire bone saw in there. I gave you a dose of antibiotics already. Take another epi-shot after two days. If you have to amputate your foot, inject an epi local anesthetic and take two more antibiots. There's morphine in here too, but follow the dosage directions—you don't want to overdose or get so stoned you die of exposure. I made you a crutch. You are going to need it either way. Once you bandage the stump, put a fresh sock over it and seal it in a heat-shrink plastic cap. The directions are in here.

"I'd like to tell you that everything will be okay, but that would be a lie. I don't know that. But I do know that I will die before I leave you out here alone, and I wouldn't be going if there was any other way."

Emerson was numb. He had stopped hearing after Chandler said, "Rescue yourself." He stared into the fire.

A half hour later, Chandler was gone. Two hours after that, it began to snow again. The flakes got larger as the day passed and turned into a blizzard just before sunset. Emmer began to feel feverish just after dark. He used the timer in the medical kit to remind him to keep the fire stoked. He swam in and out of consciousness as the snow piled up. Near dawn, he realized he must have an infection and gave himself an epi-pen antibiot shot. When he woke up several hours later, the sun was up, and the sky was cloudless. Outside the boundary of the fire, the temperature was a bracing negative eighteen Celsius.

He used the handheld heater to melt the snow away from the dome opening and peed into a cup. He had to move around on his knees because his ankle was too swollen to support his weight. He sat on a dry stone in front of the fire and reheated some porridge from the day before.

The cat appeared on the edge of his camp. She was sitting, quite relaxed, under a snow-laden clump of sumac. Emmer tensed when he saw her and reached for the revolver. She looked like an orange tabby house cat except for her size. No housecat ever grew that large; she was at least four times the normal weight; her huge paws looked like feline snow shoes. Emerson tried to remember the pictures in *The Wild Cats of the Southeast*, a book Chandler had salvaged from an abandoned library. Bobcat, lynx, cougar… her bone structure didn't look like any of those, and a mountain lion would have eaten a house cat long before any mating. He wondered about wild cats mating with house cats. *Was that even possible?* Chandler had mentioned something about coyotes and wolves. Hybrids, he called them. Like the progeny of a horse and a donkey, Emerson had seen pictures of those. His grandpa said they were prized farm labor.

"A horse would work itself to death to please its rider. A donkey is too small for most burdens, but a mule? A mule can do twice the work of a horse, but she knows her limits. They'd say mules were stubborn, but that's just because they have self-confidence. And authoritarians have a hard time controlling free thinkers. Can't reproduce, though."

Emerson saw movement in the snow near the animal's front paws. She bent and picked up a large rabbit by its broken neck. It was flopping weakly. The boy heard his grandfather's voice, "Poor thing don't know it's dead yet," in response to a berserk turkey he'd once decapitated. The snow load was too much for the spindly sumac branches, and a bushel-sized clump of snow fell on the cat. She jumped, with the now-dead rabbit in mouth, into the clearing around Emerson's fire and dropped the limp thing next to the coals.

Emerson said, "Whoa. Good morning."

The cat flicked snow from her ear and leapt back into the brush. She paused a moment with her tail straight up and disappeared when Emerson blinked. He looked at the rabbit and called out, "Thank you."

Within twenty minutes, it was skinned and spitted, rotating over hot coals. The fragrance of roasting meat hung in the still air around the dome. By afternoon, he'd removed it from the fire and was pulling off pieces with his greasy fingers. Some sort of larger animal growled nearby. Emmer reached for the gun. Before he could snap off the safety, a vicious squabbling began on the other side of the rhododendron. Two beasts were struggling; it sounded like a fight to the death. After a loud yip, Emmer figured that they'd run away. A moment later, the cat leapt back into camp and sat licking the fur on her shoulder.

Emerson pulled off a hind leg and tossed it to the large feline, and they ate together that way until all the meat was gone, and the cat began to purr. Emerson wondered, *Do wild cats purr?* He couldn't remember, but whatever this one was, it seemed anything but wild.

◆

Chandler was halfway to the trapper's shack when the flurries became a blizzard. He found a shallow cave under a rock outcropping from the side of a small hill and rolled into it. He wished he'd had enough sun to recharge the handheld heater. But soon, snow covered the opening, and the heat from his breathing melted the inside layer, which refroze next to the snow, forming an ice wall covered outside by a thick layer of snow. But it kept the heat in. There was a smell in the cave he couldn't identify. He ignored it.

The snow kept up for hours. Chandler fell asleep. When he woke, it was still dark. He couldn't tell if it was still snowing, but he didn't want to clear the snow away in case it was. The temperature in the cave was above freezing; he could stay comfortable in there as long as the snow wall was in place. He didn't know the ice had become thick.

The next time he woke, he was sure the snow had stopped. The bright morning sun shone through the snowy plug at the cave mouth. Pushing on the snow wall told him it had turned to ice. He used his fist to punch though, but it was too thick. He needed a better angle to get a good swing, but the space was too narrow. He turned his feet against the plug, and his head was bent forward, neck against what should have been the back wall of the cave. But it was not rock. It was soft and furry. *That's what that smell is,* he thought, *a bear*! Chandler had never seen a bear in these woods. Not when he was a boy or in the intervening years. He knew there were once bears in the eastern mountains, but that was hundreds of miles away. Besides, black bears were rumored to be extinct. When he pressed his neck into the animal's yielding fat, it moaned deep in its hibernating sleep.

Chandler still didn't have the leverage he needed to break the ice. He knew if he exerted the force needed, he would probably rouse the bear. He had never dealt with a bear, woken up midwinter or otherwise. But the air in the cave was becoming humid and stuffy—they were running out of time. He had no choice. Either they would both suffocate together, or he would have to kick out the ice. He bunched his thigh muscles and stuck with both legs. Nothing. The bear groaned and stretched.

With one final effort, Chandler kicked both feet against the plug and broke through. It woke the bear as well. Chandler rolled out of the cave and tried to walk backward, facing the opening. The bear roared once, like a final complaint. The old man tripped over a log buried in the snow and fell backward. He scrambled to his feet and peered into the cave, expecting to see her at any moment. But after a minute, he heard her snoring. Between yesterday and this morning, he had lost the better part of a day.

He gauged the direction of the trapper's shack looking up at the cold, bright sun. The snow was deep, which made walking difficult. "Left my damn snowshoes to save time," he grumbled, stiff from sleeping on rocks and hungry, having left most of the provisions with Emerson. The weather caused a setback, but he still had time to get back before four days. He pushed on. At least the sun was out and warmed his face as he headed east.

In a hollow, just before the final rise to the hilltop shack, Chandler discovered the stream they'd crossed on the way west was now a rushing river.

He judged it to be at least a meter and a half deep at the middle; the current was swift, pulling away soil at the banks and churning white water over rock outcroppings. Somewhere upstream, the precipitation had to be less frozen. Strange, since the temperature should have been colder and the precipitation, frozen until spring. But whatever the reason, the river was uncrossable and appeared to be getting higher by the minute.

He tried going south since there was a possibility that the water would find flat land to spread into; the land changed so fast these days that even if he'd been making maps of it for the past ten years, they would be worthless now. Weather was getting more unpredictable. And with extreme weather came severe changes to the land. More evidence of the stupidity of the prior civilization and the blindness that came with metastasizing hubris.

After travelling south for most of the day, he admitted that the rapids had become worse and turned around. North was no better. The sun was setting, and he was faced with the terrible realization that he could not get to the shack today. If he could not get the cutter by end of the next day, the third day, he would not get to Emerson in time to save his foot.

Chandler never panicked. He learned long ago that fear shut down your cerebral cortex and rendered you unable to reason. But he was exhausted, both from the travel of the last two days and from the show he'd had to put on for Emerson's benefit. He had to keep his fear from infecting the boy. Hungry, tired, and faced with a potentially fatal deadline made calm reasoning nearly impossible. He was not used to facing the limits of his age. He'd spent the last seven years pretending he was a young parent. The fact of his eighty-five-years gnawed at his joints like the cold.

His voice echoed in the hollow. "Christ. I should be dead."

The fact that there was a hollow at all should have told him the stream's history. A river like this one was a cyclic event—it must have happened before, many times. He should have seen it. That mistake could cost his grandson's foot. His mind jumped around as doubts got the better of him.

Fuck that! he thought. Maybe an annual event created the hollow, but this raging flood wasn't normal. Or maybe it was the new normal. Since the climate began to change, weather went to hell. There were no cycles anymore. If there were, he couldn't discern the pattern. He wondered, watching the water erode the banks, inches peeling away as he watched and thought: *Maybe it took humans millennia to understand the cycles and patterns of the seasons.*

"Well. That's lost now." He sighed.

A profound wave of sadness struck him, and tears spontaneously leaked from the corners of his eyes. The arrogance of men who could not fathom the systems they erased for profit and power. The loss just—crushed him. Standing there on the uncrossable boundary of saving his grandson, Chandler Estes realized how much had been lost, and it was too much to know. At that moment, he heard a sound he never thought he'd hear again. A shuttle.

The morning of the third day was warmer and but not warm enough to melt the snow. Emerson had recharged the handheld heater, but his wood supply was dwindling. The cat made sure they were both well fed. She brought small prey twice during the day, and this morning, there was a bird, a grouse maybe, which Emerson cut up into a stew to eat with buckwheat.

He was calling the animal Cat, but she needed an actual name. Emmer named plenty of pets, but this one was different. For one thing, she wasn't his pet. She had come to him on her own. And she would stay as long or as short as she wanted. It was her choice. She was more of a friend, or a companion.

Naming her was less about choosing a good name and more about discovering who she was. He said, "Chandler is gonna call you a mule. I'm not sure if that's correct, but I don't argue with the old man. I'll just name you Mule, at least until something else comes up."

He wondered *what* she was too, but she distracted him by sitting close in front of him and looking into his face with a peculiar look. It said, "I'm trying to say something important, and you aren't listening. But that's okay. I can wait."

Emmer said, "What?" as if she could speak. But she didn't. A part of him was disappointed; another wondered if he had a fever again. He'd used the last of the antibot shots, and the cable around his ankle had cut deeper into the flesh. The surrounding skin was hot and raw. It didn't help any that he crawled a little too far yesterday, trying to keep his latrine covered. It felt like the wire was grinding on his shinbone. The pain was constant now, but he was afraid to use the morphine.

Mule reached out with her furry paw in the direction of the cooking pot of stew, breaking his reverie. Emerson said, "You want some of this? It's not done yet. But you'll get yours." He lifted the lid with a branch and stirred the bubbling pot. Mule flattened her ears and turned her back on him; the tip of her tail twitched.

"It's not my fault," he said. "I can't make time go faster." Nor would he want to. It had already been three days. Chandler had to be back today. He told the cat, "It's just the snowstorm that slowed him down, you'll see." He tried not to think about his ankle, but later, when he unwrapped it, his foot didn't look right. It was blotchy and pasty-colored. He quickly wrapped it back up.

After noon, and a large bowl of stew, he became sleepy and went inside the dome for a nap. When he woke, it was hours later, and he was soaked in sweat. He stripped off most of his clothing, but he couldn't cool off. His mouth felt like dirt. He needed water, but that required melting snow. He went outside. The fire was out. In his delirium, Emerson could barely register the gravity of the situation, but a small, distant part of his brain realized that he was freezing to death. He crawled back into the dome and dressed, hugging his knees and falling asleep. A minute later, Mule entered, curled her large, furry body around the boy, and began to purr.

Emerson woke to a sound so foreign to him that he thought it must be a dream, but it got louder until it stopped so close to the dome that he imagined it was going to eat him. Chandler came in. Emerson could barely keep his eyes open. Chandler said, "Thank God you're still alive." He unwrapped the bandages and inspected the wound.

Another man entered the dome. He was dressed in a grey jumpsuit made of synthetic cloth. He was taller than Chandler and easily forty years younger. He had a tool in his hand. Chandler moved out of the way, and the man knelt next to Emerson. He said, "This looks nasty, but I think we can save the foot. I'll need to treat it here. We shouldn't move him right away."

To Emerson, he said, "My name is Dander Mitchel. I'm a trained emergency medic. I'm going to take care of you, but this first part is going to hurt." He injected Emerson with a local anesthetic, but he didn't wait for it to take effect before slipping the open jaws of the tool under the cable. Emerson cried out; Chandler held him down by his wrists.

Mitchel pumped the tool several times, trying to hold still. On the twelfth pump, the cable clicked, and the snare fell off. He gave Emmer

35

a sedative, a MRSA antibiot shot, and spread anti-infectant salve on the open wound. He opened his medical kit and removed a plastic tool that looked like a laser thermometer. He waited a minute for the swelling to go down and the local to completely numb the area. The laser-type tool was Interface Industries' latest version of a flesh knitter.

Dander sat back and held the tool in both hands while his eyes rolled back.

Chandler recognized the look of a man accessing The Interface. Yesterday, as they flew across the river to his cabin, Chandler had told the pilot the limited version of the story of who he was and why they were out in the woods. Once there, they gathered supplies, but it was dark by the time the shuttle was packed. Over a meal of replicated burgers and fries, flavors Chandler hadn't tasted in years, they discussed fur trapping and the weather. Chandler didn't offer any other information, and the pilot didn't ask. The food was a superficial imitation. The chemical residue from its manufacture burned Chandler's tastebuds and gave him gas, but he was a guest. Guests did not refuse the hospitality of a meal. It had been weeks since Chandler had slept indoors in a warm room, and he passed out soon after.

Mitchel didn't want to wake him and let him sleep past dawn. When he did wake up, hours after sunrise, Chandler was shocked and anxious about the time. Dander assured, "I know the snare where your boy is trapped. We can be there in forty minutes."

He insisted that Chandler have a cup of real coffee. And though the old man was at the end of his composure, he agreed. The coffee was also replicated and artificial. It had been decades since Chandler had tasted actual roasted coffee, but he could tell the cup of brown liquid Dander proudly gave him wasn't "real." Still, he was polite and thankful and didn't rush his host. He would tell Emmer later, "The impatient man gives away too much information for free. Always be thankful of hospitality and never respond rudely to a gift. But never trust anyone solely on the basis of their hospitality either."

Dander Mitchel was a pilot, First Class. He'd been flying for twenty years. Chandler might have recognized him if he had been an Enforcer twenty years ago, but he didn't want to go down that road. The man had already demonstrated his relationship to the truth, and though Chandler found him lacking in the tastebud department, Dander Mitchel was the key to saving Emerson. So, he withheld anything which might have sounded like judgement. He heard Chandler, *Tell 'em what they wanna hear and look for an escape.*

And Mitchel was correct about the location of the snare. It only took thirty minutes to get there.

Dander was a certified Interface user. Aside from flying the shuttle, the healing tool that he used on Emmer was controlled by it. He obviously knew how to operate the tool. Within twenty minutes, the nasty, infected gash around Emerson's ankle was nothing but a thin scar, slightly lighter than the boy's natural skin color. The pilot said, "The MRSA antibiot will take a day to completely clear the infection, and he won't be able to walk for a week. But I can give you a lift back to your place later tonight after I check my traps."

He left after monitoring Emerson's vitals. A few minutes later, the boy began to wake. Chandler said, "Take it easy, cowboy. Doctor says stay quiet. We're going home later tonight. He's going to fly us. I'm going to try and get an elk before he returns. You rest here."

He started to leave. Emerson said, "Fly? I'm really going to get to fly?"

"Yup, I guess you are."

"Ah, Grandpa? I made a friend. Maybe she can help you hunt."

Chandler stopped and turned. "What kind of friend? You were here alone for three days, Emmer, and when we got here, you were pretty out of it, talking to yourself and all."

"Yeah—I mean, no. I was out of it, yes, but this cat, I think she might have been the one that spooked the elk. She showed up after you left. First, she fought off some other animal to protect me. Then she bought me a rabbit."

"I haven't seen a rabbit in a fair while."

Emmer pointed to a leg bone near the fire and said, "Look at that. She brought me lots of other game too. Birds."

"What kind of birds?"

"I think it was a grouse, or a guinea hen. I've only seen them in pictures."

"How do you call this—cat?"

"I never called her. She just shows up."

The cat squeezed though the dome door and stepped gingerly around Chandler. Emmer exclaimed, "Mule!"

Chandler had been on his knees, about to duck out the door. When he saw Mule, he fell back. "That's no cat. I thought by some weird twist you found a housecat. But that's—that's—an ocelot crossed with a tabby."

"She can hunt better than anything."

"Are you sure she's safe? I mean, I'll wager she weighs more than me."

Mule was crouched next to Emmer, purring. The boy was twisting a lock of fur around his finger behind her ear. After a moment, Chandler added, "She looks pretty settled in. Sure she wants to hunt with me?"

At the word *hunt*, the animal leapt to the door and sat, her tail lashing but her ears straight up. Emerson said, "I think that means yes."

"And you call this animal Mule? She probably is a mule. Hybrids like her can't reproduce." To the cat he said, "You ready, Mule? Let's go get 'em." He never had cats and seriously had no idea how they acted. Emerson had a vague memory of a hairless cat one of the Lords had riding on his shoulder at a parade in The City. But he was only five and couldn't connect the image to anything.

Chandler said, "You rest. I'll be back before Dander returns."

◆

Mule seemed to understand exactly what Chandler was saying because she slipped out of sight as soon as they left the campsite. Chandler thought she'd run off. He didn't believe much of what Emmer had told him. A cat the size of a timber wolf was hard enough to believe. But one who guarded a boy alone in the woods was beyond the pale. He blew once on his cow call trying to inspire a response. Nothing. He blew again. When he didn't hear a reply, he moved slowly though the wood, crossbow out and arrow ready. After three steps, crunching through the top layer of snow was tiring and slow. He stopped and heard hooves.

Mule had located the herd before Chandler blew his call. And from the sound of it, they were bearing down quickly. The cat fishtailed around the corner of a copse of linden trees and skidded to a stop next to Chandler, who crouched down and instinctively put his hand on the animal's back.

He said, "Stay down, Mule," and sighted in the direction the stampeding elk would come from. Two seconds later, the first bull exploded through the snow. Chandler shot him through the heart, and he dropped just as the next three elk bounded around the trees. He was able to take down another smaller cow.

The animals were strung up and skinned when Dander returned near sunset. By the time they were processed and packed in cryo-sleeves, it was late. They roasted some of the meat and ate it sitting around the fire. Dander checked Emerson's healing and proclaimed him 90 percent home.

The pilot slept in his shuttle, and Chandler stayed in the dome with Emmer. Mule snuck in around midnight but left at dawn. No one noticed. She was missing as they packed up the shuttle. Chandler strapped in. Emerson said, "What about Mule?"

He called her, and Chandler tried too, but the cat did not show herself, though Emerson was pretty sure she was nearby. Dander never saw her, which was probably her intention. After twenty minutes, they left. Mule watched the silver shuttle lift and shrink as it picked up speed. There was no way she would get inside that noisy monster; she might have been huge, but she was still a cat. After she could no longer hear it, she trotted away through the forest.

◆ ◆ ◆

THE RECRUITER

Emerson was anxious about leaving Mule behind. He didn't say anything, but Chandler could tell from the way the boy tapped his feet. He put his arm around him and said, "If she needs you, she'll find you."

Emmer said, "But it took us days to get here."

"Yes, but she's capable. She's the reason we'll have elk in the meat locker."

Emerson's attention was captured by the sound of the engines, a high-pitched whine that quickly rose beyond his hearing range. Chandler pointed out the window. As they ascended, the land below them shrank. It was like his dream. He was flying. A feeling of warmth and safety washed him. He'd been in a shuttle before; it all came back.

He blinked, and they were above a cloud. A moment later, a hole opened in the cover beneath them, and he glimpsed trees and streams. As another, lower-altitude bank of clouds obscured the ground, shreds of the formation above it tore past the window, and suddenly, they were above a cloud floor that stretched to the horizon in all directions.

Emerson said, "Wow."

Dander heard him and dipped the nose of the shuttle into the clouds just enough that wisps rolled over the windshield, giving the illusion that they were skipping across an ocean. Emerson sucked in his breath, mouth wide. The pilot laughed. Chandler grinned.

◆

After unloading and inviting Dander in for dinner, which he refused with apologies, Chandler shook the pilot's hand, and he walked toward his shuttle. As the door lifted open with a faint hiss, he turned to Emerson and said, "If you want to come to The City and learn to fly, I can introduce you."

Chandler, walking back toward the house, shouted, "He's not interested," without turning around.

Emerson betrayed no emotion. Dander came close to him and said quietly, "If you ever need my help." He gave him a small silver cube. "Just push this panel and it will send me a beacon."

To Chandler, Dander said, "Well, just the same." And he left.

When the aircraft had shrunk to the size of a crow, Chandler said, "Don't listen to him. He thinks he lives in a paradise. You don't want to be there."

Emerson went to his room. He shut the door gently and sat on the edge of his bed taking deep breaths. It took all of his strength, which was considerable, and more so impressive for an almost-sixteen-year-old, to keep from yelling and breaking something. He hadn't thought about his flying dreams for a long time; he'd forgotten how they made him feel. He remembered now. Chandler's denial of his dreams burned like a hot poker. He lay on his back and tried to calm down. His ankle throbbed and itched. He thought about Mule and whispered, "Damn old man!" He would probably never see her or any other cat again.

To distract himself, he found the book on wild cats and turned to the entry for ocelots. Mule's head looked similar, but the markings were completely wrong. Mule was a fifty-kilo orange tabby. And the biggest ocelot on record was eighteen. Emmer doubted she was a mule. But he didn't know what she was.

◆ ◆ ◆

The most snow they'd gotten in the past ten years fell in four hours on solstice night. But it melted the next day, creating a mud field and new rivers and streams through the door yard. New Year's on The City's calendar passed without event for Emerson and his grandfather. Chandler pointed out to the boy that the winter solstice was a better celebration than the first of the year, though people had rejoiced in it all the world over for centuries. The City's New Year happened five days later, though the traditional Gregorian calendar set it at ten. Chandler said, "Months should follow the moon. Twenty-eight days. Thirteen months. The planet has a built-in timekeeper up in the night sky, and, as usual, people tried to make a better one. What I want to know is, better for who?"

He mumbled something about fascists and said, "That's one of the ways the Elites control you. They take away your traditions and language, rearrange your calendar and disconnect you from the planet. It's reprehensible."

Three days later, when Emerson was taking out the compost, the big cat was sitting in the path. He exclaimed, "Mule!" The animal rubbed her head against him. From the ground to the tips of her ears, she measured a meter in height; she could almost have knocked him down. He said, "You found me." She trotted off around the side of the tool shed and returned after Emerson had finished his chores with a pair of grey hares in her mouth.

Chandler was impressed. "Damn, Mule. It's good to have you around." Emerson skinned and prepped the rabbits. Chandler cooked them. He said, "This is the way my grandad would prepare rabbit. Back when we used to find them in our garden and catch them with our bare hands; most weren't this big, though." He used rosemary and a lot of wild onion and garlic in his big cast-iron Dutch oven. "The same kind of pot we had when I was a kid. I found this one in a salvage pile." Just as the vegetables were beginning to brown, he added reconstituted mushrooms from the root cellar. He stretched the brace, tied to wooden sticks, and laid them on top to steam, covered. He boiled a pot of buckwheat groats and brought up an earthenware crock of butter from the cold storage.

Emerson watched his grandfather in silence, marveling at the spaces he had created with his hands. The house was an extension of the old man. Everything was constructed or collected, by Chandler. The cabinets and most of the furniture were made of timber he had cut and milled himself; the sawmill ran on a repurposed diesel engine he'd salvaged from a tractor trailer cab. Emerson had heard origin stories about his favorite kitchen tools: the oversized Lodge cast-iron Dutch oven, the lemon-yellow KitchenAid stand mixer that he'd rewired to run off solar, his beloved stove...

Chandler told him the story. "This stove is a 1901 Red Mountain, wood-and-coal burning, farm-style cookstove made by the Birmingham Stove and Range Company. I salvaged it some years back from a homesteader's cabin that had burned to the ground. The place was still smoldering, nothing but a bunch of broken-off black sticks standing guard like sentinels over the dead.

"When I explored what was left, I discovered the burned remains of the homesteaders and my stove. Well, they didn't need it anymore. It's a heavy piece of iron; took a makeshift crane and my tractor to pull it out of there, but this baby keeps the whole house warm."

When the rabbits were ready and they sat down to eat, Mule stood up against the door and rattled the knob, peeking in the glass. Chandler said, "You better let her in before she tears it off its hinges." She padded over and sat at the corner of the table.

He chuckled, "You think she might have done this before? She seems pretty comfortable inside for a wild animal."

Emerson knew she could jump through any window without a scratch, but he kept it to himself. Mule didn't feel trapped; that's why she seemed domesticated. He identified. She had already assessed the escape routes and felt confident that she could protect herself. Otherwise, Mule wouldn't have come inside. He filled a steel bowl for her.

After dinner, he washed the dishes and put up what was left. Mule curled up and slept next to the stove like a dog. Chandler made the observation and told him dogs were pretty rare too; they were susceptible to the virus. He said, "There aren't many left besides the wild ones," and wandered off to find a book and a comfortable place to read.

Emerson finished seasoning the pot and the bowls and put the leftovers in the cold room, ten steps below the floor of the house. Chandler didn't use heat-displacing-refrigeration day to day. There was a freezer in the root cellar, but that was only for the long term. It wasn't the sort of freezer people had in their kitchens when every house had one, back when Chandler was a child. The freezer that Emerson's grandpa build was a super-insulated box buried in the floor of the cellar. It needed some electricity but not much; one of his 200-watt solar panels kept its nickel-cobalt-aluminum battery charged. He used a thermoelectric type of cooling based on the Peltier effect: when current flowed through the conductors, heat was removed at one junction and cooling occurred. It was the same technology as the hundreds of portable plastic refrigerators made and discarded in the aught-years of the twenty-first century. Grandpa made one by cobbling together several small units into a twenty-cubic-foot freezer that maintained a constant negative twenty degrees Celsius.

Chandler built everything he needed without any frills or sugar glaze. He was a utilitarian to the core, and his tastes were simple. Not that Chandler's house wasn't comfortable. He didn't believe in austerity, but changing the surface of a thing to disguise its purpose made no sense to him. To Chandler, a wood floor should not only look like planks; they should BE planks. Honesty in materials was as important to him as honesty in speech.

Nothing in Chandler's life had a veneer on it. He claimed, "If it's ugly, then let it be ugly, goddammit, as long as it does the job." He took this advice to heart. Emerson noticed that many of his grandfather's projects were misshapen. He didn't believe in trying to cover up mistakes as long as the final product worked. And he could fix anything. He once traded the year's forage of ginseng for a case of duct tape. He said, "The world will mourn the loss of this stuff. I've saved time and lives aplenty with it."

The few things he worked to make beautiful, usually gifts for Emerson, possessed a simple utility. They taught the boy more about engineering and design than any amount of words Chandler could have said. He made the child several flying machine models, fanciful contraptions with webbed paper wings and moving flaps. The old man was a genius at resurrecting dead machines, whether they were electronic or mechanical, and could seemingly reanimate anything.

He wouldn't give Emerson many details of his life in The City, though. The best the boy got were anecdotes that contained what his grandfather liked to call Instructives. To Chandler's thinking, anything important and worth remembering had a story to it. And if he didn't know the story, he'd make one up.

By the time Emmer was eight, he realized that he could tell when his grandpa was conjuring a tale and when it was an actual truth. If he had known the term, he might have called his grandfather a bullshit artist. By the time he turned twelve, he had developed a merciless sense of irony and already embraced Chandler's desert-dry sense of humor. Once he hit his teens, he stopped pretending. If he didn't want to listen to a Chandler Instructive, he'd simply walk away. It was a clear sign that balance of power in their relationship was changing.

This was the once-comfortable, at times strained, and now fraying, relationship the two had shared for nearly a decade. The arrival of the cat signaled the beginning of a new chapter. Though Chandler had never said so, he didn't like house pets. Emerson had mice and snakes and even a couple of quail for pets at one time or another. But these creatures lived in terrariums or out in the barn. Not only did Mule invite herself in, no one could exclude the one who brought dinner. But she didn't act like a pet; she acted like a roommate. Once Chandler and Emerson went to bed, Mule elected to follow the old man.

Chandler hadn't slept with anyone in more than twenty years. Near midnight, he had to tussle with her to get his blankets back. And when he got up to pee near three, he returned to the damn animal stretched across the bed diagonally, dead to the world. He gave up trying to move the comatose cat and went to sleep in his chair by the fire, which was where Emerson found him in the morning.

"Where's Mule?" Emmer asked on his way to the kitchen.

"She slept in," he said wryly.

But she was in the kitchen when he got a bowl of cold groats and a cup of chicory, rubbing against his hip, knocking him off balance. Chandler came in and got a cup. He said, "We need to check the cistern today. It's been too long."

Water was an essential part of their infrastructure. If the cistern failed, it could mean the difference between staying and leaving. Chandler said, "Survivability is dependent on how well we design and maintain our support systems. And in the same way we need to take care of our bodies so they can serve us well, we have concentric circles or zones of support that we must maintain.

"The sign of a healthy and robust system is that it has several redundancies and can be maintained with a reasonable amount of attention. If our house is zone one, and the barn and shop are in zone two, the cistern and the compost fields are in zone three, the fruit orchard is four, and the surrounding timber is in five."

Chandler had to stop and rest twice, climbing the hill to the water tank. Emerson asked, "You okay, old man?"

"Yeah, yeah. Just tired I guess."

Emerson saw that he was out of breath. But he would never tell Chandler Estes what to do. The old man never tolerated being told he'd done anything wrong, and even if the proof was glaring and obvious, Emerson knew better than to point it out. Like the window he installed wrong-side in. Chandler swore that he'd planned to put the locks on the outside. He wouldn't hear Emerson's reasons why that was absurd. Six months later, he quietly reversed the window. When Emerson asked about it, he scoffed, but didn't elaborate. Emmer never mentioned it again. These thoughts ran through his mind, but underneath, he was afraid. For the first time in his life, his grandfather looked frail. It reminded him with a chill of how alone he would be without him.

◆ ◆ ◆

After celebrating Emerson's sixteenth birthday with an extended day of hanging out and playing chess, Emmer asked, "Grandpa, how did my parents die?"

Chandler, never one to sit idly, was fidgeting with a crazy-looking metal curiosity the size of a baseball. Emerson had no idea what it was. He'd learned long ago he should only ask one question at a time; otherwise, his grandfather would have an easy excuse to ignore the one he didn't want to answer.

"I told you."

"No, you didn't."

"Hand me that spanner."

Emerson said, "No. You never answered."

"Give me the damn wrench and I'll tell you all about it."

"Tell me first."

Emerson had the old man figured out by the time he was eight. It was time for him to know. They both knew it. Chandler looked at him, silent. The shop building creaked; the wind gusted. Emerson wondered if his grandfather was having a heart attack.

Finally, he said, "Your dad was a stupid revolutionary, and your mother loved him." He looked at the ground. "I couldn't stop her. She never listened to what I said. The young people in The City are convinced they know the secret. Any kind of rational thinking is old-fashioned. They always have their ways of saying it, but it comes down to the same thing. Youth is all that matters.

"Your parents believed in exercising their rights. But the Enforcers are trained to follow orders and can only see what they are told to see. Protests are not tolerated. Children are not anyone's children. And those rights that Deborah Soo and Marc thought they had? They were long gone before I was born."

He looked at Emerson, sixteen and almost a man, and smiled. "I guess you could say they died fighting for what they believed in. I think it was a foolish waste, but that vindication is a bitter salve on my grief."

That was all he would say on the subject. He never spoke their names again.

◆ ◆ ◆

Chandler believed a balanced diet included fish whenever possible. But Chandler didn't like fish. And by the time Emerson came along, his disdain was impossible to disguise. Still, he took responsibility for the boy, and that included his diet. Dutifully, once a season, he would go fishing in the creek, which was once called Dancer's Crick, a small trickling ribbon of clear water. Nowadays and for the past twenty years or so, the creek was more of a river. When the brown, frothy water was high in the spring, it was dangerous. Most of the rest of the year, it was 100 meters across and twenty centimeters at its deepest.

Emerson never liked water. His grandfather avoided saying he was afraid, but that's what he thought. For the first three years Chandler made him come on his fishing trips. Emerson was an obedient boy, eager to please his often-confusing grandfather, but there were lines he would not cross. He went to the creek, but he stopped six meters from the bank and refused to go a step further. He'd stand without speaking, sometimes for hours while his grandfather fished. Chandler tried to ignore him; he'd given up trying to change the boy's mind. When Emerson turned eight, Chandler finally gave in to his pleading and let him stay home.

For Chandler, fishing was an act of meditation; having the boy stand, silent, for hours in protest was counter to the spiritual benefit he sought to impart. The funny thing was Emerson loved fish. He never had to be convinced to eat whatever Chandler caught. And he ribbed his grandpa about his poorly hidden dislike whenever the opportunity presented.

That year, after Chandler left for the fall fishing, Emerson waited long enough to be sure the old man was beyond hearing distance, and he turned the music system in the main room to full volume. He was used to using the earpods that Chandler adapted to his PDA with a short-range wireless technology that hadn't been used in half a century; his grandfather was able to make any type of tech communicate with any other type. He'd never explained it, just said, "I guess I gotta knack for it. Understanding machines is just natural for me."

It was the only time Emerson could be alone at home and play the old songs at the volume they were intended. His grandfather had a huge collection of music and video from centuries past, but Emerson's favorite was the British rock-and-roll period from the mid-twentieth century. Cream's "Sunshine of Your Love" rattled the cabinet glass as Emerson washed the kitchen floor, dancing with the mop, imitating the Sorcerer's Apprentice scenes from *Fantasia*.

Chandler might have believed in an uncomplicated life, but he was always keenly aware how vulnerable the records of the past were. He maintained an archive of twentieth and twenty-first century artifacts, which included digital copies of most books, films, and TV ever made. Chandler saved the best parts of mankind for his children. When Deborah Soo and Marc were killed, that inheritance became Emerson's. The boy appreciated it more than his mother ever did.

While he spun the mop around, half expecting that it would scoot off across the rough plank floor, he heard a shuttle landing near the house. Thinking it was Dander, he rushed outside. The shuttle was black and huge—at least twice the size of the trapper's craft.

The outline of a door traced itself on the side in glowing metallic blue. The hatch opened out and hinged at the bottom, forming a staircase to the hard-packed earth of Chandler's door yard. A grinning man in a dark-green uniform descended the steps, his black, knee-high boots shining like the surface of a lake. He removed his cap, a short-billed thing with an insignia of some sort in the front, and reached his hand out to Emerson.

He sucked his teeth and said, "Hi, son. I'm Captain Eric Eggert.

Dander Mitchell told me you'd make a perfect pilot for the Enforcer's
Squad. Do you want to fly, son?"

◆

Chandler and Mule made it to The Creek before noon. He set up a
pole and lay down for a short nap in the sun. The contraption Chandler
had assembled to hold his pole had a bell attached to alert him if anything
bit. He was asleep in less than a minute.

When he woke, Mule was stretched out, leaning into him.

Chandler yawned and said, "What good are you, you lazy cat?" But
he smiled and scratched her behind an ear.

When he checked his line, the worm was gone. There was no sign
of fish. He sighed and went to his creel to get more bait. The basket was
filled with trout.

He said, "Damn, Mule. I want to fish with you more often. Emmer is
going to be pleased." He paused for a moment and finished with, "Yetch!
Fish." They were packed up and ready to leave in ten minutes. He estimated
that they'd be home before dark.

◆

Captain Eggert had a barrel chest, a goatee, and a stubble of hair on
his head. He invited Emerson into the craft and showed him to a seat. He
said, "How much do you know about The Interface, son?"

Emerson was immediately suspicious. Chandler lectured him often
regarding Enforcers' duplicitous ways. He kept it to himself, though, and
said, "Not much, sir."

In truth, Chandler had taught him a comprehensive history of The
Interface. He was not surprised by anything the captain told him, though
he acted suitably impressed. He didn't have to pretend he was excited.

The captain held up a silver capsule about the thickness of a pencil lead and two centimeters long. "This is an implant. When you begin your training, this will be surgically implanted in your neck. It doesn't hurt, though. We insert them with a syringe. But for your application and initial placement, I can loan you a temporary."

He produced a pocket watch-sized black disk attached to a ribbon. Holding it up in front of Emerson, he said, "May I?" The boy nodded.

He wrapped the ribbon around Emerson's neck so the disk was pressed against the pulse below his left ear. Emerson felt a faint electric vibration. The skin beneath it became warm.

"Feel it?" Eggert said. Emerson nodded.

Eggert produced a featureless black, ten-centimeter cube. "This is the other half of The Interface. It's calibrated to your temporary Interface. Close your eyes and relax." After a moment, Emerson's breathing slowed, and Eggert said, "Look for a glowing letter I."

Emerson saw it before Eggert mentioned it. He said, "Uh-huh. It's a capital I. It's blue."

"Reach out with your mind and change the color to red."

Emerson changed the color. He said, "This is easy," and changed it back to blue, then yellow, then orange.

Eggert said, "Uh-huh." He could see what Emerson saw.

"That's great, great. Now, turn the letter from uppercase to lowercase."

Emerson caught on quickly. He changed the single letter into an entire alphabet and made each of the letters a slightly different color ranging from red to blue. He laughed and changed all of the letters to varying sizes.

"You can change your point of view too, Emerson. Rise above the letters or arrange them into a circle. Everything on the field is changeable in four dimensions."

"Four?"

"Yes, four. Up-down, left-right, forward-back, and size. The Interface is all about what you can imagine using your mind in the field. When operating complex machinery, you will need to define multi-level menus.

The fourth dimension, scaling, gives you an almost infinite depth to arrange sub-controls."

Emerson said, "When can I try running a machine?"

"Oho! Don't let's get ahead of ourselves, cadet. You have years of training before we'd let you take control of a shuttle."

Emerson opened his eyes.

Eggert said, "And now that you've opened your eyes, I want you to find the blue letter again and change it as before, but without shutting your eyes. It may take a little bit to find it…"

Emerson was already shuffling the letters like playing cards, fanning them out and changing the color and transparency. He said, "This is incredible. It's so cool…"

"We can try the simulator as soon as you fill out the application. Don't worry about the address and identification fields. You aren't a citizen of The City yet. You don't have any of that. Just put in your name and birthdate."

Emerson worked quietly for a few minutes and said, "It asks if I know anyone who can vouch for me as a citizen? What does that mean?"

Captain Eggert ran a search and said, "Your mom and dad were citizens. And so is your grandpa, Chandler."

Surprised, Emerson said, "What? No. He said he wasn't. He said he's free."

Eggert said, "You can just list your mom. Her identification is enough to admit you without a blood test. You were recommended by Dander Mitchel. That's good enough for me."

Chandler was a citizen? It was unsettling to Emerson. He'd wait until he could talk to his grandfather before revealing any more to the captain. When the application was complete, Eggert started the simulator. "This is a beginner's simulator. As such, it runs on a preset menu of controls to save you from having to create your own. When you are trained, you will design the controls to suit your style and ability."

Emerson opened his eyes inside the simulation. It looked and felt like he was sitting at the controls of a shuttle. The room felt like a cockpit. He was strapped in with a regulation harness, a helmet and gloves. The windshield looked out on the dooryard. Beyond the hard-packed dirt, he could plainly see the shop, with a twist of smoke rising from its small chimney.

Eggert said, "The simulation is projecting the images outside the shuttle into a construct, a simulation. It will feel like you are flying even though the sensations are being fed directly to your brain through the implant. It is a perfect illusion. The best part is that if you crash, you can just start over." He clapped Emerson on the shoulder.

Emerson was hardly listening, and the captain's hand gripping his arm startled him. He looked at all the controls laid out before him and felt his heartrate climb. Querying the instruments, the ignition, precheck, and prime indicators glowed green. He slid the engine controls forward, and the craft began to whine. The frame of the shuttle vibrated and rattled. The craft slowly lifted off the ground. Emerson used his palm to turn the ship, panning to the house and the barn before facing the shop again. He increased the thrust; the whine became a rushing. Clouds of dust rose off the hard-pack, and the shuttle lifted into the sky. When Emerson read the altitude of ten kilometers, he accelerated forward and shot into the clouds.

The ground looked far away; the homeplace was grey and shabby-looking from high up. Emerson banked and flew a wide pass around zones three and four, widening out in concentric circles to give him a detailed view of zone five and the forest beyond.

He saw Chandler and Mule, striding the trail, coming down off the mountain that separated home from The Creek. The shock of seeing his grandfather returning shook Emerson, and he lost concentration. Instantly, he was back in the interview chair. The engines were off. The shuttle had not moved.

Eggert said, "I've seen all I need to, boy. You are a natural. I've never seen anyone fly so well for their first time. I don't have the authority to decide if you are accepted—that is up to my superiors—but I will put in the best word I can for you, son. I'd be proud to train you."

"I don't have to leave now, do I?" Emerson was suddenly worried that his grandfather was about to return. He knew the old man would be angry.

He hoped Eggert could hurry up and go so he didn't have to explain what he was doing in an Enforcer's shuttle.

"No, not now. First, you have to be accepted. But second, and more importantly, you have to be seventeen. Don't worry, though. I'll come back next year and pick you up." He paused and finished with, "As long as your grandfather says it's okay."

Emerson was sweating. He said, "Okay, Captain, I guess we're all done now. Thanks for coming by, and I guess I'll see you next year. Okay, that's it. I think you should go now, before my grandpa gets back. See ya. Bye..."

Eggert said, "I understand. I'll leave in stealth mode."

Emerson seemed confused. He asked, "If you can be quiet, why be noisy?"

"Uses more fuel, less efficiency, and it wears out the reactor. But these babies can be silent when the need arises." He extended his hand and said, "Be ready after your birthday, Mister Emerson Lloyde. You are going to be a pilot!"

Once he was gone, Emerson cleaned up the mop and water in the kitchen and went outside to wait. About twenty minutes later, Mule and Chandler came down the path and into the dooryard. Emerson was relieved he had dodged the bullet. Chandler carried the stuffed creel. Mule crossed the dooryard but stopped frozen, sniffing the dirt where the pads of the shuttle had rested, the earth compressed into skid-shaped depressions.

Chandler said, "What's all this?"

Emerson never lied to his grandfather. He was worried that the old man would be displeased, but he was also angry that he felt guilty for wanting to fly. His grandpa knew how important it was to him. Why was he so mean about it?

He said, "A Captain Eggert stopped by to talk." He hoped Chandler would accept his vague answer he wouldn't have to elaborate.

Chandler said, "Fuck, boy. Didn't I teach you anything? You can't trust those sum-bitches. What the fuck did he want?"

"He let me try The Interface. Told me I was a natural. Said he'd come back next year, when I'm seventeen."

Chandler yelled, "The fuck he did!"

Emerson seldom heard his grandfather raise his voice. Chandler's face was red. He dropped the pole and creel and stood, flexing his fingers, making fists and releasing them. He was trying to regain control, but he couldn't. He was afraid and exhausted. All of the years of hard work protecting his grandson were for nothing. He yelled again, "FUCK, EMERSON. What in God's name were you thinking?"

Emerson was frightened by Chandler's behavior. But his fear was replaced instantly by indignation. Without thinking, he hollered back, "I WANT TO FLY, GRANDPA. In case you haven't noticed in all these years, that's all I *ever* wanted to do. Why can't you let me be myself? Why are you making me into you? Ever think I don't want that? Ever think that maybe, just maybe, I know what's best for me?"

Chandler was not able to listen and respond. He had crested the boundary into reaction. Between his exhaustion and Emerson's mutiny, he snapped, "DON'T YOU TALK BACK TO ME, YOU FUCKING ORPHAN."

Emerson couldn't believe what he had heard. He stared at his grandfather, mouth open. Chandler tried to say something to take it back, but though his mind raced, no words would form. He stood, lips trembling, his hand extended toward Emerson, fingers still grasping. His eyes rolling back, he said, "I—I—I," and fell to his side, spasming in the dooryard dirt.

Emerson cried, "GRANDPA!" and dropped to his knees by Chandler's body, which had curled in on itself amid the dead trout, covered in fine brown soil.

"GRANDPA CHANDLER!"

◆ ◆ ◆

Emerson didn't know how he got there. He'd been asleep. The sun was setting, the temperature was falling. He'd been crying; his eyes hurt. His hands were scraped; one fingernail was broken and the others were clogged with dirt. He got up and sat against a tree. Mule rustled behind him. She pushed her head against his shoulder. He tried to remember what happened.

Running. He'd been running. Then he was crawling, digging through the underbrush. He didn't know where he was going, only that he must run, outrun it, this thing. But he couldn't. He couldn't run away from the grief. He collapsed into a feverish sleep, reliving the moment over and over: his grandfather, the only father he could remember, lips trembling, falling to his knees, hand shaking.

And his final words, echoing in the empty cavern of his dream, "DON'T YOU TALK BACK TO ME, YOU FUCKING ORPHAN."

◆ ◆

Emerson spent that night and the following morning inside the house. He wouldn't look out the window. He didn't want to acknowledge Chandler's death. He knew it was true. He just didn't want to prove it. As if by not confirming the fact, he could pretend it hadn't happened.

Mule collected up the fish, and Emerson washed, gutted, and scaled them. They were in the cold room now. He tried to read, but he kept drifting off, thinking dispassionately about how weird it would be to never talk to Chandler again. Only a day and he was already getting numb to it.

He suddenly realized that the buzzards would be here soon if they weren't already, and ran out to the dooryard. Chandler's body was still there, undisturbed. Emerson stood over him. He looked small and grey.

Dead. He had never seen a dead person before.

Emerson hadn't noticed that his hair had gone completely white. He wondered how long it had been that way. A pang pierced his heart when he realized that he could never ask again. The sheer dislocation of it, standing above the body and realizing what his death meant, caused the boy a brief vertigo. He ran to the shop, dragged back an oilcloth, and covered the body with it.

He remembered the beacon Dander gave him. Without thinking, he pressed the activator and set it on the kitchen table. Mule sat near his leg as he waited. He didn't have to wait long. The whine of the shuttle started from far away and grew louder until the craft came into view and landed near the dooryard. Dander could tell what happened before Emerson spoke.

"He got upset. He was tired. He was old, Dander. He was so *old*. I don't know how he did it. I don't know what I'm going to do." Dander didn't talk. He listened, and when Emerson was talked out, he let the boy hug him.

And after his breathing returned to normal, Dander said, "Where do you keep your shovels?"

◆

They marked Chandler's grave with a block of marble Emerson pulled out of the shop. Dander used a laser cutter to etch the stone: RIP Chandler Estes 2015-2115—Father, Grandfather.

They sat in the kitchen as the light faded and laughed at Chandler's quirks, like the backward window. Emerson nearly broke down at one point, but Dander put his hand on the boy's arm, and he found a way to recover.

Emerson said, "Chandler was an amazing guy. But he used to tell me that I was smarter and faster than he was at my age. I always thought he was just saying that. Now I'm worried that he was just trying to make me feel better."

Dander said, "When I met your grandpa, he impressed the hell out of me. One of the most intense people I ever met. Sharp as a tack and honest to his own detriment, that man was stronger than me and he was forty years older than I am. So, if he told you that you were smarter than him? I'd believe it."

Emerson grilled a few trout. They ate the fish on a bed of foraged greens with a side of buckwheat mash. The sixteen-year-old thought the pilot was making fun of him because he kept raving about the food. Emerson finally said, "You're serious, aren't you?"

Between mouthfuls, Dander said, "I don't think I've ever had a meal as vibrant as this. And I've eaten trout and microgreens before. Yes, I'm fucking serious. This is amazing."

Emerson was flattered, but he still couldn't quite believe what the pilot was saying. This was plain, basic food—dredged in sorghum flour and fried in fat. He'd done nothing special. Chandler didn't like fish no matter what was done to it, and Emerson loved it no matter what. He didn't know anything about best or worst.

Dander had eaten some fresh game in his life, which was more than most of his contemporaries could claim, but the majority of his sustenance came from the fungus-based protein source processed through a replicator. The taste of all replicated food was brain-simulated flavor. Otherwise, it would be pretty cardboard and wallpaper paste. Problem was nobody remembered what real food tasted like anymore, and the further the replicator's calibration got from proper flavor profiles, the more synthetic and artificial the taste became.

With no one to check, no one could tell.

Of course, Emerson had no knowledge of this. When he finally tasted replicator food, he nearly vomited.

They slept in the fireplace room. Emerson didn't feel right letting a stranger sleep in his grandpa's bed. Neither could he bring himself to sleep in it. Before he turned over to sleep, Dander said, "Tomorrow, you can pack up what's most important, and I'll bring you back to The City to live with Roxanne and me until you come of age."

Emerson sat up. "No," he said flatly. "There is too much to do here. I can't leave just before winter. This house doesn't run itself. If I am going to leave, it has to be planned."

"I think it would be best if you…"

"That's a problem for you folk in The City, Dander. You put a lot of value on what you think. I'm not ready. I'll go when I am."

And that was the last he'd say about it. He could almost see Chandler smiling.

◆

Dander left mid-morning. He told Emerson that he would check up on him. "You can use that beacon anytime, and I'll be here as fast as possible."

Mule came out of the shadows after the shuttle's whine faded.

Emerson said, "We got some work to do if we want to be ready for winter."

They set right to it. But the weather had other plans, as Chandler was prone to say. The first snow began at midnight and didn't stop for two days. The temperature dropped to zero and stayed there for weeks. What began as a difficult preparation became nearly impossible. Emerson spent the next two weeks indoors, only going outside to empty trash and compost, slogging through several meters of snow and drift. Mule found no game. And no matter how much wood they burned, the temperature in the house never got above fifteen degrees Celsius.

Emerson spent much of his time staring into the hot coals trying to remember everything that his grandfather had told him. He began writing things down in a leather-bound notebook that Chandler had stashed on a bookshelf. But after two or three pages, he lost interest. He didn't look in the back of the journal, where Chandler had left him a note sealed in a blue envelope. He wouldn't see that letter for twenty-five years.

◆ ◆ ◆

END OF PART ONE

INTERFACE

PART TWO

THE CITY

He was flying. There was no sound, no sensation of wind. He felt naked, just his body and the sprawling vista, a million different skies. There was no way he could describe it to Sally. No matter what combination of words he assembled, she always smiled politely and said, "That's just fascinating, Emerson," in her breathy soprano. And then she would go on to say how she couldn't ever imagine flying one of those shuttles. She'd say, "It's hard enough for me to run the ovens."

They'd met at an orientation meeting for Interface users when Emerson had just arrived. She was attracted to his athletic build and boyish features. He was impressed that she wanted to spend time with him. They fell into an easy relationship that evolved into a serious relationship. Emerson, having little experience with people, let alone female people, treated it like most things. He didn't resist, but he didn't really give it much thought.

Sally made ceramic plates. She didn't actually make them; a machine made them. Sally ran the machines. Ten of them, at once. Like most of the Free Citizens of The City, Sally Mink was implanted. Every aspect of her life ran through The Interface. She didn't have a very well-developed imagination. To her, having a neural connection to the world was what set her apart from the Dreks outside the wall. She'd once told Emerson,

"Those 'unconnected' people. I can't hardly think of them as people at all." As if the unconnected were uncivilized, stupid, beasts.

Emerson understood the stereotype. He also understood that the "beasts" she was thinking of were far more "civilized" than she. Emerson learned early in their relationship that Sally couldn't imagine his greatest love. Flying didn't matter to her. She was content with spending her time absorbed in multiplayer virtual games, an added privilege of the implanted, or having sex. That part pleased Emerson, but in the six months since they had been living together, the narrow routine was getting boring. Eat, work, sex, sleep... He began staying away at the outposts longer and longer. At the ten-month mark in their relationship, he applied for an extended license to fly bigger ships. His skill level was there. It was just a matter of grinding through the paperwork. He was already the youngest pilot at twenty-one.

In the intervening years since he'd arrived, Emerson had developed into a thin man of medium height with large biceps and hairy legs and arms. He had fine, blond, almost white hair. But none grew on his face or chest. His eyes were still ice blue. His hair remained unruly at any length.

After he and Sally had been together a year, he began flying longer missions. This gave him cover to stay away even longer on camping trips. At first, he asked her if she wanted to go; she declined with skepticism.

She said, "Ew! How can you sleep on the ground with all those 'animals?'"

He didn't miss her company. She was just a warm body most of the time, plugged into some other reality. He'd begun to question why he lived with her. He didn't think it was fair to either of them, but neither of them articulated any complaints. Their relationship was comfortable and convenient, like most in The City.

The first time he flew back to the homeplace, he had not actually made the decision to go. The Shuttle Corps were responsible for supplies and personnel transfer between The City and the 300 outposts surrounding its center. He told Sally, "I'm a glorified delivery boy." At least he wasn't an infantry grunt. All those guys did was clear the gates and clean up the roads.

Being certified to fly longer distances granted Emerson several priv-
ileges, the greatest of which was free time. Nobody scrutinized his hours
as long as schedules were met and expectations were exceeded. Emerson
found himself in a situation perfectly crafted for his talents. Showing his
superior officers that his concerns were theirs made him into a black hole
of sorts—he didn't reflect any light, so to The Authority he was invisible.
He thought, *look for your escape…*

The certification unlocked the final levels of The Interface. With it,
he was able to use his imagination to fabricate controls with the finest
tolerances. And the ability to modify the look and feel of his inner control center was nothing short of astounding, even for Emerson, who was
practiced at making the most out of a design's limitations.

His initial experiments were with the shuttle's navigational systems.
The first control sets were imitations of Emerson's idea of a manual con-
troller. He imagined the inside of a traditional pre-collapse cockpit with
its levers and gauges, switches and knobs and a steering wheel he saw once
in a book about B-52 bombers.

After the certification unlocked an unlimited imaginative capability,
he did away with all controls and connected the data reading directly to
number displays when he thought of them. There was no longer any need
to consider proximity to his control sets. When he needed something, it was
available. The thought to turn something on or off or to raise and lower power
was now simply a matter of thinking specifically about the designation. He
didn't even think of the control set as levels or labels anymore. Up became
a feeling. Speed an urge. Deceleration was a tightening in his back muscles,
and turns were simply the idea to lean. And because The Interface was a form
of AI, Emerson's relationship grew deeper and more interconnected as time
passed. The Interface improved itself automatically; it worked with him.

After a few weeks, he stopped making the physical movements that
automatically accompanied these ideas. At that point, the control of the
shuttle was reduced to subtle shifts in thought. He stopped thinking about
what he wanted and became the ship. The control sets could be frozen

as well, like a mental hold button, so that he could pause and move his attention to other matters, other systems inside or outside the ship.

The certification gave any pilot these capabilities, but from talking to the instructor and others in his training unit, Emerson realized that he used these abilities more completely. He was more competent than his teacher, but he kept the fact to himself.

He remembered when he was seventeen, getting his implant before he went to the first training class. Emerson had spent the past year, in sometimes agitated anticipation, waiting for this moment when he could begin working with The Interface.

But sitting in the waiting room, he realized that all of his grandfather's warnings were about to become his reality. The power of the implant went both ways. He got the ability to control things with his mind; they got control of his mind. He had never really thought about giving up his sovereignty before that moment. The thought paralyzed him. And when he was called into to the examination room, the doctor greeted him warmly. She had an odd habit of spitting juice into a cup. She tried to hide her red-stained teeth, but Emerson saw.

When she touched his arm and spoke, he instantly felt more relaxed. He actually sighed. She said, "Hello, Emerson Lloyde. It is *so* good to see you again."

He looked at her face, the faded traces of a tattoo, the circle quartered by a cross, on her dark skin. Emerson said, "Again? I don't think we've ever met."

While she spoke, she loaded an implant syringe and swabbed his neck with a cold alcohol swab, a few inches below the left ear. "Oh, I met you when you were just a little white-haired boy. I gave you a sedative before your grandpa came to pick you up. I knew Chandler. I knew your grandmother, Ciara."

Emerson was captivated by the Doctor's sonorous voice. He didn't notice that she was implanting him until it was over and she was putting her tools away. She put a patch over the tiny incision and said, "You can take that off in a day. It's waterproof. You can shower. As a matter of fact, in your case, I encourage it." She laughed.

Emerson said, "You knew my grandmother?"

"Let's just say I promised to look out for you. Your implant is locked. That should protect you while you're here." She closed a drawer in a glass-fronted cabinet and called for the next patient.

Emerson was mute. He didn't know what she meant. The doctor said, "Take care of yourself, Emerson, and good luck."

He hadn't thought about it much back then, but the mystery of it nagged him. Someone that knew his grandmother lived in The City.

◆

He was returning from a supply run to the far southeast outpost number 240, not thinking of any destination in particular. He was supposed to be going home, but he'd already decided not to and was flying low, which was his habit when he had nowhere to be. He claimed it helped him think. A furred animal snagged his attention, and he replayed the image. It was just a white chuck. He heard Chandler's voice add, "Rare but not unheard of in this region," and smiled. Emerson's mind wandered.

◆ ◆ ◆

THE HOMEPLACE

He'd spent his last winter and the beginning of spring at the homeplace putting it in order. He cleaned and organized the shop, cleared out the last of his frozen food stores, and disconnected the freezer. The water lines were purged and closed down from the cistern; the overflow gates were opened. All solar panels were removed and crated. The windows shuttered, fireplace cleaned, and the kitchen sanitized and organized.

Chandler had several Interface-type controlled devices built into the house. He explained to Emerson that the true Interface was geographically limited to proprietary devices. In order to create local ones, he had to build a wireless server for the house. The locks were central to his design. He'd taken great pride in them and repeated the story of how they operated several times. "The Interface is a neural connection. Plain and simple. Nothing more. If a man knows the wiring, a man can do the same thing as their fancy-shmancy Interface cube." He made all of the locks in the house respond to his and Emerson's brainwave patterns. He maintained, "This is all yours anyway, Emerson. It ought to be your brain that unlocks it after I'm gone."

During that last season, when the spring leaves emerged, and the overall tone of the forest shifted from grey to green, Mule arrived with an offering of rabbits. As Emerson kneeled down to accept, three orange-and-white kittens appeared from behind their mother and entered the house parading with the same tail-up bravado as Mule did her first time in the house. The big cat made her bed next to the stove while her kittens nursed. They were obviously new, their noses pushed in and eyes still crystal blue. But they were big, already the size of full-grown housecats.

Emerson remembered saying, "I told you she wasn't a mule, Grandpa. But you couldn't hear me." He talked to Chandler often because he felt him nearby. He was so used to it that until Mule arrived, he hardly noticed talking to himself. One of the kits jumped up onto Emerson's lap and purred herself to sleep. They sat that way together for the rest of the evening. In the last days, while Emerson packed things to bring, Mule and her kits followed him everywhere. And when Eggert arrived to bring him to his new life, Mule showed herself one last time, standing alone at the edge of the zone four tree line. Her tail twitched twice as the big shuttle began to lift. She was gone before it had turned toward The City.

♦

Back in the present and without thinking, Emerson changed the coordinates and veered sharply left. Even though he was still an hour away, he believed he could already see the change in the landscape. He was going home. The thought filled him with a strange lightness that he hadn't felt for a long time; he must have been very young when he originally felt it because there were no words to accompany the feeling. Chandler could have told him he was feeling hope.

Scrub grass and brambles had grown up in the dooryard. The heat from his pressure field scorched a wide arc around the shuttle, leaving the greasy odor of singed grass. Emerson called out to Mule as he strode to the house. The locks would need a power source in order to function. He plugged a diagnostic power pack onto the trim where the front door should have been and called up his general panel. The notification log showed nothing major in the years since he'd been there. The house unlocked with a click.

The systems powered up; the house came alive. Windows appeared from behind shutters, doors and vents opened, and the house air recirculation system took a purging breath. Before Emerson hooked up a portable wind generator and climbed the hill to restart the cistern, he gave in to the urge to wander around the house, fingering items and remembering his time there, thinking about his grandfather. It suddenly seemed important to understand why Chandler was so dead set against him flying.

He built a fire by muscle memory and sat in his grandfather's chair. He felt close to the old man in this place, as though his spirit was crafted into every plank and fitting. His grandfather *was* the house. When he was a boy, he thought Chandler was afraid of The City. And thinking about it that way served him as a child. He could understand fear, even if his desire made him believe that he was strong enough to bear it, whatever that fear was.

But when he got into his teens, Emerson realized that nothing frightened Chandler Estes. The old man would dig in rather than turn away from a charging bear. It felt to Emerson that his grandfather didn't understand his love of flight. But that wasn't true either. Chandler went out of his way to find him books on flying. Chandler made him carved flying contraptions with moveable flaps and doors that opened and closed. Emerson went to his room and found the wooden box that contained his most treasured toys. When he picked it up, something heavy slid to one side. Emerson pulled back the latches. Inside were several of Chandler's handmade machines. But in addition, there was a matte-black metal cube, ten centimeters square: an Interface. Emerson sent the open commands. He instantly found himself back in the fireplace room. The fire was much larger, and there was a smell of candle wax, roasting ramps, and potatoes.

Looking over to his grandfather's chair confirmed his suspicion.

Chandler sat there grinning. He said, "I knew you'd go looking for that toy. You played with that thing every day for years."

Emerson said, "It's good to see you, Grandpa," and they hugged. It felt real. It was real. Yes, Chandler was many years dead. The routine he created for The Interface was a direct neural communication. Emerson was trained, but he'd known the central fact when he was a boy: everything we experienced was happening inside our brains. Our bodies were just energy converters, input devices. The Interface overlayed our physical nervous system and took the place of reality.

He didn't waste any time being awed by the technology. Since moving to The City, he had been in countless simulations that used similar routines. Though he'd never gone, there was supposedly a club where people swapped bodies with strangers of different sexes.

He asked, "How did you know I'd come back?"

"This is your home. That's not the question you want to ask, though, is it?"

Emerson was suddenly overcome with emotion. Could he ask this simulation all the things he never got to ask?

"Well, of course you can, foolish boy. Why would I make such a routine if it wasn't to offer you answers?"

"Okay, I have one. Since you obviously knew I would go to The City and get the implant and learn to fly and fulfill my heart's desires, why were you always trying to keep me from going?" Emerson was crying.

"I wasn't keeping you from going, son. I was teaching you to use your mind, to think. You made it clear in the first twenty-four hours with me, you knew what you wanted in life and that you'd get it whether I helped or not. But life is a convoluted maze, and nothing is as simple as a child sees it. I had to show you many things before you would be able to see through the illusions The City spins. I taught you to never give yourself away. To be suspicious. To always understand what people really want and to know how to make it look like you are giving it to them. Because when they make the bet that you are valuable, they will do anything to make sure they collect.

"I knew you wanted to be a flyer the day I met you. And I knew you would have to go to The City to realize that dream. But The City only wants to tear you down and use you up. To be who you were meant to be, you needed to be strong enough to stay true to yourself.

"Just remember that you are your own. No matter what they think your value is to them. And they can't take anything you don't want to give them. You are special, Emerson. Don't forget it."

Emerson broke down and cried. The grief came rushing back on him like waves of rain, drenching him, knocking the wind out of him. The simulation ended.

◆

Before closing up and leaving the next morning, Emerson walked out to Chandler's grave and sat on a stump listening to the wind. He had Chandler's Interface cube in his pocket, but he didn't want to see a neural simulation. No matter how lovingly created it was, it was not Chandler. Emerson didn't want to speak. He sat quietly for a while. Then he locked up the house and flew back to The City.

◆ ◆ ◆

The trip back was the first time Emerson had flown that route since Captain Eggert picked him up. Chandler would have reminded him that he was born in The City and he was officially coming home, but knowing that didn't help. When he had first come this way, Eggert was playing tour guide, helping him feel less nervous.

When they came up on the fifty-kilometer mark, the captain had said, "Take a look out the port side, Emmer. That's the beginning of The City down there." He sucked his teeth.

Emerson said, "Which way is port? And my name is Emerson Lloyde. Don't call me Emmer. My grandpa called me that."

The balding pilot said, "Left. Sorry. Do you see the houses starting to pop up? That was the wealthy district around the original city."

"What was the original name?"

"Ah, nobody remembers. I don't anyway. But you can see how many of them there are, probably millions. All empty and slowly rotting into the dirt."

Eggert took the shuttle down lower and said, pointing, "There were little towns all over the place, servicing these huge wasteful houses. As we get closer, you can see the buildings change. The structures get smaller, closer together."

Eventually, the districts became scored with tiny streets, cluttered with garbage. Emerson thought he saw a figure running for cover, but when he looked again, there was no other movement.

Eggert continued, "We have to be careful around the skin of The City. The Dreks that live out here are hostile. Some say they resorted to cannibalism when the Lords closed the wall. They are always trying to bring down our shuttles."

Eggert gained altitude and established radio contact with the guard wall. "Wall. This is shuttle 35002, requesting flyover."

Emerson didn't hear the reply. The pilot said, "Rodger dodger, wall." And to Emerson he said, "Come up here and sit with me. Emerson." When he was strapped in the copilot's seat, Eggert said, "This is The City inside the wall."

An ordered grid of streets and slate-colored buildings rolled out before them. The avenues were arranged in a semicircle; there were no animals or mechanized transports. It was clean and orderly and bustling with activity. Brightly dressed people moved purposefully. The pilot lifted the nose up and revealed the mountains ahead. A wide blue lake stretched inside and beyond the western edge of the village. The wall extended 100 meters into it at the south and north border. The vast middle was clear open water. An uncontrollable shiver crept up Emerson's spine. The water was strangely attractive and repulsive at once. Eggert said, "That's the reservoir."

Emerson asked, "It's open in the middle. What stops people from just coming in?"

"You'd have to be a fool to try and cross that water. Everyone knows that."

They turned north from the center of The City and crossed another inner wall carved into the side of the mountain. Emerson was glad to be flying away from water.

Eggert said, "This is where the Founders live. Beyond this are rock cliffs. On the other side of this range is a deep canyon. And there's nothing on the far side of that except the north outposts, and you'll visit them soon enough."

Emerson had a million questions, but Chandler had trained him to wait quietly. The old man would wink and say, "All answers come with time." Emerson yearned to know about trade, electricity, machinery, communication, and people. Where would he meet people? The idea of being in a room with more than one other person was exhilarating and terrifying at once. The feeling was seductive.

These memories felt like yesterday, as though the five intervening years were just a dream.

◆ ◆

About halfway to The City from Chandler's homeplace, Emerson flew over Carter's Farm. Old Mister Carter grew sorghum and corn in spirals, using hand-operated machinery. The man was a mechanical savant who designed wind-aided walking machines that looked like giant horses. His grandfather told him, "Most farmers had to be geniuses in order to survive. The markets ruled everything as though it was alright to squeeze good men to death for us to eat. That's the capitalist system. Damn thing ran on blood."

Chandler would make a biannual pilgrimage to Carter's with a

75

nano-carbon-fiber cart to carry grain. He'd gotten his original buckwheat seed from the farmer. The place looked deserted now, no smoke from the stove pipe. Carter was at least a decade older than Chandler. He probably died years before. Emerson wanted to investigate, but didn't.

Twenty minutes later, an alarm notified Emerson that his shuttle crossed The City's boundary. He radioed in. Below, the strip malls and small shops appeared. He scanned the horizon and switched on the autopilot. Freed from the wheel for a few moments, he took a long drink of water from a canteen clamped next to his seat and looked down at one of the overgrown streets. He saw movement next to a brick house. A flash from a piece of glass or a faceplate.

The catapult operator was deadly accurate. The bottle, most likely filled with potato vodka or some other highly volatile distillation, smashed on the windshield and burst into flames. It startled him more than anything. The ship's skin was designed for suborbital flight; a little alcohol fire and smashed glass wouldn't even leave a mark. He snapped off the autopilot and swooped down to the house where he'd seen the flash, hovering, and turned slowly for a moment. But there was no further movement. He left on his original route.

◆ ◆ ◆

THE RED PALACE

After he landed and his shuttle was checked in, he called Sally. The call went directly to voicemail. Emerson figured she was plugged into some multiplayer reality and went to find some dinner on his own.

As he was waiting on line at a replication station, the woman behind him said, "Don't you get tired of this swill they keep trying to feed you?"

Emerson turned to face her; she was about six inches shorter than him. Her striking black hair and leather jacket marked her as an Elite. Some of them wanted to be called Lords, but most people referred to them as the Founders. She was young, obviously somebody's daughter.

He said, "This isn't food."

She looked at him intently and said, "No, it's not. I don't recognize you. What's your pod?"

"I don't have a pod; I grew up outside the walls."

The man behind her said, "Can we go around? I need to get back to my machine."

Emerson and the woman stepped out of the queue. She said, "Let's go get some real food. I'm Elli Rattlesnake, but my friends call me Quinn." She strode off, the heels of her boots clacking on the cobbles. Emerson followed.

Quinn was thin. Her arms, legs and even her neck were unusually

77

long, and she wore a large red stone hung on a fine silver chain around her neck. She had straight, black, shoulder-length hair and violet eyes. She wore a silver ring in her right ear and a stud with jewel of some sort on the side of her thin patrician nose. Her teeth were bright white, unlike many of The City's residents. In a city of citizens surviving on replicator food, Elli Rattlesnake ate well.

He had learned that most people lived in arranged family pods in which the parents were just the primary registrants. The City regulated who could be together by license. The registration in turn dictated people's relationships. Detailed records were kept on what pod they were registered to and when anyone left or was added.

The City Authority claimed the records were maintained in the public interest, and no one Emerson ever spoke to had stories about The Authority taking action on all that data. There was no apparent reason for anyone to suspect a nefarious use. As a result, no one looked for evidence. Chandler taught him that this was the way they managed the population. The Authority's hand was firm, but people were otherwise free. There was certainly no one in need or any evidence of the disgruntled poor.

Chandler would say, "Happy people don't rebel. They are blind to any betrayal because they are rewarded when they ignore it."

Sally wanted him to register a new pod with her. She explained how the process worked. Emerson was careful not to betray his revulsion. She explained, "Children are raised by The City until they are granted to a pod. Most fertile women are conscripted into the Birth Corps sometime after they are eighteen. I hear it's like a year-long spa treatment. And they harvest all your eggs too, so there's no more periods after. I can't wait."

She went on, "The Birth Corps implant fertilized embryos in a highly managed clinical environment. All the calculations of The City's population balance are controlled along with DNA screening for necessary traits and health before a fertilized ovum is put into the queue. The moms live in a private village with medical staff until delivering the child. Attachment is pharmaceutically mitigated."

Emerson covered his smirk. *Pharmaceutically mitigated, huh?* That meant drug-induced detachment or attachment as needed. Conveniently controlled by The Authority.

Sally had launched ahead. "Birthing women usually leave after one child, but some stay on to help midwife for others. Because of carefully managed health and nutrition protocols, most of the negative impact of birth on women's bodies has been mitigated. I know lots of Birth Corps moms; you can hardly tell."

Emerson knew it was the way things were done even though the whole idea seemed gross. No one in The City questioned the processes because everyone was happy and satisfied. Needs were met resulting in a low desire for change. He asked, "Does anyone ever get pregnant the old-fashioned way?"

"Well, most girls can't even have babies, but really, The Interface disrupts conception until we become moms. The Authority takes care of the population. Our implants even regulate the impulse to procreate. Most women are called in as soon as their hormones reach certain levels. The Interface monitors us. And after giving birth, moms never get pregnant again."

Chandler had told him stories of resistance. And though he never pointed directly at Emerson's parents, the boy figured it out after coming to The City. His grandfather's opinion was that The Authority used the Enforcers to isolate and remove dissidence before it became noticeable. Chandler also believed that the Elites ran everything.

But Sally was a Middle, a member of The City's large middle-class. As she explained, "Everything is free in The City—at least, there's no money. When we are kids, we are taught that the machine runs well when the people run well. When we work together, our load is light."

They were raised to believe it, and for them, it was true. Middles thought of themselves as the more fortunate ones left in the world. They had warm homes and clothing. Everyone only worked to their own degree at jobs which interested them. But no work was required. Most people did a job because it needed to be done. And they did a good job because The City gave them all they needed.

Quinn lived in a very different world.

He and Quinn climbed a series of stone-step switchbacks built into the side of the hill. She stopped at a heavy wooden wall banded together with metal bands. Looking back behind him and down the hill, the main district of The City rolled out from the mountainside to the wall. Ruins of the storefronts and tenements poked up from the other side looking like broken teeth. The young woman tipped her head and whispered something close to the door. The bands unwrapped the planks which folded back on themselves like an accordion door, opening a passage. She looked at Emerson and tapped the spot where her implant pulsed just beneath the skin. Emerson tapped his own. He noticed Quinn's bright purple irises. She had to duck her head to go through the low tunnel.

A momentary fear of being trapped rippled up Emerson's spine. He automatically looked for an escape route. But he told himself he was being paranoid and followed her.

After they passed through the arch, the bands rewrapped, and wood reassembled to appear as impenetrable as it was before. Quinn said, "I have always lived outside that system too. My parents are my birth parents. However, I didn't grow up with my mother, and the woman who lives with my father is more of a servant. Quinn is just my family name. I have little to do with either of them." But Quinn was an Elite, which meant she could go anywhere and do anything she wanted.

Founder's Quarter looked different, lighter, warmer. If Emerson had ever seen a picture, he'd recognize that part of The City looked more like Florence, Italy in the 1600s. At least the aristocracy's Florence. Most windows dripped with flowers. The cobblestone streets were spotless. A few people walked purposefully on their private business. Others lounged around on the wooden benches in front of buildings or on the wide green lawns.

Through the stone arch and around a brick corner they entered a broad sandstone-paved plaza. Looking north, the mountains loomed directly behind the stone buildings separated by the strips of green lawn. A marble fountain in the center of the plaza bubbled. As they walked past it, Quinn said, "My dad arranged to have this fountain flown here in pieces from Palermo, Sicily."

Emerson had very little knowledge of geography. Chandler might have archived every book ever written, but he had little interest in the names of dead places. Emmer didn't want to betray his ignorance, so he didn't respond. Quinn saw through it and said, "You know where that is?"

Emerson said, "No."

Quinn said, "I'll send you a map. Better still, I'll give you an upload." She'd stopped in front of a small shop with a broad glass window. There was no sign. She opened the door and said, "After you, sir." The smells inside were intoxicating: fresh bread, roasting meats, savory casseroles.

The comfortable café was a single room. The floor was a tile mosaic, and walls were hung with large dimly lit oil paintings. Most of the tables were occupied by couples speaking in low tones. Soft music played from somewhere, and there were real candles burning on each table. Quinn and Emerson found a seat; he looked around. The music came from a single acoustic guitarist. Emerson had never seen a real guitar before and started to look but stopped himself when a woman in a white apron arrived with glasses of water. Quinn said, "I want a beef steak, rare, and French fries with Heinz ketchup. Oh yeah, and a Coke on ice, with a straw."

Emerson looked from the white-aproned woman to Quinn, who said, "You can get anything you want."

Emerson said, "Anything?"

"Yeah. And this is real, buddy. None of that replicator bullshit."

"And anyone can just come in here?"

"Well, yes and no. They would have to know it's here, and they would have to be able to gain access to The Quarter. You have to be a Founder or work for one to enter."

"I'll have what you're having."

As the waitress turned to leave, Emerson said, "On second thought, I'd like an elk burger and a cinnamon bun."

Quinn said, "A cinnamon bun? That's random."

"I had a book about a cinnamon roll when I was a kid. I don't remember a thing about it except that my Grandpa Chandler didn't have any cinnamon. I always wanted to try one."

"And so you will! Bravo, Emerson…" She paused.

He said, "Lloyde."

"Emerson Lloyde! Congratulations. This calls for an extra celebration. But first, while we wait, let me upload some books to you. Let's see, *Twentieth Century Geography, The City*, a worthwhile fiction even if it is just propaganda, and this one, perfect: *The Underground Girl's Guide to The Interface.*

"The upload process is similar to getting a pedicure," she said, "You know? Like someone is playing with your toes, which is distracting, but it's not bad. And this will only take a minute. Nothing like getting waxed."

"Waxed?"

"We'll get to that. Here's our food. I hope you enjoy your burger and bun."

The food was amazing, and both of them cleaned and licked their plates. The burger was perfect. The bun was interesting. He said, "It's stickier than I imagined. Cinnamon is weird. It burns my nose. And this was so sweet I can't taste anything, now."

"That's honey. You never had honey?"

"Grandpa didn't like insects. Oh. I think the upload is done."

"You read those books and come talk to me after." She winked. "C'mon, I want you to meet my friends." She pulled him by the wrist out the door and into a narrow alley around the side of the building. They crossed a wide road and up another set of stairs. Quinn didn't knock. She threw the door open and announced, "I'm home, I'm bored, I'm horny!"

The group of twelve or more young men and women sitting on couches and stuffed chairs repeated the greeting: "I'm home, I'm bored, I'm horny!" And everyone laughed, talking at the same time. Quinn pulled Emerson to a loveseat occupied by a man and woman. Emerson said, "Hi." But when he looked at their faces, he was stunned. The man had broad shoulders and the woman a modest bust, but both had straight, shoulder-length red hair and exactly the same face. Emerson stared.

"Never seen twins before, I take it?" Quinn looked at him with her crooked grin.

Emerson continued to look into the couple's faces. He said, "I didn't see anyone besides my grandpa for ten years. Sure, I've seen pictures, but I've never seen an actual twin."

"Meet Suzy and Sam. They're the latest generation of the Bax line." They laughed. She continued, "Only an Elite could have a twin. They are genetically excluded by the Birth Corps protocols."

Before Emerson could speak, Quinn announced that they were going to the Palace, and the room emptied. He lost track of her in the crowd. A young man wearing a stretch hat walked alongside him, who put out his hand and said, "Hey, I'm Max."

Emerson took his hand briefly and said, "Emerson. I read in old times strangers would shake hands to prove that they weren't holding weapons."

"Yeah, I heard that too. But not all weapons are in the hand, are they?"

Emerson was going to ask where they were going when Quinn called to him. She was waving. He waved back.

Max said, "Yeah, she likes you. You're healthy and smart. New blood from outside the wall. See ya."

Emerson walked to Quinn. He considered what Max said for a moment. There was something odd about it even though it sounded like he was just stating the obvious. But the thought left his mind when Quinn smiled at him and took his hand again. They had arrived at a three-story granite block building. The doors to the main foyer were behind a row of massive Doric columns. Quinn led him to the reception desk. The others followed in a slow-moving clot, talking and laughing. Emerson looked at a few faces, trying to gauge what he was getting himself into. He asked, "What are we doing?"

She didn't look at him and said, "You'll find out." To the receptionist, she said, "All of us, Simone. I think there are eleven today, no, twelve."

Simone was bored. She sucked on a vape cartridge between each sentence. "The cathedral room then, hon. You know the drill. Everyone gets scanned. Don't enter until you hear the beep."

Quinn gave Emerson a piece of shriveled fungus. She said, "Chew this up and swallow it."

"What the fuck is it, Quinn?"

"Psylocibin, just a micro-dose. It helps with the process."

"Process? What process?"

Quinn grabbed Emerson's hand and pulled him out of the receptionist's vape cloud to the entrance, a dark archway covered in red velvet drapes. She called the others, "Come on, boys and girls. Let's get a move on."

Emerson said, "I don't think this is such a great idea for me." He looked around for a way to escape.

Quinn took his hand and looked into his eyes and pressed her chest into his, kissing him gently, probing his lips with her tongue. As she pulled back an inch, she whispered, "Trust me."

"Yeah, that's the thing. I don't."

She used a scanner to read Emerson's implant. An indicator near the door switched from red to green, and the scanner beeped. She said, "That's all there is to it." Once his implant was read, she pulled him in. He tried to resist, and she kissed him again. As he turned, Quinn poked his wrist with something sharp.

"Ow! Shit. What was that?"

"Just a little stick. Because you're not part of the Founder's bloodlines, I needed to take a sample. You know, to make sure you're not carrying anything." She held up a slide with a dot of red in the center.

"You could have told me."

"Some people are weird about blood. I thought it would be better to just get it over with."

As they entered the main hall, he muttered, "Better for who?"

The room was red velvet, floors, ceiling and walls. The lights were amber and flickering, candle-like. There was a floor-to-ceiling fireplace with a blazing fire at the far end. The atmosphere was moist and hot, like a greenhouse. Emerson could tell from fifty meters away that the fire was fake, an image on a large screen. The heat and humidity drifted down from ceiling vents.

A double row of red velvet chaise lounges lined the walls. Each had its own small end table with a dim lamp and a cup of clear liquid. Quinn was already half undressed, pulling off her shirt, when she noticed Emerson standing helpless, looking around the room. Other friends were getting comfortable on the lounges, laughing and talking loudly. The room absorbed most of the sound. And there was string quartet music playing low somewhere. Quinn said, "It's OK, Emerson. No one is looking at you."

Emerson stared at a woman with waist-length blond hair. He had never seen anyone with skin so pale before. Her rouged nipples captured his attention, and his erection pressed against the inside of his pants. Quinn said, "You'll be more comfortable without your clothes."

He was beginning to sweat. Quinn lay face up on a couch nearby; Emerson sat on the edge of an adjacent one, removing his boots. He sat in his boxers with his erection straining against the thin cloth. Quinn snickered. He looked at her as if to say, "Must I?"

She laughed and said to the room. "OK, guys, concentrate…"

The lights dimmed; the song changed into a single tone. Emerson realized that he was entering The Interface. He'd heard of these places. Some of the other cadets in pilot training joked about them. He imagined they were brothels like the ones at the outposts. The idea of trading for sex seemed reprehensible to him. He was raised to believe that sex was part of a relationship and preferably practiced between two or more people who were attracted to each other.

This was something entirely different. When he woke up inside the construct, he felt like it was his normal body. The friends were together out-doors, on a mountainside. A broad white-sand beach stretched from horizon to horizon before them; foam-topped turquoise waves lapped the shore. The others were nearby at tables or in cabanas. Some sat on the grass. Everyone was dressed in white, formal eveningwear. Waiters and waitresses in cerule-an-blue tuxedos drifted effortlessly through the crowd as if they were on roller skates. They carried large trays covered with foods and drinks, glasses of red wine, fruit, cheeses. A group of monkeys played nearby on a climbing gym.

Emerson reached for a glass and turned to sit in a wicker chair. Quinn, wearing a multilayered white chiffon gown with a canary yellow sash, moved close and kissed him deeply on the lips. When she pulled away, he saw rainbows in her eyes. Her red lipstick was sweet and sticky. He reached his hand behind her head and brought her face close again. She spoke inside his mind, "We can have sex here, Emerson."

He smiled and kissed her again. She said, "I can be you, and you can be me. We can be anyone here. Watch." She put her arms around his back and hugged him tightly. Instead of pressure in his chest, he felt his body pass through Quinn. When he looked up at her face, he saw himself instead. She said, "See?"

He pulled back, holding her shoulders, but she was him, and he was her. Quinn-as-Emerson opened the first few buttons of Emerson-as-Quinn's blouse. He/she was not wearing a bra; she/he slipped a hand beneath each breast, cupping them in her/his palms and bending to kiss one, sucking a nipple in. Emerson felt a ping of arousal in the middle of his/her body. The skin between his thighs moistened. His/her nipple hardened in her/his mouth.

It felt exciting. It felt weird, a physical disassociation. His/her chest flushed, and a valve opened somewhere inside. She was kissing him again, only he was her. Her lipstick smeared, or was it his? They were suddenly overdressed and began pulling each other's clothing off. Soon, they were naked and rolling on the grass. Aroused and slippery.

Quinn said, "I want you inside me." Emerson, thought, irrationally, *I want me inside you too.* He heard others moaning. He glanced over to see two women caressing Max. He glanced back at the same moment and grinned. He was not wearing his ever-present hat.

The lights blinked once. All of his sensations smeared; he almost lost consciousness. It felt like something was tearing inside his mind, not painful exactly, but uncomfortable, dizzying, nauseating. When he opened his eyes, everything was red. As the images swam into focus, he realized that he was back in the cathedral room, lying prone on a lounge, with a painful erection.

Quinn screamed, "What in God's-ever-loving fuckwhistles was that, Simone!" She jumped off the chaise, naked and red-faced, her black page-boy shaking with rage.

Simone stood in the red velvet archway, motioning the raven-haired banshee to calm down. She said, "Elli, please, get dressed. This isn't my doing."

Quinn didn't hear her. She yelled, "WHAT THE FUCK!"

A large, wide-shouldered man, flanked by two equally wide-shouldered bodyguards, touched Simone's shoulder and turned her back to the foyer. When Quinn saw him, she became instantly calm and said, "Oh. It's you, Father."

Emerson pulled on his pants and boots and plotted an escape, but Lord Quinn's entourage was blocking the exit.

Not only was Boston Quinn big, he was tall. Emerson didn't realize how tall until the lord was standing in front of him just as he got his second boot on. Emerson stood; he had to look up to see Lord Quinn's face. The 182-centimeters-tall young man stood about eye level with Boston Quinn's top shirt button. Elli Rattlesnake's father was a thick man with narrow hips and a block jaw. But there was something wrong with his hair. It didn't look like it fit on his head. He thumbed a gold ring with a large sparkling stone on his left hand. Emerson assumed it was a diamond.

Emerson said, "Sir?"

Boston said, "Emerson Lloyde. Raised by Chandler Estes. Mother and father, Soo and Marc Lloyde, suspected terrorists: deceased. How in the name of God did you get in here, son, let alone get your penis into my daughter?"

Quinn said, "You understand virtual sex, right, Father?" She slung her leather jacket over one shoulder. Even with lifted boots, she looked like a child next to her father. Judging from the color of her face and upper chest, she was still extremely aroused. As far as she was concerned, an angry yelling match with her father might serve her as well as an orgasm, though she had gotten control of herself for the moment. She said, "Hi, Daddy. What the actual fuck are you doing here? I'm a legal adult now."

"I'd laugh, but I'm late for a meeting. Let's just agree I am the law and leave it at that. Where did he latch on to you, and how did he get you to let him in here? You're not that stupid. Oh, and Christ, Elli, get dressed!"

"What? I'm wearing pants. You afraid of my tits, dear Daddy? Besides, you're not supposed to read the records of The Palace without a warrant."

"Again. Stop confusing the story we tell the Middles with some sort of reality. Rights like those disappeared with the United States of America. Did you think I wouldn't know when some Drek sticks his filthy prick into my heir?"

Emerson recognized that Boston Quinn could have him killed if he desired. He wanted to protest and glanced over at Quinn. She cautioned him to silence with a look.

To Boston, Elli said, "I brought Emerson here. He is my guest." She pulled her shirt over her head.

He became angry and shot back, "Don't think you can pull that old hospitality shit on me. That's just old fashion bull…"

"You know Mother doesn't think so."

"Your mother isn't here."

"Should I call her? I have her contact right here. Wait. It's ringing now."

"Fine. Leave off. He can stay as your guest. But no sex. I still get to choose my second heir. That's part of the same hospitality rules, girl."

"You will meet the father of my first child when I introduce him to you, dear Father. And stop subverting the rules to your own favor. You know very well that I, the woman, have the sole discretion of choice in all matters concerning my ancestry. Don't try to lay your patriarchal crap over that, Lord *Quinn*. You have a whole world outside this quarter to impose that stupid shit on. Inside here, *we women* rule, and you know it." She readjusted her left breast by putting her right hand inside the shirt, tightened her belt, and said, "And I'll fuck whoever I like, wherever I like."

She called, "C'mon, people. This place stinks. I'm ready to eat again. Mush."

And as everyone filed out, they greeted Lord Quinn as they passed. They were children of Founders and had known him their whole lives.

Emerson said, "Goodnight, sir."

Boston sniffed.

Outside, Quinn said, "I know someplace else to go where things are more private."

Emerson said, "I need to get home. It was really interesting, to say the least."

Quinn looked at her PDA and at the top of the stone tower across the plaza. She said, still not looking at him, "Well, that's okay. I have what I need."

Emerson said, "Hey, don't do that. Look at me. What was that back there... Was that real?"

She said, "Yes and no. Most of what happened was between your brain and The Interface. Maybe seventy-five percent was fake."

"Twenty-five percent of waking experience is a lot. What was real about it?"

She said, "How did it feel?"

"It felt great. Was it real?"

"Does it matter?"

Emerson took her hand. "I want to see you again."

"Are you going to tell Sally about me?"

"You know I'm not."

Quinn took his other hand, "Maybe you can come and live here with me."

"I *do* want to see you, but I have to go. How can I find you?"

"I sent you contact info when I upped the books." She turned and walked away from him. "I also gave you access to the plank wall." She and her friends walked slowly toward one of the green lawns. The sun was nearly down. Emerson went back into The City proper and home to Sally's house. He was not sure what the afternoon meant, but he was sure that he would never register a pod with Sally Mink. As he walked, he realized what was up with Boston Quinn's hair. "He wears a toupee."

◆ ◆ ◆

THE SOHO MOON

Emerson's relationship with Sally Mink deteriorated rapidly. After he met Quinn, he stopped concealing his impatience with Sally. They had been together for over a year, and from her point of view, Emerson changed drastically. Emerson, of course, saw it from his own angle. Sally was smothering him, pushing him to make commitments he didn't want to make. He wasn't able to see life through Sally's eyes, and he was frustrated that she couldn't explain it to him. He had grown up a free male, outside the restrictive City culture, raised by a man who was entitled and privileged. Chandler believed he understood how nature worked, and he taught that system of thinking to Emerson. But Chandler couldn't see all of the picture, though he believed he could.

One huge part of that picture was the fear any woman or girl must exist with. Sally had to live within the roles The City prescribed for her. To rebel against those restrictions was as dangerous as it was unthinkable. If she pushed against that culture, her culture, it would exclude her. She would be exiled. Alone, she imagined, she would die.

Like most City women of her age, Sally didn't harbor any illusions about love or romanticism. The years following the collapse left deep scars on the few survivors; the trauma, as always, was passed down to their children. When the Founders established safe havens, they were the people's salvation. It would be a betrayal to criticize their saviors. The memory of starvation was too fresh in the gene pool. And that trauma was what allowed The Authority to control them.

The gulf between Emerson and Sally widened daily. He craved meaningful conversation with someone who could spar with him. He was also raised to avoid meanness. So, he waited, and the gulf grew wider. Sally always felt that Emerson was giving her a gift by just noticing her. She liked to be seen with him. Emerson didn't understand or care about appearances. Sally's behavior confused him, but she couldn't or wouldn't discuss it. Sally felt he was her wild man tamed. But he needed a thinking companion. Chandler had set a high intellectual bar.

Now Quinn had captured his attention. When Emerson began criticizing Sally, he couldn't stop himself. Even after he'd made her cry. He would apologize later, but that just confused her more. If he didn't want to be with her, he should leave. But Emerson didn't want to hurt Sally. She seemed fragile to him. Not knowing his intentions made her erratic and unsure, which led to speculation of the worst kind. And of course, her fear made Emerson more critical. And the cycle would repeat.

During one particularly violent argument, Emerson let himself channel Chandler in all his drunken eloquence. They were drinking mead, a delicacy usually only available in the Founder's Quarter, but Emerson had his connections. Sally wanted to talk about forming a pod, and Emerson hadn't eaten. The replicator food made him sick. Most times, he would avoid eating at all. But that had its consequences too since Emerson was already thin and lanky. He needed food. Four glasses might not have been a huge amount of mead. But on an empty stomach, honey wine was a powerful drug.

He began by calling the pod system the most ludicrous idea he'd ever heard. He continued to drink, but he spilled a considerable amount on the tile floor, which he expected Sally would clean up. It was her house, after all. He slurred his words, "Women are mothers, not incubators for The City. My God Sally. How can you think that it's good for any child to grow up that way?"

"I grew up that way."

Instantly sober, Emerson said, "Oh, fuck. I'm sorry, baby."

Sally couldn't stand it anymore. She screamed, "Get out. You are driving me crazy; I need to be alone. I need you to go. Don't speak. Just go. Now. Go!"

He tried to say something anyway. She stopped him with her palm and said, "No."

Emerson stormed out of the house and disappeared.

Ten minutes later, she regretted sending him away, but her implant was tuned to head off depression in women her age. She wanted to send the Enforcers to look for him but went to bed instead. Though she missed Emerson, the anti-depression mode distracted her from thinking about him each time she tried. Over the next few weeks, the gaps grew longer until she stopped thinking about him at all. Sally never saw Emerson again and never gave it another thought.

◆

After Quinn and Emerson had their encounter at the Red Palace, she gave the blood sample slide to her servant, Tanya, and told her to bring it to Doctor Sailor. Less than twenty minutes later, the doctor called Quinn's PDA.

Quinn opened the connection. Sailor said, "How did you get this?"

Quinn said, "Hello to you too." The doctor ignored her. "I told him that it was required for people born outside the founder's families."

"You are a lying bitch, Elli Rattlesnake, but you better sit down for this news. The DNA from this man is perfect. Somehow, his line was not damaged like everybody else. I don't understand it, but he might be the key to repairing the damage in others. Don't let this one get away."

Quinn was silent for a moment and said, "Don't tell my father."

"No. Of course not."

"Swear."

"Of course, I'll swear, child. I've known you all your life. I couldn't lie to you."

Quinn disconnected. She immediately sent a message to Emerson:

`The last time sadly wasn't real enough for me. My moon has passed. Tonight is the first night under the Soho moon. Come do me.`

He received it as he was storming away from Sally's house. He was still pretty drunk and didn't think to respond; he just went to look for her. At Founder's Quarter he asked after Quinn in the little storefront restaurant. A different woman in a white apron didn't know where she was, so Emerson moved on. He knew the Red Palace and could have asked if anyone knew where it was, but she wouldn't be there. He barely remembered the outside of the building where she met her friends. The only chance he had was to retrace their steps. He went around the side of the building, through the narrow alleyway and up a set of stairs across the wide road. The structure was a squat, green, ranch-type building with a wide, shaded porch. The porch floor was painted red. The doors were open. Emerson stepped up on the porch and into the main room. The floor was wide-plank polished oak. It was larger than he thought. Leather couches and recliners, flanking low, inlayed wooden tables, were scattered around the room.

Quinn sat alone at a concert grand piano, playing a short, repeating melody. Emerson said, "Hey." She stopped.

"What took you?"

"Your moon?"

"My blood, she comes with the new moon. After, I'm ovulating. I call it my Soho moon because I get SoHo: soooo horny. But I texted you that hours ago."

"Yeah. Sorry." He dropped into a leather recliner. A servant brought them each a glass of brown liquid.

Quinn said, "Scotch. Single malt from 2025. Some of the last."

Emerson sipped; it opened his eyes. "Damn. That's a lot of alcohol." He sniffed it and put the glass down. "Where do you get this stuff? Like the Coke. Nobody has made Coca-Cola in decades."

Quinn drained her glass and reached for Emerson's. "You can't waste something this precious." She threw it back and set his glass down. "The world was a fucking mega-consumer circus, Emerson. When everybody died, they left all their shit in ships and warehouses. My people go out and collect it. We'll run out someday, but until then, we can party like it's 1999."

"I don't get it."

"The song. By Prince?"

"I never heard it."

"Oh. Wait." The song played on a built-in sound system.

Emerson smiled. "Ok. This is pretty good. I usually listen to '60s rock, but this is... Yeah."

Quinn stood, grabbed both of Emerson's hands, and began swaying and moving seductively, stepping from one foot to the other. "C'mon, boy, dance with me."

Emerson stood still while she danced around him. He said, "I can't dance. I don't know the first thing about..." Quinn grabbed his hips and pulled him into her. He didn't pass though her or change into her body, which was a weird relief. He met her pressure with his own. She put his left arm around her waist and his right on her shoulder.

She put her hands on his hips and said, "Move your body with me. I'll lead."

The music pounded. He could feel the bass in his lower belly. Quinn pulled him closer and put her head on his chest. She said, "That's it, feel the rhythm through my body. My feet are stepping in time. We can move inside the beat this way." She swayed her body from side to side, lifted her head to look at him, and closed her eyes. Emerson knew she wanted him to kiss her, but Quinn's way of expecting his compliance with little or no explanation annoyed him, and yet he didn't want to articulate it. Instead, he broke away.

The music stopped. Quinn said, "Okay. Not a music lover. Got it."

Emerson said, "It's not that. I just don't know what you want from me, Quinn. What *do* you want?"

She said, "I want to show you my room," and began to walk away.

He stayed and said, "See. That's what I'm talking about. Why not ask me? Why do you need to tell me what to do? I like you, Quinn. You're smart. Can we just *be* with each other and see where it goes?"

She sat back down.

He said, "OK. Tell me, Miss Quinn. Why Elli Rattlesnake? And how did your family get to be one of the founding families of this glorious empire you forged out of the death and collapse of modern civilization?"

"Want another drink? I do."

"No, not really. I want to get to know you, not get more drunk."

"That's fair. Elli Rattlesnake is my name, but that's a story for another day and copious amounts of inebriants. If you'd read that book on The City I upped to you, you would at least know the official story. But I suppose the true story is more important. And more interesting."

"OK." She rattled the ice in her empty glass. A waiter scurried in with a full one as she spoke. "My dad's family owned most of the transportation on the planet. Jets, trains, container ships…"

Emerson said, "I studied them. I was fascinated with shipping when I was a kid. Funny thing is I'm really afraid of water…"

"Yeah, well, there aren't any more of them. They were all sunk near the time of the collapse. A terrorist group decided that eliminating ocean shipping would reset the world economy and the climate. They got support from countries who were paying too much due to low volume. But once the containers were gone, there was no way for goods to travel. The virus helped crush that industry to death. And I don't blame you about water. I hate the stuff myself. W.C. Fields would say 'Fishhhh… swim in it!'" They laughed together.

She went on, "But really, there's reason for that water fear. It's a cultural taboo. The Founders developed it. For the culture of The City to function, it has to appear to be a closed system to the inhabitants. But for the logistics of The City to function, they had to understand that nothing can survive in a closed system. If no one believes that there is anywhere else to go, they are more likely to put up with inequality in the society.

"Even when they eliminated fiat currency, the system still required inputs. So, the Founders set up a distinct separation of classes. The top, the middle and the bottom. Sounds similar to most of man's history, eh? Sure, sure. But here in The City they controlled populations as well. And genetics. Anyone who fell into the poor category had no purpose. They reduced the need for outside input to a bare minimum, gave everyone in the middle class the sort of wealth that calms the hearts of wild beasts, and eliminated the poor by putting them outside the wall and forgetting them.

"The Interface had taken all the power out of the people's hands already; the virus just sounded the death knell."

Emerson said, "What made the Founders the Founders?"

Quinn said, "When the world was dying from the virus, my father's grandfather made an alliance with seven other families. Representatives from these eight formed The Founders and sequestered themselves and their families in shelters. These shelters were originally envisioned by the oligarchs from the mid-twentieth century as fallout and bomb shelters. But over the years, the underground rooms became more extensive, more expansive. The Founders moved everyone to the shelter that still exists under this part of The City. They brought several families from outside with them. While the contagion consumed most of humanity, they set up supply chains and designed The City's structure. And when the virus finally burned itself out by killing over 75 percent of the earth's population in a three-month period, they emerged and built the wall."

Emerson considered her story. He said, "Yes, I'd like to see where you live."

Quinn and Emerson walked across the wide road and up a steep staircase cut into the rock between two three-story residential buildings. Quinn said, "Servants. The people who live in these buildings are the maids and waiters, butlers, cooks and builders for the Founding families. We support hundreds of individuals. Some have even formed pods. This is a miniature version of Founder's Quarter. The people who work here do not leave the quarter and never speak to anyone outside its boundaries."

Emerson said, "That seems unrealistic. What happens if they leave or tell?"

Quinn stopped walking, looked at Emerson, and shook her head. "Tell me you don't know the answer to that question."

He considered it for a moment and said, "They actually kill them?"

"The Lords prefer the term *remove*, but yes, in essence, if Interface Behavior Modification doesn't work, they are removed. There is no dissent in The City because those who complain outside of accepted channels disappear. No one talks about it, but the guidelines are very clear. It is never a mistake. And everyone knows in a crisis, extreme measures are justifiable. Of course, there is no crisis anymore."

At the top of the stair, Quinn turned and disappeared through a stone wall. Emerson said, "Hey."

She poked her face back through and said, "It's an illusion. Come on." She grabbed his wrist and pulled him into the wall, which was, as she said, only an illusion. It was a strange feeling, though. And Emerson felt dizzy when they were through.

"Yeah, it does that, at first. But you'll get used to it." She tapped her implant scar. "For anyone else, the wall is actually there. But The Interface allows your cells to permeate the type of synthetic rock the wall is made from. You are passing through stone, essentially, and your consciousness reads that sort of passage like you are breaking a physical law. Your mind can't make sense of such a thing. So, after a short time, you have to let go and ignore the feeling. Otherwise it will drive you crazy. Come." She pulled him along the narrow corridor.

They stopped, and she put her hand on a matte-black panel in the smooth clay wall. A door traced itself and opened. Quinn said, "After you, Emerson Lloyde."

A woman's voice from inside her apartment said, "Glad to make your acquaintance, Emerson Lloyde. I see from your file that you have no permanent address in The City. Would you like to update your records?"

Quinn said, "May I?"

Emerson said, "I guess, sure."

Quinn said, "Siobhan, update, authorization: Quinn, Rattlesnake, zero, one, two, six. Enter permanent address, Quinn residence, save, close." She smiled and looked at him. "There. Now you live in Founder's Quarter. No one will ever question you again. Thank me later."

◆

She brought two cups of tea from the next room, and said, "It's real. Real honey too. And not too much."

Emerson raised an eyebrow, "You brewed this yourself?"

"Me? No! I wouldn't know where to begin. I have a maid. Her name is Tanya. No one ever sees her."

Emerson took a sip. "This is good. We were never able to cure tea leaves properly. At least not to satisfy Chandler. He wouldn't touch commercial food from before. So, we just drank really bad tea. Have you ever tasted stevia? It grows wild in the scrub forests in this region."

"No. why?"

"Chandler used it as a sweetener, but it tastes like dogwood root, which is to say it tastes like shit. Sickeningly sweet followed by a lingering bitter aftertaste. It was the only sweetener we had. I avoided it."

They drank their tea for a while. The honey-thick wedge of sun streaming in Quinn's high, west-facing windows changed angle like a massive sundial. Emerson looked around her room. It was a spare, high-ceilinged attic chamber. The walls were smooth plaster, and the ceiling was wood plank. Other windows around the room were tall floor-to-ceiling antiques. Upon a little closer look, Emerson realized that no, they were not antiques. They were new, handmade, leaded glass, double-sash windows. He burst out, "Holy shit. These windows are amazing!"

Quinn sipped her tea and smiled. "Everything is that way in Founder's. Experiencing this life, this last flash of brilliance from humanity's past, is our purpose in life. Everything feeds and supports us in this, and when it is gone, its greatness will only fade with our memories." She looked at him. She wanted him to share her vision. "By our estimates, at the current population threshold, our warehouse will last 200 years. Which, by the way, we might live to see because of the transplant possibilities our private doctors have reopened.

"My mother thinks she's immortal already, which makes sense when you see how she treats her body. But damn, Emerson. Wouldn't you want to live like this for the next 200 years?"

Emerson was getting better at navigating Quinn's manipulations. Rather than say "fuck no" like he wanted to, he gave a noncommittal, "Hmm," and before she could speak, he said, "Can we get some more of this tea?"

Quinn returned with a tray of chocolate chip cookies and two more cups of tea. She said, "Come sit with me. There is another reason why I want you to stay."

She patted the space next to her on the loveseat and crossed her ankles. When he sat, she slid closer so their hips were touching. Emerson said, "You know, Quinn. You're still not telling me what you're after. How do you know I wouldn't just give it to you?"

"You really don't want to live in the last breath of paradise with a willing, young, sexy girl like me?"

"That's beside the point, Quinn. What do you want from me?"

"You don't see how special you are, do you, Emerson Lloyde? Let me enlighten you to the facts. Number one. You are a captive in a very elaborate prison. I am offering to make you the warden. From where you stand, you don't know where the walls are, so you can never escape.

"Two. You have clean DNA. Even though your parents lived in The City when you were born, they did not come from here. And neither did your grandmother and grandfather's family. You're a survivor from a lost leg of humanity, and I'm City royalty. Do you understand what kind of power we could wield together?"

Emerson knew this was another of Quinn's trick questions. But he didn't know about his DNA. All he could say was, "How do you know that?"

She laughed and began undressing. "We know everything, Emerson.

Everything about everything. The only way we can stay in power is because nobody knows more than we do. If they did, they would take what we have. You see?" She was completely naked. "Whew! That's better. I am *so* much more comfortable now. Fuck. I would abolish clothing if I could. Hey, maybe that should be our first edict as lord and lady."

Emerson said, "What in the fuck are you talking about, Quinn? And what the fuck are you doing?"

She said, "Look, boy. I'm doing whatever I please. Always have and always will. You better remember that." She ran the fingertips of her right hand through her vulva and licked each of them slowly.

She said quietly, "You see, Emerson, you gave me permission to access your neural implant. I can make you do or see anything I want. That's how The Authority Control works. So, if you don't want me to simply take it, then you can save yourself a lot of pain and humiliation and give it to me freely. You have to admit—you get the prize either way."

Emerson couldn't argue with his erection. The thought bubbled up in his mind—*Being naked would be so much more comfortable*—followed by a fleeting worry that Quinn was manipulating his thoughts. She was leaning back now, arms above her head, laughing. He leaned over and hugged her around the middle, pressing his chest into hers, and kissed her, covering her mouth with his, probing her tongue, grinding against her body.

When Emerson came up for air, Quinn said, "Please take your clothes off. You're giving me a rash."

◆

They were in bed for the next eighteen hours. Emerson had never experienced such luxury. He'd never even read about it and so had nothing to compare except his austere childhood. Quinn fed him fruit that he didn't know existed. He drank liquors that had been bottled before the United States Declaration of Independence was signed. And Quinn showed him things they could do in bed, positions they could take. If she was manipulating his reality, he didn't care. Emerson was so happy he felt anesthetized. Between the cognac and the Kama Sutra, he had never felt his body so clearly, and never been as high. He didn't realize until much later that complete anesthesia left a mythic hangover.

Quinn left for a bath on the evening of the second day.

Emerson dozed. He was engorged again by the time she returned. But she was dressed in her black leather with a pink bowler. He tried to sit up, but couldn't focus. There was something across his chest. He mumbled, "What the fuck, Quinn? What did you do now?"

He was able to get the silk sheets pushed away from him enough to see that it was a woman's leg across his chest. He woke up a few more notches. "Quinn?" She blew kisses at him and walked toward the door. "Quinn! Who is this? What did you do?"

"Whatever I wanted, Emmer. Like I said." The woman moved her face down to Emerson's crotch, which put his face near hers. Quinn closed the door behind her. Emerson yelled, "Quinn!"

The woman turned around and sat across his waist. She was completely nude. Her bust was larger than Quinn's; her hips were expansive. She was blond, at least the hair on her head was, white actually. Her eyebrows, the only other hair on her body, were brown.

She said, "I'm Amber, Quinn's bestie. She said you wouldn't mind."

He said, "Mind? Mind what? That I go to sleep and when I wake, my girlfriend has given me to her friend for sex? Why would I mind that?" He was getting loud; his pitch rose at least an octave.

Amber said, "She said you understood the stakes. Listen, I'm not gonna fuck a Drek for Quinn's sick sense of humor. She said you were clean, right? Unique DNA. I gotta have some of that. I'm sure you get it, boy. I'm a founder's daughter. I'm an heir to this shithole. I have to look out for my descendants' best interests. So, if I want to fuck you for your sperm, you damn well will let me." Now she was getting loud.

Emerson said, "You are very pretty, Amber. And I'm like twenty-two, so I'm already hard as an oak branch…"

"Yes, that's not a secret, you know." She nudged him with her knee. He smiled.

"Yeah, well. So, you know it's not that I can't, but I don't *want* to give you my sperm. I'm not sure I have any more left after what Quinn did to me last night. So, if it's all the same to you, I'd like to get up and shower now."

Amber began sliding her wet bottom against the lower half of his body. She said, "Hmm. What do you think now, boy? You're not any different from any other cock and balls; when a woman wants a man, a woman takes him."

Emerson was aroused, but he was also frustrated. He didn't want to hurt the woman, but she was assaulting him. He'd said no, and she kept on. Just to be sure she understood, he said, "Amber. Stop. I don't want this." This was what happened when he trusted people. *Fuck!*

She had her head tipped back and was sliding her hips around; wetness squelched with each thrust. Emerson's anger rose. After so many years of controlling himself around his grandfather, he had come to know when he was cresting his limit. His body gave a last warning when he was about to lose it: his ears burned. Once that happened, there would be no turning back. As Amber fell deeper into her ecstatic trance, Emerson struggled to relax.

Chandler had impressed the finality of losing control upon the boy by having him throw a fine china plate on the tile floor, shattering it into a thousand shards. He said, "Emmer, once the plate is broken, can you fix it by saying sorry?" The eight-year-old Emerson shook his head, not sure if was his turn to speak. Chandler said, "No, boy. You cannot. All the sorrys in the world can't remake something you break in a fit of emotion. Remember that."

He had learned the lesson well. Amber was no longer listening. At this point she probably couldn't even hear him. She still had her head back, eyes closed and mouth open, mouthing some nonsense song. Emerson made one last try. He yelled. "AMBER, GET THE FUCK OFF ME!"

Something inside his mind snapped like an over-stretched rubber belt. When it recoiled, Emerson spasmed and threw Amber off the bed and onto the slate floor. Her head hit the tile, and she rolled over, unconscious. Emerson leapt to her curled body and felt for her pulse, which was steady and strong. He looked at her pupils, which reacted properly to the light. "Thank God," he mumbled.

He called out, "Quinn. If you are near here, come now." She didn't answer. Amber's breathing was slow but steady. He covered her with a sheet and called Quinn's PDA, which went to voicemail. He left her his message as he buttoned his shirt and skipped down the stone steps, "What the fuck, Quinn. I just knocked your friend unconscious. Amber? Yeah. Nice friends you have. You told her I'd happily give her my sperm? Where in the actual fuck did you get that idea? Fuck you. I'm going to work."

◆ ◆ ◆

OUTPOST 212

Dander Mitchel was in the locker room when Emerson came in. They greeted one another with hugs like they were brothers. Indeed, Emerson felt close to Dander, and the older pilot looked out for him. Dander zipped into his jumpsuit and said, "There's a mission to Outpost 212, due west out to the Inland Sea. It requires two shuttles, but there are no return riders. I have some traps near there, and I thought you'd like to be my second, get out of the city, and maybe do some hunting."

They did the necessary paperwork and had their ships stocked. The flight out was uneventful. Emerson read the three books Quinn had given him. He saw a notification that she had called, but the service in The City didn't reach far enough out. He would have to listen to the message later.

The geography book was a good reference. He wondered about the logistics of dismantling a marble fountain half a world away, bringing it back, and reassembling it. His questions would fill a book, but mainly, he was curious about flying over the ocean. What was the other side of the world like now?

Quinn was right about The City book. It was full of lies and misrepresentations. He'd only been there a short while, and it was already obvious to him. Then, he thought, it was more likely that he could see the freedoms the Middles *believed* they had but did not. *The Girl's Guide* was an eye opener and, he suspected, mostly satire. He wanted to talk to Quinn about some of The City spots it listed like Carolina's Lard Hotel.

His feelings for her were confused. On the one hand, he was attracted to her self-assured power and intelligence. On the other, she was selfish and rude. He didn't know what to make of her. The sex was incredible. Quinn did things to him that would have made Sally cringe. He wanted to understand her, but he wasn't sure he should ever go near her again.

At the end of the file was a video labeled, FOR EMERSON'S EYES ONLY. Emerson opened it. Elli Rattlesnake Quinn, from the waist up, filled the frame. She was shirtless and smiling.

"Hey, Tiger. Sorry about Amber. I told her you might be open to the idea. I'm not responsible for what that woman does, but she doesn't listen very well. Anyway. I just wanted to tell you that I didn't take over your neural connection when we made love. That was all you. <kiss-kiss!>

"Your Interface connection as installed by the Enforcers could make you vulnerable to manipulation, but when I scanned you at the Red Palace, your implant was already locked. You have friends in high places, Emerson Lloyde. It would be a serious breach of sovereignty to take over a lord, and that's what you are in The City. Especially now since I registered you that way when I made your address as mine.

"The Authority has trained technicians who guide the desires of the Middles. It's a subtle art and takes years to perfect. That's why there is no dissent among the masses. The Authority diverts poor decisions whenever possible; it's for their own good. Call me when you get this." Quinn blew him a kiss and held her left breast while she took a deep breath and sighed. The video ended.

Their deployment at 212 was routine. Emerson watched the muddy town carry on its daily business through the second-story windows of the shuttle cafeteria. The lounge was insulated from the town that grew up around it. Outsiders were not allowed in, and the Enforcers were supposed to stay away, but nobody paid any attention to those rules unless they needed an excuse. Push carts with repurposed bicycle wheels crowded the muddy streets, and people, many drunk or drugged, slipped and slid trying to go from one tent or stall to the next. There was a brothel directly across from the Flight Center. A strategic placement, no doubt. A sign, The Fly Saloon, written with an unsteady hand in red paint, hung over the stairs. He'd heard that the women in the outposts were all kidnapped and held against their will. Most were addicted to drugs, which made them easier to control.

Emerson watched Dander step up on the porch. A pale redheaded woman in a pink garter and nothing else brought him inside by the arm. A minute later, an Enforcer lieutenant burst through the doors, hopping on one foot, trying to put on his boot, with a naked, blond woman hanging onto his back, screaming in a foreign language, hitting him over the head with a heavy book.

Outposts were strictly Enforcer-manned installations. There weren't supposed to be any civilians. The shanty towns grew up around each outpost. They had no paved roads, no infrastructure. Water had to be trucked in or found and purified in order to be safe, which much was not. There were no supplies for the non-Enforcer population. The people who lived in Outpost 212 were non-citizens. As far as The Authority was concerned, they were outside the wall, Dreks. Valueless.

But surrounding each Flight Center, there was a thriving market with a class structure of its own. The official rules were ignored. 212 had a fish market. Emerson decided to buy a whole cod to make for dinner out in the woods. He would smoke strips on a rack and maybe make jerky. For that he'd also need spices and salt.

He asked the fishmonger, "You have a boat? Where do you fish?"

The toothless fisherman laughed and said, "No boat! I stand on the shore. The fish jump out of the water into my net. No boats anymore! Besides, you fall in that water, you die!" He laughed again and accepted a vial of antivenom as a trade for the cod.

While Emerson was down in the street, a fight broke out between two local men. One of them, the heavy one, was having the piss kicked out of him by a skinny bald guy who was apparently stoned out of his skull.

The result looked preordained until the heavy guy pulled out a short-barreled shotgun and killed Skinny by putting a large hole in his chest. Guns were rare but not unheard of. Activity in the street didn't register that a man had been killed. The dead body sank into the mud and disappeared. Two Enforcer infantrymen descended on the gunman and dragged him away as he yelled about justice. Emerson continued on to the spice shop.

He met up with Dander later that afternoon. They packed and provisioned their shuttles and went to the cafeteria so Dander could eat. Emerson fasted. Eating replicator food had become impossible for him.

As they rose above the outpost later that evening, Emerson hovered over the edge of the shore and asked, "Dander, why don't we fly over it and see what's on the other side?"

"You know the answer, Emerson. We can't carry enough fuel to fly that far, man."

"That's bullshit. I know that if we can get to Italy, we can get across a flooded river."

"Well, you asked, and that's the reason. You can disagree with it all you like, but take it up with somebody else 'cause I ain't got no dog in that fight."

Dander built cabins in several places in the vast lands surrounding The City. They landed and unlocked the systems. Emerson had a fire going and fish sizzling in the time it took Dander to unload their gear. They were looking forward to a few days of wandering around in the woods, checking on traps and hunting. Before he did anything, Emerson changed into his woods clothes and his grandfather's jacket. Chandler made the insulating material by copying the design of a bird's wing. By copying the way air was trapped inside hollow feathers, he grew the structures in his shop. Chandler had a talent for synthesizing. His insight appeared as though he could see around corners and into the future. When Emerson wore the clothes, his body maintained a constant temperature and humidity. It was fitted as an over suit. Emerson looked bloated when he wore it.

Sitting around the fire, later that evening, Emerson said, "You don't believe all that bullshit about fuel, do you? There's probably enough capacity in your little ship to get you to Italy and back."

Dander threw the stick he'd been fooling with into the fire and sighed, "No, I don't. But you have to be aware, Emerson. Talking on the radio is like talking directly to The Authority. You need to remember that. Speaking out against the established way is dangerous. Those people have no mercy, and they don't offer second chances."

Emerson put another log on. The fire snapped. He breathed in deeply. "Which people are you talking about, Dander?"

"I think you know."

"No, Dander. I don't."

"The ones in charge, of course."

"And who are they?"

"You know this already, boy. What are you getting at?"

"I've been in Founder's Quarter. I'm dating a Founder girl, ah, woman. Quinn."

"Shut the fuck up. You're fucking a Founder? I rest my case, man. You are too stupid to be alive."

"I don't know, man. She seems pretty regular to me."

"Like you would know." He did a bad imitation of Yoda, though he had never seen a Star Wars film. "So worldly you are."

The fire was beginning to die. Dander slapped a mosquito. Emerson said, "I know a way to repel those bastards. Remind me when we get back and I'll dig up the recipe. And yes, I know. Quinn has a thick shell, but I can get through it. I'm working on it. I'll break through."

Dander stood, dusted off his pants and went inside. Emerson lay back and looked at the stars. He could still identify the important groups. With the stars and an accurate clock, he could navigate to anywhere on the planet, part of the Chandler education method. In many things, the old man really knew what he was doing.

When Emerson was sure the fire was going out, he went inside, but came back out with a bedroll a few minutes later and lay down by the smoldering embers.

◆ ◆ ◆

In the morning, after three beautiful late summer days in the woods, seeing no one and only talking when necessary, thick clouds covered the sky, pressing down on Emerson. He felt like the barometer was blowing up a balloon inside his head. He and Dander started packing without saying a word. As he was locking up, Dander said, "I have another mission to perform on the way back. You're welcome to come with or just head on back."

"What kind of mission?" Emerson had just changed back into his pilot's coveralls.

"I do some work on the side for a higher-up in The Authority. I think he actually skims off the top. Then he passes what we find on to the Founders."

"Right. Quinn told me about this. I didn't know they were using pilots from the Enforcers, but it makes sense. Who else would be able to poke around for stuff?"

"It's a little more complicated than poking around. I have maps. Clues I've have been systematically tracking down. The Founders collect everything, whether it is permanent or transitory."

"You mean whether it's art, machine, or food, right?"

He nodded and said, "So, you want to come? Follow me. Most of these places are abandoned, but there are sometimes Dreks. You know, bandits and squatters. You need to keep your weapon ready."

Emerson snickered when Dander said weapon, but he turned away so the other pilot would not see him. *Weapon*, he thought. *I'm more effective with a rock and leather belt than I will ever be with a short sword. And what in the hell would I do with that if the other guy had a gun, like Skinny?* He didn't voice these thoughts. Instead, he said, "I'd rather have my grandpa's crossbow." He patted the nano-polymer package clipped to his tool belt. To Dander, it looked like a thin, black notepad, but when unfolded, it turned into a deadly accurate weapon. Emerson had adapted it to his Interface; he could sight through the viewfinder in his helmet.

"We should all have these bows," Emerson said. But Dander was already boarding. He turned back. "Turn off your transponder and stay off the radio, Emerson. The Authority doesn't need to have a record of this."

"Won't that set off an alarm if I shut down my tracker?"

Dander said, "I have our serial numbers programmed in a transponder circuit here at the cabin. After we are done, I can switch it off remotely. Don't worry about it, man. I have you covered."

Emerson strapped in and switched off his transponder. No one would be able to find him with it off. And until Dander switched off the remote copy, he had to leave it off, as it would send up a major red flag if there were suddenly two.

He followed Dander's shuttle above the trees and then above the cloud cover. Once above, the sky opened up clear and endless. Dander shot off to the north, and Emerson caught up to him in a minute. They flew for an hour. Dander rocked his shuttle to signal Emerson he was landing. They touched down in a scrub grass and thistle clearing, which must have been a paved parking lot before the collapse.

They got out together. Dander said, "There is a building complex below this parking lot. My intel says the door should have been near here." He took a four-meter-long metal pole out and held it like a wizard's staff, rapping the end on the ground. It made a dull thudding noise. He walked around in a spiral, each circle growing wider until the one final strike that hit metal. It produced a hollow echo from somewhere underground.

Dander said, "We'll bring the shuttles close. I have some tools. We should be able to get this open in short order."

After scraping most of the dirt away, Dander used a laser cutter to remove the lock panel. It took both of them to lift the steel door open on its hinges; they let it fall over on the weeds. The sunlight illuminated a rusty spiral staircase coiling down into the black shaft out of sight.

Emerson shined his light into the space. "Let's go check it out," he said.

At the bottom he looked up at the square of blue sky. He estimated it to be about three stories deep. He shined his light around. Corridors stretched into the darkness to his left and right. They were lined with overhead-type doors.

Dander said, "We don't have to look in all of them. We just have to bring back evidence. Someone higher up will justify a retrieval mission."

He removed the lock from the nearest garage and rolled up the door. Emerson shined the light. Inside were several wooden crates of varying sizes. Most were stenciled in black with Chinese characters. Dander looked at Emerson.

Emerson said, "I have no clue."

"Only one way to find out." He slid a prybar out of his tool belt and wedged the lid off one crate. Inside, six, compact plasma guns made of a rainbow-colored alloy gleamed back at them. Both men said, "Damn," together.

Dander picked up a rifle. He said, "This is an Interface weapon. If the rest of these crates are filled with similar artillery, this room alone would justify a full-scale retrieval." He picked up another and gave it to Emerson. "You should keep this baby in your shuttle whenever you fly outside the walls. A weapon like this could cut a shuttle in half at 500 meters."

They opened a different-sized box. Inside were four five-gallon buckets marked with three Chinese letters. Emerson pointed. "This character means paint. I've seen it on cans my grandad salvaged. I don't know the others." He broke the seal and poured a little on the floor. It formed a small shiny black puddle. Emerson screwed the top back on.

But as the liquid dried before their eyes, the shininess was replaced by deep flat blackness. Emerson bent and touched it. "Damn, Dander, this is anti-reflective paint. It absorbs light. I read about it somewhere. It was called the blackest black ever made. So black that it's actually cold."

Dander said, "I'll make sure to put it in my report. This must have been a secret munitions storehouse. My intel said it contained humanitarian supplies."

He resealed the door with an official Authority tag, an Interface locking device that recorded movement and kept a time log. They ascended the stair to the surface. Dander resealed the main doors with a similar lock. He and Emerson kicked dirt over the plate-steel door.

Dander said, "I'll make a report when I get back. You keep quiet about it since I wasn't supposed to bring you here." They boarded their respective shuttles and headed back to The City. Emerson made a note of the location just to cover his ass if anything went south with Dander's exclamation for the Lords. Neither of them made it back to The City.

◆ ◆ ◆

JUICE HACKERS

lli Rattlesnake Quinn looked at the pregnancy test again and shook the pink plastic stick, willing the second line to appear, but it did not. She wondered if the expiration date on the box meant it was completely useless or if it was just a date stamp to show the retailer when to throw it away and buy replacements. Either way, the test expired on 2/28/50, nearly fifty years ago. She thew the tester on the floor and opened another box; she had a half case of them left. She squatted over her toilet and strained to squeeze out a drop, but there was nothing.

"Fuck," she spat and pulled up her leather pants. She looked at her body's profile in the floor-to-ceiling dressing mirror. Tanya appeared and asked if she needed any help. Quinn said, "No." When her maid turned to leave, she said, "Wait, yes. Go to Doctor Sailor's and get me a pregnancy test that works."

Tanya said, "Don't you have a whole box of them? I'd think that would be enough."

Quinn shouted, "I didn't ask you to think, shithead, I told you to go get me a fresh one. Pronto! Now, git."

The woman looked at Quinn for a longsuffering moment and walked slowly to the door. Before she opened it, she turned and said, "I'm not your slave, you know," and left, closing the door gently behind her.

Quinn scoffed. "Oh, but you are, dear girl. We all have to serve someone." She laughed, smoothed her hands down her flat stomach, and sighed. She sent a text to Emerson:

> Come and get it. Third time's a charm, Tiger.

The system couldn't connect, signaling her that he was outside the wall. She said, "Fuck," to the empty room and went to find something to drink and take her mind off her uncooperative reproductive system.

Tanya returned with a test. The lot number was the same as the whole case Quinn had. She said, "Figures," and gave it back to her maid. "Put it with the others." Tanya shook her head and mumbled something that Quinn didn't bother to make out. She poured herself a glass of bourbon and downed it in one gulp. She texted Emerson again. She was being impatient, but she had a feeling; it was hard to identify. She was used to caring mainly about herself. She couldn't tell if she was worried about Emerson because she needed his sperm or if she actually liked him. He *was* cute and charming, in an innocent kind of way. But she couldn't shake the feeling that something was wrong.

> Hey, what's up? Where are you?

◆ ◆ ◆

Dander told Emerson that he had released the shuttle transponder codes and said, "Follow me in from here; we can arrive together, and it will look as though we came directly from Outpost 212."

Emerson set the autopilot and opened the book from Quinn about The City's history. He was looking for a reference to her family name: Quinn. The chapter on The Lords of The City listed Boston Quinn as the latest generation. There was nothing about Elli Rattlesnake or any other Elite child in the book, only Lucia Rattlesnake, who he assumed was Quinn's mother.

The landscape below them began to change, buildings appeared, and neighborhoods began to spring up signaling the final approach. Dander dropped altitude for final entry, and Emerson followed. He had a moment of apprehension remembering the Molotov cocktail rocket from the last time. But there was no movement on the ground. He went back to his book. Dander radioed their approach.

The rockets made no noise until they struck their targets. Emerson could clearly see Dander in the cockpit of his shuttle when the first stream hit him. When the blast enveloped the midsection of the vessel, it broke in two and fell out of the sky. Emerson only had a moment before his craft was struck. He shouted, "Holy fuck, Mitchel. Are you…" A second later, the rapidly disintegrating pieces of Dander's shuttle fell onto the streets below, leaving a fiery trail of shards and twisted wreckage. No one could have survived.

Emerson's shuttle lost power and began to drop. He snapped on the mayday beacon and struggled to keep the nose up, but it was futile. The controls disconnected, and the vessel continued to fall. Emerson strapped his body in tighter, put his Interface on automatic, and braced for a rough landing. A minute that seemed like an hour later, the craft hit the ground and skidded to a stop along a cluttered suburban street, clipping piles of metal trash and burned-out car carcasses, finally slamming into a brick retaining wall. The engine was burned up, and the windshield was cracked, but the outer shell was intact, so cabin pressure remained consistent. He ran a system check to be sure nothing was about to explode and unstrapped. The radio was dead. He was still too far away from The City to use his PDA. Taking stock of his situation, he realized that he had just watched one of his oldest friends die. Grief nearly knocked the wind out of him.

It was getting dark. He did a short-range movement and heat-signature scan and opened the hatch. The shuttle smoked from underneath, but he decided that was from scraping along the road and not an immediate worry. He began to leave but remembered the plasma rifle and went back for it.

He left his helmet on, hoping it would provide some protection if someone tried to hurt him. He cautiously stepped onto the street.

◆ ◆

Quinn called her father and asked that he put a search notice out for Emerson.

Boston said, "And why would I do that?"

"He's your future heir's father. Is that enough for you?"

"What?!"

She hung up on him. Twenty minutes later, she got a message from a Lieutenant Captain Monroe: Emerson Lloyde's shuttle dropped off the scopes just before crossing the wall. He was down, somewhere in the wastelands, his whereabouts and health unknown. But his Interface was up. They assumed he was alive.

She called Boston back. "Daddy. You have to do something."

"You never call me daddy, Elli."

"I'm appealing to your loyalty. To family. Please find Emerson and bring him back to me."

"I'll see what I can do, but Enforcer business is out of my hands."

"That's bullshit, and you know it. You are a lord. The *Elder* lord, God dammit. Who cares what the others think? You can do anything you want. I'm telling you: this man is part of your family. You have to do everything possible to save him!"

Though her father agreed to try, Quinn had a pit in her stomach. Something *was* wrong. She'd felt it, and now it was confirmed. The feeling didn't go away. Something was desperately wrong. All she could do was wait. She dimly realized that she had lied to her father. She hoped Emerson would be returned to her before the truth was obvious. She never depended on people; she couldn't tolerate the risk.

The Authority confirmed that Dander Mitchel was dead. His shuttle was disintegrated. But Emerson's was intact, disabled, but in one piece.

The command protocol was automatically put into action. The highest priority was to keep the technology out of the hands of the Juice Hackers, a decentralized group of Outsiders who'd stolen and reprogrammed Interface cubes and implants, presumably removed from corpses. The protocol was to target the downed shuttles and retrieve them. But in this case, the tech was spread all over the quadrant. There was nothing left of Dander's craft to target. The second choice was to eliminate the population. It was more costly in resources, but it would solve the problem quickly. Most importantly, it was a justifiable action. The most important thing was to contain the tech.

A team of Enforcers, on foot, placed a set of low-frequency emitters throughout the area. When activated, the tones produced would shatter the eardrums of any living creature and disincorporate nervous communication, effectively killing every living thing with a brain for a one-kilometer-wide circle around each of the ten devices. The troop was deployed within twenty minutes of the first crash.

Quinn was not told about the decision until the following morning. She locked herself in her apartment and drank herself to sleep.

♦♦

Emerson used the infrared filter on his helmet's visor to scan the area. He took his survival day pack and the plasma gun. He also brought his grandfather's jacket and mittens. It might be a while before he reentered The City. If he could stay alive, he might be free. The prospect was wildly exciting. He cautiously looked around a corner. A short arrow whizzed past his head and stuck in a door frame. He turned in the direction of the shooter and blindly fired, searing a two-foot-high gash in the side of a garage. When the smoke cleared, he could see inside; a similar-sized, orange gash in a car's side sparked and glowed. He spun around to a noise behind him. He found himself pointing the weapon at a cringing red-haired girl, dressed in rags, cowering next to a pile of plastic boxes. The gun beeped, signaling a full charge. Emerson shut the weapon down and extended his hand.

He said, "If we stay here, we die. Come with me now." Another arrow glanced off the metal side of the shuttle. The girl ran to him. He opened the door, pulled her inside, and sealed it as a volley of arrows clattered against the outer skin.

◆ ◆ ◆

The Enforcer team set emitters around the quadrant and pulled back. One man caught an arrow in his shoulder, and an Enforcer fired at the source, but they never saw anyone. An hour later, when the team was safely back within the walls, they activated the emitters. Emerson and the girl could only feel a faint vibration. Everything outside their vessel within the entire quadrant died screaming in agony. Emerson and the child stayed inside until morning. He altered his jumpsuit to fit her, but she had no shoes, and there were sores under the filth covering her neck, face, and hands. Emerson cleaned her as best he could with moist towels from the latrine. She didn't resist. The child was pliable like a Gumby doll; she let Emerson move her anyway he wanted. He was apprehensive, not knowing where it was alright to touch her body. When he was done, she wasn't much cleaner.

He went to the replicator, but the ship's power was too low. When he turned around, she let the jumpsuit fall around her ankles and stood naked with her hands at her sides. He'd thought she was much younger when he brought her on board, but standing in front of him, he could see the faint wisps of her pubic hair. She didn't speak.

When he tried to give her back the jumpsuit, she bent over the cot, presenting her butt to him and wiggling her thin hips back and forth. Emerson said, "No, no. I don't want that. Put your clothes back on." He took her by the shoulders, stood her up, and turned her around. He said, "You're safe now." Her face did not register his words. She put the jumpsuit on again and rolled up the pants and sleeves. Emerson used elastic bands to hold them in place.

He gave her some dried cod, which she swallowed without chewing, and told her to lay in his cot and try to sleep. He sat in the cockpit and explored the communicators. But the only application he could access was the locater beacon. He didn't have any hope of being rescued. The Enforcers who set the emitters had seen the beacon. They weren't interested in saving his life. He realized with no small amount of satisfaction that he was on his own. *Good,* he thought. *It's time to get out of this place anyway.*

◆ ◆

When Quinn was notified of the low-frequency deployment, she tried to reach out with her mind to locate Emerson, but she never had an extrasensory ability. Still, she couldn't accept Emerson's death. It didn't seem possible. He was inside of her just the other day. He couldn't be dead. He was supposed to father her baby. The doctors had created a synthesized herbal decoction of valerian root. She took a pill. It usually gave her a rest. After twenty minutes, she took another. And then another. She slept four hours, got up to pee, and get a drink, and then she took four more and went back to bed.

◆ ◆ ◆

Emerson and the girl packed up whatever they could carry in two slings and left the shuttle early the following morning. Evidence of the mass death caused by the emitters was everywhere. Everything from rats to children had died gruesome deaths in the streets. The bodies were jumbled together as if in their last moments, differences became irrelevant; they died clinging to each other, the last living beings they could touch. Emerson covered the girl's eyes from the anguished death masks, but she didn't respond any differently, sighted or blind. A short time later, she stopped at the corpse of a woman of similar size to her and took shirt, pants, and shoes. She dropped the jumpsuit on top of the corpses.

Emerson knew how The Authority thought. His shuttle was at the center. The emitters would have been set to eliminate all life within a day's walk. It was early. He estimated they would be outside the circle before sundown. "Early enough to make camp," he said, remembering the way the words sounded in Chandler's mouth, wondering if they felt to the old man the same way as they did to him. The girl did not respond. She walked dispassionately.

Emerson worried that she would fall into a hole if he didn't stop her, but later that morning, she leapt over a pile of dead mice and skipped twice after. Her face betrayed no joy, no emotion of any kind, but her body was alive and deft. He realized that her silence was her protection; lack of engagement was a shield.

He understood staying shielded. Even though he loved his grandfather, he never fully trusted him. After the old man nearly died saving his life, his fears were only confirmed. To get through to this girl, he would need to earn her trust.

He asked, "Do you have a name? Because I need to call you something. If you don't tell me, I'll have to make something up. So, what will it be?" She didn't speak or look at him. After a few steps, he said, "I'm gonna call you Elli. She's a friend who lives in The City."

The girl did not make any motion that she heard or understood Emerson. He continued, "I'm Emerson, by the way. I lived in The City, but I grew up outside the wall." He waited. "Okay then. Elli, meet Emerson, Emerson, Elli."

In the high-pitched voice of a stick-doll pilot character he made up as a young boy, he said, "Glad to meet you, Emerson. I'm Elli."

She didn't laugh, but he saw the corner of her mouth twitch, though it could have been his imagination. He took it as a good sign and said, "The sooner we are out of the kill zone, the better I'll feel. Let's go a little faster, 'k?" He began to jog; the girl, Elli, jogged alongside him. She didn't look at him. She sped up so she was nearly trotting. Emerson had to run to catch her. He smiled when they were side by side again. Elli didn't react to him. She faced forward with her disinterested expression, as though she had seen it all at the ripe old age of… what? At first, he'd thought she was no more than ten. But after her come-on in the shuttle, when he'd gotten a closer look at her body, he knew she was older. Fifteen, maybe?

He said, "Elli, how old are you?"

She looked at him, if only for a second. She stared into his eyes. Emerson saw her clearly for the first time. She was *much* older, even if she didn't have many years on her. He let it rest; small talk was what people did when they didn't want to face the truth. Her eyes told enough of that story to know it would be a while before she could say any of it out loud.

He said, "That's alright. But really, next to you, I'm old. Let's slow down just a bit, or I won't be able to walk at all tomorrow." He heard Chandler's voice when he said that too. He knew he wasn't really that old. It was just a story he made up to ask her to slow down. He thought, *I do spend a lot of my time sitting on my ass.* He imagined Chandler's scowl.

They jogged across the boundary of the kill zone near sunset. Skies were clear; there would be enough light to set up camp for at least another hour. Emerson had been scoping out suitable shelter for a while. He said, "We need to collect some firewood. I can probably make a lean-to out of some of this scrap."

Elli didn't listen to him; she walked to the nearest building and went inside, closing the door behind her. Emerson went after her as soon as he realized she was gone. When he opened the door to the brick townhouse, she was standing in the middle of a decaying, high-ceilinged entry hall with another young person. She put up her hand to stop Emerson before he could speak. The young man standing across from her said, "Hi, I'm Jacob. She says you need shelter. I'm obligated to help if I can, and there's plenty of room in this house. I live here alone."

It took Emerson a moment to understand what Jacob was saying. He could tell from the boy's voice that he was young. His accent was thick. He was slight of build but tall enough to be a man. Emerson said. "She spoke to you?"

Jacob said, "Not with words, but I knew what she was asking. These times require the old way."

"Old way?"

"Hospitality. Never turn anyone away if you can help."

"Yes, my granddad taught me that. People in The City don't know anything about it. Everyone is a potential enemy there."

Jacob said, "I've heard the stories. We support each other here. There are other quadrants where…" He trailed off. Emerson could imagine what he wasn't saying. Some of those people killed Dander; to them, he was the enemy. They offered no hospitality.

◆ ◆

Enforcer cleanup crew 05 arrived at Emerson's shuttle near noon. Six other crews were deployed around the quadrant gathering debris left by Dander's disintegrated ship. They confirmed Dander Mitchel's death about an hour later. By sundown, Emerson's shuttle was airlifted out, and Emerson was listed as missing, not confirmed dead. It seemed that Emerson's implant was locked; they required several layers of permission from him to access his Interface. They didn't include that in their report.

That news was passed on to Quinn after she woke up at ten that night. She asked Tanya to get her a cup of coffee and to summon her friend and fellow Elite child, Maxamillion Hamp. She always told Max everything; he would help her see the big picture.

By the time she had showered and put on a sheer silk dressing gown, drinking the last of her second cup, Tanya told her that Max was in the drawing room. They embraced when she entered. She pulled him into her private lounge and pushed him down into a stuffed leather chair. She sat on the coffee table across from him with her hands on her knees. Max tried not to stare at her body through the silk, but he was doing a poor job.

She said, "I didn't think it was possible, Max. But it seems I've fallen in love. At least I think it's love. I can't stop worrying about him. His shuttle was shot down on the outside. The other pilot was killed. And now he's missing. I'm afraid, Max."

124

Max said, "Yes, hello to you too, Elli. Slow down a tad, eh? Why wouldn't he identify himself to the cleanup crews? How far could he possibly be? A day's walk? He'll show up in a couple days."

Quinn chewed the cuticle on her thumbnail, stopped herself, and sat on her hand. "That's the thing. I don't think he wants to be found. I don't think he's coming back."

"Oh, I see."

"No, you don't. It's worse. I told my dad I'm pregnant."

"You bedded him already? Fuck me, girl. You move fast."

"You were there the first time. And it's been three months; you call that fast?"

"I forget who we're talking about."

"Beside the point. I lied to the Elder Lord Boston Quinn, himself."

"He'll forgive you. You're his only daughter."

"I asked him for a favor, and I pushed him with a lie. I'm fucked, Max. I need to be pregnant."

"Well, you know I can't help you there. My line ends with me, I'm afraid."

"Not that I don't love you dearly, Maxamillion, but I don't want to fuck your sterile dick."

"Ouch."

"Sorry. I want Emerson Lloyde. I want to have his baby. I never felt anything this strongly in my life."

"Oh, I dunno, Miz Rattlesnake. I've seen you at your most passionate, remember? At the Red Palace, there's no place to hide."

"Ha, ha. This is different, Max. This is real. I need to find him before someone else does. By now, The Authority considers him a high-level security risk—he's a trained shuttle pilot. I can't ask my father for anything else."

"You shouldn't have asked him for anything in the first place."

She continued as if he hadn't spoken. "I need a team that answers only to me. I need them to go into the outside and track him down. I need to talk to him."

Max thought for a moment and said, "I'll ask around. Shake a few trees, see what falls out."

"Where do you get these archaic expressions?"

"That's what I'm studying, Elli. Idioms from before the collapse. Now tell me, can I get some of that sixty-six-year-old bourbon?"

"A little early, yes? Maybe you'd like Tanya to put it in some coffee."

"Ah, it's close to midnight, Quinn,"

"Not for me. You're in my world now. So, coffee?"

"Real coffee? Yes, that sounds great. I forget your family avoids the replicators. There's some logic in that. Especially when there's real coffee."

"Like we used to say when we were kids, Max: someday this will all be gone."

Tanya brought him a cup, as though she had been listening around the corner with the pot ready. Quinn said, "Let me know when you have my team ready."

He sipped his coffee. "Aaaah. Yes. Will do."

"And stop staring at my tits."

"Ah, ok."

Quinn stood up, "You can go now."

"But I haven't finished my coffee…"

She strode away. "Tanya will see you out. Goodnight, Max."

◆ ◆ ◆

Emerson and Elli stayed with Jacob overnight. They slept on the floor in the empty living room. At dawn Emerson gave her a strip of elk jerky. His stash was almost empty. This was the end of the last batch that he and Chandler stretched. Thinking about hunting put a smile on his face. Elli took the dried meat and gnawed off an end. Emerson said, "I'm leaving. You can stay here if you want, or you can come with me."

Elli stared into the corner, chewing on the jerky with her hands in her lap.

Emerson said, "OK, then. I guess this is goodbye." He was only ten paces down the street when she caught up to him; neither spoke. She knew he'd seen her. They walked on in silence for most of the morning. Near noon, they arrived at a swollen swamp. Years ago, it had been a scenic park overlooking a trickling stream. The river marked the border of the old city from before the wall. The road they traveled was once a main street.

The bridge crossing the water was somewhat intact, meaning steel rebar showed though the cracked and flaking cement in several places, and the steel girders spanning its length were rusted and decaying. Vines of kudzu and blackberries draped the siderails.

But the pavement looked sound, if you didn't step into a pothole, of which there were several. And when Emerson stamped his boot on the roadway, the bridge didn't shake. He deemed it safe enough, though they crossed without a pause, not quite running, but not dawdling either. As they passed one hole, Emerson noticed that he could see through to the churning water below.

The other side was more overgrown. The foliage had taken the street, and the woods encroached. The path was dark and overgrown. They walked for several hours until large houses began to appear off the trail. Worn paths crisscrossed the spaces between, signaling Emerson that people lived here. Though they didn't see anyone, they avoided the buildings. By the end of the day the few houses, they encountered were vacant. The vegetation was thicker. A few moments later, they saw a brick home with a wraparound porch near the road. Emerson said, "We should go inside before it's dark."

The inside looked like the people who lived there had left for work or school in a hurry and just never came back. Cereal bowls on the kitchen table, moldy dried scum in the Mr. Coffee. Dishes in the sink, food in the fridge. Of course, it didn't look like food; anything organic had rotted or been eaten. Empty cardboard boxes with holes chewed in them scattered the floor.

Emerson verified that there were no bodies in the house, and after a little searching, he found a linen closet with blankets that weren't too ravaged. Mice had chewed some of the fiber filling, but they were long dead; even their scat had turned to dust.

He set up a sleeping area near the front door and built a fire in the fireplace. The chimney drew poorly, and the house filled with smoke at first. But once it warmed, the air cleared. Emerson went out with his crossbow in search of game. Elli wasn't interested in moving from the fire. He gave her his last strip of jerky and the waterskin. "Drink more when you eat a lot of that stuff. It will suck up all the water in your body."

Emerson walked deeper into the forest seeking game. Elli ate the jerky and drank all the water. By the time it was dark, she had to pee. Two heavily dressed men met her on the walk back to the house. They wore camouflage and carried crossbows with stretch masks covering their heads and faces. Elli was startled but betrayed no emotion.

The thin one said, "Hey, what have we here, Rosco?"

The other said, "Leave her alone, Barton. We're not hunting little girls."

"Easy for you to say, Rosco. You're married."

Emerson appeared silently and held a knife under Barton's chin. He said, "I can kill him before you get an arrow nocked. Don't try. How 'bout you drop your bows and pull off those hats so I can see your faces?"

Rosco had short black hair and a bushy full beard which went well with his barrel chest and rotund gut. Barton was smaller, skinny even, with a shaggy blond mop. He had a clean-shaven, scrubbed look to him, but his cheeks looked swollen, which made his eyes seem small and sunken.

Elli walked back to the house, unconcerned.

Rosco said, "Don't let my brother's foolish mouth cause you to do something unnecessary. I'm Rosco, and he's Barton, and we are just hunting the woods. We didn't know anyone was livin' here."

Emerson slowly lowered his blade. "I'm Emerson. Me and the girl are just passing through. I grew up the outside the wall a ways south of here. We're just going home." He watched for any aggressive movement, the tensing of a muscle, the shift of gaze, before relaxing. Emerson was satisfied that the brothers posed no immediate threat, but he was never fully relaxed around people.

Rosco said, "We have a doe hung up down the path a piece. We can share a meal and you can help us butcher. A fair deal."

Emerson said, "We don't really need any help. But thanks for the offer."

Rosco said, "Bullshit. You aren't in The City anymore. Out here, loners die. Alone."

It was dark. He wouldn't find any game tonight anyway. He said, "OK, thanks. I'm a little touchy—lots of weird shit has been happening."

◆

They brought the carcass into the house and cut it up. Rosco complimented Emerson on his knife skills. Barton cooked a filet, and Emerson boiled a pot of groats on the fire. The four sat on a powder-blue, velveteen sectional eating venison with their fingers off Mikasa Bone China. To them, there was nothing ironic about the situation.

Rosco said, "We have hooch if you're into it." Elli got four teacups with saucers, and Barton filled each with a greasy-looking liquid.

Barton stood and said, "Miss Elli, please accept my humblest apology. I would never force a girl to do anything beyond her will." He raised his teacup and said, "To full bellies and new friends."

Elli looked him up and down as if gauging whether she could take him in a fight. Though he was thin, his body was wiry. He looked at her hungrily, small, beady eyes set in his round face. His lips were pouty, and his fingers short and stubby. She gave him a satisfied nod.

He believed his half-assed apology was sufficient and forgot about being called out. She decided he had a glass jaw; in a fair fight, Barton would be out before the first bell.

Emerson took a sip; the stuff was nearly pure alcohol. He looked around, realizing they were all still drinking. He quickly finished his. As soon as they put their cups on the coffee table, Barton refilled them. When they were finished, he tried to refill Emerson's, who stopped him saying, "Enough. Enough." He laughed. But the others were already downing their next.

It took a minute for Emerson to realize just how drunk he was. Elli leaned over the arm of the couch and vomited. She sat back up, grinning widely.

Barton said, "Lightweight," and laughed, bellowing like a bear.

Elli pulled down the waistband of her pants, exposing a dark blue triangle tattoo. She wiggled her hips and said, "You can fuck me if you want to."

Emerson raised his eyebrows and said, "Don't listen to her. She's drunk." It was the first time he'd heard her speak.

Elli said, "Emerson doesn't like girls." She giggled.

Emerson said, "Very drunk." To Elli, he said, "Nice to hear your voice. Just keep your pants on."

"They're not my pants. I stole them off a dead girl." She stuck out her tongue at him and said, "Hey, Barton, you got any more hooch?"

Before he could answer, because of course he did (at this point he would build a still and make more if it meant he'd could get closer to Elli), Emerson said, "I got a plasma rifle. Wanna see?" He showed it to them, laid it across his knees, capturing everyone's attention. Elli made a raspberry with her lips. Barton laughed.

Rosco said, "May I?"

He picked it up and held it in his hands for a moment. The rifle beeped, and the charge meter lit. Rosco said. "Cool. An Interface weapon."

Emerson was shocked. He said, "You have an implant?"

Rosco tapped the pulse beneath his ear and said, "We're Juice Hackers, Emerson. That's how we survive."

Rosco said, "Mind if I fire it?"

◆

Elli stumbled down the front steps. Barton caught her arm, and she leaned on his shoulder. They walked a few meters from the house. Emerson sighted a tree 100 meters away and fired. The pulse incinerated the first six meters of the trunk, and the tree fell forward, crashing to the ground just beyond the trail.

Rosco tried it next. He sighted the top of a Douglas fir and narrowed the beam and sliced the top two meters off.

Barton declined to try. Elli wanted to, but Emerson explained that she didn't have an implant and thus couldn't fire an Interface weapon. Rosco told him that wasn't exactly true. He handed the gun to Elli and said, "Put the stock against the hollow of your shoulder and put your finger on the trigger. Sight that white dogwood flower over there." He put his hand on top of the sight, and the charge meter lit, reducing the power to low yellow. Rosco said, "Squeeze the trigger."

The single blossom vanished with a small puff of smoke.

"Damn," Elli said.

Emerson said, "I didn't know you could do that."

"There's a lot The Authority people don't want you to know." He took the rifle and handed it to Emerson, who locked it. "If you stay with us for a little while, we can show you. We have a community just down the road. There's plenty for a man with an implant to do. But we better get Miss Elli to bed. I think she's already gone to sleep."

Elli snored, still leaning against Barton. He smiled sheepishly and said, "I'll carry her in."

Emerson said, "That's OK. I'll take her." He held the gun in one hand and put her over his shoulder like a bag of flour.

On the walk up the stairs, Rosco said, "We'd welcome you. And you could stay as long as you like, leave whenever you want to."

Emerson said, "I'll sleep on it and let you know in the morning."

Rosco said, "Fair enough."

◆ ◆ ◆ ◆

END OF PART TWO

INTERFACE

PART THREE

INTERFACE

PART THREE

QUINN'S TEAM

ax sent Quinn a note the next day to say he'd got the team together: three ex-Enforcers, two men and a woman. He said they had Emerson's Interface registration code, retina scan, and some history on his background; they needed to know how to stay in touch with her.

She texted him back:

```
Come see me. Bring the woman.
```

Later that evening, Tanya told her that she had visitors. They met in the sitting room. Quinn said, "You know who I am, right?"

The woman nodded. She had a thickly muscled neck with very short, brown hair, wore loose-fitted black drawstring pants, and an oversized black long-sleeve shirt that hung mid-thigh. Her loose clothing concealed her strength. Max had told Quinn the woman was a martial arts expert. She had been a tracker with the Enforcers until she twisted her knee. Injured soldiers were released without a hearing.

The woman stood at ease. Quinn told her to sit, sipped some tea, and said, "What's your name?"

"Nimue."[1]

"Right. Nimue, this man is my lover. He is going to be my husband. If anything happens to him, you will pay with your life. Am I clear? I must talk to him, just talk. Got it?"

She nodded again and said, "May I ask, ma'am, how are you going to communicate with him? All radio bands are monitored. Personal communication devices don't reach beyond the wall. Should we bring him to you?"

Quinn opened a wooden chest and removed two satellite phones. They were compact, not much larger than a PDA. She said, "The satellites that these phones use are still orbiting the earth. These are exceptionally rare. Call me when you find him and let me speak to him. Then return the phone to me."

The woman said, "Excuse me, lordling, but let me compliment you on your pregnancy. My podmother worked with birthing women. She taught me to see the differences in skin tone and color. I could tell you were pregnant when I first saw you. About ten weeks, correct?"

Quinn's face was red, though it was not clear to Max if it was anger or embarrassment. He prepared himself for her retaliation.

But Quinn surprised him. She said, "You are mistaken. I spent some time under a sunlamp, an ancient tool for darkening the melanin in my skin. Nothing more." She looked at the woman for a long moment; their eyes locked. The woman nodded.

Max promised various contraband items, titanium bars and rare electronic tech. "But not the phone," Quinn added. "These are mine."

As the woman left, Quinn said, "Thank you."

Max stayed behind. Quinn said, "I expect them to find Emerson within the week. Make sure they know it."

Max said, "Righto, captain. Listen, do you think you could get me a Switch or a Game Boy?"

---

1   Pronounced Nim-Wah, means Lady of the Lake.

Quinn pretended she didn't hear him. She said, "I figured you might want a drink."

Max said, "How do you always read my mind?"

"You are a man, Maxamillion. Men are easy. You guys either want pussy or altered states, am I right?"

"Like I said, Miz Rattlesnake, you read my mind."

◆ ◆ ◆

Col. Brent McGee was the head of security. He effectively ran The Authority. His office controlled the Enforcers. He received the salvage report from the collection teams. The delivery agent handed him the sealed envelope and left McGee's office. The colonel tore it open and read the one-page report.

He muttered, "Fuck," and sent his office manager a note that he would be gone for the remainder of the day. It took him half an hour to walk to Boston Quinn's house. By the time he arrived, the staff was serving lunch, and the colonel had calmed his jittery heartrate.

Boston said, "Come, sit. Have a meal with me. What's so important that you walked all the way up here without calling?"

McGee wasn't hungry. If anything, the news he brought made him nauseous. He nodded and sat. Boston Quinn had a reputation for serving foods that were no longer available. Brent knew firsthand how he acquired his copious stock of provisions. Today the staff brought hamburgers on poppyseed buns with potatoes cut into thin strips and fried in hot oil. The smell was intoxicating. The meal was delivered with ketchup packets and iced drinks in waxed paper cups.

The cups had obviously been used before. Brent pushed the fries around on his plate and had a sip of the drink, nearly gagged, and set the cup down. He noticed that it was leaking on Boston's inlayed wood table but didn't point it out, already nervous enough at the prospect of giving Lord Quinn bad news.

Boston ignored him. He ate three burgers and a handful of fries, drained his cup, and pushed his plate away. He tipped his chair back on two legs and stretched his legs. "So, McGee, what's the house fire?"

Col. McGee swallowed. His mouth was dry. He drained his leaky cup. It dribbled into his lap, leaving a conspicuous wet spot in his crotch. He took a breath and said, "The collection team got Emerson Lloyde's shuttle. There wasn't much left of Dander Mitchel. We got his implant and any part of his craft that was larger than a half meter. But we also found something unexpected." He paused to catch his breath. Apparently, he hadn't been breathing.

Boston, more impatient than usual, said, "Fuck, man. What was it? I need to piss."

McGee continued, "They found parts of a pre-collapse weapon. An Interface-driven plasma rifle."

Boston said, "And? You got it, right? Where the fuck did Mitchel get a gun like that?"

"That's the thing, sir. Dander Mitchel was our scavenger. He investigated caches of old items for us. It was a closely held secret. Only you and I know about the program, and only a couple of Authority agents work with the intelligence."

"Right. As it should be. What's the fucking problem, McGee? What the hell are you trying to say?"

"Emerson Lloyde, sir. He and Dander Mitchel were close. We assume that Lloyde went on salvage missions with him, and Mitchel didn't report it since it would have got him killed. There is a high probability that Emerson has one of these weapons. He also knows where they are. And the last place Mitchel investigated was rumored to be huge."

"That is interesting, Brent. Thank you. You can go."

Brent McGee was a high-ranking official. Boston Quinn didn't need to dismiss him twice. But before he got out the door, Quinn called to him, "McGee. Find him. Now. Bring him to me."

McGee sighed, relieved that he'd gotten away easily. Lord Quinn used his Interface connection to take the colonel's occipital lobe offline. The soldier walked into the door jamb, hitting his head and crumbling to the floor. He said, "Oh my God, I'm blind!" His nose was bleeding.

Boston brought his sight back and said, "Don't disappoint me again, McGee. Now git!"

The colonel stumbled trying to get away, as if distance would interrupt The Authority Control Lord Quinn had over him and every other Middle in The City.

He considered telling his daughter about Emerson, but rejected the idea. He thought, *This Emerson kid might turn out to be useful.*

♦ ♦ ♦

Emerson and Elli went with Rosco and Barton the next morning. Elli had a slamming headache and wasn't speaking. Her eyes were bloodshot, and she cringed at any noise. They had packed the butchered venison into saver bags. Rosco explained to Emerson that the polymers used in the bags was salvaged tech. The Juice Hackers accessed The Interface controls. The temperature inside the bags would drop to four degrees Celsius within minutes of being sealed. The bags automatically purged excess air.

Emerson said, "My grandfather had saver bags. I thought he invented them."

Rosco said, "Chandler Estes was your grandfather? Damn, son, these are his design. Most of the nano-plastic adaptations our people have made are based on Chandler's work. Your granddad was a genius!"

They arrived at the village of Blue Hole just before noon. The activity on the path had increased steadily for the last hour. Emerson stood silently taking in the wall; other pilgrims and traders passed him. Pine trees, pounded into the ground, surrounded the enclave. It stretched out as far as he could see in both directions away from the road. Rosco said, "She's big, ain't she? Ten meters above and five below."

Emerson said, still looking at the towering structure, "How did you build it?"

Rosco tapped his implant and smiled. "We're a resilient bunch."

They entered the village through a high gate guarded by two large men in military-looking Kevlar suits. The doors were made of the same thick pine logs and hung in balance, allowing each to be moved by a single person.

Within the walls, gridded streets of a suburban neighborhood sprawled out before them. The houses were converted into shops and warehouses. Garage doors were open, creating stalls where all manner of goods and foods were laid out.

Emerson said, "My grandpa took me to a market like this one a few times when I was a child. He would have loved this place."

One stall contained stacks of aluminum motors. Another had drawers of communication devices and solar chargers. Another displayed several varieties of squash. There was a fenced yard containing goats. Vertical gardens grew on every building. Rosco mentioned that there were large greenhouses for every kind of hydroponic. One stall had hanging cages of rabbits, mice, and ferrets. Elli stood near the rodent cages and watched the animals. Emerson had to go back and get her.

In front of a modest, wood-frame, two-story building with a wide front porch, Rosco said, "This is my house." There were vines hanging from every post and railing; it dripped flowers. "You and Elli are welcome to stay here until you find a place of your own. There are plenty."

Barton said, "I live on the other side of Blue Hole in a group house with a bunch of other single guys. I'm going to bring my meat home. I'll catch up with you later." He didn't leave, but hovered near Emerson and Rosco, listening. A broad-hipped woman with long grey tresses came down the narrow staircase.

Emerson thanked Rosco, who went on to say, "And this is my mate. Grendel, this is Emerson and Elli. They came from the first quadrant over the swamp. Enforcers murdered everyone. They were lucky to have escaped. Emerson is a pilot." He raised his eyebrows.

Grendel and Rosco kissed. Like her husband, she was a light brown thirtysomething woman. With her dark, greying dreadlocks, high cheek-bones, and several strands of beads, she looked like a wise woman from a fantasy world. She and Rosco had been together since they were children. She had told many people, "In this world, nothing is guaranteed, so, when you find someone, keep them close."

She was shorter and thinner than Rosco, but her hair, thick and long, made a balanced counterpart to his bear-like wildness. She carried a scar on her forehead from a fall trying to out-perform Rosco rock climbing, when she was barely a teen. The grey streaks in her hair began after she lost their first child nearly ten years ago; others followed.

Grendel ignored Emerson and took Elli's hand. She said, "This Moon child needs to bathe," and pulled her into the house. As they walked away, Grendel said, "Who cut your hair, child? Looks like it was hacked off with a machete."

Emerson said, "Moon child?"

Grendel said, "We call all orphans with no memory of their parents children of the moon. It often becomes a surname and gets passed on to future generations."

Rosco said, "She's my momma hen." He paused and said, "Hey, we have hot running water. You look like you could use a shower."

Emerson said, "In a minute. First, tell me, how long have you been living this way? It's incredible. No one in The City would believe it."

"When the Elites sealed The City walls, my family was on the outside along with thousands of others. They left us to die. My parents' parents nearly starved that first winter. Together with a group of other families, mostly engineers and doctors, they found this place and made it their own. Over the decades, we've been able to build the wall. Bandits and shysters taught us how to protect ourselves. We use The Interface to make new machines.

"My great-great-grandad was implanted. He passed it on to his son and so on until it became mine. Lots of folks here inherited their implants. The Interface is the most powerful weapon the Elites in The City covet. My people believe that power belongs to everyone."

Barton said, "Or no one."

Rosco turned to him, scowling, and said, "I thought you were taking your meat home."

Barton sulked. "Yeah. I'm going now."

After he left, Emerson said, "I take it you think your brother is an idealist."

"I don't think it's a philosophy. See, if anything, I'm a realist. Barton is just young and independent-minded. His brand of independence creates problems in a community like ours. He isn't implanted. Refuses it on *ethical grounds*, whatever that means. Lot of people aren't implanted, you know. I think it's a personal choice what a person does with their own body. As long as we work with everyone else."

"And Barton?"

"Oh, he'll come around. He's a good kid."

◆

Grendel took Elli to the baths. It would be a good way to introduce her to the village. Besides being dirty, the girl needed stability. Grendel understood where Elli came from, the sort of life she had led. And as her grandma would say, old habits died hard. Grendel watched out for the girl. Protecting her, yes. But protecting the people in her close family too. It was *her* old habit to neutralize threats in the kindest way: through healing.

The baths were crowded day and night. Fed by hot springs, they were made up of several smooth rock basins naturally carved into the rock of the hillside by the last glacier. Each one emptied into the next, forming a gentle, natural waterslide into the central pool. The minerals from the spring tinted the water blue. The entire complex of slides and ponds sprawled under a massive rock overhang. It felt like being inside the mouth of an enormous cave. The echoes from every conversation in the baths filled the cavernous space with a constant reverberation of murmurs, kind of a background white noise.

Grendel said, "The echo in the baths produces a sound many believe is healing. It's the sound of the very people it heals. These waters are never still, and this space is always filled. We come here to let go of the world outside and remember what's real."

To Elli, it felt like she floated above the ground by just being in the cavernous space. There had to be 200 people nearby. Her anxiety drained away with the flowing water. She smiled.

Grendel continued, "Everybody has their own reasons for forgetting what is most important, but we all do it. The baths will help." She removed her sarong and necklaces and placed them on an outcropping of slate, stepped into the water, and floated out. The current spilled down the successive steps, flowing into each of the various pools, finally emptying into the main basin with the other floating humans.

Elli wanted to dive into the water, to feel that healing energy surround her body. But she had never been in water deeper than a bathtub. She removed her clothes but froze at the edge of the basin, trembling.

Grendel saw her complication and paddled back. She said, "The water can be intimidating. But it comes from a mineral spring. You will float. Here, let me help you." She stood in the water, which was only waist deep, and beckoned with both hands for Elli to enter. "Come," she said, "I'll hold you up."

Elli stepped into the shallows nearest the edge. Grendel said, "Lean back into my arms. Relax, I've got you." Grendel noticed the dark blue tattoo on the back of Elli's right hip, a triangle pointing down with a red dot in the center. She'd seen the mark before; she knew it was a brand. Elli closed her eyes and leaned. Grendel took her shoulders, laid her down into the water, and slipped her hands under the girl's back to support her. She said, "There. You're floating. Feel my hands? I'm right there. I've got you."

They stayed that way for a while. Elli floated in her mind while her body floated in the warm water. She nearly fell asleep. She decided she wasn't that other girl anymore. Her body felt connected to her mind now. She could be whoever she wanted. When she opened her eyes, Grendel was standing a few meters away near the edge, her arms folded beneath her breasts. Elli said, "I'm floating."

Grendel smiled, "Yes. Are you ready to take the slide? Here, we'll hold hands."

She took Elli's hand, lay down on her back, and pushed off the side. The girl tightened her grip as they slid over the spill-edge into the next basin. The spillover to the next basin was swifter, and Elli squealed. They both laughed. The following three drops were quicker until they splashed over the final two-foot waterfall into the main pool.

Both women went under for a moment, but bobbed to the surface like corks. Elli came up laughing and sputtering. Grendel still held her hand. They stood up; the water was only up to their chins. They leaned into back floats and relaxed in the murmuring rush. They stayed that way for over an hour.

◆ ◆

Emerson went to work with Rosco in the machine shop, where he taught new Interface users how to treat it as an extension of their body. Elli went with Grendel to the school, which was a loose collection of younger and older kids learning to read, cipher, and do research. Elli could read a little. Grendel helped her find books. Orwell's *Animal Farm* and *Peter Pan* caught her interest. After Grendel left, Elli went in search of Emerson but spent the rest of the day wandering around. No one looked at the girl twice; she'd never felt so free.

Two days into Emerson's new routine, Quinn's team—the woman in black, Nimue, and two men—arrived at the wall. One man wore an eye patch; the other had a leg prosthesis. The guards, Carter and Tango, stopped them, standing in front of the trio with arms crossing their chests. Tango said, "State your business."

The woman, her loose-fitting black pants and shirt flapping in the slight breeze, leaned on a polished, crooked branch as a cane. She said, "Official City business. We are passing through and looking for a man."

Tango said, "There are roads around the village. I don't know you. Do you know anyone who lives here who can vouch?"

She said, "I have my orders directly from the elder lord. Let us pass."

Tango's voice betrayed his fraying composure. "No. You are not welcome here. We do not recognize your *Lords*."

"Are you harboring a citizen named Emerson Lloyde?"

Tango didn't know Emerson personally, but news in the enclave traveled fast. Everyone knew about the stranger and the girl. He knew better than to reveal anything. Instead, he said, "I know nobody with that name. If you will not go around the wall, I will call for reinforcements. You will be imprisoned until we can determine your true intentions."

The one-eyed man shouted, "Enough! I demand to speak to the village lord, the mayor, somebody in authority. NOW!" The other guards had closed the gate doors.

Carter and Tango stood up taller, and Carter made a call on his PDA. He spoke into the device, "Yes, sir. At the North gate. Yes, that was him, making a ruckus."

Five minutes later, Rosco arrived at the gate. He came through, and they closed it behind him.

Nimue said, "We are here to speak to Emerson Lloyde. That is all. Can you tell me if he is inside your walls?"

Rosco took the measure of the three and decided on diplomacy over force. He said, "Maybe he is, maybe he isn't. I'll ask around. What do you want to talk to him about? I mean, if I find him, he may want to know before he comes out here. You guys are a little intimidating."

"Tell Emerson Lloyde that Elli Rattlesnake Quinn is calling him." She held up the satphone.

◆

When he heard, Emerson blurted, "Quinn? What the hell does she want?" He was instantly suspicious.

Grendel, who had Rosco on the line said, "One way to find out. I'll keep an eye on Elli. I'm assuming this Elli Rattlesnake is why you named her that."

Emerson swallowed. "She's one of the Elite children. If she knows I am here, The Authority probably knows too. I have to leave; I am putting you all in danger."

Over the line, Rosco said, "Bullshit, Emerson. We have guarded our sovereignty for fifty years. We know how to deal with The Authority. You should come down here and see what they want. If you require protection, I've got your back."

When Emerson came through the gate door, Rosco was talking with the woman; the two men were resting nearby in the shade, smoking. The village guards were still tense, and Rosco had his hand on his short sword, but the tension was not coming from anyone on Quinn's team.

Nimue said, "Emerson Lloyde?"

He nodded.

She opened the satellite phone and pressed a sequence of numbers. Rosco said, "Whoa. I wondered if the satellite communications network was still working. Damn. What I wouldn't give to try and reverse engineer that baby."

She handed the phone to Emerson.

He said, "Hello, Quinn? What are you doing? Are you tracking me for your father?"

Quinn said, "No, he doesn't know anything about this. I was worried. Are you okay?"

"Rich. You're worried about me. Uh-huh."

"Ouch, Emerson. We made love. We are a part of each other now."

"Sex means nothing to you people. Don't screw with me."

"Sex has consequences, Emerson. And the product of those consequences has been known to alter the history of whole civilizations."

"What are you saying?"

"I'm pregnant. With your baby. You are going to be a father with the daughter of an elder lord. You may not realize it now, but that's more power than anyone else in the world has. You will be the father of a future lord."

"That would sound nice if I believed you, which I don't. You lie, Quinn."

"Keep the phone. I'll find a way to send you proof. My team works only for me, and I won't tell anyone that I found you."

◆ ◆ ◆

She disconnected after telling the woman to come home, never telling anyone of what they'd found. Nimue said, "Anyone on my team would choose to die rather than betray you, Elli Rattlesnake." She instructed her to leave the phone with Emerson.

◆

Max was halfway through his third bourbon. He'd pulled his hat down over his eyes and had his arm stretched out, trying to find his nose with his finger. He said, "You're not preggo, Elli. He's going to find out soon enough."

"He won't find out if we don't tell him." But the scope of her lie was growing, and she didn't want to think about how the story would end.

Max said, "Maybe I'm not the sterile one, you know? Maybe we should give it a try. See if, you know, Celeste is the barren one. I might not be shooting blanks after all."

Quinn raised one eyebrow. Max said, "Okay then. But keep it in mind. When Daddy finds out, you might wish you took me up on the offer. Just saying."

Quinn said, "Fuck you, Maxamillion. And shut up about Celeste. You shouldn't talk that way about your sister."

"Touché."

Later that night, Quinn tested her pee again. The test came up negative again. But she was late. Her cycle was usually so regular she could tell the date from her weight. Today marked a week past due. She looked at her PDA calendar and confirmed it. One week. *Shit*. Maybe the tests *were* expired. Maybe she really *was* pregnant. She put her hand on her lower belly, closed her eyes, and said, "Hey, baby. You in there? Send me a sign." A bubble of gas suddenly moved in her gut, and she farted unexpectedly. The sound was hollow and loud. A giggle boiled up in her throat.

She said, "That's some kind of sign, anyway."

◆ ◆ ◆

PLASMA RIFLE

merson's days fell into a quiet routine. He spent them working at the machine shop with Rosco. He taught new Interface users the basics. Anastacia Moon was an Interface programmer at the shop. Emerson was impressed by her work. She was attracted to him from the moment she saw him. When he was working, he had a habit of rolling the sleeves of his shirts above the shoulder. Between his upper arms and his occasionally bare lower back, she was distracted by him for a whole day. They didn't speak until sundown when he approached her to ask what she was working on.

She said, "I'm cleaning up the interface for running the Bridgeport lathe. But I'm considering starting over. The connections are all wonky." She pursed her lips in her own unique way.

Emerson said, "The programmers in The City believe that they are the pinnacle of sophistication, but they are writing demos compared with your code."

Ana blushed. Emerson smiled. He said, "You're cute—no, really. I'm not kidding."

And she was fast. She and Emerson talked about the simulators that he learned to fly on, and together, over the course of a week, she mocked up a demonstration. It was realistic and adaptable. Emerson told her, "You put The City programmers to shame. Most of the routines and many of the tool interfaces the Enforcers use are rude sketches. You have an incredible talent for simplicity and stacked purposes." He thought her mouth looked like a tiny pink rosebud. It made him want to kiss her.

He remembered the inside of the Red Palace and added, "There are some real artists there too, but you would do better work given the environment."

Ana and Emerson stayed together after they left the shop each day. They also began taking longer and longer breaks. Near the end of their marathon week of simulator development, Emerson told Rosco and Grendel that he and Anastacia were going to move into a house nearby. When the two left after dinner that evening, Rosco told Grendel, "They didn't come back from the noon break today. And have you noticed how Ana is glowing, lately? Somebody's getting laid…"

Grendel kicked his leg with her bare foot and said, "Well at least somebody around here is." He kissed her. Elli pushed her plate away and left the table without clearing and stomped out of the room.

Rosco said, "Is she OK? Should I…"

Grendel said, "No. Let her be. She's trying to decide if she's staying with us or going with Emmer. Don't get involved."

"My mama hen."

She squinted at him. "You do remember that there are no domestic birds anymore, right?"

He just smiled.

◆ ◆

Ana didn't have relatives in the village. She and her mom arrived as refugees from another quadrant when she was only six. She never learned why they left. Her mom died soon after, and she was raised by Grendel's aunt. Anastacia Moon had known Rosco and Grendel her whole life. Moon was a surname given by the citizens of Blue Hole to orphans with no memory of their parents. No one ever found out where she came from or why her mom had to leave. But it didn't make any difference to the community. They made Ana feel welcome, and she, like most people in Blue Hole, had everything she needed.

Growing up, she'd kept to herself. But Rosco noticed her talent for fabricating imaginary constructs when she was only ten. He arranged for her to get an implant; she had been connected with what, up to that time, had been the village's only temporary. Thanks to her designs, they now had three temps and a training program for young kids.

Grendel had seen Anastacia grow from a gawky teenaged tomboy into a strong, independent, and competent woman. She was still thin—long-boned, Grendel's aunt called her—but there wasn't an ounce of fat on her muscular arms and legs. Her straight auburn hair was cut shoulder-length these days. It looked like a curtain opening when she turned her head.

The house she chose as her nest was a split level, three-bedroom brick structure with a garage. Anastacia imagined that she and Emmer would grow old together, though she hadn't revealed these dreams to him. She would have been happy to stay home and have babies, but like many young women after the collapse, she did not menstruate and was considered by Pamela P, the village doctor, to be sterile.

By the time she settled with Emerson, she had bedded many young men, but she never considered staying with any of them. And even though birth control was readily available, she had never used it or gotten pregnant. Anastacia accepted that she would never have a baby of her own. She'd tell herself that there were plenty of children who needed a parent and resigned herself to her fate. She believed that fate was the gift the universe gave you at birth. What you did with it was up to you.

She treated Elli with passive watchfulness. She tried not to judge her, but even without speaking, Elli pushed all of Ana's buttons. The girl didn't speak and would sometimes just walk away in the middle of a conversation. The two women didn't have much chance to get close. Ana had never asked Emerson about his feelings regarding Elli and just assumed he wanted the girl to come and live with them. Ana wanted to treat her like a daughter. But Elli acted like Ana wasn't there. It infuriated her.

Pamela P was a grey-haired woman who walked with a limp. Her back was twisted from a childhood illness left untreated. As a girl, it gave her the perfect opportunity to devote herself to learning; unable to run around, her adventures came through reading. She apprenticed with Old Samuel, who was doctor before her, and inherited his databases and medical books when he died. She'd been practicing in Blue Hole for thirty years. It was long enough, she'd say. Time to find someone to train! She hoped she had enough time.

Pam had a strong intuition. "Inner tuition," she called it. "Voices that tell me what I should do. And it's like my hands know if I let 'em. I had to learn to get out of the way first." She knew she had some terminal disease, probably a deep cancer. *A lot of bad shit deep in us survivor's bones.* She didn't need to know any other particulars. There wasn't anything she could do about it. But the approaching deadline stepped up the urgency with which she lived. She needed to have a couple of years with the next doctor. Otherwise, her death would leave a hole in the community, and her love of the people she served would not let that happen without a struggle.

Pamela asked Grendel to bring Emerson and Elli to see her. She liked to meet new arrivals. Ana came along. By this time, she was seldom seen without Emmer. Elli would go anywhere with Grendel unquestioningly. However, when she realized they were at a doctor, she tried to leave.

Grendel said, "Hey, hey, girl. Nothing to worry about. Pamela P is a gentle healer. She just wants to meet you, that's all." Elli stood close to the door when Pam invited her in and offered her some dried figs, which were a rare treat. The girl ate them quickly, messily.

"That's okay. You can take all the time you need," Pam said and gave her a towel.

She brought Emerson into her private office and closed the door. He faced her in a plain wooden chair; she sat behind her desk shuffling through papers. She asked him standard questions like, "Where were you born, any injuries you can tell me about, pains, complaints?"

After answering, she listened to his heart and looked in his nose, ears, and mouth, took his temperature, and tested reflexes in one leg. "You're in great health, Emerson Lloyde. It's interesting that you have two names. Is that common in The City?"

Emerson said, "No, not really. It is a family tradition. I was raised by my mom's dad after my parents died. Chandler believed last names were important. He wanted me to remember my father's family line, even though I hardly knew him."

She said, "Fine, fine. Just one more thing. Masturbate into this jar please. I want to get a sperm count and assess your motility. I'll wait."

"Right now? Here?"

"You can go to the WC, but the compost needs to be emptied. Or I can go out and wait in the exam room. Or maybe I should ask Ana to come in?" She raised her eyebrows and smiled.

"That might make it easier."

It did. Just sitting in the room with her watching sped up his usual twenty-four-year-old lightning-fast arousal. Kissing him and showing a nipple pushed him over the top. Ana called the doctor back in.

Pamela P came back in and said, "That was fast." She smirked when she said it. Ana laughed, and Emerson tried to ignore them, but he was no poker player. Everything he thought was written on his face.

Pam turned the jar sideways and said, "Prodigious amount, too. Miz Ana, you got yourself a keeper."

Ana didn't laugh. She said, "Excuse me," and left the room quickly.

Pam said, "I guess I put my foot in it. I wasn't taking about sperm. I meant you are probably an amorous lover. Shit." She looked at Emerson and shook her head. "I'm not very good with the English."

Emerson said, "Oh? What languages do you speak?"

She said, "English," and held up the jar of Emerson's semen. "Let's have a look at these little buggers, shall we?"

She made a quick slide and put it under a digital electron camera. She used her Interface to route the output to a projection on the wall. The sperm in the image were each a half meter long, propelling themselves frantically in all directions. The sample was thick with them.

Emerson said, "I've never seen that high a resolution with such brilliant color."

She said, "This is tech we salvaged before the Elites got their grubby little mitts on it. Pretty amazing, eh? You can see all the little swimmers. You have no lack in that department either, son. I'm surprised that those goons that run The City ever let you go. Your genetics must be rare. I wish we had sequencing capabilities."

Emerson thought of Quinn but said nothing. She had his DNA. He looked down, which signaled to Doctor Pam that he was concealing something. He said, "Just lucky, I guess," but he went silent. He wondered if Quinn was part of a bigger scheme to imprison him. It seemed ridiculous, but she was Elli Rattlesnake Quinn after all.

Elli and Grendel were in the exam room when Emerson and Pamela came out. Emerson said, "What happened to Ana?"

Grendel said, "She left in a hurry. What did you say to her?"

Pam said, "It was me. I told her Emerson was a keeper because he produced a lot of semen. It was stupid. I need to apologize."

Emerson said, "I'm going to go find her," and left.

Pam sat on the edge of her exam table. She said, "Hi, Elli, I want to examine you, but I will not even touch you without your consent. Do you hear me? People where you used to live hurt you. Is that right?"

She nodded. Grendel said, "She can speak, and she has. But normally, she doesn't."

Pam said, "I figure you are about seventeen, is that right?"

She nodded again.

"Have you had your moon?"

She looked questioningly at Grendel, who said, "Menstruation, child. Do you bleed?"

She shook her head and looked at the floor. She whispered something to Grendel, who said, "She hasn't bled, but other girls in her quadrant started younger. She was…" She whispered something to Elli, who responded more quietly than Pam could hear. Grendel repeated, "Selected."

Pam said, "I see. Okay. I think that's enough for today. If you ever want to talk to me about what's happening to your body, my door is always open."

The girl smiled and fingered the doctor's stethoscope. Pam said, "You want to see how this works?" She put the ear pieces in her ears and asked, holding up the diaphragm, "When I press this part to your chest, I will hear your heart. Is that okay?"

She nodded. Pam listened to a few places and murmured, "Hmmm. OK, now you try."

She put the ear pieces in Elli's ears and pressed the diaphragm to the same spots on the girl's chest. She said, "Can you hear it? That's your heart. The first sound is the beginning of the systole when your heart contracts, pushing blood through your body. The closure of the mitral and tricuspid valves makes a low, slightly prolonged 'lub' sound. The second, sharper, higher-pitched 'dub' sound is caused by closure of the aortic and pulmonary valves at the end of systole when blood refills your heart."

Elli listened, fascinated. Pam said, "My door is always open to you, Elli. You can come and learn about what I'm doing anytime."

As they were leaving, Grendel said, "I forgot how good you are with kids, Pam."

"I give that same speech to every kid in Blue Hole, every time I see one."

Grendel said, "I remember. You gave it to me."

"Do you know how many take me up on my offer?" She didn't wait for Grendel to answer. "None. Nobody. No one in the thirty years I've been doing this. But I saw something in Elli's eyes when I was telling her about how her heart works. I think she'll be back."

Grendel thought about it but didn't reply. She hoped something would grab the girl's interest and pull her out of herself. She held no judgement for what that might be.

◆ ◆ ◆

Eric Eggert took the assignment to search for Emerson Lloyde. After recruiting the boy, the two had lost contact. But the captain tracked all of his recruits' careers, so he knew when Emerson had gone missing. He unsealed his orders after crossing the wall. They expected Lloyde to connect with one of the Juice Hacker enclaves and explicitly commanded Eggert to stay silent. The Hackers were tech-savvy, it said, and could be monitoring Enforcer communications. He was to bring back any tech including a plasma rifle. Lloyde was labeled expendable.

Eggert was a career Enforcer. He never questioned orders. But he was confident that he could appeal to Emerson and bring him home. He knew something about plasma weapons too, having used a similar weapon when he was in special training; plasma guns left a trace that could be tracked. When one was discharged, it left a lingering field of energy, detectable as ultraviolet light, surrounding the strike point and radiating out up to three miles. The field lingered for about three weeks. After finding the hole in the garage wall confirming the exact signature of the gun, Eggert spent a week scanning in different directions away from the crash point. The gash still radiated strongly enough for Eggert to see the faint orange glow without a scope.

The field emanating from Emerson's demonstration for Rosco and Barton was still faintly visible. But because a plasma field drifted with wind and rain, it was difficult to tell where the strike had actually occurred until he found the mutilated tree.

Eggert landed a safe distance away from the Blue Hole gate and cloaked his shuttle. He went into the woods surrounding the road and doubled back to the wall a few hundred meters away from the gate using a copse of rhododendron as a blind. Shuttle pilot helmets had a telescopic feature built in that allowed him to use his Interface as a spyglass.

He watched the guards for a while and contemplated scaling the wall but decided against it. A merchant pulling a wagon approached. Eggert turned up his distance hearing. The man was carrying herbs and oils, and the guards were aggressive. They made him empty his entire cart while two others trained crossbows on him from vantage points above the wall. Once the guards were satisfied, he repacked and was allowed in. They told him that after the market closed, he would have to pay a fee or leave for the night. When the gate opened, another guard accompanied him.

Eggert wondered why no one had built an inn outside the gate, but forgot about it as soon as it closed. Going in the front door was probably the best way; he would ask for Emerson and talk to him. The longer the tech was unaccounted for, the better the chance it would be reverse-engineered or, worse, used against the wall around The City.

Eggert went back to the main road and approached from the North.

As expected, the guards held him at arrow-point while they sent someone to find Emerson. Eggert waited.

One guard asked what his business was.

"It's a private matter, for Emerson's ears only." He sucked his teeth.

The guard scoffed. No one spoke for ten tense minutes. The gate opened, and Emerson appeared.

He said, "Eric. How have you been?"

The captain got right to the point. "I need the plasma gun, and you need to tell me where you and Dander got it."

Emerson's smile evaporated. "And if I refuse?"

"That wouldn't be wise. If you don't cooperate fully, the Authority will come and take it by force."

"You mean attack this community? Over a rifle?"

"The Authority is very careful with weaponized technology."

"I'd rather talk about this over a pitcher of mead, Eggert. Why don't you come in? I'll vouch for you."

The guard said, "I can't let him in. He's a high-ranking Enforcer."

Emerson said, "I'm an Enforcer. You let me in."

The guards looked unsure. They called Rosco. Nobody spoke while they waited. Emerson tried to think of a resolution to this standoff. When Rosco arrived, he said, "It didn't matter when I brought you inside. I took responsibility. You're new here. You don't have that kind of trust yet. I can accompany you and Captain Eggert, but he will have to leave his weapons, gear, and communications outside the wall. We'll go to Fran's Café, have a drink and see what's what."

Eggert agreed to leave his stuff, and the three went to Fran's. Rosco's jovial nature put everyone at ease. But Emerson remained tense. They sat at a wooden table near the window. Emerson watched a group of children in a park across the street playing a game with a large rubber ball while Rosco ordered tea. Eggert had water. Emerson asked for tea as well, not wanting anything.

Eggert said, "The facts are pretty clear, Emerson."

Rosco cut in, "How do you two know each other, Captain?"

"I recruited Emerson, after his grandfather died. But that won't change the consequences if he doesn't address The Authority's demands." He sucked his teeth. Twice.

Rosco laughed. "Captain Eggert. We're just talking here, trying to see where we each stand. So, let's all settle down. Why don't you tell me what you're after, eh?"

Eggert stood up suddenly, knocking over his chair. His water glass shattered on the tile floor.

He said, "Don't double-speak me, Juice Hacker. Emerson! Be realistic, man. Give it up."

Before Rosco or Emerson could move, two burly guards bearing short, black crossbows appeared through the doorway, backing Eggert against the wall.

Rosco sipped his tea. Emerson tried to wrap his head around the last few seconds.

Eggert shouted, "My people know my exact location." Which was, of course, a bluff. "So, you can end this charade now. Kill me and they will come down on you so hard you won't know what hit you. Your only hope was to give me the rifle and the coordinates. But you've screwed that up now and sealed your fate!"

Rosco nodded, swallowed the last of tea and set the cup down. The waitress, Ruth, came over and asked if they wanted anything else. The guards had Eggert pinned in the corner; she glanced at him but didn't say anything about it.

Rosco said, "No, hon. Sorry about the mess. We're good. Thanks." She nodded, looked at Emerson, expressionless, and walked away. He hadn't touched his cup.

Rosco looked at Eggert and said, "Who trained you to negotiate, Captain? You people watch too many old cop shows." He made a dismissive sound. "Sheesh. Do you think we are just a bunch of stupid hicks? What do they teach you in The City? That we are poor primitive fools stumbling around in the dark?" He shook his head and laughed. "This building is inside of Blue Hole Village; the walls of the perimeter structures are wired. While we're inside, it's like being in a big Faraday cage. No radio, no beacons, no service but our service. When you entered the gate, your stuff was put in a smaller cage, and as far as any sensors are concerned, you disappeared. Not only that, bud, but I know there is no constant monitoring of your position. How do I know this? Because the GPS system has deteriorated so much that the remaining satellites will only work at certain hours of the day. And," he looked at his PDA, "they were offline from about two hours before your arrived until fifteen minutes ago." He stood up and said to the guards, "Put him in the VIP housing. Get him anything he wants. Captain Eggert is going to be our guest for a while." He and Emerson began to leave. Eggert hadn't regained his powers of speech.

Rosco turned to him and said, "And we have your shuttle. The cloaking thing is BS. Any tracker worth a damn could see the air disturbance when he looked at it. The edges of those fields always pixelate. We aren't children, you know." And he walked out.

On the way back to the shop, Emerson said, "They will be looking for him."

"Yeah, I know. He's a problem that isn't going away. But now that he knows about us, we can't let him go. You should talk to him after he's had some time to realize what just happened. Maybe you can convince him to join us."

"Fat chance of that. Eric Eggert is a true believer. You don't convince those people of anything. They've already been sold."

◆ ◆ ◆

By the time she was seven weeks late, Quinn was sure she was pregnant. She had to pee all the time, and the thought of food, even when she was starving, made her queasy. Part of her was happy, but it was a hollow victory. At first, she told herself that she was just using Emerson. But now that his baby was growing inside her, she realized she was worried about him. More than worried. Quinn was scared for his life. She had never felt that way about anyone.

She heard through her contacts in the Enforcers that he had a plasma weapon. Normally, a missing pilot's implant would send the enforcers on a seek-and-destroy mission. A pre-collapse weapon like the plasma gun was considered a high-level threat to The City. And no matter what Boston told her, which wasn't much, even though he knew Quinn was pregnant, she couldn't trust him. When Boston Quinn felt threatened, he would do anything to secure his interests. She needed to talk to Emerson and make sure he was still alright. He wanted proof that she was pregnant. She had been thinking out loud. Tanya was a safe place to work out her thoughts; she was sworn to secrecy.

"Tanya, tell Doctor Sailor I need a confidential visit. Set a time when I will not be seen."

"Yes, ma'am. And that fear that you're feeling? That's called love. You are in love with that man, and you should tell him."

◆

Stephanie Sailor was a healer. She was brought to The City by Lord Quinn years before, but she still spoke English with a strong accent from her homeland. In return for leaving willingly, she lived like an Elite. She was also able to get insulin, without which she would have died a painful death many years prior. She was an impossibly tall woman with a shaved head. Tattoos of protection in dark red and black ink faded on her shoulders and wrists. A dark blue circle-within-a-cross on her left cheek marking her as a healer in her village was only a rough patch on her skin.

Her belly and breasts told the story of the many children that grew within her. If they still lived, all of them would be grandparents by now. Her eyes were dark and brooding. When she came to The City, she brought with her a penchant for betel nuts, which she chewed incessantly, spitting orange juice into a tin cup that was never far away.

Through his salvage efforts, The City and Lord Quinn had acquired enough advanced medical equipment and supplies to fully stock the small hospital in Founder's Quarter. Sailor made the lord agree to let her train other medical practitioners. She wanted to build a medical school for Middles but was discouraged from taking things that far. Advanced medical procedures were beyond the reach of most City inhabitants, but the Lords always had the best. Steph knew that the supplies would run out some day; for now, they had enough stock to treat the residents of Founder's Quarter for 100 years. The situation disgusted her, but she kept it to herself.

Doctor Sailor also ran the Birth Corps and the genetics lab. She was closely monitored, which riled her already gruff disposition. She made no secret of her opinions regarding the population control protocols or the "new" family system of legal and extended pods. It was a grim tradeoff. At least she had the proper equipment to save lives when needed.

"Jesus, Elli. Why didn't you come in here right away? Seven weeks late? You are joking, yes?"

Quinn didn't speak, didn't think she had to. Sailor had known her all of her life, and they were friends. Elli Rattlesnake sat uncharacteristically quiet and accepted her tongue lashing; she deserved it. And Sailor was just getting started.

She spat. "At least then I could have run a DNA profile on his semen. You know better than this, El. And you know how dangerous it is for women in your line to conceive, let alone bring a child to term. Blast it to hell, you stupid girl!" She was getting herself too worked up, and she knew it was unwise to stress her heart. After a few deep breaths, she said, "Sorry. I didn't say congratulations, dear. I know you have always craved children."

"You're done berating me then?"

"Yes, give me a hug."

While the younger woman was locked in her tight embrace, Sailor said, "Damn, girl," and sighed. "Who is the father?"

Quinn said, "The father is the man that blood slide came from. I got him to get me pregnant, see? Aren't you proud of me? His name is Emerson Lloyde."

Sailor stopped and said, "Oh?"

"Yes. Why, do you know him?"

"No, no. It's just an interesting name. I knew a couple once named Lloyde. I wonder if they're related. So, what's your *difficult* favor?"

"Let's go out on the balcony. I have another gift."

They closed the double doors behind them. Quinn leaned back against the railing; Sailor sat in a chair. Quinn removed an unopened box of Marlboro Reds from her pack and peeled the cellophane seal. She put the box to her nose and breathed in the scent, tapped two out, and gave one to the doctor. Quinn lit them with a silver Zippo lighter.

Sailor exhaled a cloud and said, "I'd ask you where you get such things, but I know. It pains me as it gives me pleasure. I can't reconcile it. I've quit trying."

"My father made you an offer you couldn't refuse. You had no choice." She took a drag and put the cigarette out by twisting the glowing ember off and putting it back in the box. "I need to send Emerson Lloyde an ultrasound. He needs proof that I'm pregnant."

"He'll want to know if it's his, you know."

"Yeah, I thought of that."

"I bet you did."

"Right. I need a report with markers proving heredity and an ultrasound, in an encoded digital file that I can send to him."

"What's the difficult part?"

"I need to keep it a secret. Especially from my father."

◆

She called Emerson that night, but his satphone hadn't been charged. No one picked up. She had Tanya get Max. There was a new job for Nimue.

◆ ◆ ◆

After Emerson and Ana had moved in together, Elli stayed with Grendel and Rosco. But after a couple of days, she went to Ana and Emerson's house and sat at the kitchen table until she was noticed. She chose a bedroom, gave Ana a hug, and that was that. She spent most of her time at Doctor Pam's, only showing up occasionally for meals.

The girl was more of a ghost. If Ana asked her to clear the table or clean up, she'd either ignore her completely or walk away. After the first day, Elli would answer with a longsuffering look and a tsk before leaving.

Ana said to Emerson later at dinner, "Where's Elli? I thought she was with you."

"She's been following the doctor around."

"Well, someday soon, the honeymoon is going to end for her. I know she had a tough life and all, but she needs to take her turn around here. I'm not a servant."

Emerson nodded, his mouth full of stew. He didn't want to get in the middle of their drama. He said, "She's getting used to being a teenager. Cut her a little more slack, okay? She'll come around."

Ana was skeptical, but she kept it to herself. She knew girls like Elli when she was her age. The ones that seemed to never have enough justified stealing by saying they were persecuted. Though Elli didn't speak to her, her face said it loud enough.

Near lunch a week or so later, Rosco came onto the shop floor and signaled for Emerson to come and talk. "You have a visitor," he said. "Down at Fran's."

The black-clad woman stood when Emerson came in the door. He'd noticed the pair of guards outside. It made sense now. He said, "What does she want now?"

She extended her hand and said, "We began poorly. May I start over? Good day, Emerson Lloyde. My name is Nimue. I have a message from Elli Rattlesnake. She implores you to hear the truth."

Emerson held her hand in the customary greeting of her homeland. But he did not smile. She bade him sit. Fran asked if he wanted anything; he declined.

"What is this message?"

"It is just this." She held up a military-grade tablet. The screen was cracked, and the case was scuffed and dented.

Emerson took it and said, "It figures that she would have one of these. I've only seen one in pictures."

"This one is a loan from Doctor Sailor. I must return it. She and Quinn made you a video."

Emerson tapped the screen, which displayed a three-dimensional ultrasound in color. An accented woman's voice in the background said, "My name is Doctor Stephanie Sailor. What you are seeing is the fluid-filled gestational sac for the approximately seven-week-old fetus in the womb of Elli Rattlesnake Quinn." An arrow entered the field and pointed at a twitching blob in the center. "That is your baby."

The screen changed to a shot of Doctor Sailor and Quinn sitting side by side. Emerson recognized her. She was the doctor who implanted him; she knew his grandmother. Quinn said, "That's our baby, baby. But I know you have a skeptical nature, so…"

Sailor finished her thought. "I ran a DNA sequence on you and Miz Quinn here."

The image changed to a scrolling sequence report for a moment and then back to the women. She continued, "You're 100 percent guaranteed to be this child's father. That is if the child survives."

Quinn said, "Emerson, I need you to come and take care of me."

Sailor spat into her cup. Emerson caught a glimpse of her red-stained teeth. She said, "Your baby mama has a blood disease. They used to call these things rare. Now women without it are the rare ones." She spat again. "So, I'm telling you, for Elli, getting pregnant is dangerous."

Quinn said, "I need you to come home. Come back to me."

Sailor said, "The report is on this tablet if you want to inspect it. But it's the real thing. I don't know you. But I've known Elli her whole life. If she says she needs you? You should believe her. Emerson. Come home."

The screen went black. A moment later, Quinn's image came up. She said, "I miss you, Tiger. In all the ways. Goodbye. And charge the damn satphone. I want to be able to see and talk to you. Ciao."

The file ended.

Emerson sat staring at the screen for a long moment. He waved at Fran. When she came over, he said, "You have hooch, yes?"

Fran nodded.

"Please bring me enough for friends. I just found out I am going to be a father."

Nimue took the tablet and placed it in her pack. She said, "Congratulations, Emerson Lloyde. I must return to The City."

Emerson said, "Thank you. Can you give her a hug for me?"

Nimue said curtly, "No, I do not touch the lord's children. But I will tell her you send your affections, if that is adequate."

"Of course."

She left without another word, striding toward the gate. The two guards had to run to catch up.

Emerson hugged Fran when she brought him the bottle. She uncorked it with her teeth and poured them both a half shot, toasting, "To new life!" as was the Blue Hole custom.

◆

Emerson was pretty drunk by the time he got home. He'd met Rosco and Grendel on the way, and they had to toast the new arrival even though the due date was far off. He stopped by the shop, but Ana had left. There were a few engineers still on the floor which called for another toast, and since it was the end of the day, they shouted, "To new life!" each time before slamming back the unaged whiskey. On the road home, he toasted three more times with several complete strangers. By the time he arrived home, he was squiffed, stumbling, and slurring. It took Ana three tries to find out what had happened. Emerson tried to toast with her, but the bottle was empty.

She wasn't sure how she felt about Quinn, but she toasted to the baby anyway. After the collapse, any suggestion of new life was cause to rejoice. When she looked down at him, Emerson had passed out. She let him sleep beside the couch.

◆ ◆ ◆

As the days warmed, they fell into a pleasant routine. Blue Hole was a community of sharing. The fruit trees, gardens, compost bins, and electrical grid were run by revolving groups of community members. And like the councilmen and women positions in town politics, jobs were on a cyclical basis, staffed with appropriate overlap so as not to leave anyone unprepared. In addition, there was a communication tree for most processes that kept the elders connected even if they no longer worked on that process. The atmosphere around most interactions was convivial and communal. Small groups often worked out their differences without help, but in those cases of extreme contention, the council would refer complainants to mediation. The system had evolved based on needs. No one was interested in having power. Needs were met within reason, and reason was generally agreed upon.

Emerson and Ana were treated as any other Blue Hole couple. If somebody felt they were being singled out because of their race or ethnicity, a subcommittee on equity was assembled on a cyclical basis and would hear both sides.

Elli was not treated as a child, which might have contributed to her wildness. She never really got a chance to experience puberty. At present, in Blue Hole, Grendel was only one of two people Elli spoke to. She was mute with everyone else except for Pamela P. The doctor said, "Elli talks all the time when we're together. She's fascinated by the human body. Her own and any other one I see. All life captivates Elli."

One afternoon at the baths, she began telling Grendel her history. They had to dip in the water to keep from getting cold. Much of the story was told neck-deep in one of the mineral pools.

Elli said, "My name wasn't always Elli, you know. Michel named me Mew Mew. Cute, huh? Like I was a little kitten. I didn't have no mother. No father. They both died, or was killed in Nickel Crick. That's where I came from. Now it's a deadland. Prolly better off, I say. When I was thirteen, before I got my blood, just as these little bumps you see were raising on my narrow chest, Michel tol' me I needed these vitamin shots.

"He wasn't no good with them needles either. I got infections a few times." She showed Grendel the scars on her shoulder. "I got headaches. My breasts got a little bigger, but this is it." She pointed at the lump on her chest with an inverted nipple. "No blood." She stared at the overhang above them for a moment, took a deep breath, and sighed. "It wasn't no fucking vitamin. I'll tell you that much. And Michel wasn't looking out for my health none, either, Fee-male A-nee-mee-a. Bullshit.

"You've seen this tat, right?" She turned over, face under the water for a moment, and pushed her butt in the air at Grendel's face. Elli had developed a deep love for the water; her fear was completely gone. "That's a brand. Pam says girls like me were in big demand in her homeland. No mama or daddy. No one to look out for you. I was worth more for sex if I never got any older. And so, Michel made sure I didn't.

"At first, I was just supposed to hang out and be one of the boys. Michel took care of me, fed me, got me clothes... I didn't have no friends. Just Michel. When I turned sixteen, he made me go with one those boys. I guess they didn't just like me for my bubbling personality. It hurt, but

I got used to it. Doctor Pam says I probably learned to like it. I dunno. I don't know how a girl could ever like a man doing that to her. But it was the only way I knew, you know? I never had no choice."

As they were leaving, Elli picked up a smooth grey stone from the water's edge. She said, "I'm going to keep this rock as a reminder that I don't gotta be that child anymore. I belong to myself now."

Pam told Grendel the shots were a puberty blocker called leuprolide acetate. It was made originally by a company up north called Merck. She'd heard rumors of warehouses full of pharmaceuticals that were collected and traded for high stakes. Pam expected Elli's shots came from that network. Elli had he had been receiving them for so long that it might have permanently stunted her development.

Elli told Grendel, "Since Emerson brought me here, I ain't had no shots. Doctor Pam says my body might start developing all of sudden. She feeds me all kinds o' nasty herb teas and stuff. Says it's like giving my body the fertilizer she needs to grow again. So far, nothing. I'm not sure I want anything to grow. I kinda like being in between, you know? Not a boy, but not really a girl either. It's nobody's fuckin' business anyway."

Grendel told Rosco, and Rosco let Emerson know what Elli had gone through. But Emerson didn't tell Ana. Maybe because she seemed so attached to being the girl's mother. He didn't want to tell her how much worse it really was. He wasn't sure; something was off. So, he kept quiet. It was the way he dealt with Chandler for whom silence was golden, even if it choked you to death.

◆

The first thing Emerson did after his evening of celebration was to recharge the satphone. A few days later, he'd devised a way to leave the village: he needed to bring Eggert's shuttle to a hangar in Blue Hole. Rosco wanted to go with him, which nearly blew up his plan, but at the last minute, a crisis with the boilers stole his attention.

Emerson said, "Do you need me to help, here?"

Rosco said, "No, I think we can handle it. Just get the shuttle in here. We can take it out later."

Once he was out of sight from the watchers at the wall, he called Quinn. She answered before the first ring completed.

"Emerson, thank the Goddess!"

"I didn't know you were religious, Quinn."

"Oh, I'm not, but I'm trying to break the habit of saying thank God all the time. I can't believe in the hairy thunderer either, but at least the Goddess is a woman. And it's better than saying fuck all the time."

"So, you're really pregnant."

"Fuck yes! And it's hell. But I have a bump now, so everybody knows."

"What do you care?"

"I don't. But that's all anyone wants to talk about. It's maddening. I need to stay in bed most of the time, which is a drag. And Tanya makes me smoothies with real milk and fruit, which is, like, the best part. My dad won't come and see me, but my mom moved into the next-door apartment, so she's helping."

Emerson said, "But, Quinn, I have no idea how you expect this to work. I'm a fugitive. An Enforcer showed up here to take me back. We have him locked up. I can't go back there."

"I can fix everything, Emmer. Just come back to me. My dad is a big softy when you get to know him."

Emerson knew she was exaggerating. He'd met Boston. The only thing soft about the man was his belly fat. The rest of him was hard as a bull's horn and sly as a fox. He told Quinn he'd think about it.

She said, "I love you, Emerson."

He said, "I gotta go…"

"Do you love me?"

"Yeah, sure," he said absently. "Of course. But I really have to go. Bye."

◆ ◆ ◆

THE FALL

Ana had a rosebud mouth and a clear, pale complexion sprinkled over with freckles. Her laugh was wicked, and she talked with her hands, waving her long fingers around. She grew up in Blue Hole and knew her way around.

"Like any community," she told Emerson as they walked the mostly deserted main avenue in the moonlight, "Blue Hole has aspects that are not fully acceptable to the majority. But since we pride ourselves on open-minded attitudes and have an anarchic bent to our method of governance, people stay mostly out of one another's business." She turned down a small overgrown path that Emerson didn't even see. "Even here in Blue Hole, The Fall is somewhat controversial."

They walked for a while through the forest, or what had grown up out of the suburban wasteland over the past fifty years. She went on, "There are people who disagree with the prevailing regard. I've seen signs lately that they are sowing dissent where there really isn't any. It's becoming a problem."

After moving in silence for a while, Emerson saw the flickering of a fire in the distance through the trees. Ana said, "This part of the forest is an experiment in regrowth. Blue Hole planted these trees when I was a girl. They are towering now." Emerson looked at the tops. They looked healthy.

They arrived at the fire; a cabin was nestled into the trees nearby. Ana led him to the door and knocked in a strange rhythm. The lock clicked, and the door opened on a dimly lit foyer. The door closed automatically, and Ana turned to him and said, "Surprise! And welcome to The Fall."

Emerson said, "I think I've been in a place like this before. Quinn took me to the Red Palace."

Ana used a handheld scanner to read her interface implant and gave the gun to Emerson. She said, "The Red Palace. I've all heard of it. It's where the idea came from, but The Fall is different." Emerson scanned himself. They went through a lacquered black door with Chinese characters painted on the surface. As Emerson looked at them, they seemed to swim into different shapes until he could read what they represented. The first three were, "Peace, Home, Life…" Ana pulled him through the door before he read the last.

Inside the room was dim with indirect blue lights. The couches were salvaged from nearby houses. Some were missing legs; other had worn spots in the cushions.

Emerson said, "What was this place? Before."

"A brothel, I think. An opium den and a bar. Why?"

"I smell alcohol."

"You have a good nose. Lay down."

"Hey, Anastacia, I don't want to have virtual sex with you, OK? I've done that, and it was creepy."

"As I recall, you got a baby out of it, did you not? Besides, this isn't about virtual or any other kind of sex. Lie down and relax."

He felt compelled to explain virtual sex, but as soon as his head touched the couch, he awoke in a completely different world. The gravity was different; the light was intense and had a yellow tint. He called, "Ana? Hello? Are you here somewhere?"

She appeared at his shoulder and held his hand. He turned to her, and they embraced. Emerson said, "You said no sex."

"I said no virtual sex. This is real."

"What do you mean?"

She took out a pocket knife and said, "Show me your wrist." She held his hand, palm down. "What do you think I mean?" She pulled the blade slowly across the flesh on the back of his wrist. The skin peeled back and showed an intricate maze of fractals. Looking closer, he recognized the flow of energy up and down his arm. He flexed his hand and watched the muscles and vessels move and pulse.

"This can't be real."

"Go with it, Emerson. The fun is just the beginning."

When he looked back at his wrist, the skin was knitting itself back together until it was just a thin scar, which faded as he watched. Ana brought his chin up and kissed him hard. His body felt as though it were filling with gas, making him stronger and fuller. Ana looked the way he felt: flushed skin, muscles rippling, and the light on her hair reflecting off in little rainbows.

Soon they were naked, legs and arms intertwined on a king-sized bed. Ana was moving under him. He felt strong. Emerson stood and lifted Ana off the bed like she was a doll. She hugged him around his neck as he supported her thighs with both hands. He pulsed with a kaleidoscope of feelings and colors. The sound of the ocean rolled over them. Their movements were synchronized and forcefully rhythmic.

When the sweat had dried and they'd rested, Ana pulled Emerson through the open doors of the bedroom and onto the grass leading up to the sea. They held hands, walking barefooted across the dew-damp grass. The salt and iodine of the sea washed over them. Ana pulled Emerson toward the end of the grass.

She said, "Come. Come. This is the best part."

At the edge of the lawn, there was a four-meter-wide sand path. Along the sea side of the path was a weathered split-rail fence. Though it looked from the house that the ocean began at the end of the lawn, in reality, the ocean was at the bottom of a 100-meter cliff. There was a crumbly-looking edge about a meter wide between the fence and the drop.

Ana said, "I love you, Emerson."

"I love you too, Ana. This is so beautiful. But what's the best part?"

She ignored him. "How much do you love me, Emerson? Would you die for me?"

Emerson had an itch at the back of his neck. It felt like a mosquito. But it wasn't buzzing. It was more like a whisper, too low to make out. He said, "Sure, Ana. If it came to that, I would. I'd die for you."

He wasn't trying to be romantic. Emerson didn't know what romantic was. He was just being honest the way his grandpa taught him. Chandler also taught him to keep his eyes open, but the state he was in made that difficult. He felt like he was on the verge of falling asleep. Something kept pulling him away.

And of course, he would save Ana if her life was in danger. Even if he lost his life doing it. That's the sort of person Emerson was.

Ana said, "Prove it," and jumped over the fence. The rough clods of dirt and rock holding the edge together crumbled away, and she grabbed the fence just as the edge disappeared. "Emerson! Oh my god! Help." She looked over her shoulder and began to moan.

Emerson said, "Hang on, Ana," and grabbed her wrists, bracing himself against a post. At first, he thought she had fainted; her hands slipped off the top rail. The only thing holding her was Emerson. She looked up, terrified, and screamed. She twisted her hands around and grabbed Emerson's wrists and used her legs to scramble up, but instead, in her panic, she pushed off the cliff face. Before he could speak, Emerson lost his footing and flipped over the rail. Ana's hair swirled around her head like a flame as they plummeted toward the rocks at the edge of the sea.

◆ ◆ ◆

Boston Quinn received information from every corner of The City. He had spies in most of the more established settlements all the way to the Inland Sea. Doctor Sailor verified Elli's pregnancy and Emerson Lloyde's paternity. Boston told Stephanie that Elli would eventually come, and if she told him about it, he'd make sure her supply of insulin and betel nuts would not be interrupted. She'd kept her word to El not to let him find out where

Emerson was, but Lord Quinn already knew that anyway. Eggert, one of his toy soldiers, was out doing the requisite search. The Juice Hackers were smarter than him; they probably locked him up in some Faraday cage by now.

If he left the hackers alone long enough, they would prove themselves to be the danger he knew they were. But he grew tired of waiting, even though his mole said they were close; they had the shuttle and the pilot. All that was left was to bring him on board. After the "incident," it would be easy to convince the other idiot Lords to take care of the Juice Hacker problem permanently.

The fact that Emerson Lloyde was his heir's father made keeping his secret even more important. Speaking of heirs…

He called for his secretary. "Arrange a dinner with my daughter and her mother. Tonight."

Elli and Lucia spoke even less than he and Elli. The two were more like rival sisters than mother and daughter. *No matter*, he thought. *Even that can be turned to my advantage.*

◆

Elli and Lucia Rattlesnake both took the invitation as a summons. Elli spat and said, "Tanya, tell that fatass to go fuck himself!"

Lucia's response was only slightly different and in Italian. She told her serving man, "Merda, Cristo mio! Crede ancora di possedermi? Quel grasso cazzo," which, loosely translated, said, Shit, my Christ! Does that fat fuck still think he owns me?

Both servants changed their replies:

See you there.

Ricardo and Tanya had more sense than to deliver such messages.

◆

The dinner went as expected. Elli feigned boredom in her best imitation of a bipolar teen, and Lucia complained about everything that had transpired in her life since Boston kicked her out. The truth was she left on her own. The separation was mutually agreeable. But Quinn's power continued to grow, while Lucia felt like a nun relegated to her tower.

The meal was an onion-glazed pork loin roast with wine-soaked roasted potatoes and a green salad on the side. Elli, uncharacteristically, ate two platefuls and asked for dessert.

Lucia hardly touched her plate. Boston ate too much too fast, washing it down with glasses of wine. When he was done, dinner was cleared for everyone. He lit a cigar and said, "Elli has something to tell us. And it's the truth. I've seen the proof."

Elli knew she had been betrayed by the doctor; no other proof was needed. She would deal with it later. For now, her mother was staring at her. Elli said, "I'm pregnant, Mom."

Lucia showed no sign of surprise. She said, "Who's the father—do you even know?"

Elli fought to remain calm. Her mother knew where her buttons were hidden and how to press them. After a breath, she said, "His name is Emerson Lloyde. He comes from outsider blood. His DNA is robust. Maybe exceptional. It carries none of the damage that everyone else seems to have."

Lucia said, "Why isn't he here, eh?" and directly to Boston, "What aren't you telling me? Bastardo! You and your daughter are two peas in a pod."

Boston said, "He disappeared. He has contraband weapons. He's a pilot with tech. We believe he is hiding out with a Juice Hackers group." He added, looking at his daughter, "We don't know which one."

Lucia said, "There are dozens of Juice Hacker groups. Are you looking for him?"

He said, "We are pursuing all possible avenues."

Elli said, "And we all know what that means."

Lucia said, "Why did you bring me here? What do you want? Certainly not my opinion."

He said, "Your daughter is pregnant, but there is no guarantee that our heir will be born or that she can survive the labor or birth. Elli has the virus in her blood, Lucia. Like you and your mother before you. It was a miracle that she was even born. She needs you, 'donna. Our little girl needs her mommy."

Lucia went to Elli and hugged her from behind. Elli began to cry uncontrollably. She said, "It must be the hormones."

Lucia said, "You really are a bastard, Boston."

◆ ◆ ◆

Emerson thought his heart would stop. He was holding Ana's hand, but she was limp, in shock. He had never been so scared. They fell toward the rocks. When he looked down, the ground sped towards him so fast that he had to look away, out over the ocean. The sun was setting, and in that moment, the orange orb dipped just below the horizon, streaking the wisps of cloud with lavender and red. For a millisecond he forgot that they were plummeting to their death. When he looked back at the ground, the rocks were inches from his eyes.

The world went black and soundless. Slowly, a blue light grew around him. He heard his heart, felt his breath. It was slow and steady. He remembered the moment before hitting the rocks, and the terror shocked him, causing a fast, deep, inhale. *Did that really happen?* he thought. The room was lighter now; he was lying on the couch. He looked at his hands and wiggled his fingers. *It seems like my body*, he thought. Suddenly, he was stuck with the oddity of that thought. Why wouldn't he trust that he was in his own body? He suddenly wished he had a mirror and half expected one to appear in his hand.

Ana moaned from the couch next to him. She stretched and yawned. They both sat up. Emerson remembered where he was. Emotions flooded him, and he began to cry. Ana was more reserved, but she had tears in her eyes as well.

He said, "Did we just die together?"

She sat next to him and hugged him around the shoulder. She said, "Yes, we did, love. Do you want to do it again?"

Emerson became excited at the suggestion. Almost as fast, he doubted himself. He said, "Isn't that morbid? I mean, the object of life isn't death."

She said, "No? What is it then?"

Emerson had no ready answer for that. Though it felt irrational, the idea was deliciously exciting. He said, "I want to, but I don't know why. I'm also exhausted and starving. How long were we in there?"

Ana said, "About three hours. Now that you mention it, I'm pretty hungry too. Brain activity burns a lot of calories. The Fall is intense. But life-altering. At least that's what I'd heard."

"You've never done this before?"

"I knew what I was supposed to do, but I didn't know what was going to happen. In that world, circumstance and causation are exactly the same as our normal reality. That's the baseline of this model. But our choices are not predefined. We can tweak any aspect of the reality that we want. But I hear playing with this program is addictive. Worse than heroin. There are stories about coders getting lost.

"There was a group when I was a child that believed the program offered powerful spiritual experience. Other people say it opens the mind to the possibility of unlimited power. Either way, it's an amazing tool."

Emerson thought for a moment and said, "It was truly unbelievable. The most terrifying experience I've ever had."

Ana said, "Makes me feel more alive, more grateful to be alive. I have an awareness of the value of my life that I never really had before. I want to honor that part of me and have more respect for all life."

Emerson said, "There was something a little off about the way you got to me save you."

Ana said, "I know. I felt bad. But I was told that coming into the experience with no prior knowledge was far more powerful if you are surprised. And since you never heard of it before, I wanted to give you that opportunity. Can you forgive me?"

Emerson hugged her and said, "Of course," but the whole experience felt sideways in his heart. He let it go, but it would not let go of him. One thing he was certain of—he and Ana now shared the strongest bond he could imagine. Was it love? He didn't know.

◆ ◆ ◆

EVERYMEN

Emerson had a great curiosity for everything life offered him. He was too full of wonder to complain much. In his experience, waiting fixed most problems. This gave him the aura of a man drawing on an infinite well of patience. The truth was Emerson was just used to waiting. Ana shared his curiosity and would listen to him talk about growing up in the woods with Chandler for hours. In turn, she explained Blue Hole customs. He never interrupted her, even if he already knew about what she was describing.

Ana told him that all public duties in Blue Hole were filled using a revolving method. Any citizen over the age of eighteen who was capable of carrying out the duties would be conscripted to serve up to four years. A similar method was used for technical positions, designers and coders and the like. After apprenticing for a time, a tech would work on the job where they showed a natural ability for a period of up to four years. After that, they could choose to move on or remain. Technicals who wanted to retire would remain on call for a time to offer elder wisdom to those who were actively doing the tasks.

There was no money. All trade was done using a gifting model. Because of the basic viewpoint that the entire citizenry was a dependent collective, each person would choose what they wanted, or even that they didn't want to do anything, though people who seemed unbalanced or showed reclusive behaviors were checked on. Otherwise, most everyone contributed to the village and reaped the harvests in support, energy, food, water, and tech. There was a lively trade between Blue Hole and surrounding enclaves which rounded out supplies of goods that the village could not produce in isolation.

Emerson asked, "I've seen windmills and solar panels, but it seems like the village has unlimited electricity. How do you heat the buildings in the winter?"

She said, "There is a hydroelectric generator on the Blue Hole creek. It produces much more power than we need. So, we built heating and cooling towers using super-insulated coatings. Once the water is heated to 100 Celsius, the wind and solar can maintain it. We have been plumbing the whole town for years. Soon, it will provide heat and cooling for everyone."

After a moment, she said, "Have you considered becoming a full resident? I'd like that; it would be like a commitment to me and the rest of the town. We're a tight community."

He said, "I didn't even know there was such a thing. Sure. How do we do it? I like it here. But, you know, Quinn is pregnant, and I don't know how that's going to turn out."

"It's not a prison sentence, Emerson. It's more like a home base. Once you are accepted, you can always come home. But if you're not a citizen, you can only stay for six months."

"Sign me up."

"It's not quite that simple. You have to apply and be approved. I don't expect any problem. Rosco heads the council now. He should be able to convince the others."

Emerson said, "How many people are on the council?"

"Four. Rosco and Barton and two others. I don't know them."

"Where do I find the application?"

"I'll run the routine for you tomorrow. It is an Interface module."

"Don't tell me. You wrote it?"

"You know me too well."

She was peeved that he brought up Quinn, but the woman was carrying his child, so she kept quiet. She vowed to do whatever it took to keep Emerson with her. Maybe they could bring the baby to live in Blue Hole. The thought warmed her heart. She imagined getting a crib and fixing up a bedroom for the new arrival. She would have to displace that girl, Elli. Emerson wouldn't object. She never spoke to him either, the surly teen.

◆

When Elli wasn't with Pam, she was usually hanging around with Grendel. She didn't trust Ana, so she spent as little time in her house as possible. Emerson talked to her about it, and she listened politely but walked away without acknowledging anything when he finished. It made him sigh. He recognized the signs of her trauma. He didn't know how anyone could survive such a life and not come away damaged. Elli had never been able to go anywhere or do what she wanted. Her entire life before was organized around what Michel required. By the time he was forcing her to have sex with men, she had retreated so far into herself that she stopped imagining her escape.

At Blue Hole, she was completely free, and she wasn't going to give that up to anyone, especially another broken orphan like Anastacia Moon. She thought, "I can see you, girl. You can't pretend the empty away. I know. I've tried."

But still, Elli was restless. She began following random people. She followed Pam to the market and to a little opium café where she would spend hours. She followed Ana to a coders' meeting. But the woman was as boring in secret as she was normally. Elli followed Grendel to a house on the far southern edge of town, where a man she didn't recognize invited Rosco's mate to come in. Elli got tired of waiting for her to come out and went home. She occasionally followed strangers just to see how different people lived. But she never talked about her investigative adventures with anyone. It was her secret obsession, yet she didn't spend any time thinking about it.

One of the few times she was home for dinner with Ana and Emerson, he talked about a meeting Barton had invited him to. Ana said, "Maybe they're interested in nominating you for a council seat in the next cycle. You have to be a citizen to serve."

"Maybe so," he mused. "Barton didn't say much about it, only that everyone agreed that I would be a benefit to their group. Good thing we made that application."

Elli heard every word but showed no interest. After the meal, when Emerson left, she slipped out the back door and followed him. Ana called after her to clear the table, but the girl ignored her. She followed Emerson from a safe distance, theatrically ducking behind boxes and corners when she thought he might turn around.

The meeting was across town in a red brick building. It must have been a warehouse once. There were wood crates stacked to the ceiling in a huge room. Elli hid outside when Emerson went in, closing the door behind.

She followed him by looking through the succession of ground floor windows as he walked to the back. He sat at table with Barton and three other men who were already there. Rosco was not. It didn't seem to Elli like an official meeting. They greeted Emerson with a nod. It looked like a secret meeting. A pane of the window glass was broken out, making it easy for her to hear what they said. The underbrush was thick, obscuring most of the view from inside, though Elli had to be careful not to rustle anything. She held her breath.

Barton said, "Emerson, I want to welcome you to this meeting of the Everymen. You know me. These three gentlemen are Roy Nichols, Just Sam, and Peter Rust." Each of them extended a hand in Emerson's direction when their names were spoken. Emerson shook and murmured hello and good to meet you. Roy offered him a cup of steaming liquid from a large thermos. The others had mugs.

Emerson said, "No, no, no. You're too kind, but thank you," following the custom of hospitality to refuse three times.

Roy poured him a cup. It was a delicious brew of herbs and fermented apples. Emerson hadn't had an apple since Chandler found a nearly dead tree in an overgrown orchard when he was ten. That one was riddled with worm holes and rotted brown on one side. It was one of the best things he'd ever eaten, sweet, tart, and juicy all at once.

He said, "You have apples?"

Peter said, "They call it miruvor. We trade tech for it with a band from the east. They have the fruit and the stills. We have The Interface."

Emerson took a sip and said, "It's marvelous."

Barton said, "Yes, yes. Well. Let me start by thanking you for coming. We represent a group of men and women who believe The City is *our* home. We advocate taking it back, by force if necessary. We have a plan to make that a reality. The Enforcer shuttle was a missing piece until that captain arrived."

Just Sam chimed in, "Since he won't be needing it no more."

Barton continued, "What we need now is a trained pilot. And that's where you come in."

Emerson said, "What do you want me to do?"

Peter said, "We have a series of low-frequency emitters. The plan is to fly into Founder's Quarter so our team can deploy them. Once in position, we can use them to force the Elites to surrender. A bloodless coup."

Elli could hear everything clearly. She was getting a cramp in her foot from standing still for so long. She began to sweat, which ran into her eyes. She couldn't move because they were right on the other side of the window, but she couldn't stand still much longer.

Emerson said, "I think I'll pass. I don't have any argument with the Elites, as you call them."

Barton said, "I thought they were after you because you stole tech, the stuff in your head and that rifle."

Roy said, "That rifle is part of the plan as well. You see, the early-warning system for the Wall security and the communications antennas need to be destroyed before we can just fly in there like we own the place. But we'll take care of that. Just Sam here is an expert marksman. All you gotta do is fly, boy. Fly in there and fly back out. Easy, right?"

Emerson said, "I really appreciate the invitation, but I still gotta pass. I don't need to be crossing swords with the Enforcers. I trained and worked with those guys. Some of them are my friends. I know you'll understand. I can help train someone to fly. But I'm not your pilot."

"That's disappointing to hear," Barton said. "But I thought you liked it here in Blue Hole. You and sweet little Anastacia are playing house together. That little slut, Elli, is pretending to be your troubled teen, right? How are you gonna take care of them if we throw you out? They've been here a few weeks. Right, Roy?" Roy nodded a little too eagerly. "I think we can safely say your application for permanent residence is on its way to being denied."

"How can you say that, Barton? You are only one voice on the council."

"Yes," he smiled, showing an uneven row of yellowed teeth, "Rosco will undoubtably vote for you to stay. But Mercury Slone and Deb Crow are Everymen. They hold the other two seats and always vote with me. So, my friend, without my blessing, you will be out of here by midnight tonight, I'm afraid."

Emerson was livid, but he kept himself under control. He looked around the table slowly. He wanted to tell them to go to hell, but Chandler's words came back to him: "Never show them what's in your heart, boy. Just act agreeable until you see a way to escape."

Emerson said, "Nobody gets hurt, right?"

Barton said, "I give you my word."

After looking at everyone again, he said, "You got me then, boss."

They talked about logistics for a few more minutes. Emerson touched hands with each man and left. Elli had to stay still until the others were done. Once Emerson was out and the door was closed, Barton said, "These goody-goody boys are always the easiest to manipulate. Stupid fucker. He thinks he has power because he's from the goddamn City."

Roy said, "He thinks no one is getting hurt. What a moron."

Just Sam said, "He doesn't know Boston Quinn. The only way to stop that snake is to cut his fuckin' head off."

Barton said, "He probably knows, the pansy. Low-frequency emitters can't be adjusted. You turn them on, and they kill everything withing a half kilometer."

Peter laughed. "Looks like you have this under control, Barton. I'll arrange for Jock to meet with you at the tunnels. My community service is teaching archery this quarter so I'm going to be busy. You're on your own."

◆

The Everymen left after drinking the rest of the thermos. Elli had to tell Emerson. She didn't know who else she could trust. What could Pam do? Grendel and Rosco were married, and Barton was Rosco's kin. She knew better than to get between kin. She thought, *Good way to die quick.* But she had never spoken to Emerson. She was scared he would be angry about her following him and listening in on private conversations. Michel beat her when she went against him; broke her arm with a broomstick once. She needed to work up her courage, and time was running out.

Several days passed. She hung around the house more often, trying to find an opportunity to get Emerson alone. Ana noticed and became suspicious; she felt Elli's distrust and met it with her own. Ana believed her relationship with Emerson would last until old age. That he was her true love even if he didn't know it. She'd hoped Elli would move out entirely. Her loitering and lack of contributions wore on Ana.

Anastacia couldn't conceal her resentment and began dropping snide comments. Elli seemed oblivious, but the hostile atmosphere compounded by her need to warn Emerson stressed her.

When Emerson left to take the compost out, Elli stood to follow, leaving her half-eaten dinner. Compost was Ana's responsibility as a child, and it was a job she felt should have been Elli's. She said, "You can follow my man around like a dog sniffing for a bone, but you can't help take out the damn trash? You're a fucking tramp."

Elli had never heard the word tramp. But she recognized the tone. She turned before going out the door and spat on the floor. Ana exploded in a rage. "YOU DISGUSTING BRAT. Come in here and wipe that up." Elli strode out, leaving the door open. Emerson was too far away to hear. Ana yelled, "Don't you dare come back here, bitch."

Elli trotted to Emerson and pulled on the back of his shirt when she caught him. He turned, and she said, "Your Ana doesn't like me very much. She thinks I want to fuck you."

Emerson stopped and stared at her, mouth open. It had been months since she'd said anything in his presence, and she was owled the last time. He said, "Ana doesn't know you, and she's a jealous sort because she's insecure about being abandoned. You just have to give her time."

"She threw me out."

"Oh, she didn't mean it."

"Oh, I think she did. She really believes I am after you."

"I'll talk to her about it."

He dumped the bucket and covered it with shavings, then turned the rotator a few times to stir up the contents of the barrel. He said, "It's nice to hear your voice. Especially sober. You are much more pleasant this way."

She smiled and said, "I followed you. To that secret meeting. I heard everything."

He frowned. "That's unethical, Elli. You weren't invited. It was private business between me and those men."

"The Everymen? I have known men like them all my life. Do you trust them? 'Cause you shouldn't. I got stuck in the bushes. After you left, they said things you should know."

"What did you hear?"

"They are planning on killing everyone. And I know your girlfriend, Quinn, is pregnant with your baby. They want her dead."

Emerson thought about it for the rest of the walk back to the house. Before he went in, he said, "Why don't you go see what Grendel is doing?

I want to talk to Anastacia alone tonight. I'll meet up with you tomorrow, and we can decide what's best."

Elli had never touched Emerson before. At least not since the first night when she let him undress and bathe her. Before he went through the door, she hugged him tight around the chest and put her head on his shoulder. She whispered, "Please don't leave me, Emerson. I need you. Please?"

Emerson pulled her back, looked into her eyes, and said, "I will never leave you, Elli. You can count on me."

She said, "You're a good man, Emerson. But you shouldn't make promises that you can't keep."

◆ ◆ ◆

Emerson left Blue Hole on the pretense of cleaning up the burn left in the woods from moving the shuttle. After he finished, he used the satphone to call Quinn, who took a few rings to answer this time. When she picked up, she said, "I felt your baby kick me today. She wants to come out and meet you."

Emerson said, "I have some news. I've been blackmailed into flying a mission to take over the City."

"The fuck?"

"Yeah. I shouldn't be telling you. But this radical group, the Everymen, want to kill all of you, and I have to figure out how to stop them."

"Why don't you just leave? You have a shuttle. You can just steal it, right?"

"It's not that simple. I have people who count on me. Besides, leaving won't stop them."

"You can take care of me and our baby. I count on you."

"Only if I survive this mess, Quinn. Look, when I have a solid plan, I'll let you know. Don't tell anyone, okay? Trust me."

◆ ◆

Elli Rattlesnake hadn't spent much time with her birth mother since she was six. But she needed help now, and her mom seemed to know her particular situation. She was an active young woman with friends who followed her every idea with great anticipation. But once she started to show, they became anxious and fidgety. At first, they only stayed a little while. After the baby began pressing on all of Quinn's organs, cutting off circulation and pinching nerves, no one came around at all. It was no wonder. She had never been one to stoically bear discomfort. Contrarily, she liked to complain, loudly and for as long as her discomfort lasted, which was most of the time after the first trimester.

Quinn knew her issues were a natural part of pregnancy; her rants always focused on an element of minutia. Lucia didn't pay her any mind. During one of Quinn's tirades about soup, Lucia stopped her with a look and asked if she needed a back rub.

Over the course of the pregnancy, Elli's nose and tastebuds gave her all the excuses she required. The soup was bland, spicy, or rotten, too salty or not salted enough. But Lucia saw her daughter clearly. Elli didn't understand how and asked about it.

Lucia said, "You are my daughter, la mia bella ragazza. I love you. And love knows what love needs."

When she wasn't in pain, they spoke about the state of the world, the lives of women, and the uncertainty for the future that the Middles never experienced.

Quinn said, "People in The City eat all replicated food. But health is spotty, and survival is based on strength and the hospital's opinion. But they aren't dying from stress."

Lucia said, "The real world is kept secret from them. The Lords can eat what they want, which is often the pre-collapse diet complete with diet soda and sugary treats. Processed foods, my God, it is a wonder they all don't die of heart failure."

Quinn rolled her eyes and said, "Doctor Sailor is cloning transplant organs."

"They think they can control life. They are fools." Lucia went on to say, "We are growing fresh meat and some veggies in controlled areas. Up north, they patrol huge fenced preserves where different stock lives a monitored life. Even with all that, most of them don't eat it. They prefer the exotic frozen foods and cooking oils that were stored in bunkers around the country. They think it's safe, but the older preserved foods are poisoned with pesticides and the like. There is still a problem with water in many places."

Quinn said, "Sailor said fresh-grown hydroponics and meats raised on wild forage are the healthiest. That was the last time I saw her. We haven't spoken since she betrayed me."

Lucia stroked her daughter's hair and said, "You should forgive her. She is a very old friend. And you know that your father forced her. She would never willingly hurt you."

"Speaking of Father, have you noticed the Lords' current infatuation with opulence? They are dressing like twelfth-century aristocracy and decorating like a Trump!"

Lucia agreed, "I mean, Boston actually has good aesthetic sense, whereas all the others have no idea of what quality is. Their thirst for power is unmasked out of stupidity."

Quinn replied, "But even Daddy is dressing with sashes and medals now."

They both laughed heartily. Lucia called Tanya to bring some sandwiches. "Make them from rare beef and fresh greens, dear. My baby needs all the iron she can get from living foods."

◆

As the baby grew, her pain got worse. Her feet swelled if she stood, and her back ached no matter what position she was in. There was no relief. Lucia arranged for Max to visit. She made her daughter promise to stay silent for ten minutes so as not to drive her only friend away; she gave the two some privacy and had tea in the sitting room.

Max said, "Not going to ask you how you feel. I care, but I want to spend time talking, not listening to you bitch, sorry."

Quinn said, "You want a scotch?" She yelled, "Tanya, Max needs a drink."

"You'll join me, of course. A little alcohol should soothe your pains."

Quinn pointed to her swollen belly. "No scotch for baby."

"Ew, motherhood is boring."

"It's worse than boring. But take my mind off it. What did Nimue say? I haven't seen you in months."

"She played the file for Emerson and left. She asked me to give you a message." He bent over her large belly, tenderly hugged her around the shoulders, and said, "Emerson sends his love."

Quinn smiled and said, "Thank you, Maxamillion. We've spoken. I still don't know what's going on, but at least he knows about this." She indicated her bulge.

"She also said he looks comfortable. Happy, even."

Tanya brought his drink. Quinn sighed. "I'm worn out already, Max. I don't know how I'm going to get through another four months." She lowered her voice to an almost-whisper. "He's fallen in with some insurrectionists. They want him to fly an army into Founder's Quarter to wipe us out."

"Is that some kind of joke? How would they get by the Wall sentries without being blown to bits? And the guard would be there in less time than it takes to fly in. The defenses of The City are unassailable. This Emerson guy is insane if he thinks that will work."

Quinn sat up and said with a cross tone, "He's not stupid, Max. That's my point. He won't do anything that stupid. But I can't predict how his blackmailers are going to respond. It worries me. I asked him to just leave. He has a shuttle. But he said others depend on him."

Max laughed, "That's your boy, Quinn. Heart of gold. I understand why you love him. Besides, of course, the seed he planted in you. You know none of these sods around here would give a crap. They're too busy looking out for themselves."

Quinn thought about Emerson's eyes and his shaggy blond hair. He once told her he didn't bother brushing it because it went right back to looking messy. She smiled at the memory.

Max said, "Hello? Quinn? Where'd you go, girl?"

"They used to call it gathering wool. I don't imagine anyone around here would even know what that means. Emerson uses all sorts of archaic expressions. He used to listen to archived recordings when he was a kid. You two should talk."

"Seems like you want to be alone. I gotta get goin' anyway." He kissed the top of her head. "Take care of yourself."

"Yeah, I need to rest."

He left; Lucia came back. She said, "You are in love with this boy. If he comes back here with an army, your father will execute him."

"I know, Mother. I hope he's not that pigheaded."

"Like you?"

Quinn smiled and closed her eyes; she was sleeping a moment later.

◆ ◆ ◆

END OF PART THREE

INTERFACE

PART FOUR

INTERFACE

PART FOUR

EGGERT'S DILEMMA

Captain Eric Eggert might have been under house arrest, but the space they gave him to stay in was nicer than any apartment he had ever had. He had a refrigerator stocked with fresh food and drink, and a woman named Margret brought him dinners each evening. They were balanced meals including a green vegetable, often lettuce or broccoli, and a protein of rabbit or quail, beans, or fish. Eggert had never eaten real rabbit or quail. He thought he liked beans, but the pintos and Anasazi beans tasted like an entirely different food from what he ate in The City. He had pre-collapse frozen breaded fish at a Founder's party once, but it was nothing like the buttery delicacy of the plain pan-fried river trout she brought once a week.

The alcohol back in The City was weak and watery. At Blue Hole, mead and beer were in ready supply. And the hooch, a pure unaged whiskey, would clean your clock. He had lived on replicator food all of his life. Within a week, his chronic gassiness and hip pain were gone. A month later, he was regular as a clock. Even his body odor was sweeter.

The bathroom was a marvel. The house he lived in was originally an extended-stay hotel. The Blue Hole engineers had reconnected the electricity and rerouted the heating and cooling lines so the Village's central plant maintained a constant twenty-four Celsius. He had plenty of hot water, and the pressure was perfect. He had grown attached of the plain oat-and-oil soap and was stashing extra bars in case the supply ran out. Margret explained that they made it themselves. She said, "When it runs out, we just make more."

The towels were thick cotton, absorbent and soft; the Enforcers-issued ones in The City were thin and left you feeling wet. The screen in the main room was Interface-adapted and hooked into the Blue Hole network. He had a range of archaic television and documentaries to watch in addition to a historical database.

The range of entertainment and books available was amazing. There were titles available in Blue Hole that he had never seen in The City. And since he had little to do, he spent most of his time reading, watching, and learning. Emerson came to talk regularly. They would sometime share meals or coffee. Eggert made a French press for his visitor with unmasked glee, grinding the beans in an antique burr grinder and boiling water in an electric tea kettle. To Emerson, he was transformed into a boy.

Blue Hole traded with groups all over the continent. The City was more insulated. If there was similar trade going on there, Eggert had never seen it. Emerson told him about their supply train, which ran from the village into the southeast.

He said, "They've been clearing off the tracks for years. The train is a solar contraption put together with public transportation parts salvaged from various cities. It's only used for shipping goods; people seldom leave the confines of the walls."

Eggert sipped his coffee. "We were told your enclaves were primitive and rude. No one outside The City is supposed to have this sort of technology. But of course, no one can see for themselves. So, it's easy to control what the people believe. I don't know if anyone would stay there if they saw how you are living here. And I'm a captive." He closed his eyes, breathed in the scent of the steamy dark liquid in his cup, and sighed. "This is real. I never knew." After a moment looking out the window at a group of teens talking and laughing, he said, "The people in The City? They'd be appalled. I'm appalled. What you have built here is impossible in the story we've been told. If I hadn't seen it, I would have thought it was some kind of trick." He sucked his teeth and had another sip.

Emerson said, "I feel you. It sucks to have your eyes pried open."

Eggert said, "Yeah, it's a dilemma for sure."

◆

After he had been kept in for a couple months, Rosco told Emerson to unlock Eggert's doors and give him a key. He said, "He has experienced enough of our ways now to see we're not monsters."

When Emerson gave it to him at his next visit, Eggert was surprised. He said, "This is the weirdest society I've ever heard of. You take me prisoner and then release me with the key to my prison. What's to keep me from just walking out of here?"

Emerson smirked. "Go ahead and try. Rosco thought it was a good risk. I disagreed, but he reminded me that the wall works both ways." He drained his cup and said, "Ahhh. And your shuttle is in a hangar in the village. If you did get out, you would have to walk."

Eggert shook his head. "He's right, you know. If this is prison you can throw away the key. It's obvious that my whole life is a lie. I have lived in a darkness that my beloved City fostered and maintained. That's a pretty major betrayal. So yeah, I don't have any reason to leave. They didn't care enough to try and rescue me. I say fuck 'em."

A few days later, Eric Eggert showed up at the machine shop looking to be useful. Rosco showed him around. He and Emerson ended up working together on an educational coding project for the kids. Emerson felt like his world had been off its axis and was just now settling back. He felt more normal than he had since Chandler died.

Barton made sure to rekindle his anxiety. He arrived at the house and escorted Emerson to a meeting. Elli had been living with Grendel and Roscoe, spending most of her time at the doctor's, and did not know. Ana believed it was a council-related thing and didn't give it a thought.

Once there, Roy gave him a cup of miruvor, and they greeted one another like they were old friends. It took most of Emerson's resolve to keep from telling them how he really felt. But even if he decided to leave Blue Hole, he needed their complete trust in order to do it.

Barton said, "We have the emitters stowed in Captain Eggert's shuttle. You need to design the plan to get past the guards and into Founder's Quarter before they shoot you out of the air. Otherwise, Just Sam will be your copilot."

Sam looked grim. He wasn't excited about flying into a potential war zone and was hoping Emerson's pacifist attitude would inspire a solution that didn't include his marksman's talents.

Emerson said, "The shuttles use a responder code. They can track us with them. It allows The Authority to verify who is who. What we need to do is make Eggert's shuttle invisible. They use three towers to determine the locations. A signal is sent out like a radar wave, and the onboard responders send back the ship's information and a location can be determined.

"We could cut the lines from the towers. But that will alert The Authority, and they will mobilize. We need to be quiet. Sneak in and surprise them."

Just Sam said, "Maybe we can block them in a way that makes the engineers suspect system failure rather than intrusion."

Emerson said, "I think Ana and I could craft something like that."

Barton was suspicious. "Can she keep quiet?"

"Such a program would be a good defensive tool for Blue Hole. She'll be into it. I don't have to tell her what it's for."

"Sounds good," said Just Sam. "If you need anything, we will provide it. I want you to meet the platoon for the mission. Be here tomorrow afternoon."

Emerson said, "I want to inspect Eggert's craft and make sure he didn't rig anything that could betray us."

Barton said, "I'll send word to the guards to allow you into the hangar."

◆ ◆

On his way, he ran into Elli. She was running an errand for Dr. Pam with a list of herbs and medicines to get around town. Emerson saw her coming out of Carello's Herbal Apothecary and called out, "Elli, walk with me."

He said, "They pulled me into another meeting. I need you to watch them to make sure I am not betrayed. But they can't know. Are you game?"

She nodded. He gave her a PDA. "This is good inside the borders of Blue Hole. My number is programmed in it. I'll send you a note whenever I am meeting with them."

She gave him a little hug and walked in the opposite direction. Emerson went to the hangar. The emitters were stowed in the rear cargo space. Eggert's ship was twice the size of his, but thanks to the extended travel certification, he was trained to handle it, meaning he could unlock all security levels on the ship's systems. He used his Interface to inspect the circuits on the emitters. The units were simple and archaic. Since he figured that the platoon would not arm them until they were placed, he knew he needed to be able to disable them remotely afterward. He inserted a kill-switch. It would be undetectable to the soldiers that placed them. He could shut them off if he was within a range of 100 meters.

He met Barton leaving the hangar. "Everything OK?"

Emerson was surprised by his sudden appearance. He said, "Are you following me?"

"What if I am? You know, Lloyde, I have a hard time trusting anyone who put a knife to my neck."

Emerson thought, *The sentiment is mutual,* but kept quiet. Instead, he said, "Check for yourself. I'm doing what you asked."

"Oh, I will. You can be sure of that." He began to walk away but stopped and turned around. "You best watch your attitude. You wouldn't want anything to happen to pretty little Anastacia or that dirty slut, Elli." He didn't wait for Emerson to respond and continued walking. Emerson wondered how much meat Barton carried on his skinny frame. As he walked, he contemplated the steps required to butcher Rosco's brother into useable cuts. Such was his growing hatred for Barton.

Before going out the next day to meet with the platoon, Emerson sent Elli a text message. Ana asked where he was going. He gave her a short kiss and said, "Barton wants me to meet some people. He seems to have plans for me."

"Barton has always creeped me out. He has those little piggy eyes in his puffy face."

Emerson assured her, "I think my whole deal with him will be short-lived."

◆

He didn't see Elli, but he was pretty sure she was there. When he arrived at the back of the warehouse, five uniformed men stood around the table. Barton sat; the other three conspirators were absent. Emerson greeted them. Barton said, "The black-haired one is Jock. He is the platoon leader. The others answer to him only. If you have anything to say, say it to Jock."

Emerson noticed that they were standing stiffly in line facing him from behind the table; they appeared to believe the stance they'd adopted was attention. It wasn't.

There wasn't anything to say, so Emerson nodded, and Barton continued, "This is a new team, and Jock here will need a little while to get them trained up. Isn't that right, Jock?"

Jock said, "Right."

Emerson thought the scene looked like a satirical movie from the late 1990s and had to resist grinning. He ventured, "Ah, how long will our mission be on hold, sir? I was given the impression that we were ready to go."

Barton snapped, "I don't answer to you, Lloyde. And I'm not responsible for your impressions. We only just acquired the shuttle and a pilot. I can only move so fast."

"No, sir," Emerson agreed. "So how long is that, sir?"

Barton and Emerson looked at Jock, who, after a moment, suddenly realized he should be speaking and blurted, "Two, three months, sirs. Ah, sir."

"There," said Barton. "You have your answer."

The others were dismissed and sauntered away, whispering. Barton bade Emerson sit. He said, "I'm sorry about all that. You are helping our cause. I know that. I just get a little worked up sometimes. You understand, right? No hard feelings?"

Emerson wondered about that expression. What would a soft feeling be? He certainly didn't love Barton. He assumed the feeling was mutual. The man was a two-headed viper.

"Of course not, Barton. You must have a lot on your mind. Two months gives us more time to perfect the software we'll need to get in."

Barton smiled in a way he must have taken to be warm and gentle. To Emerson it appeared to be more of a snarl. He took the offered hand and nodded. He was relieved. This would give him more time to get out of going at all.

◆ ◆ ◆

THREE MONTHS OF HELL

Weather in Blue Hole had its own microclimate. When Chandler's great-great-grandmother, Susan Estes, would drive the Interstate highway near where present-day Blue Hole was, she'd encounter a dip in the land where it was often raining when the weather was clear. Or, inversely, clear when the weather everywhere else in the state was raining. Cell service was a dead zone. When the climate began to spin wildly out of balanced cycles, the microclimate of the region became erratic as well, but it was often its own isolated brand of extreme. Fast forward 100 years.

It rained steadily for the next three months. Usually a light rain, just enough to make the atmosphere feel like a greenhouse; it was hot and humid, and the light was always diffuse, giving the trees and plants a weird iridescent glow during the day. However, the mist turned into a severe thunderstorm every few days. Its arrival was unpredictable and sudden. Within minutes, anything not bolted down in a low area would be washed or blown away. The streets filled with water. All transportation was switched to makeshift rafts and flat-boats. A lot of commerce was conducted on great wooden barges pushed around by poles or towed by shirtless men and women wearing harnesses.

The development in the shop moved upstairs. The water added a layer of difficulty to life, but things went on. People adapted. They built docks where front porches had been and rigged garages to be boat houses. Ana and Emerson moved into a different building as the house they'd chosen was in a lower elevation; the first floor was completely underwater. Rosco and Grendel also moved into the same building. Elli stayed with Doctor Pam, an older, lifelong resident who had the wisdom to choose a building on a hill.

Elli became an adept boatwoman. Her upper arms and back became muscled from piloting her modified kayak through the town. She still only spoke when necessary, but she was lively and engaged. Emerson often saw her laughing.

Barton stayed away for the most part. And Elli reported back to Emerson about his and the others' movements. Most of it was worthless information, but Elli felt purpose in the doing. She kept meticulous notes and stayed hidden. No one suspected they were under surveillance. She had developed a keen sense of humor and had given each of the players nicknames. Barton was Piggie. Roy was Moose. Just Sam was The Turtle. She thought Jockstrap was an appropriate nickname.

She said, "When I was little, I used to follow Michel around. I got pretty good at avoiding notice. I was a nothing of a girl, and his unpredictable anger taught me to keep quiet. These guys? Moose and The Turtle? They're more boring than he was. They go to the store, they go to some office, they go to cafés and talk about bullshit. I don't know how their wives can stand it. Except for Piggie. Ooh, he's a sneaky bastard. I kept losing him until I figured it out.

"Tunnels. There's a whole mess of watertight tunnels under Blue Hole. As near as I can tell, they only run under the businesses section. Downtown, the locals call it." She shrugged. "Don't look no different from nowhere else around here. Back in Essex—that's what they called it where you found me—there were skyscrapers. Miles of row houses, sewers, you know? Real city streets. Real wildlife like rats and snakes. The people were *mean* too, like…"

Emerson got her attention by waving. He was glad she was opening up, but he depended on her to tell him what was going on.

She said, "Yeah, yeah, okay. We need to get into the tunnels."

Emerson said, "Is there any reason to believe that there really is anything going on down there? I'll ask Rosco about them. I bet they're not a secret." He never did.

Elli looked disappointed, but she didn't say anything. Emerson didn't notice. She wanted to be useful, but wasn't sure she should bring up Grendel. Before she could convince herself that it was a bad idea, she launched ahead. "I followed Grendel. She's visiting some man in the south of town."

"Visiting?" Emerson said. "No. I don't want to know. And you shouldn't be following her around. She's got a right to privacy."

Elli was stung. She said, "What the fuck am I doing for *you*? Huh?"

Emerson softened. "I'm sorry, Elli. I like Grendel and I wouldn't want anyone following me. But I bet she has her reasons, and we should respect that."

He wished he knew more about what Barton was doing but didn't want to contact the man. The less he had to see him, the better. He said, "No, what you are doing is good. Keep it up. Let me know if anything happens. Especially with…" he paused and smiled, "Piggie."

But there was no news. And the rain kept up. It felt as though the sun would never shine again. Doctor Pam treated an epidemic of foot fungus cases, and Elli was busy with her most of the time. When she did follow one of the Animal Farm Gang, as she sometime referred to them, they didn't do anything exciting. She had begun following Ana too, another boring and predictable person. She craved some sort of excitement.

Elli didn't elaborate on Grendel's afternoon long visits to the lone house in southside. She followed the woman there several times and had begun tailing the mysterious man too.

He was strangely deformed. She found him a grotesque, brittle man with a big head and a hunched back. He dragged one foot. They visited the doctor once, but Elli couldn't ask Pam about him. She didn't know where to begin. And now the mystery of the tunnels worried the back of her mind like a tongue sore. Whenever she found herself in the "downtown" area, and she rolled her eyes whenever she said "downtown," it took all her strength not to follow little Piggie down his hole. She resisted; she told Emerson that none of the others ever entered the tunnels.

The weather depressed most of the inhabitants. Faces were glum. Elli liked the mist and the watery air. To her, it felt like she was living inside of a secret land where the air was thick and green, and everyone lived floating on the water. It was a perfect fantasy because it felt so real. She imagined herself a sort of pirate. Her hair was getting longer, finally! And she would comb it down over her eyes so no one would see her face.

Emerson and Ana finished the code to their spoofing routine. Ana proudly explained it to Rosco, "Most alarm systems have a trip mechanism, like a proximity sensor or a radar or something. Programs designed to defeat security would disable the input or the output, which in our case would alert them to a breach. The key to our program is that it does not interrupt the signals. A diagnostic would show the system was optimal. And it really would be. What our code does is intercept notifications, any and all internal notification really, and silence them. As far as the people watching are concerned, the system is alerting to nothing. When they try to find out why, everything will be fine."

Ana was getting excited; Emerson loved that side of her. But she did get carried away sometimes.

"We simply spoof an entire system, interrupting *all* the alarms, cell phones, door locks, lights, etc. and substitute a timed program that cycles through and fires them off at random times. It would drive an operator crazy. Whoever this is used on would have to be a pretty technologically advanced group, I expect, but I know it would be undetectable and could stay hidden until it's needed."

Emerson began to sweat. She was about to speculate to Rosco what the program was really made for, which might lead to a bunch of difficult questions.

She went on, "Which is why I believe that someone else in another part of the world could be interested in trading for this. It's is very valuable."

Rosco smiled and said, "Genius, pure genius."

Emerson relaxed a notch. The program was essential. Maybe the damn weather would keep up, and everyone could forget about invasions and power struggles. He knew he was just dreaming. Leave it to humans to fuck up their own paradise. It always seemed obvious to him that cooperation was better.

◆ ◆

Quinn carried her hell with her, not that she could carry anything anywhere. Between Doctor Sailor's concerns for placenta previa and the slow onset of hyperemesis gravidarum, Elli Rattlesnake Quinn was confined to bed. By the time she was six months in, she felt as big as a house and couldn't eat much of anything without giving it right back. The only exercise she got was the short walk to the bathroom for the toilet or a bath. She took a lot of baths, far more than any Middle's water quota, not that the Elites ever paid much attention to it; Quinn's bath-taking was excessive, even for a lord. Getting in and out of the tub got harder every day, but it still didn't amount to much exercise.

She'd learned by trial and violent regurgitation, mostly the latter, the only food she could reliably keep down was a cracker developed by one of the midwives at the Birth Corps. The woman, Bette Craine, claimed it came from a recipe she'd discovered in an old obstetrics manual. "Just fell out on the floor," she'd say when telling the story. It was called a morning cracker and claimed to settle the most violent cases. Quinn's stomach would not be completely settled until after her hungry passenger left, but at least she didn't have to starve to death while waiting.

Since the Birth Corps was created, the midwives kept a supply of morning crackers on hand. Even modified with the sorghum flour the cooks used instead of extinct winter wheat, the crackers calmed her enough to feed her. Morning crackers comprised most of what she ate.

When she wasn't bathing, retching, or sleeping, Quinn worried. The satphone had stopped working soon after she and Emerson's second call. She talked to Max, and they decided the satellite network had probably degraded. She resisted asking her dad. "I'm a mess, Max," she complained. "I can't eat. I pee all the time. I feel like my guts are packed into a sardine can. I hate this. And I think, Jesus—Emerson did this to me—the fucker."

She burst out crying. Max sat on the bed next to her and tried to hug her around the shoulders, but he leaned on her breast, and she yelled. "Get the fuck off me, asshole. Shit!"

She sniffed and wiped her nose on the back of her hand. "I'm afraid he's dead. Max. What if Emerson is dead, and I have to do this by myself?"

"You have Lucia and Doctor Sailor. You're strong."

"Not the birth, you dolt. Raising a fucking baby. I can't do this alone. I don't trust any of these people."

"I hear you there. I'd be worried too."

She hit him with her pillow. "Nice encouragement, fuck head."

"Are you going to keep yelling at me? Because I like you, Quinn, but I don't want to be treated like that."

She burst into tears again. Max stood by and watched warily. She wailed through her tears, "I'm ugly-crying, and I can't stop. Aaaah."

"They used to call a person acting like you a basket case."

She stopped crying and said, "What?"

"You said you were a mess. A pre-collapse euphemism for a person with a messed-up situation was a basket case."

"Why? I don't see the connection."

"It's terrible, really."

"Tell me." She was sitting up now, all emotions on hold.

"It turns out the phrase is mostly propaganda, but it was coined as a name for quadruple-amputee World War One veterans. It came about as the result of a fictitious news story about quad amputees being warehoused.

The fact is no one came back from that war with no arms or legs, and no quadriplegic was ever carried in a basket. The phrase came to mean a mentally unbalanced person, which in common slang was applied to anyone having a chaotic period in life where multiple events go the wrong way."

"That's very eloquent, Maxamillion. Are you contemplating writing educational programs?"

"I'm trying to stay busy so this place doesn't turn *me* into a basket case, Quinn. You will give birth one day, and all this will end. I will continue to slog along here like a rich prince who will never inherit the throne."

"Aww, poor baby," she said and kissed him on the cheek. "Tanya, Max is here. Bring him a drink." She pulled his hat over his eyes.

He said, "Can you make it a double?"

◆ ◆

The rain in the Blue Hole microclimate did not lift until late July. Just in time for any remaining plants to be scorched by the sun. It seemed that climate change had surreptitiously moved the line of Earth's latitude. Where Blue Hole used to lay on the thirty-sixth parallel, summers now felt more like the twenty-ninth. The rain-soaked town barely began to dry when a dust storm swept the streets clear of anything not already carried away by the rain.

The only positive news for Emerson was that Jock contacted him to say the platoon was ready to go. Barton called a meeting. Emmer told Ellie to listen in. He arrived to the back of the warehouse just after the others. Ellie was hiding below the broken window, ten meters away.

Barton said, "Jock tells me they are ready to launch."

Jock sat at the table. The others slouched in what Emerson assumed they believed at-ease looked like. Elli's nicknames seemed so appropriate that he nearly chuckled but coughed and sniffed to cover it. The platoon leader said, "We set up a tower outside the wall. We will begin spoofing The City navigation from there at sundown on the next new moon. By the time The Authority is considering shutting the whole system down, it should be dark, and any real incursion will be ignored. Meanwhile, Emerson flies the shuttle into Founder's Quarter."

Emerson said, "What do we do if the Elite Guard confronts us the moment we land?"

Jock looked at Barton and then back to Emerson. "We didn't know there was an Elite Guard."

"Uh-huh. There is. And they will be on us the second we touch down. Nope, boys. We will need to not only confuse the alarms; we are going to have to cloak the ship. Which means landing away from the main square."

"Wait a second, Lloyde. What are you trying to sell us?" Barton was squinting his piggy eyes, causing Emerson to swallow another snort.

Emerson produced a map of Founder's Quarter. He said, "There is a dead-end street here," he pointed on the paper, "two blocks from where you need to position the emitters on the center plaza. There's a huge fountain in a private garden at the dead end. We can cloak the ship near it, and the mist from the fountain will confuse anyone looking at. In the bright, artificial light of the square, the cloak would be noticed as a shifting rainbow of reflections tracing the hull. Anyone walking by would be able to tell immediately what it was."

Jock nodded. "Sounds reasonable."

Emerson said, "There is a nonreflective black paint that will help the craft stay hidden. If we paint the shuttle, it will increase our chance at success."

Just Sam said, "Can we get such a thing?"

Emerson said, "I know where, but I will need the shuttle to get there."

◆ ◆

Quinn's labor started at three o'clock in the morning; her water broke soon after she stood up to go to the toilet. The midwives and Doctor Sailor came to the apartment. Tanya was there, as always, working as her doula, and Lucia provided support.

Contractions were sluggish. At about five hours in, Quinn was only at three centimeters, and she was exhausted. Doctor Sailor looked stressed. The midwives consulted quietly among themselves and returned to tell Quinn what they believed.

Marcy Stratton, the head of Birth Corps, waited until the contraction ended before telling Quinn, "If you aren't able to make some serious progress soon, we are going to have to do a cesarian."

Quinn had no opinions. She was so tired she couldn't think properly. She wished that Emerson was there. *He would know what to do; he knew how to take control.*

But at eight that morning, Emerson was in Blue Hole preparing to go on a reconnaissance mission to retrieve the stealth paint. He went to Eric Eggert's apartment to ask for his help. Eric delighted in making the younger man coffee. While Emerson waited and watched the people filling the street, he became dizzy and had to put his head on the table.

Eggert asked him if he was alright.

"Yeah, just a little lightheaded as my gramps used to say. I'll be okay, maybe some bread."

While Eggert toasted a slice for Emerson, Quinn drifted in a semi-aware state.

Emerson, meanwhile, excused himself to go pee. As he closed the bathroom door, he was assaulted by another wave of nausea, and his knees buckled. He knocked a ceramic dish full of soap bars onto the tile floor, and it shattered, throwing shards and soap across the floor. Emerson fell and hit his head on the porcelain bathtub. Eggert called for him and, when he didn't answer, pushed into the room, shoving Emerson's legs out of the way. The younger man was out cold.

◆

He woke in a field of wildflowers. A faint breeze blew. When he sat up, his perception shifted in a way that told him he was in a construct. He recognized this place; it was the grassy meadow he and Quinn visited in the Red Palace. He knew it was impossible for The Interface to capture him from so far away. Besides, all of Blue Hole was essentially behind a firewall. There was no logical way he could be there. But there he was. He stood up and looked around. At the far edge was a tent pavilion he hadn't seen before. He arrived at it in a single step, further verifying the artificial nature of the environment. He couldn't figure out the logistics of this construct while he was in it; too large a part of the human brain was occupied during full-body Interface engagement. It took up too much bandwidth to do analytical exploration. He entered the pavilion.

When he passed through the door, he entered Quinn's apartment. She was naked, squatting on the tile floor. The midwives circled her. Her breasts were large and swollen, areolas dark brown, hair stringy with sweat and fatigue. She looked more beautiful than any other woman he had ever seen. A woman he assumed was Quinn's mother, Lucia, sat behind her, holding her arms and whispering encouragement in Italian. Tanya stood in the doorway with a towel and a jug of water.

Doctor Sailor paced and spat her red juice into a crystal scotch glass. Emerson could not hear any noise from the apartment. He surmised that he was projected there by some weird glitch and that the others couldn't see him. He approached the bed.

Marcy saw him first and said, "There's a strange man in the room. Can anyone else see him?" She pointed directly at Emerson, who waved and smiled. She said loudly, "Can you hear me?"

Quinn's contraction ended; the other midwife checked her dilation and shook her head. "Still at five, Marce."

Emerson approached. Quinn looked up and relaxed. She said, "I hoped you'd come." But another contraction gripped her, and she moaned. The sound modulated into a guttural bellow, frightening Emerson. Marcy looked at him and mouthed, "Can you hear me?"

Emerson shook his head, but he had heard Quinn. He held her shoulders, looking into her eyes, and said, "I don't know how I am here, but I am. I can see they're worried, Rattlesnake. But you've got this. We're gonna get this baby out together."

Quinn panted to catch her breath. She looked into Emerson's face and whispered, "Kiss me. Kiss me like you mean it. Kiss me and tell me you love me."

He took her head in his hands, kneeling in front of her, and covered her mouth with his. He felt the power of birth surge through his face, neck, chest, core. He remembered being Quinn and imagined her contraction in his body. The core of his being tightened. Their uterus was gathering all the strength of their extremities and beyond, growing like the roots of a mighty tree, calling out to mycelium in the soil, concentrating in the trunk where the largest muscle in the human body performed the work. Nothing existed beyond this collapsing muscle, contracting with the strength of the universe. Emerson thought he might lose himself in it, like a collapsing star, but then like an ocean wave, the contraction receded. He gasped. Quinn opened her eyes. "That was better. You're helping. Stay here with me."

Eggert dragged Emerson's body out of his bathroom and onto the couch. He slapped his cheek and shook him, but his body remained limp, obviously unconscious. Eggert left in search of help.

Quinn was taken by another wave of contracting. Within seconds of it receding, another crashed upon them. Emerson and Quinn held their breath, while Lucia took deep breaths and encouraged Quinn to breathe through. The second midwife checked dilation and announced, "We're at ten!"

Marcy said, "You're doing great, Elli. This is transition. Remember what I told you about shifting?"

Transition felt like a whirlpool of energy as the uterus shifted from opening the doorway to preparing the push. Emerson and Quinn separated in this quiet turmoil in the center of the storm.

He felt a hand on his shoulder and twisted his neck around. A woman, her pupils bottomless emerald pools, peered into his eyes. She wore an elaborately embroidered skirt. Her silver hair was tightly braided and tucked beneath a kerchief. She bent down and whispered into his ear. Deep wrinkles creased her sun-browned skin. Emerson glanced at the floor; her long feet were wrapped in colorful felt slippers.

She said, "No matter what these knowledgeable women say, let her body shift naturally to bringing this baby forward. She will just breathe this baby into the world. The child knows this secret from her ancestors. Be present as she slides naturally, massaged by her mother's womb through the doorway. She will remember this moment and thank you for it when she is old enough. Remember this, great-great-grandson. Trauma is not the reason we live. This one is free." The elder vanished.

The midwives, not aware of the visitation, began coaching Quinn to push. Her own mother led the chorus. Emerson leaned in and touched his forehead to Quinn's. Immediately, the three became one with the presence of Emerson's great-great-grandmother. She sheltered them beneath her arms as their guardian. The voices urging Quinn to push faded into the background as mother, father, and child danced with the contracting uterus, massaging the young one through the soft walls of Quinn's vagina, bumping against her pelvic bone and turning.

The deep guttural sounds that emerged from Quinn's throat overtook the whispering of outside encouragements. The sound was primordial, connecting through time from daughter, to mother, to father, to all grandmothers in infinity, flooding through the embodied lineage of Quinn and Emerson's heritage, converging into the full potential of the small one appearing for the first time Earthside.

She emerged, a tiny, pink human, face up with eyes wide, sliding, gently, into Marcy's hands. The babe did not cry but looked around the room. And when she saw Emerson, she grinned her toothless newborn grin.

Quinn reached out, calling, "My daughter!" Marcy handed the baby to Quinn with the umbilical cord still attached. Emerson faded. Quinn whispered, "I love you. We'll name her after your great-great-grandmother."

Emerson, almost completely transparent now, said, "Marya. Her name was Marya."

The last thing he heard was Quinn, saying, "Marya? Welcome, baby girl. Welcome to the world, Marya!"

Doctor Pam had just taken his pulse when Emerson's eyes snapped open. She said, "Welcome back. Where did you go?"

Emerson sat up and said, "I don't think you would believe me if I told you."

◆ ◆

Eggert and Emerson took the shuttle west to the location of the bunker he and Dander had unearthed. The transponders were disabled. As they flew, they were undetectable. On the way, Emerson explained what they would find. Eggert said, "You locked me out of the controls. That was smart, but I'm not interested in going back."

"I can't be too safe."

He told the older pilot about his experience with Quinn's labor. Neither could explain the phenomenon. He explained the mission Barton had forced him into. He said, "That's why I wanted to come out here. There's more in that bunker than stealth paint."

Eggert said, "Hearing that makes me want to stop them myself. I hope you are smart enough to find a way."

Emerson said, "My child and her mother's lives depend on it."

Once inside, they cracked open several crates and removed at least 50 plasma rifles and ten buckets of paint. It took the rest of the day. Eggert showed him a hidden storage compartment in the rear of the shuttle where they stashed the guns. He also showed the younger pilot the escape pod and the hidden rocket systems.

He said, "I had this ship modified for combat. Not that I ever saw any. She also has a hidden extra capacity fuel tank." Emerson wanted to ask if the captain had ever been across the Inland Sea, but a storm was brewing, and he needed to give the controls his complete attention. The trip was choppy and rough. They arrived back at Blue Hole near midnight, and Eggert helped him hide the rifles under the shuttle's floor panels.

Emerson tried the satphone, but it would not work. He brought it to Rosco, who was a wizard with the ancient art of solder and wires. There was a shop set up in his new garage. Emerson talked while Rosco took the case completely apart. Within a few minutes, the satphone was dismantled and in pieces under Rosco's halogen work lamps.

Emerson described the birth. Rosco couldn't explain it either. He took detailed pictures of the phone and connected the main board to his test equipment. He said, "I'm analyzing the circuits. When I'm done, I can recreate the phone in a virtual sandbox here in my terminal, reverse-engineer it, and make more."

Emerson said, "I need to see my daughter. I feel like I was actually there, touching her mother while she was being born. I know it sounds strange, but I felt her enter the world. We're connected. It's the damnedest thing."

Rosco finished up reassembling the phone. "You sound like every parent I know. Don't worry about how you bonded. Know that you did. That's good enough." He switched on the phone and handed it back to Emerson. "Only one way to test it. Let's go for a walk."

Rosco talked as they walked to the main gate. "Something's up with Grendel. She says it's nothing, but I've known her my whole life."

Emerson remembered Elli talking about Grendel visiting a man, but he kept quiet. When Emerson didn't respond, Rosco changed the subject. "You realize we have always traded with the Lords in The City, right?"

Emerson said, "What?"

Rosco continued, "Not everybody knows. Barton, for example, would freak out if he thought we had normal relations with them. He thinks they stole our birthright or some such shit. He and his buddies think The City is theirs, and they want to take it back. They're loony. The Lords allow us to exist. If they didn't want us here, we'd be gone."

Emerson was shocked at first. But when Rosco explained all the technical work he provided to the Founders and the foods and medicine they got in return, he realized how much sense it made. Indeed, he was surprised he didn't realize it sooner.

When they were 100 meters outside the boundary, he said, "Try it now."

Emerson called Quinn. She didn't answer. He tried again, but the phone wouldn't connect. He sent her a text:

`Call me.`

After walking up the path for a half hour, they turned to go back. The phone dinged. Emerson said, "She says she can't talk. Breastfeeding." He grinned, "We'll connect when Marya is asleep, which she hopes will be soon." Emerson sent,

`I'll be waiting.`

Rosco said, "Well, my work here is done. See you later, Dad." He walked back toward the gate. While he waited, Emerson sent Elli a message:

`The mission is good to go tomorrow. Our last meeting is at four this afternoon in the warehouse. Be there.`

Elli didn't receive that message until Emerson reentered the Blue Hole network on the other side of the gate a half-hour later. While he was outside waiting for Quinn, she was tailing Piggie, who had just ducked into a tunnel. She decided to follow him.

Quinn called him ten minutes later.

He said, "Was I there, or did I dream that?"

"You know you were there."

"Yeah. Kiss Miss Marya for me. But how was I there? That's what I don't get."

"You were here. That's a fact. So, when are you coming home?"

"There are some problems. I am supposed to bring a platoon to plant low-frequency emitters around Founder's Quarter. They claim they just want to knock everyone out and take over, but I don't think their intentions are so benign. I installed a switch to disable them, but I need to get away from the platoon when we arrive undercover. Then you and the baby can escape."

She said, "When is this assault supposed to take place?"

"Tomorrow evening. Can you be ready?"

"Sure, sure. But ready for what, exactly? If you're going to stop them, then just turn them over when you land and walk away, right?"

"It's not that simple, Quinn. I have people who depend on me. I can't just vanish. It wouldn't be fair. Besides, I'm being blackmailed. They might hurt my friends if I don't succeed."

He felt guilty for not calling Ana what she was to him. But he figured that would just complicate things. So, he kept it to himself.

Quinn said, "Do you think this is fair to me? I'm alone with a new baby, Emerson. I need you."

"I have a plan. We'll talk face to face tomorrow. I can't wait to hold my daughter."

"I'm not sure I like this plan, Emerson."

"Don't worry. It'll be tomorrow before you know it. I have to go back now."

The call disconnected.

Quinn sent a message to Max:

```
I need your help tonight.
```

◆ ◆ ◆

Just Sam and Roy met Emerson at the warehouse in the late afternoon. The platoon had painted the shuttle. Emerson added her name in script, remembering pictures he'd seen of The Enola Gay, a World War Two-era bomber. Near the nose, he spelled out The Black Mariah in high-gloss urethane, which gave the letters a ghostly embossed look. The shuttle was fueled and ready. Its new coat of flat black made it look like a floating shadow. The air surrounding the craft was cold; it was like a black hole sucking the heat out of the room.

Emerson arrived. He had texted Elli several times since returning from his satellite call with Quinn, but she was not responding. He told her the time of this meeting and hoped that she was listening. Barton was not there.

"I suppose he is at the hangar?" Emerson said as he sat. There was no cup of steaming liquor. The two other conspirators seemed unmoored without their leader present. They looked at each other.

Just Sam said, "They found Barton bludgeoned to death late this morning."

Emerson said, "Then the deal's off." He turned to leave.

Roy said, "W-w-w-w—wait." He seemed to have developed a stutter.

Emerson turned back. Roy said, "Barton hired someone to kill Ana and Elli if you failed. He was going to tell you about it before you left."

Just Sam said, "As an assurance that you wouldn't back out at the last moment."

Emerson said, "How can this assassin be stopped if Barton is dead?"

Roy said, "That's just it. W-w-we d-d-don't know."

Emerson said, "Fuck. I have to go. The mission will happen as planned, gentlemen, though I'm not sorry to hear about Barton's demise."

They both called. "Good luck!" together, but Emerson was halfway to the door. He muttered, "Fuck you." He gathered his day pack and went to the shuttle. It was the first time Emerson had worn the jacket since he'd moved to Blue Hole.

◆ ◆ ◆

THE DARK AT THE END OF
THE TUNNEL

He called Ana on his PDA. She answered on the second ring. He didn't give her a second to speak. He said, "Meet me at the hangar at Mersy Rock. No questions now. Hurry."

He tried Elli again, but she didn't connect. He texted her to meet him at the hangar ASAP. He arrived, and Ana showed up a few minutes later. She said, "I've never seen that jacket before." He brought her inside where the platoon was suited and ready and said, "Get strapped in. We lift in ten. I'll tell you about it later."

Jock eyed Ana. Emerson said, "My ship, my rules. We give Elli ten. Then she's on her own. Strap in." He boarded the shuttle and showed Ana where she should sit.

Ana said, "What is this all about?"

Emerson said, "I'll tell you later. Right now, just stay quiet and keep your head down." He logged into the main controls and unlocked the ship's flight instruments. Emerson's instrument array allowed him to walk around and run systems at the same time. He powered up the reactors and opened a screen displaying the shuttle from above with a wide angle that showed the door to the hanger.

The ten-minute timer beeped. Emerson said, "Time's up," and began to seal the doors. Elli entered the hanger and trotted toward the shuttle. The reactors whined like a siren. When she was midway, a man in a deerskin jacket came in carrying a pistol. She looked over her shoulder and began to run. Emerson opened a loudspeaker channel and said, "Stop. Drop your weapon." The man didn't slow, but raised the gun in Elli's direction. She was still twenty meters from the hatch.

Emerson spoke louder. "HALT. DROP YOUR WEAPON, OR I'LL SHOOT."

He activated the front cannons. The reactor had reached full charge; the whine was deafening. The deerskin man used both hands to take aim. Emerson fired. The rocket caught him in the stomach. He seemed unaware that there was a six-inch-wide hole in his middle.

Ana said, "Oh my God," and turned away from the gory spectacle.

The assassin's legs collapsed before he could pull the trigger. The missile took out the hanger door and exploded across the field at the base of a brick storehouse. Elli entered the shuttle, and Emerson sealed the door.

The shuttle rose off the ground and slowly turned to line up with the doorway. Elli said, "I was wondering how you were going to open that."

She strapped in. Emerson said, "Hang tight."

The force of acceleration pressed them into their shock-absorbing seats. The outside blurred, and the craft shot out of the hanger and into the night sky. Within moments, they were above the buildings and then the clouds. Below, through the breaks in the cloud, Emerson saw glimpses of electric lights and open fires on the ground. The spoof app had run for hours now. If he and Ana's estimates were correct, the security systems in The City were off.

He set a course for Founder's Quarter, engaged autopilot, and removed his helmet. When he turned in his seat, Jock was pointing a plasma rifle in his face.

◆ ◆

Quinn was a jumble of emotions. She thought for nearly nine months and three weeks that when the baby came, life would go back to normal. It was becoming clear that she would never see normal again. The City prided itself on raising infants in a controlled, nurturing environment. All babies placed in pods were well adjusted, happy children. New pod leaders were given the full range of bonding treatments. They were assured of a commitment from the new parents, no matter how many there were. They were monitored all their lives via implant. If a child showed any signs of distress, the Birth Corps became involved and would rehome a child if necessary. But behavior modification was used liberally.

There was no chance for women to give birth to their own children. Only the daughters of the Elites had this option, and as a result, there was little support for new mothers. The traditions had been broken. Neonatal parenting was a forgotten skill.

Before the bleeding stopped, while Marya lay across her mother's swollen belly, her cord still pulsing, Doctor Sailor suggested Elli give her daughter to the Birth Corps. She said, "We can make sure she has all she needs until she's four or five. There will be many brothers and sisters and a whole crew of dedicated mothers round the clock. And when she has developed enough, we will reintroduce her to you with all the bonding serums and treatment. She won't know the difference."

Quinn was exhausted, but she knew exactly what the doctor was saying. She said, "I'd know. And what am I supposed to do? Do you have a drug for me?"

Sailor said, "Well, yes, actually. We do."

Quinn would normally have exploded, but she couldn't get loud because it would wake her baby; she whispered, "Get the fuck out of here, Stephanie. I am not giving you my daughter, and I am not taking a fucking amnesia shot so I'll forget her. My body will never forget. Fuck you."

Lucia was no help either. She left as soon as Marya was born. After Elli's birth, she went on a two-week vacation somewhere in the south of the country. Quinn was raised by a wet nurse named Nan and one of a revolving parade of Boston's servants until she turned twelve and informed him that she was living on her own. She hardly ever saw Lucia.

Emerson's attack weighed on her; she couldn't stop thinking, *What if he fails? What if they set off the emitters and everyone dies from massive brain hemorrhages?* She couldn't take it. Between all the birth hormones still coursing through her bloodstream, the postpartum depression, and her dread of total abandonment or possible death, Elli broke down and called her father. She told him about the attack, about what Emerson had planned, and how scared she was.

Boston wasn't surprised. It was as if he already knew. *But he always acted that way,* she thought, though usually she could see through it when he pretended. He was quietly smug. She cried to him on the phone. He comforted her. They disconnected. She felt better for a couple of minutes; then she was drowned in a wave of terror that she'd signed Emerson's death warrant. Elli tried to call her father back, and he wouldn't pick up, which scared her even more. Marya woke up and demanded the breast. The child was fussy, and Quinn couldn't get comfortable with the bulky pad between her thighs. By the time she got the baby back to sleep, she was exhausted and passed out herself.

◆ ◆

Emerson said, "What's up, boss? Why the gun?"

Jock said, "Barton didn't trust you. And now he's dead."

"You a pilot, Jock?"

"No. Why?"

"'Cause as far as I know, you're threatening the only pilot on a shuttle flying 100 meters an hour at 10,000 meters. Want to reconsider?"

He said, "I don't trust you," But he didn't seem too sure. Jock was realizing that he hadn't thought it through sufficiently.

"Well, you are going to have to. Otherwise, I'm pretty sure you're going to die."

He lowered the rifle and said, "I still don't trust you." He sat back down.

Emerson turned back to the windshield and said, "The gun is locked, by the way. That's what the red bar over the charge strip means. Strap back in and brace yourself. I need to take her up in order to avoid being seen. Once we are over the wall, I'll drop us down in the quarter. Be ready." He put his helmet back on and closed the visor, enclosing his head in a sealed bubble.

The shuttle began a steep incline. Emerson increased speed and slowly changed the oxygen-to-carbon dioxide ratio until he was sure all of the passengers were unconscious. He leveled at an altitude of 75,000 meters and resumed the autopilot. He actuated seat harness locks on each member of the platoon. As the room became more oxygenated and the passengers began to come around, Emerson knelt in front of Ana and Elli and said, "You are going to have a headache."

Elli already had one. She snapped, "Why the fuck am I here, Emerson?"

Emerson lowered his voice and said, "To keep you safe. I'll tell you later."

Ana nodded. Elli turned her head away. Emerson addressed the platoon.

"I am the captain of this ship. By ancient nautical tradition, that makes me lord and master when my ship is underway. I am the law here. Your leader, Jock, tried to take control away from me. That is called mutiny. I am well within my rights to open that hatch and throw each of you out. I don't know what to do with you yet. But as long as you are here, I don't want to hear from you."

Jock said, "Wait until the council hears about this. You'll be…"

He was cut off midsentence by a silver strap that shot across his mouth, effectively gagging him. Emerson said, "Anyone else have anything to say? Good. We will be landing in approximately twenty minutes. Be ready."

One of the soldiers opened his mouth. When Emerson looked at him, he closed it. Emerson went back to his seat. He said, "The Enforcers didn't shoot us down yet. That's a plus."

He began his descent and muted the reactor. Around 6,000 meters they broke through the cloud cover, and the lights of Founder's Quarter came into view. He adjusted the cameras and shunted the feed to a wall-sized projection area. The streets were clearly visible now. Emerson focused in on the fountain and turned on the cloak. The shuttle settled gently to the cobblestone street. Emerson shut the reactor down and scanned the area.

"OK, now, boys. We made it. Time to go place your emitters. You have exactly twenty minutes before I leave." The straps unlocked and retracted.

Jock turned on his communicator and said, "Unlock the rifle, Emerson. Don't send me out there with no way to protect myself."

The red bar turned green. It felt like a mistake, but he couldn't refuse the man. Emerson said, "Don't do anything stupid." The door outline emerged in blue and opened out. The four platoon members left, each carrying an emitter. Emerson said, "I have to go find Quinn and our daughter. You guys stay here, and you'll be safe."

He gave Ana a hug and said, "I don't advise it, but there is a fully stocked replicator."

Ana said, "Wait. I know you are in a hurry, but why are we here?"

Emerson said, "Barton hired a man to kill you. I couldn't protect you if you were not with me."

Elli looked at the floor and said, "Come back, OK?"

Emerson went to her and stood her up so he could hug her properly. He raised her face to his and said, "I'll do my best," and left. The door closed and sealed. They would not see Emerson again for days.

◆ ◆ ◆

Each member of the platoon carried his emitter; they looked like small, black wastebaskets with a carrying handle on top. They reached the entrance of the dead-end street twenty meters ahead of Emerson. At the intersection of the main square, they split up, two going left and two, including Jock, who was carrying the rifle, going right.

As they rounded the corner, a blinding bank of spotlights switched on. A loud, amplified voice said, "DROP YOUR WEAPONS AND YOU WILL NOT BE HARMED."

Emerson ran to the nearest wall, crouched down, and watched. Jock yelled, "FOR THE EVERYMEN!" and fired the plasma rifle at full power, spraying the beam into the spotlights in a sweeping arc before Emerson could open his mouth.

The hot beam evaporated the lights, twenty of the Elite Guard, and the building behind them, which was home to most of the kitchen and serving staff, all Middles, permanently assigned as support. It was after eleven p.m. Most were home in bed when they were erased from existence. Of the fifty-six men and sixty women, no trace was ever found.

The flanking twenty Elite Guard, poised and ready to the sides of their fellow guardsmen who were now dead, immediately opened fire using conventional M15 ordnance. The Everymen platoon were dead within seconds.

Senior Guardsman Deepak Minz entered the dead end alone and unarmed. He walked directly to Emerson. He said, "Emerson Lloyde, you are under arrest on charges of sedition and murder. Come with me now, or I will restrain you using your implant and take you anyway."

Emerson hoped Deepak didn't know about the shuttle parked 100 meters from where they spoke. Rather than chance anyone noticing it, he said, "Of course I'll come with you. I was forced to do this. And the emitters were disabled by me. No need for restraints. I'm on your side."

Minz took him by the arm and led him away. As he walked onto the main street, Emerson couldn't help but see the bullet-riddled bodies of the four platoon members. Jock had a look of surprise frozen on his dead face. The guard had already retrieved the plasma gun and emitters. When Emerson looked across the street to the glowing, smoldering rubble of the support housing, he realized his attack was far more serious than he originally thought. He was suddenly worried that they were simply going to execute him.

"Where are you taking me?" he asked the guardsman.

"To the dungeon, of course. I bet you didn't know we had a dungeon, did you?"

Emerson thought, *This would be a good time to join me, Quinn.* But she didn't. She might not have known he was in the quarter.

As they marched him through the central square, Max pressed himself into the shadows of a stone wall. He heard the guard and Emerson talking. They walked toward the Elder's Hall; he knew where they were going. After they passed, Max went directly to Quinn.

♦

Tanya woke Elli from a deep sleep. It took her a moment to realize where she was. She'd been dreaming of a place in a shaded forest near a pond. There were geese. She asked Tanya, "Are there still geese?"

Tanya ignored her. She said, "Elli, your father is here."

She helped Elli into a dressing gown. Marya slept in her arms. Tanya helped her walk. She was perfectly capable, but Tanya knew Elli needed any edge she could get when she spoke to the Elder Lord.

They entered the sitting room. Tanya said, "May I get you anything, Lord Quinn?"

Elli said, "Get him a scotch. Get me one too."

Boston said, "Should you be drinking? You're breastfeeding, I assume?"

Elli said, "Fuck you, Father. What are you here for?"

"I guess we'll get right down to it. My second heir. She will be raised by the Birth Corps. You are not responsible or mature enough to take care of a future queen. Sailor says she can be transferred to a wet nurse as soon as she's had all of her colostrum. That's the word, right? Supposed to pass immunities on, better than vaccinations or some such shit. I leave this sort of thing to the women. But that should be the end of the week. So, get your time in with her. Sailor will come round to pick her up and give you the first unbonding shots."

Elli didn't know what to say. She looked at her father, shaking her head. She realized that he was dead serious. She had to get away and take the baby. Emerson was supposed to be there later that night. She'd wanted to convince him to stay, but that was off the table now.

Boston finished his drink; Elli hadn't touched hers. He stood and turned to leave. As he walked to the door, he said, "You'll be happier in the end; you can't raise her by yourself." He closed the door.

Elli yelled, "I'm not alone." But it was getting late, and she hadn't heard anything. *Maybe I am alone.*

Max arrived before she could get back into bed. She handed Marya to Tanya and said, "Don't wake her. Walk around. I need to step out."

Tanya looked at her in that longsuffering way she had, but said nothing. Max was out of breath. He said, "We need to talk."

They went to a bench next to a nearby lawn. He said, "Emerson is in the dungeon. The platoon from Blue Hole is dead. They murdered most of the serving and cookstaff with a plasma weapon. I've never seen a gun do so much damage so fast. Whizbang." He snapped his fingers. "Like, 100 people extinguished, just like that. They're never going to let him out, Quinn. We are going to have to spring him. And I want to come with you when you go."

It took Quinn a few minutes to comprehend all that Max said. She smiled and said, "Having a child gives you brain damage." After a long pause where she stared at the sandstone walk stones, she said, "We are going to need more help. Who can you trust? This may get us killed."

"No one is going to kill you, Quinn. If they did, your father would cut small pieces off of them until they begged to die. And he'd do it himself and slowly."

She said, "You're right. No one else will be spared. If they catch us, you're dead."

Max said, "Then no. I wouldn't ask anyone else to sacrifice themselves for you."

She said, "Why would you be willing to die for me?"

He didn't hesitate at all but removed his hat and held it over his heart. "Because I love you, Quinn."

She was dumbstruck. When she recovered her wits, she said, "I love you too, Maxamillion."

"No, you love Emerson. And I'm not sure he loves you like I do. I've loved you since we were babies."

"I need you to help me, Max. Will you help me?"

"I said I would die for you, Quinn."

She looked at him blankly. He waited to hear her response.

Finally, she said, "Lucia. Lucia will help me. She loves me too. But I bet my father is monitoring her communications. Max, will you take a message to her? Tell her Boston is threatening to take Marya, and I need her help to free Emerson from the dungeon."

Max was crestfallen. He tried not show it. It was Quinn, after all; what did he really expect with his ovation of love? Instead, he brought her hand close to his lips and kissed the back. He said, "Yes, my queen."

◆

The dungeon was your standard damp stone room with only tiny barred windows near the high ceilings. There was a built-in bed and a stainless-steel toilet/sink contraption. The floor was cement. There were electric lights, a feather pillow, and a thick comforter too. Emerson had never been in a real dungeon; he had nothing to compare it to. But in reality, it was a ten-by-ten-meter jail cell. A pretty comfortable one at that.

The City as a whole had very little need for a jail. The people were raised to be satisfied, and as a result, most were subdued. And those that weren't calm and satisfied were modified. In fifty years, the jail in Founder's Quarter had never once been occupied.

Emerson had been locked up all night. When they closed the barred door, he was sure Quinn would arrive any minute. He didn't sleep. His fear increased in the silence; he lay in the narrow bed and stared at the light fixture above him. As the sun rose, casting cold blue light across the ceiling, he worried that no one was going to come and began to get depressed.

Max whispered down to Emerson from the high barred window, "Emerson, it's Max, Quinn's friend. She sent me with a message."

Emerson said, "Max! Get me out of here."

"We're working on it. But a lot of people died. Boston doesn't telegraph his punches, but I'm sure he will offer you up as a sacrifice to the other outraged, and frankly terrified, Lords. They will shout for blood because you got in and could have killed them all. Lord Quinn needs to make an example of you."

"I figured. But I need to get to my people. They are trapped in the shuttle which is cloaked and hidden at the end of Fountain Garden Circle if they haven't impounded it yet."

"Boston wants to take your daughter from Elli at the end of the week. But I think I have a plan. Trust me."

"I am sending my access key to you. Find Elli and Ana. Bring them to a safe place."

"Her name is Elli?"

"It's a long story. When I get out of here, I'll tell you all about it."

"Do you need anything? I'll be back after dark."

"Tell Quinn to get ready."

◆

The door to the outside of the shuttle beeped twice, signaling the beginning of the opening cycle. A thin, iridescent blue line traced its outline on the wall. Ana and Elli grabbed the only weapons within reach: a steel water bottle and a blocking stick from the cargo locker. As the hatch folded open, they lunged at the figure standing outside.

Max covered his head and babbled, "Emerson sent me. Emerson sent me. How do you think I opened the door? Don't hit me."

They lowered their weapons. Ana said, "Why didn't you warn us? Don't you know how to use the intercom?"

Max said, "No. Emerson just gave me the door code. He's in the dungeon. You are Elli and Ana. Come. It's not safe here."

Elli got in Max's face and said, "Where do you think you're taking us?"

"To Quinn. You'll be safe there."

◆

Boston Quinn entered the dungeon level flanked by two of the Elite Guard, a man and a woman in full dress uniform. They stopped in front of Emerson's cell. The man produced a paper scroll and read aloud, "Emerson Lloyde, stand."

When he did, the guard continued, "You are found guilty of murder and sedition. Your sentence is death. You will be disintegrated by plasma stream at noon Friday." He rolled the paper up and turned, with his cohort, and left.

Boston said, "Of course, I can rescind that order if I want. But that depends upon what you will give me. I know you are the father of my second heir. I know my daughter is convinced she loves you. I will give you a chance to live here with her."

Emerson said, "What do you want?"

Boston smiled, showing even white teeth. He said, "The shuttle and the location of the storehouse where you and Dander Mitchell found those rifles."

"Can I think about it?"

"Until noon Friday."

"Okay." Emerson said and lay back down in his bed.

Boston turned and left.

◆

Tanya woke Quinn, "Elli, Max is here with…" She paused, afraid to describe the two Outsiders that Max had brought into her apartments. She continued, "News."

She helped Quinn dress by holding the baby and put her arm on the woman to steady herself as they went into the sitting room. When Quinn saw the two women, dressed in clothing different from anything she'd seen in The City, she woke up. She kept her voice low but said, "Who the fuck are you and why are you in my home? Max, what the fuck?"

Max said, "Quinn, this is, ah… Elli and Ana. They came with Emerson. He asked me to take them to safety. I couldn't think of anyplace safer."

She said, "Fuck." Baby Marya began to fuss. Quinn took her from Tanya and pulled out a breast. The baby girl latched on like a vacuum pump and fell back to sleep. Quinn sat and waved her hand for everyone to join her.

She extended her hand to Ana and said, "Glad to make your acquaintance, Ana. Any friend of Emerson's…"

Ana took her hand and said, "Anastacia Moon. And I'm Emerson's mate."

Quinn withdrew her hand and raised her eyebrows. She extended it to Elli and said, "Hi, I'm Elli. I didn't think it was a common name, but here you are."

Elli sniffed. She didn't take Quinn's hand. She looked at the floor and said, "I'm named after you."

Quinn said, "I'm sure there's a story there." She waited, but Elli did not look up.

Ana said, "She's had some trouble in her life."

Quinn said, "Hmmm." She turned to Max and said, "This is the safest place you know for the two women in my lover's harem. Cool."

When Ana opened her mouth to protest, Quinn stopped her with a hand and said, "Not important. What matters is getting Emerson out of the dungeon and getting away from here."

The three murmured their agreement. Tanya went to the door and let Lucia in. Quinn's mother said, "Give me my perfect granddaughter." She went straight to the baby and took her from Quinn's arms. Marya sucked an invisible breast contentedly in her sleep.

Quinn said, "Mother, we need to break Emerson out of the dungeon. Will you help?"

Lucia kissed Marya's forehead and said, "I assume you are leaving. Take me away from this snake pit. I'll help you any way I can."

Max said, "Good! I have a plan. Does anyone need coffee, snacks?"

Quinn said, "Alcohol, Tanya. Break out the good stuff."

◆ ◆ ◆

THE PLAN

As the night progressed, Max explained his idea. "The jail was built fifty years ago. No one has ever been in it before. I dug up the original plans to the building before it was renovated. There is another part of the cellar that was sealed over. Guess where it is?" He didn't wait for anyone to answer. Max was in his element at the center of attention. "Right next to the jail cell. It looks like it's made of stone, but that's just a façade. It's only a thin layer of stones glued on top of a regular wall."

Ana said, "Regular? Like sheetrock?"

"Uh-huh. All we have to do is get into the other part of the cellar. Here, I have a map." He routed the feed to a screen over the fireplace and used one of Quinn's pool cues to point with. "Here's the cell. It's locked with an actual key. Outside there is a hallway that leads to a stairwell up to the main level where the guards sit. They monitor the hall and the cell with cameras.

"The beauty of the plan is we won't go near the door or the hall, so we'll stay off the video. We go into the cellar of the Museum of Fine Artifacts and open a hole to the cell from there."

Ana said, "That sounds easy enough."

Quinn said, "The museum has alarms."

Max smiled, "Right, but with Ana's genius and our access, we can shut them off. Right?"

Ana frowned. "That will take some time."

Max said, "You made that spoof program. I bet they still don't know how that works."

Ana said, "That was built off a program that I already had and understood. This is a foreign system. I won't know until I look at it."

Quinn passed her access via Interface and said, "How fast can you assess the system? If you can't do it, we'll have to come up with a backup."

◆

After the sun set, Max went to see Emerson, who told him about his execution Friday at noon. Max told him they were working out a plan, but he couldn't relay the details yet. Max left him with, "Elli and Ana are safe with Quinn. Stay calm. We'll get you out."

Back at Quinn's, Ana told Max that the alarm system seemed pretty simple, with the exception of the fact that the notifications were sent directly to Lord Quinn. Any tampering would alert him first. Lucia said, "Unless he was distracted in a very engaging way."

Max said, "How does that work?"

Lucia answered him. "I think you know."

He said, flummoxed, "Not you, Lucia, Ana."

Ana replied, "There is a special subroutine that notifies Lord Quinn if anyone tampers with the program. It's pretty sophisticated code. I assume he has something very valuable in that building."

Quinn said, "That's where he keeps the gold."

"Gold?" Ana and Elli said together.

"He uses it to pacify outside groups when force appears too costly. He has several metric tons of it." Quinn blew a raspberry. "Worthless as lead. Only an idiot would want it."

Max said, "So we are betting that he will be so hot and bothered from your seduction that he will ignore it? I think that's a stretch."

Elli Rattlesnake said, "Mom, that's like putting your head in the lion's mouth. It's too dangerous."

Lucia said, "Boston knows I still love him, and he still loves me. And I have come to him from time to time over the years. We are old, old lovers, la mia bambina, and love is a trance. I know how to distract him." She lifted her right breast. "You can be sure of it."

Max said, "Can you keep him busy all night?"

Lucia smiled slyly. "No problem."

Ana said, "As soon as he realizes what has happened, he will trigger the alarms."

"Okay," Max said, "while I'm breaking Emerson out, Elli, Elli, and Ana, you will make your way to the shuttle and seal yourselves inside." He gave Quinn the codes. "Lucia, whatever you do, make sure Lord Quinn is occupied for a half hour at midnight. That's when I'll go in. Ana, set the interruption to last thirty-five minutes, beginning exactly at twelve. Then you and the others get to the shuttle and wait. I need to get some rest. If it all goes as planned, Lord Quinn will never know we were ever there. We can meet together here at sunset tomorrow."

Elli said, "That's Thursday. They are going to kill Emerson on Friday. It's too close. What if something goes wrong?"

Ana said, "Elli's right. We need a backup plan."

Elli said, "I know where there is another plasma rifle on board the shuttle."

No one spoke for a long minute. She went on. "We don't have to kill anyone. The rifles have delicate power adjustments. I used one once to shoot the blossom off a dogwood. I can cut through anything in a pinpoint. There's only one problem. It's an Interface weapon, and I am not implanted."

Max said, "How did you use a plasma rifle with no implant?"

"Juice Hackers are the shit. Don't fuck with a Juice Hacker."

Quinn said, "I can give you an implant. I have a drawer full of them. They're self-implanting, no surgery necessary. It's the newest thing."

Max said, "So what if you can get the gun and fire it with pinpoint precision, how will that help?"

Elli said, "I don't know, but I'll feel better with some kind of backup."

Quinn said, "We will meet here at sunset then?"

Everyone agreed.

◆

At noon the following day, Lord Boston visited Emerson without the guards. He unfolded a chair in front of Emerson's cell, crossed his legs at the ankles, and lit a cigar.

Emerson said, "I've made a decision."

Boston said, "Slow down. I'm not here about that."

"I'm listening."

"You need to know that you were a pawn in this whole game, son."

Emerson sat on the edge of his bed. He said, "Go on."

"Barton was my agent. He told me everything. Before he disappeared, we would speak every day."

"How? Blue Hole is a Faraday Cage."

"There is a tower in the woods hardwired to a communicator inside Blue Hole. I use it to work out trade with Rosco. We've been trading for twenty-five years. Rosco is the third agent I've had there. Barton promoted the plan to attack The City that I gave him. The emitters were never real. But that fucked-up weasel, Jock, wasn't supposed to have one of those guns. No one was to be hurt. At least, no one from here."

Emerson said, "You wanted an incident."

"Hmm. I did. And I got one. And I got you back too. I'm not going to execute my future son-in-law, Emerson. I need you to help my Elli to raise the future queen of this kingdom. Don't look surprised. That's the way it has always been."

He puffed up the stogie until the end was glowing and blew a thick cloud into Emerson's cell.

"You know what they say? Someday this will all be gone. We are using it up, Emerson. There's no way to replace it. The Middles will be hard to control when the riches run dry. By then, we will need a reason for the people to love and fear us, and the way to that reality is by making ourselves royalty. We have to, in order for everyone to survive."

Emerson said, "With you riding on our shoulders?"

"Someone has to do it."

"No thanks. Besides, how can you trust me?"

Boston laughed hard, which caused a coughing fit that he ended by spitting phlegm on the cement floor. "I can trust you, Emerson. That's why I am taking your daughter. As long as you do what I want, she will be returned to you when she is five. If you don't, I always have plan B."

"Plan B?"

"I kill all of you and get someone else to raise the child."

"So essentially, I have no choice."

"Everyone always has a choice, Emerson. Some choices are better than others. I'll let you think about it overnight. We can talk more in the morning,"

He left his cigar butt smoldering on the floor and left without refolding the chair. Emerson lay back and looked at the ceiling. He thought, *Fuck, Max, hurry up and get me away from all these crazy people.*

◆ ◆

Max brought Elli to the shuttle, and she retrieved the rifle. She wrapped it in a pillowcase she'd borrowed from Quinn's. Even though it was a compact weapon, the barrel stuck out of the top a couple inches. Luckily, no one saw them. At sunset, together again in Quinn's parlor, they went over the timing. Lucia left to shower and get ready for her date with Lord Boston.

Quinn implanted Elli, and Ana initiated the connection routines. Elli was opening doors and turning on screens with a half-hour of practice. She showed Max the power setting and the lock on the rifle. He told her, "Don't kill anyone, or they will execute us all."

She said, "If they can catch us."

Max wasn't pleased with her answer. He said, "Do you have a plan yet?"

"No," she said, "but I'm pretty good at making things up. I specialized in fantasy roleplay." She winked at him.

At 10 p.m., Max left for the museum; Quinn and Ana went to the shuttle. Tanya carried Marya's bag. Elli stayed in the apartment studying the map of Founder's Quarter.

She had the vague tracings of a plan in her mind. The Founders were crippled without electricity. They relied heavily on it. If she could find the place where power entered the quarter, she could cause a major distraction by cutting it off. Studying the map showed her where the conduits passed into the city proper. That was the place to strike. She thought, *All in one neat place, how convenient.*

Near eleven, she put on a bulky coat she found in Quinn's closet, stashed the rifle underneath, and made her way to the southwest corner of the quarter. At the same moment she was leaving Quinn's, Ana, safely closed in the shuttle, started the timer on the alarm disrupter. She hoped that Lucia was keeping Boston busy enough. At exactly midnight, it would switch the alarm system off.

Tanya was crying. Quinn tried to calm her as they hurried across the square. She and Ana stowed her bag as Quinn embraced the woman who lived with and cared for her since she was twelve. She said, "Tell them you *know* I'll be back. Stay in my apartment and keep it ready for my return."

Tanya had tears in her eyes. She said, "Will you be back?"

Quinn held her shoulders and looked in her face. "No, Tanya, I won't be coming back."

◆

EMERSON

Max entered the front door of the museum at exactly 12:01. He was able to easily unlock the all the doors; there was no sign of an alarm. Two minutes later, Emerson heard scratching from the other side of the back wall to his cell. The noise got louder until one of the stones fell off and clattered to the floor. Another followed. Emerson grabbed the others before they detached completely and dropped them on a pillow to lessen the noise. No one came. And within fifteen minutes, a one-meter square hole was opened in the wall.

Max stuck his head through and said, "Let's go."

Emerson scrambled into the museum's cellar. He followed Max up the stairs and out through the lobby. When they were ten meters from the door, the alarms began to sound. Spotlights flooded the courtyard, pinning them in plain sight.

Emerson said, "What now?"

◆

LUCIA

Lucia arrived at Boston Quinn's residence at 7 p.m. sharp. He complimented her timeliness and greeted her with a kiss on the cheek. He said, "Beatrix could never be on time for anything. Neither could Patricia. It's one of the things I've always loved about you." He reached out, pinched her nipple, and said, "Hello. I've missed you."

Lucia turned from him and slipped off her jacket, revealing her naked shoulders. The dress was low-cut to begin with, and the bustier pushed her breasts together and up, creating tantalizing cleavage. Lucia felt like she was being pressed out of a toothpaste tube. They went into the dining room and sat together at the same end of his long table. The staff served fresh oysters on the half shell and flutes of chilled Krug champagne.

Boston said, "1928. One of the best ever made." They toasted by touching rims. And the glasses kept coming. Throughout the evening, as Boston and Lucia got drunk, they sipped wine, crunched down toast points smeared with Beluga Caviar, and, as a special present to Lucia, slices of authentic Italian soppressata and Ciliengine with cantaloupe grown in his private hydroponic garden.

Near ten, after the staff had cleared, Boston poured two brouilleurs of absinthe and added ice to the tops. They moved to his sitting room, and he lit a cigar as the freezing water dripped into the emerald fluid, slowly turning it a milky green. Lucia sipped her drink. She was very high. The food had been amazing. Boston had outdone himself. She knew what he expected in return. Her only problem would be delaying him long enough.

She excused herself to the bathroom, figuring that would kill some time. Lord Quinn sighed impatiently. She stayed on the toilet for ten minutes. Just before returning, she removed her undergarments and stuffed them in her clutch. Back in the sitting room, she said, "I'm not used to such rich food, mi amore. But I took off my tight clothes, and I feel much better."

Boston leered at her. She went behind him, put his cigar in the ashtray, and leaned over his back, kissing him. Her dress was loose in the absence of the bustier, and her large breasts slipped out. Boston put his hands on either breast and pressed his cheek into one. He nearly purred. Lucia, having captured his interest again, stood up and said, "I've had enough alcohol. Can you get me a coffee?"

Boston called for his serving man. Meanwhile, Lucia resituated her breasts and sat in the leather recliner next to him. She said, "Can we have a fire, baby? I never get to smell a wood fire anymore."

Boston tsked. He had one lit. He said, "Whatever your little heart desires." They sipped their coffees. It was eleven forty-five. Lucia said, "Why did I ever leave you, mi amore? We had such a beautiful life together." Boston shifted his weight uncomfortably, grimaced, and looked at the time.

◆

ANA & QUINN

Ana, Quinn, and Marya settled into the bunks at the back of the shuttle and tried to sleep. Marya succeeded with the help of her unlimited warm milk supply. Ana and Quinn stared at the dim blue light illuminating the ceiling. Ana said, "I can't have children."

Quinn said, "That's a problem with many women. The poisons from 100 years of industrial agriculture have accumulated in our bones."

Ana said, "There is nowhere for me to put my anger at what they did. I've carried it my whole life. I don't know who I'd be without it."

Quinn wondered if Ana's *they* were her ancestors. That didn't seem to be who Ana was implying, but the possibility assaulted her with a momentary wave of guilt.

They were silent, considering the state of the world. Ana continued, "I know Emerson wants to raise Marya with you. I thought we'd be married and grow old together, but you've captured him."

Quinn said, "Captured, eh? With what, my uterus?"

Ana was stung. She was trying to be honest. Quinn sat up. "I didn't *capture* Emerson. If anything, I seduced him. At first in the Red Palace and later back at my place. He seemed pretty willing, but I knew he wasn't that attached. Once he got to Blue Hole, he was more concerned for your safety than mine. I told him he should just leave, and he refused. All that's changed now, but don't sell yourself short."

Ana bit her lip and said, "He brought us to protect us, but I don't think he loves me."

Quinn said, "Emerson is a special man. He's not like anyone I've ever met. I'm sure he loves you. It's just in his own particular way. He feels responsible for Elli, too. And he just found her in the rubble. Emerson has a big heart, Ana. Big enough for all of us."

◆

ELLI

At eleven thirty, Elli was standing in the shadows near an empty church. Fifty meters away at the inside corner of a high stone wall, six twenty-five-centimeter-wide conduits protruded from the wall and curved down into the ground. She had the plasma rifle power adjusted to its lowest setting. She'd spent the last hour experimenting with the controls using her implant. The visual enhancements she found while playing with the sight amazed her. Focus, depth, resolution, color enhancement, non-visual frequencies. If she could imagine it, The Interface allowed her to create a control set for it. Hearing had the same depth of control.

A digital clock appeared on her inner screen. "Oh shit!" she said out loud and then covered her mouth with her hand as the sound of her voice echoed off the stone in the damp air. It was way past midnight. "Twelve-thirty." She should have been paying closer attention. She felt something ripple through The Interface. A feeling she'd never experienced, like something tugging at a loose thread in the center of her brain. It made her squint like a sour taste.

A second later, the alarm blared, and spotlights went on all over Founder's Quarter and lit up the sky like a night game at Giants Stadium. She sighted the conduits, checked her power again, and squeezed the trigger.

The world went dark and silent.

◆

LUCIA

Boston suddenly rose and picked up Lucia. She couldn't tell if it frightened or thrilled her. Boston was a big man. His fist could fit around Lucia's neck. He carried her body to the bedroom. Her breasts slipped out of her dress again. His coarse beard scratched her skin where he nuzzled between her shoulder and neck.

He yanked the dress from her body in a fluid movement, like he was pulling a case off a pillow, and threw it on the floor. She sat up to unbuckle his pants, but he pushed her back onto the bed and slowly undressed. His erection stood out stiff in front of him. He stroked himself. Part of Lucia's brain was entranced. It wasn't hard; she was very drunk, and she hadn't been with a man in a long while. Still, she was fully aware of what she was doing and what would happen if she was caught. Boston put his face between her legs and made it difficult for her to think about anything.

She glanced at his bedside clock. She was too early. But there was no stopping now. After licking at her for a minute, sloppily missing all the right places, he abruptly flipped her on her knees and mounted her from behind, thrusting into her. Lucia braced her hands against the headboard to keep Boston from smashing her face into the wall.

He pounded relentlessly. She remembered why she'd left. She would have bruises. Even when she was young, Boston left her in pain. She needed to prolong it, but she was pinned with no room to move. Lord Quinn was in a trance state, completely focused on pistoning into her. Sex was one of the few escapes that he had, a few moments where he could shut off his mind, take his cerebral cortex offline, and let the amygdala, his lizard brain, take control. He grunted with each stroke. Sweat seeped from his artificial hairline.

Probably due to the amount of alcohol plus the fact that he was over-weight and out of shape, Lord Quinn took longer than usual, but when he finally finished, it was only twenty minutes past midnight. Lucia was already sore and nauseated. It was too early. She needed to keep him dis-tracted. As he began to relax, Lucia spun around under him and wrapped her legs around his waist. He fell forward, holding himself up with his hands on either side of her head. She put her arms around his neck and whispered, "More, baby. I know you can. Give me more."

Boston entered her again, but he was already fading. When he was twenty-five, he seldom could do what Lucia was asking. Fifty-five-year-old Boston Quinn would need a good night's sleep. He tried, but as willing as his mind was, his body would not respond. It was embarrassing. Lord

Quinn didn't get embarrassed; he got angry. He withdrew without looking at her and strode to the bathroom. Lucia looked at the clock. Twelve-thirty.

A second later, Lord Boston bellowed. He sounded more like an angry rhino than an out-of-shape human. The alarm blared from every corner. Lucia rolled out of the bed and sprinted naked from the room before he could return. She grabbed her coat and ran into blinding lights, leaving the door open.

◆

EMERSON & MAX

Max said, "Fuck."

Emerson looked around, but he saw nothing. He said, "Not helpful, man. Where do we go? I'm blind!"

Max looked around, sightlessly trying to get his bearings. He yelled, "Fuck!"

They heard footsteps. Emerson said, "We have to move; someone's coming."

Max said, "Okay. Okay. This way." He ran into the lights opposite of the sound. Emerson followed. The alarm still blared.

The world around them suddenly went dark and silent. They kept running. The shuttle was parked 500 meters across the center square. As they ran, they saw flashlights and heard shouting. Elli was standing at the end of the dead end. She held the rifle; the power bar glowed red. Emerson and Max stood next to her, and a moment later, Lucia arrived, breathless. Lord Quinn was right behind her.

◆

QUINN AND ANA AND ELLI

Quinn heard the alarm through the closed shuttle; she shut down the interior lights and waited. After what seemed like forever, she opened the front windshield at the very moment the lights went black. The shuttle had spotlights but she didn't want to give away their hiding spot. She said, "Ana, if we actually get out of here, remind me to make Emerson teach me to fly."

They watched the camera feed display from inside the shuttle. The display was an enhanced infrared. Quinn turned on the sound from outside and raised the volume. There were some flashlights. She saw someone stop at the end of the street; they looked directly at the ship. Ana said, "That's Elli." Quinn opened the shuttle door and stepped out. Her eyes adjusted to the dark. Ana whispered, "Quinn. No."

She could see two other people standing with Elli. She thought, *Emerson*, and began to walk to them. She had already gone halfway when her mother and father arrived. Quinn pressed her body against a building and crouched in the shadow. She could see them, but they didn't know she was there.

Boston grabbed Lucia by the neck and threw her into the brick corner like a limp doll. She crumpled to the sidewalk, her neck in an unnatural position and her coat open. Lucia's naked body spilled out of her opened coat onto the sidewalk. Quinn yelled, "Mother! NO!" and ran toward them.

Elli stepped back. Emerson ran to Lucia; Max froze. Quinn looked from her dead mother to her father and spat in his face. He advanced on her, flexing his fists. Elli pointed the rifle at his face and said, "Back off, motherfucker." Boston's eyes were rimmed with rage. His pupils were red from the indicator glow. He looked like he would lunge at her at any moment.

Elli said, "Oh, please move, you fat shit, so I can carve your stinking eye out. And believe me, I can do it." She set the power to low and burned a small heart in the sidewalk at Boston's feet.

Emerson called out, "Quinn, Max, Lucia's dead. We have to go."

Boston said, "You better kill me, girl. Because if you don't, I will track you to the ends of this Earth. You might think you've won, but you're a baby. Know this. I will *never* rest until I have erased you, your family, and everyone else you know."

Elli laughed; there was no humor in it. She mocked, "Oooh. You're scary." She spat, "Fuck you. I have no family. And I'm tempted to vaporize you. But Emerson would be mad at me." She laughed again. "I can't just let you go, can I?" Emerson was behind him now. She continued, "You look tired. Maybe you should take a little nap."

Emerson pinched a nerve in the big man's neck, a technique he learned in Enforcer training. Boston's eyes rolled back, and he collapsed in the street. They heard footsteps, running toward them.

Quinn grabbed the rifle from Elli and aimed it at Boston's head. "FUCK YOU, FATHER," she yelled.

Emerson yelled, "Don't!"

The rifle fired, gouging a smoldering ten-centimeter-long trough in the sidewalk next to Boston's ear. She yelled, "Killing you would make me no better than you!" She spat on his face.

After they ran to the shuttle, a large, black, Norwegian rat emerged from the storm drain near Lord Quinn. It peeled his toupee from his shiny bald head and dragged it, waddling backward into the sewer, just as the platoon of Elite Guard arrived.

◆ ◆ ◆

The shuttle rose silently into the dark sky. Quinn held Marya in her lap. Max held Quinn's hand. Elli held the plasma rifle across her chest like she was guarding the exit. Ana had her eyes closed. She appeared to be praying.

Once they reached 21,000 meters, Emerson set the autopilot. There was still a chance the Enforcers would come after them, so he set proximity alarms and radar sweeps. He hoped the spoofing program still had The City's security in a shambles.

With his chair turned, he could see the others. Tears dried on Quinn's face. Max looked hypnotized. Elli faced forward, eyes front. Ana had fallen asleep in her seat, chin to chest. Before he could speak, Elli said, "I killed Barton. The traitor."

Emerson said, "What?"

She paused. "I followed him into the tunnels. I know you said not to, but I couldn't help myself."

Ana murmured, "Fuck, girl."

Elli said, "He was talking to Lord Quinn. He went for me, and I hit him with a pipe."

Quinn said, "Sounds like you were defending yourself." There were affirmative murmurs.

Ana said, "That man always creeped me out."

Emerson said, "I'm really sorry that happened. He was a predator and a traitor, but you are no executioner."

Elli said, "Yeah. I almost got Ana and me killed over it. So, I gotta live with that too."

Ana unstrapped and moved next to Elli to hug her. She said, "I'm sorry I pushed you away. I was afraid you would suck up all of Emerson's attention." Elli patted Ana's back, but she looked away.

After a moment of silence, Quinn seemed to wake up. She had her shirt pulled up; Marya nursed. She said, "Hey, Lloyde. Nice jacket."

◆

They crossed the wall, and Emerson altered the trajectory to reach Blue Hole at low altitude in about an hour. Marya woke up and demanded to be fed. Quinn said, "Just like her mother, eh?" Emerson sat next to her and watched, amazed. He began wondering what sort of life they might have in Blue Hole, so close to The City. He thought, *Boston won't give up until he finds us. Maybe we should go far away.* At that moment, he recognized that he always wanted to go. He heard Chandler's voice in his mind say, *It's like an idea I forgot I had.*

He began planning to himself, wondering who he'd invite, worrying that inviting citizens away from the village might make him a pariah. He'd like Doctor Pam to come, but he doubted she would. Rosco and Grendel were his closest friends now, but Elli confessed to killing Rosco's brother. So, some sort of reckoning would surely have to come out of that.

Eggert retrofitted the shuttle for long distances. He wondered how long. *Could I make it to the other side of the Inland Sea?* The thought was captivating. He became lost in the branching possibilities. The proximity alarm startled him from his dream; he'd fallen asleep. Something was coming directly at the shuttle. He hardly had time to see it, let alone figure out what it was. Before they collided, the object stopped and hovered near the windshield. It was a large, black, four-engine drone. Emerson said, absently, "We're going 200 kilometers an hour." There was a notification.

Emerson accepted the request for communications. The video was blank, but the audio was clear. A pleasant female AI voice announced, "Good evening. This is a drone piloted by shuttle 292931 registered to Enforcer Captain Eric Eggert. It was awakened by your passing signal. Access code accepted. Follow this drone to 292931's current location." The communication channel closed, and the drone shot off to the west and down.

Emerson said, "Mysterious. I say we follow."

Ana said, "Well that's responsible," but no one acknowledged her.

♦ ♦ ♦

END OF PART FOUR

INTERFACE

PART FIVE

INTERFACE

PART FIVE

BLUE HOLE

The first missile flew low over their heads moments after the shuttle door opened. Emerson and Quinn watched it streak across the early morning sky. Max said, "That's too high; it will land way beyond the village."

Quinn said, "They don't have many missiles." She nibbled her cuticle.

Emerson figured she meant they would be more careful with their aim next time, but there wouldn't be too many more next times. He was about to say that when they heard the second missile. It went down east of the hangar. Ana said, "Not too many people live over there."

Quinn said, "We're under attack. Can you warn people? When the missiles run out, the shuttles and ground forces will arrive. Blue Hole is as good as gone."

Max said, "The way to save lives is to evacuate. They outgun and outman you."

Emerson used his PDA to call Rosco. Elli tried Doctor Pam. Ana found a quiet corner inside the hangar door and opened an Interface channel with shuttle 292931, Eggert's secondary craft. Emerson had planned to give it to Eggert, but that would have to wait.

She opened a channel to the Shuttle's drone and programmed an announcement. The drone arrived before the shuttle. Ana set a route to weave back and forth across the village and sent it off. Before it reached forty meters, the broadcast began. A pleasant female voice called out: RESIDENTS OF BLUE HOLE, WE ARE UNDER ATTACK. GO TO THE EVACUATION SITE DOWNTOWN. DROP EVERYTHING. BRING ONLY WHAT YOU CAN CARRY. GO NOW.

They started a phone-tree-like system and told as many people as possible that the town was under attack. Emerson said, "Have everyone gather downtown, take nothing, and hurry." Everyone but Quinn and the baby went to the downtown area.

Moments later, 292931 touched down in the open field near The Black Mariah. Eggert was one of the first to arrive. He had grown a full beard, not as lush as Rosco's, but with his newly shaved head, the two could have been brothers.

Emerson said, "Blue Hole has been good to you."

Eggert ignored him and exclaimed, "Ah, Little Wing! You've come home to Papa!" laughing heartily. He frowned suddenly, "Yes, very good. Though, I'm afraid that soon Blue Hole may be gone."

He went on, "Listen, Emerson, both shuttles together will not be enough to get these people out."

Ana said, "We have to take as many as we can."

Eggert said, "The supply train could take more."

Emerson gave him one of the rifles.

◆

The train loading docks were at the south end of downtown near the hangar. The tunnels where Elli killed Barton were built to service the docks a century before the collapse. Rosco guided people to the tracks.

Ten minutes later, a missile hit a building a block away. Part of the tunnel ceiling fell in from the vibration, filling it with a cloud of grey dust. The entire block was burning rubble, bricks were strewn in the street, and dead or dying citizens dotted the scene amid bits of burning wood and hot twisted metal.

Doctor Pam tended the injured; Elli gave her plasma rifle to Emerson and said, "I'm going to help Pam. Hold this for me." Emerson didn't notice when the doctor had arrived. He nodded and called out, "Set up a triage in the Hangar. Minor injuries should get to the supply train."

They could hear the announcement drone on its flight back criss-crossing the entire town. "…DOWNTOWN. DROP EVERYTHING. BRING ONLY…"

Emerson started back to the shuttle and met Rosco and Grendel. She told him that she had to locate someone. Rosco said, "Your mysterious liaison."

She said, "I knew you could tell something was off, and I was going to tell you, but the time never seemed right."

Rosco said, "And?"

"It's my stepdad, Paul. He returned to Blue Hole from his native enclave a few months ago. Has a weird genetic disease. I was trying to find a cure. But he is afraid to go out in public. A gang beat him pretty badly. He's never been very strong."

Rosco said, "You can always tell me anything, babe. You know that."

"He was so pitiful, Roz. I thought if I could just help him feel better, he would loosen up, you know?"

"I'm going with you. But we better hurry." Rosco looked at Emerson and said, "You good?"

Emerson said, "If you don't make it back here in an hour, we have to leave." He gave Rosco his satphone and a plasma rifle. "Call me if we get separated. I'll come and get you."

"Communicators are working here now, eh?"

"I figure the Faraday cage is down."

Ana, her face smudged with dirt, yelled for people to hurry toward the opposite entrance. A long line of terrified people clutching sacks and children shuffled in. Another missile approached. Everyone ducked. But it flew over downtown, landing close, shaking the ground. A three-story brick structure on the other side of the square collapsed. Water sprayed out of a broken pipe, and severed electric lines sparked and spat.

Amid the fires and the acrid smoke, the drone passed again: "…WE ARE UNDER ATTACK. GO…"

Ana yelled, "Come on people, move! Save yourselves."

Max went with Emerson. On the way, he said, "We should get Elli Rattlesnake out of here now!"

Emerson said, "That's what I'm trying to do."

When they returned to the shuttle, Max and Emerson got the guns out from under the floor boards and put them in the rear holding locker. He took two, gave Max two, and told Quinn, "We are going to get the able bodied on the train. Anyone with a minor injury who needs assistance can load into The Black Mariah. I'll send Ana to help, and we'll be there as soon as possible. The very hurt will go on Little Wing."

◆

After Rosco and Grendel left the public square area, Rosco asked, "How far do we have to go?"

"He's at the edge of the village, near the southern gate."

It would take them most of the hour to walk there and back. Rosco said, "Let's speed up." They trotted for a while. When they came around the last corner, Grendel stopped and grabbed Rosco's arm. The entire block of houses against the wall were collapsed in burning rubble.

She cried out, "Papa!" and ran to the pile of smoldering sticks and toppled stones where her stepfather's house had been.

Rosco shouted, "Grendel, stop. It's not stable."

But she was already throwing boards aside, yelling, "Papa? Papa Egan?" Her movements became frantic. Rosco worried the floor wouldn't hold even without him adding his formidable weight. Grendel ignored him.

He yelled, "Grendel, stop thrashing around, goddammit. The floor will collapse!"

She didn't hear him. Her voice became shrill; tears streamed. Boards shifted somewhere nearby, and a pile of bricks that he assumed had once been the chimney fell into the dark basement. Water sprayed somewhere; the cellar hole was filling. The floor under Grendel sagged. The beams broke beneath the strain with a loud crack. Grendel fell six inches and froze. Rosco abandoned his caution and stepped toward his mate. He said, "Give me your hand." She reached toward him just as the floor gave way, and she fell into the water-filled basement.

He called into the darkness. "Grendel!" but there was no reply, just the passing drone announcement: "…WE ARE UNDER ATTACK…"

◆

Fifty minutes after Grendel and Rosco left, Emerson and Ana were back at The Black Mariah, strapping the last of the injured into beds and seats. Doctor Pam and Elli were ministering to the critically wounded in Little Wing. The craft would fly on automatic once Emerson launched it remotely. He'd monitor her audio; Little Wing would give him updates on location and situation. Pam told him, "We need supplies. Take me by my office first."

Emerson said, "You're tempting fate."

She replied, "Better than watching people die."

Max entered, and the door sealed behind him. He said, "Little Wing is good to go, Emerson. The supply train left and will be beyond the village walls in a half hour."

Emerson asked Pam for a status. She said, "Mostly stable, one or two won't make it. A couple others are iffy."

"Strap in. Get ready for takeoff."

The reactors of both craft cycled up; anyone nearby would have had to cover their ears. Emerson got an alarm that City shuttles had crossed the boundary into Blue Hole; ground forces would be through the gates in moments. He launched Little Wing on a course across town. When Pam had what she could grab, the craft would leave on a steep incline to 40,000 meters. Emerson hoped the attacking shuttles would not see her. Once she was gone, he moved The Black Mariah out into the empty field in front of the hangar and rotated 360 degrees, scanning for movement and location. He called to the others, "Four warships are advancing on downtown. They will arrive in ten minutes."

Ana said, "We need to stop them. Our people are too close."

Quinn agreed, "Or at least slow them down."

Max said, "You can't endanger Quinn and Marya. Let me out with a rifle and get away from here."

Quinn said, "Max, that's suicide."

He said, "Have you seen what these weapons can do? I wouldn't be so sure."

She wasn't convinced. They touched down in the middle of the square. The rubble was still burning. After unsealing the door, the sound of the approaching shuttles was clear. Max went to Quinn and gave her his hat. He kissed her hard on the mouth and said in a passable Humphrey Bogart imitation, "Hold on to this for me, sweetheart." She looked sorrowful but managed a faint smile.

Emerson said, "Shoot a full-power beam into the sky at night and we'll come pick you up."

Ana said, "Good luck!"

Max jumped out, the door sealed, and the shuttle sped away like it was shot out of a cannon.

◆

The City shuttles came into view a second later. Max hid on the second floor of a half-destroyed building. He had a good view of the horizon where the crafts were, and the sun was getting low, shining over his back, reflecting off their windshields. *Perfect*, he thought.

He waited until they were close. His plan was to slice all four of them in half horizontally with a single shot. They had slowed and were scanning for movement and heat signatures. One shuttle fired a rocket into the tunnel entrance and sealed it. Another sighted a rat, scurrying up against a gutter, and blew a ten-meter-wide crater in the street trying to kill it. Max snickered when he saw its scaly tail disappear into a sewer grate.

They shuttles landed, and platoons of three enforcers from each jumped out, deploying a series of two-meter cubes around the square. When Max realized what they were, he tried to contact Emerson via Interface. The connection was poor. The missiles must have damaged Blue Hole's wireless network. He connected, but Emerson's replies were garbled.

He sent a message: THEY ARE SETTING MASS WAVE GENER-ATORS. THEY PLAN TO LEVEL THE VILLAGE. GET OUT NOW!

Max didn't know if Emerson received the transmission. If he didn't get far enough away, the wave would collapse the matter bonds holding everything together and reduce anything more solid than soil to carbon particles and trace minerals. The result would ignite a cloud of super-oxygenated gas, combusting anything left at an excess of 500 degrees. Essentially, nothing would be left but fine volcanic ash.

Emerson's scratchy voice said, "How far?"

Max did a quick calculation and said, "Ten kilometers in a 360-degree radius. I'm going to try to disable them, but if I fail, I might set off a chain reaction."

He didn't get another reply from Emerson. The enforcer platoon was returning to their shuttles followed by the ground forces. Max cranked up his hearing. An infantry captain said, "The village is confirmed abandoned, Colonel."

The colonel replied, "Get strapped in. We launch in thirty seconds."

Max sighted the shuttles and adjusted for distance and wind. He set the power to maximum. A weird litany began in his mind, repeating the phrase, "Maxamillion maximum, Maxamillion maximum…" He felt like he was going insane. If he clipped one of the wave generators, he would be as good as vaporized. But if he removed the enforcers before they initiated the countdown, he could avert destruction. And save his own life too.

He aimed at the center of the far-left shuttle's nose and fired, sweeping the crackling orange beam across each vessel. The ships exploded one after another as the plasma touched them. A half moment later, there was nothing but four scorch marks in the shape of shuttle landing legs on the cobbles. The wave generators stood untouched.

Max nearly burst into tears. He sent another message to Emerson: GOT THEM ALL. STILL ALIVE.

There was no reply. Max climbed down to the ground level. He walked toward the south gate. When the sun set, he'd signal Emerson.

◆

Rosco yelled, "Grendel! Can you hear me?"

He heard her weak moan, and he carefully stepped off the broken boards. He called the satphone. Quinn picked up on the first ring. "Are you okay?"

"No, tell Emerson to come to the south gate. Grendel's hurt." She passed the phone to him.

Emerson said, "Little Wing is closer, and Doctor Pam is on board. I can navigate her remotely, but I'll need to set autopilot for us to stay at a high-altitude loop. We'll be there as soon as possible. Can you stabilize her?"

"I don't know. She fell through the floor into a flooded cellar. I need to get down there; it's deep."

Emerson radioed Pam to tell her what he was planning. Elli answered; Pam was tending a hemorrhage. She confirmed that they were ready. The Black Mariah entered a loop pattern on autopilot at 50,000 meters. He opened a direct control connection with Little Wing. As long as Emerson focused on his Interface, it felt like he was inside the other shuttle.

Emerson routed the satphone to his helmet and called Rosco, who answered immediately. He said, "Be there in ten. How's Grendel?"

After the first call, Rosco found a hole in the broken floor near a corner and climbed down a splintered beam. The water was up to his knees. He used his PDA as a light and scanned the cellar. It smelled dank with mold, old fuel oil, and something foul. Something died, and it had been down there for a while. Grendel was near the middle of the room; she was lying on the section of floor that was beneath her when it collapsed. She was unconscious, the lower half of her body submerged in the greasy water. Rosco knelt beside her and put his hand on her forehead. She opened her eyes and said, "I never listen."

He smoothed hair from her forehead and said, "You never listen."

"I think my leg is broken. It feels like my shinbone snapped when I hit the ground. I hit my head."

"Emerson sent a shuttle. Doctor Pam is on board. They'll be here soon."

"I'm cold and sleepy, baby."

"I'm afraid to move you, honey. Hold on. They'll be here…" The satphone chimed.

Emerson asked about Grendel. He said, "Her leg is broken, maybe a compound fracture. She hit her head and wants to go to sleep, so I'm keeping her awake. And there's nasty water in this hole. I need to get her out, but I'm afraid to move her."

Emerson said, "Almost there."

Rosco heard Little Wing powering down as she hovered above. A nano-carbon cord descended from an open hatch in the bottom. Elli rode the harness down standing on a strap and holding on to the cable. When she was close, she jumped into the water and put the harness under Grendel as Rosco lifted her hips.

Grendel whimpered, and Rosco soothed her with his voice. "I know, baby, be done in a second. There."

Once she was on board and strapped in, the shuttle took off. Emerson spoke to them over the monitor in Little Wing. He said, "I see everyone is breathing. How badly is she hurt?"

Pam said, "Grendel needs surgery, stat. She is stable, but that could change. I've got her on an IV for fluids and a MERSA-grade antibiotic, but her skin was pierced in a compound fracture under water containing questionable nasty shit. She has a concussion. I won't know how bad that is until the swelling goes down. I can't do any more while we are flying 200 kilometers per hour. I need a hospital. A stationary one."

Ana said, "We have to meet everyone else at Terminus Station. There's not much there, but it's off The City's radar for now."

Emerson thought, *And it's on the way to Chandler's homeplace*, but didn't mention it.

"The sooner the better." She went back to work. Elli said, "It's a mess, Emerson. Grendel is awake, but she hasn't spoken. I'm worried."

Emerson said, "Do what you can. I'm routing us to Terminus now."

◆ ◆

When Emerson arrived at the market stalls of Terminus Station, Eggert had taken control of setting up the medical area and operating room. Little Wing landed a half hour earlier; all the patients had been assessed and their injuries ranked from serious to mild. The serious cases were prepped for surgery in a makeshift operating room. Elli found a storage shack and covered the floor, walls, and ceiling from a roll of plastic sheeting she found. Elli and Pam scrubbed up with Ana, who helped as their charge nurse. While Marya slept, Quinn wiped up as much blood as she could, but found a severed finger in the corner. Emerson came in and didn't notice. He asked, "You okay? Marya okay?"

She nodded, "I almost threw up. There's a finger over there." She pointed, looking away.

"Yeah. This is a disaster. But the sun is setting. We need to watch the horizon for Max's signal. If he got away, he'll show us where he when it's dark. Can you sit outside and watch the sky while I make sure everything is under control?"

"Probably better than in here with all this blood."

"We'll do something about it once we are further away from The City."

Quinn tore the cuticle off her finger with her teeth and made it bleed. "I told you, Boston won't give up. We need to find somewhere to hide and regroup. The other Lords will insist he scorch the earth. The technology the Juice Hackers have is a threat to him. That's why he created this incident."

"Right. It makes perfect sense that Boston would create a false flag in order to justify wiping out an entire society."

"Now that he has shut up the other Lords, he will set his sights on you. You can set a clock by Boston Quinn's behavior. This is the way he thinks: if he eliminates you, he will get me back. The cost in innocent life is irrelevant. He needs me to perpetuate his fucking *royal* line. His legacy. That's all that matters to him now."

They walked away from the shuttle and out into the field to sit in the grass. The sun had set, and the light was tinted amber. Emerson pointed north and said, "Max will fire the rifle straight up as soon as it's dark. We'll go and get him. You stay here for now; I'll check back with you in a little while. I need to see about Grendel and Elli."

◆

Rosco stayed by Grendel's side until Pam took her into surgery. Emerson came by to see how she was. Rosco said, "I need the whole story now, Emerson. We had no problems with The City people. We had a good working arrangement. Why in hell did they attack us?"

Emerson sat on a wood crate and bid Rosco do the same. He said, "This is going to be hard." He considered telling the whole long story but decided to cut to the important part. "Barton betrayed you. He'd been spying for Boston Quinn, who convinced him to stage a coup. This was Boston's doing. He created an incident to justify removing Blue Hole from his little chessboard. God knows what that fat snake offered your brother."

Rosco said, "How were you involved in it? Where did the other shuttle come from? And damn, man, where the fuck *is* my little brother? I'm going to wring his neck."

"Barton is dead."

"Dead? How? How do you know? He wasn't downtown, was he?"

"He attacked Elli. She surprised him in the tunnel when he was talking to Boston."

"He had a hard-on for that girl the moment he saw her. I should have known."

"He was plotting with Boston. It was all his doing. I'm really sorry, Rosco."

"The communication lines. Fuck, he knew about that, must have followed me. Fuck, fuck, fuck!"

"It's worse than that."

"How could it be worse?"

"Jock led the team to place the fake emitters."

"Oh Christ! We used to tease him when he was a kid. Called him Duh."

Emerson continued, "He had my plasma rifle. When they surprised him, he yelled something about the damn Everymen and killed a bunch of Elite Guards. But he had the power jacked all the way up, and the beam obliterated the servants' housing too, killing about 100 innocent people in their sleep. Boston's guard executed the platoon. It's a miracle they didn't kill us all."

"Oh fuck. Maybe Barton is better off. I would have had to kill him. But why would you agree to this madness?"

"Blackmail. He hired a hitman to kill Ana and Elli if I failed. But then he died before the mission. I had to take the women with me, and we would have failed without their help. I eliminated the hitman before we left. But I don't know about the other conspirators: Roy, Just Sam, and the other one, Peter Rust."

"I know all of them. Cowards with big mouths. Just like Barton. I'm so sorry, man. I had no idea. I was supposed to keep him under control; I thought he was getting better."

"Elli is pretty upset about it. It was self-defense, you know. She wasn't trying to kill him, just get away. Apparently, he thought she only existed for his sexual use, tried to take her. But you should talk to her. When Grendel wakes up, let her know. She brought Elli back to herself."

"Thanks, man. Pam's not sure if she will wake up. I don't know what I'm going to do."

"You'll do what you must, Rosco. Just like the rest of us."

◆◆

Max fell asleep waiting for the sunset. He thought he'd eliminated the threat, and he was exhausted. The fires burned on, out of control, belching greasy black smoke into the air from incinerated plastic. He was pretty well concealed, tucked between some crates and a brick wall, up on the only hill in south central Blue Hole. He didn't anticipate the backup placement team. But when they arrived, they didn't think anyone was still alive, so they didn't move quietly. As a result, they woke Max up just after dark.

He whispered, "Fuck!" under his breath. There were more than thirty of them. They'd marched in on foot, leaving the transport shuttles hidden in another part of town. He guessed they'd planned for minimum resistance. He unlocked the rifle and used The Interface scope to establish clear shots. But he couldn't be sure that the wave generators wouldn't go off if he shot them. If he left any of them live, the hidden shuttles could activate the remote keys.

He also knew he couldn't get away. Calling Emerson now would put him and anyone with him in danger. Quinn was probably there; he couldn't bring her into it. He sighted each of the generators. If he didn't hit each of them in exactly the right spot, they would surely trigger. If he sprayed plasma indiscriminately, he would kill all the Enforcers, but probably clip one of the generators and set all of them off in a chain reaction. But if he didn't kill them first, they might stop him, and it would all be a waste.

Maxamillion Hamp was an intuitive thinker. He could naturally see the risk/reward equation in most choices; in this case, the odds were not in his favor. The movement in the square changed. The generators were set; they were preparing to leave. He had to act. He removed the lock and modulated the gun, scanning the area again.

He still had a clear shot at each generator. It would be a race. Max took a deep breath and squeezed the trigger. The first generator vaporized in a flash of orange light. The enforcers froze and pulled their weapons, searching in all directions. They would see where he was when he took the next shot.

Two Enforcers saw a glint from his rifle scope—but they missed him by a long margin. He vaporized the next two generators. Enforcers began running in his direction. He eliminated four of them; the rest took cover. He aimed and smoked the next three wave generators. The enforcers had his position now; their shots were dangerously close, spraying him with cement chips. He sighted the last black box and fired.

◆

Quinn watched a shooting star cross the sky from west to east. The flash of it startled her; she almost jumped up. A split second later, the entire northern sky lit up like an early dawn. The sounds reached her a half minute later; she felt it more than heard. The vibration rose up from the ground and met a hot wind blowing in her face. It felt like her bones were being ground into dust, but only for a second. She realized with horror that Max was dead. She broke down sobbing, oblivious to Marya's wailing. Emerson found her that way twenty minutes later. He calmed his daughter and sat on the grass where Quinn kneeled, pressing his forehead to hers. They stayed that way until Rosco interrupted them.

He said, "Grendel is out of surgery. Now we wait."

Emerson stood up and said, "Blue Hole is gone. Wave generators turned everything to ash. There's nothing left but barren ground now. Best we forget it."

Quinn's sobs quieted, and she said, "He was my oldest friend. I can't believe he's gone."

Rosco said, "Hats off to Maxamillion. Let's hope his death was not in vain."

The three of them stood in the darkness under the star-strewn onyx night. A sliver of moon appeared on the eastern horizon. They huddled against each other for a long moment. But the almost 5,000 refugees of Blue Hole arrived with nothing, and there was much to do before anyone could rest. They had no food, clothing, or shelter. Rosco said, "We need a meeting to set up an interim council. I'm thinking a big fire and any roasted game we can find."

Emerson said, "I saw some people with birds. Maybe we could find them, see if we can collect eggs."

Rosco shook his head. "That's an acquired taste, man. Cloned chickens, bah! They couldn't make the broken DNA viable, so they substituted frog DNA 'cause it fills in nicely, but they aren't exactly chickens. I think the ones you saw are pets. Parents give them to kids. When they lose interest, they just let them go. The buggers are really dumb. They drown in puddles."

Quinn said, "Can you use the shuttle like a crane? We could cut trees with a plasma rifle, and you could bring them to the field over there."

Rosco said, "Now you're thinking like a Juice Hacker."

Emerson asked Quinn, "Are you sure you're alright?"

Quinn said, "Two conditions: one, give me and Ana a rifle. Two, teach me to fly."

Emerson kissed her; Marya reached up and touched his cheek. He said, "Deal."

◆ ◆

Boston Quinn paced in front of his current commander, General Towns, muttering as the nervous man explained the status of the invasion. When he said, "The town is gone, sir," Boston stopped and stared at him.

"My daughter. You found my daughter first, right? You were not to hurt her."

The man stuttered, "I'm sorry, sir. The first team was eliminated, and the second team wasn't told about her. They are all gone, sir. No one left in that village survived."

Boston didn't speak for a minute. He removed the gun from his pocket and showed it to Towns. He said, "This is a German Luger. It's an antique, I'm sure you know."

The commander's lips trembled. The gun had robbed him of his powers of speech.

Lord Quinn said, "What's the problem, Towns? Cat got your tongue?"

The commander said, "What?"

Quinn replied, "The saying is also an antique, like the Luger," and shot the man in his chest.

Commander Towns looked at Quinn in shock and disbelief before falling over dead.

Lord Quinn yelled, "Somebody come and clean this pile of shit off my floor. Send me the next in command. NOW!"

◆ ◆ ◆

THE HOMEPLACE REVISITED

While Emerson went with Rosco to cut trees for the bonfire, Ana programmed the drone to announce the fire and meeting. The hospital shack had attracted several family members of the injured. A few of the women gathered around Quinn to meet Marya, and Mary Mapes, the Blue Hole midwife, told her she would take care of Marya.

Mary had the extra advantage of having never allowed her milk to dry up. She told Quinn, "I'm a natural babysitter, I am," slipped a breast out, and the tiny girl latched on, sucking contentedly.

Ana said, "This frees us up to go hunting."

Quinn said, "I never hunted anything more than boys."

Ana laughed. Quinn said, "I'm not joking,"

Elli said, "I'll come. Pam's got plenty of help now." She already had her rifle slung across her chest.

Ana and Quinn shouldered theirs and went to the edge of the forest. On the way Elli said, "The rifles are pretty simple, but you have to remember to watch the power. Keep the setting on low until you are sure of what they can do."

◆

Emerson found Eric Eggert in a merchant's stall pounding hooch with Margret, the woman who brought him his meals while he was locked up. Apparently, she had continued to feed him, and recently, they had moved in together. The bar stall was one of the more solid buildings at Terminus, probably owing to the fact that the permanent residents spent most of their time there. The station was the end of the line, but the town, if you could call it that, looked like a refugee camp even before the remaining citizens of Blue Hole arrived. In truth, it wasn't thought of as a town by any of the traders who congregated there when goods were exchanged; it was just a clearing in the woods where the rails ended.

There were a few latrines, fire pits in rusting metal drums, and rows of roofed stalls, most of which were dry-rotted and in various stages of collapse. When the supply train had been there, the stalls were filled with distant Outsiders, displaying anything they grew, made, or found in surplus.

Eggert saw Emerson, jumped up with a hand on Margaret's shoulder, and said, "We found each other. It's a miracle, right? Come! Sit! We can drink to Max." He was uncharacteristically loud and ebullient.

Emerson said, "You seem happy for a refugee who just barely escaped alive."

Eggert looked him in the eye and said, "Death has a way of making you appreciate life, eh?" He poured a jar of greasy-looking liquid and continued, "Now drink!"

A grizzled old man with a stringy grey beard sat on the bench near Eggert and Margaret. He raised his metal cup with them. He wore torn pants and a faded, felt serape. Most of his teeth were missing, and his bloodshot eyes were unfocused when he said, "Been meeting here for near fifty years! Most came on foot. Some pulled or pushed carts.

"The Carver brothers came from way over east, past the first range. They had a rusted-out flatbed Chevy modified to run on ethanol. It had no fenders or doors. No muffler either!" He laughed, his toothless mouth wide. "Made whisky from their own corn, aged in real Jack Daniel's barrels. They used to give rides to the kids, flying around like damn banshees in the woods here." He waved his hand absently and drained his cup. "Trading days were like a festival. Gonna be hard now. Gonna miss the Blue Hole crew."

Emerson said, "Well, for now we need to feed and shelter about 4800 of that Blue Hole Crew. That will be the first step to rebuilding their home." To Eggert he said, "We have a bonfire going, and Ana, Elli and Quinn are out hunting for something to feed people. A meal and a fire will do a lot to bring everyone together and calm them down. Rosco wants to impanel an interim council and sort folks into districts. We need a decision-making body.

"But until then, we need to make sure people are safe. Most of them have never lived outside their houses or the village. Even with their resilient natures, this is going to be tough. I need another experienced shuttle pilot to take charge of building shelters."

Eggert saluted to Emerson and finished the last of his drink. He said, "I accept the charge! But I am too knackered to see straight right now, so flying will have to wait until tomorrow."

◆

Elli helped Quinn put the rifle in the correct position against her shoulder and said, "Hold steady and use The Interface to focus the sight on what you are aiming at."

Quinn nodded once.

Elli said, "Squeeze the trigger."

A twenty-millimeter-wide sandstone rock perched on a stump 100 meters away disappeared in a puff of orange mist.

The three women laughed together. Ana said, "Hell yeah, girl."

Elli said, "I think we're ready."

Ana had the most experience hunting animals and birds, though Elli was enthusiastic and infatuated with shooting. She had not inspected her own feelings enough to know if it was because of the exhilaration of making the shot or satisfaction from killing. Either way, she had become an accomplished shooter in a short time. Ana had learned to hunt with a short crossbow, which was considerably harder than using the guns. The precision and power of an Interface-enabled plasma weapon amplified her already well-honed aim.

Quinn had the least experience. Before that day, she'd never even considered shooting, let alone shooting a living target. But the invasion of Blue Hole changed her. All her life she had operated inside the restrictive, highly artificial boundaries of Founder's Quarter and the isolating constraints of being the eldest daughter of the Elder Lord Quinn. Any Middle, and most of her friends, would have thought she possessed ultimate freedom and power. And when she thought of friends, the shard of Maxamillion Hamp lodged in her heart shifted, causing a jagged, searing pain.

But her emancipation from The City burst open vast new possibilities. Dreams she'd never imagined, let alone considered. Like Elli, Quinn recognized that she was suddenly, actually, free! And the idea was intoxicating.

Max knew me better, she thought, as she brought the rifle to her shoulder, aimed, and fired. The wild turkey fell dead with a clean, cauterized hole the diameter of a pencil through its heart. The other two stopped speaking mid-sentence. Elli said, "Holy shit."

Ana said, "Quinn, one. Elli and Ana, zero. Better shake it, girls."

It was corny, yes, but Elli smiled because Ana said it. It was a very Ana thing to do.

◆

An hour later, they were on their way back to Terminus with several turkeys, eight rabbits, a couple of grouse-like birds, and a strange stunted buck that Elli took from 100 meters thinking it was farther away. They were surprised to find the animal was only a meter tall at the shoulder when they reached it. Still, walking back was a struggle; they were exhausted. The pole they'd hung their haul on cut into the neck and shoulder of anyone carrying it. It was heavy. While one woman rested, holding the guns, the other two walked with the pole. It was slow going. They had to rest often.

Ana said, "Quinn, I didn't want to like you. Emerson and I have bonded deeply, and I felt threatened by you. I thought that, being a lord's daughter, you'd be pretty stuck up and full of yourself. But I *really* like you. You are not who I thought you were at all. And baby Marya stole my heart."

Quinn smiled, but the day was wearing on her.

Elli watched Ana and was surprised to find a grin on her own face. She was developing more respect for both of the women. It was obvious that Emerson regarded her as a daughter and had no sexual interest, which was good because Elli was disgusted by the idea of a man's ardor.

Quinn was shouldering the pole at that point, and it pinched a nerve in her neck. She never did any kind of physical labor in her life. Even though her outlook had broadened, her body was still out of shape. It was worse that she'd *just* given birth after months laying around in bed. She felt fat and miserable. Even if being in the woods was invigorating, she reached her limit and crumbled. Elli caught the pole before it could hit the ground. Such a simple gesture of cooperation hit her hard; she began to cry. Ana and Elli stopped, put the pole down, and surrounded her in a hug.

Quinn let her guard fall completely as the others held her up. At first, she tried to keep it in, breath hitching, unable to speak. But her pain would not be contained, and she burst into a wail, wetting Ana's shirt. They hugged her tighter. Years of pain and confusion compounded by Max's and Lucia's death poured out of her.

When the sobs subsided, they lay back shoulder to shoulder and watched the sky darken from blue to black while Venus and the first diamond-chip stars began to peek through.

Ana said, "Are you good?"

Quinn said, "I never wanted to be a queen."

Ana said, "All I ever wanted was to be a mom."

Elli sighed and said, "I feel like I've just been born."

◆

By the time they got back, it was past dark, but they received a hearty welcome and immediate relief; several hands took the pole and the meat away to cook.

Mary brought Marya to her mother. She sat on the bench next to Quinn and said confidentially, "You little one is an angel. She slept or drank the entire time. I changed her nappy twice. The second time she pooed, the precious one. But while I was rustling around in your bag for a diaper, I knocked open a box, and *these* are scattered all over the bottom now."

A silver capsule about ten millimeters long rested in her palm.

Quinn said, "Yes. They are un-programmed."

Mary said, "They have a value, don't they?" It wasn't really a question.

"Yes, a great value."

Quinn let sleeping Marya rest in her lap. She gathered the handfuls of implants and resettled them in their container. Taking Mary's hand in her own hand, she spilled several implants into the palm. Quinn said, "We live in unsettled times. Take these. Use them to help."

Mary thanked her, wished her well, and left.

Quinn said, "Whew! I'm toast." Ten minutes later, she was asleep in a bed onboard The Black Mariah with Marya at her breast.

When Ana and Elli arrived, Emerson was just finishing up the spits. Soon, the meat would be slowly rotating near a pit of red-hot coals. The drone message had done the job. Most of the camp was gathered around the fire, which was a twenty-meter-wide circle of burning logs stacked in a twelve-meter-high cone.

Emerson said, "Rosco cut them with the rifle, and I used The Black Mariah like a crane to stack them in position."

Rosco wheeled Grendel. He made a wheelchair out of a wheelbarrow and cut-up seat. Her right leg was splinted, and her calf was wrapped with makeshift bandages torn from shirts. She said, "I got to use a rifle to light it. And gloriosky! I can see why everyone is excited about those guns. It was like spraying fire from twenty meters. Hooboy!"

Elli hugged her fiercely. She buried her face in the soft shoulder of the older woman's chest and murmured, "I'm so happy that you're okay. I was scared to lose you."

"Ah, I'm okay, honey. It will take more than a little fall to kill me."

Ana put her arm around Emerson and said, "I have decided that we are a family. And everyone in a family is included. No one is left out!"

Emerson said, "Ohana means Family. Family means nobody gets left behind."

Ana said, "Ohana?"

"It's a line in an animated film from the late twentieth century that my grandpa used to play for me. I adored that movie. Probably watched it a thousand times! It's about a weird little alien creature named Stitch, who comes to live with a little girl named Lilo who was being raised by her sister in the Hawaiian Islands. Ohana is from the Hawaiian language—I wonder if anyone speaks it anymore?"

Elli said, "Are there islands anymore?"

No one had an answer for that. After an uncomfortable moment, Ana said, "You're a weird little alien, Emerson."

Quinn returned to the gathering as everyone began to eat. Other hunters had collected game too. Some of the refugees made soup from bones with foraged wild onions and herbs. Others stretched jerky. Apparently, the community of Blue Hole kept several of the old ways alive. Emerson was relieved that he wasn't the only experienced woodsman.

Marya was awake and alert, twisting in her mother's arms trying to see everything. Quinn slid her exposed breast back into her shirt. Emerson gave her a hindquarter of a rabbit. Buckets of drink were passed around. People had whatever jars and metal cups they could find.

Quinn stood on Emerson's other side from Ana. She leaned her head on his shoulder. Elli appeared by her other side and let Marya grab hold of her finger, which was greasy from the fowl that she had just devoured.

Quinn said, "You know they're coming for you, Emerson. My father has probably put a bounty on your head. With the destruction of Blue

Hole, he knows he's made his point. He felt threatened by the technological advantage they had.

"Now that he proved his strength, he will put his attention on finding Marya and me and bringing us home—we are the key to his plan."

Emerson said, "What plan does that maniac have?"

"He is turning The City into a monarchy. He thinks that when supplies from before the collapse run out, he will need a better control on the people. Right now, he makes sure they get what they need. When he can't provide that anymore, he figures they'll revolt."

"Yeah, he told me. But you said it would take 200 years."

"Like any megalomaniac autocrat, Boston Quinn plays the long game. And aside from protecting me until he drags me back, you have no purpose. The Middles don't know you are Marya's father. Hell, they may not even know I'm gone. He can't keep that charade up forever. Eventually, people will want to see his heir. I expect they are already looking for you. We can't trust anyone. And for everyone's safety, I suggest we leave. As quietly as soon as we can."

Later that evening, when the fire had burned down and conversation had quieted, Rosco amplified his voice though the drone as it flew around the glowing fire pit. He reminded people that they needed to adhere to safe practices.

He said, "Our biggest concerns should be the big three: food, water and sewage. We have to eat, we have to drink, and if our sewage gets in either, we will die. Painfully."

He picked the interim council and gathered volunteers to build shelters and designate new latrines. He went on to give an inspired speech about cooperation and strength in numbers. Emerson chose that moment to slip away. He met Grendel in the hospital shack with Pamela P. Quinn, Elli, and Ana stood by him. He said, "Lord Quinn is hunting me, Elli Rattlesnake, and Marya. It will be safer for us to leave now before we get too involved. I know you have responsibilities here, but if you ever want to join us, we'd welcome you. I will come back and get you wherever we are."

"Where will you go?" Grendel asked.

"Probably to Chandler's homeplace to get ready and then west. West over the Inland Sea!"

He gave Grendel the satphone and said to Elli, "That goes for you too. You can stay or go as you wish. But if you ever change your mind, contact me through Grendel, and I'll come get you."

She didn't respond but looked at the floor. Emerson thought she was crying silently. Ana moved to hug her shoulders from behind. Grendel said, "Rosco is committed to the community, and my place is with my husband. But I'll pass your offer and the satphone on to him. We will call you if we need you. When will you go west?"

"I need to visit my grandfather's homeplace and collect things we will need. He was a recluse and a survivalist, even though he never thought so himself. His innovations will make the transition much easier for us. Beyond that, I hope to wait out the winter there and leave for the west in the spring."

She hugged him first and then each of the others in turn, Elli last, lingering in the embrace. With her mouth near Elli's ear, she said, "You are the daughter I could never have. I know you love Emerson like a father. Go with him. Take the call to adventure."

Pam stepped up and took over hugging Elli. She said, "I wanted you to be my apprentice, but since we got to Terminus, I have Carol and Helga Taylor and Charles B. for nurses, and I think they've been bit by the healer bug. What I'm saying is—follow your heart, little one. If a healer is what you're meant to be, then you won't be able to avoid it. Go. Live your own life. Don't worry about us. We will be fine." Both women cried together.

Elli said finally, "I love you."

Rosco finished up his inspirational. Ana called the drone in. Emerson granted control back to Eggert. He said to Rosco, "Make sure he drinks a lot of water tomorrow. He's seeing snakes right now, and he's gonna have a hell of a hangover."

Rosco said, "He's got Margaret to take care of him; she knows what to do."

Emerson said, "It will take us about thirty minutes to prep The Black Mariah for travel. After that, we're gone, boss. Grendel's got the satphone. You call if you need us."

It was Rosco's turn to hug everyone. He even hugged his mate, murmuring into the warm skin of her neck, "What a fucking day, babe."

As Emerson was walking away, Doctor Pam caught up with him. She said, "Let me walk with you for a second."

Emerson nodded; he was already thinking about how he would pack up the solar kits. Pam said, "Emerson. You are a special man, and it's not just your sperm, son."

He stopped and hugged her, resting his head on her shoulder.

"You have a huge heart too, but that's not what I'm talking about." They sat on a large log just off the path. Pam went on, "When everything collapsed, Emerson, it traumatized everyone. My parents didn't know how they were going survive at the most basic level. That kind of trauma persists. And we all inherited it. It is not just the external world that drastically changed—it's our internal world."

She tipped her head and looked at him for so long that he almost interrupted her stare. She said, "This kind of trauma can shape and reshape the brain. In the early twenty-first, the term neurodivergence was a popular, non-specific way to describe it. The brains of young people were responding to massive changes in their environment. Together, these influences became a recipe for radically different cognition.

"I believe it was an evolution. And after the collapse, it was this ability to adapt and evolve that saved many of us. That and our body's high parasite threshold. But you, Emerson, are someone who has harnessed his neurodivergence in a unique way. And when people see it, they will instinctively want to know you."

Emerson was taken aback by Pam's words. He thanked her.

She shook her head, "I think you're missing the point, son. You are a visionary. They are going to follow you, but you have to know where you are going. It's a big responsibility to be the catalyst for a new world."

Emerson said, "Oh, I'm no catalyst."

They stood up, and Pam turned to go back to the medical tent. She said, "Whatever you want to call it, you've been a spark for great changes, Emerson. The question is, what are the changes you will continue to inspire? Take care of yourself and don't get killed." She limped back toward the camp; Emerson went to his shuttle.

◆ ◆ ◆

The flight to the Homeplace was quiet and peaceful. Everyone including Emerson slept. Autopilot kept them on course and apprised of any issues. But nothing could keep Emerson awake. He couldn't remember the last time he'd slept.

As the sun rose, cold and damp over the eastern forest, Emerson woke. Sunrise at 12,000 meters was an experience like no other. The giant globe of orange crested the edge of the planet, casting beams of light across the surface. A moment later, it looked like sunrise for 360 degrees. After a while, the mist burned away, and the cistern hill came into sight. Quinn joined him in the cockpit and sat, unstrapped in the copilot's seat.

She said, "Don't forget you are going to teach me to fly."

Without a hint of what he'd done, Emerson said, "Fine. It's yours. You are now flying The Black Mariah."

Quinn panicked. "No. Take it back. I don't know what… Shit! Emerson, are we falling? Don't fucking do this to me."

He laughed, "Slow down, Roger Ramjet, the Black is on autopilot. You have to turn that off before you can do anything."

Quinn shook her head. "Damn you, I don't have any idea how to do anything."

He said, "Okay, want me to turn it off?"

"Don't you dare."

Elli arrived; Ana followed with Marya. She said, "This one wants something I cannot provide."

Elli said, "Pam has hormone shots that can fix that. I hear anybody can breastfeed, even you, Emerson." She poked his ribs.

Ana said, "That's not what I mean. This sweet angel babe is carrying a load. I'm not equipped to change shitty nappies before caffeine."

Emerson said, "There's a loaded replicator, but I warn you, it's not real coffee."

Quinn said, "I'll pass."

Ana said, "Caffeine is caffeine."

Elli said, "I'll try anything once," and left to get a cup. Less than a minute later, they heard her spit a mouthful into the galley sink. "Jesus fuck, what in hell is that shit?"

Emerson said, "Happy returns, Elli. Replicator food makes me yak, too."

They began their decent arriving at the overgrown door yard to Chandler's cabin hovering just over twenty meters from the ground. Emerson set down and shut off the reactor. He ran a quick scan for heat signatures and opened the door. The sleepy, stiff passengers disembarked, yawning and stretching.

Elli squatted and relieved her bladder. She said, "Oh, gaaahd, I hate air travel."

Emerson said, "There is a head in the back of the shuttle, you know."

She said, her stream still flowing strong, "I don't know. I'm just superstitious that way. Afraid I'll get sucked out."

Emerson used a portable power cube to unlock the house.

Ana said, "Your grandfather was amazing. He reprogrammed Interfaces and set up more advanced systems than we had in Blue Hole."

Emerson said, "He was far ahead of any coder in The City. Check this out." He ported the data stream from the house system to Ana's Interface. "This is the house log. The red bars are events of interest. Looks like Mule's been hanging around. There are images of anything that got close to the doors. I wonder if she'll come out with this many people around."

Ana said, "Who's Mule?"

As if Ana had called the big feline, she chose that moment to appear beside Emerson's leg. Ana was shocked and turned to run. Elli raised her rifle.

Emerson said, "Whoa, whoa, put that down. This is Mule. She saved my life when I was a boy."

Elli said, "What in the hell is that?"

Emerson said, "Not sure, exactly. A kind of mutated house cat. She's not a hybrid—and there are others around besides her kits."

In moments, Quinn and Elli were there petting the big cat's head and talking baby talk to her; she was entranced, eyes closed and chin up, purring as loud as a motor. Emerson said, "I got caught in a titanium snare in a snowstorm, and Grandpa Chandler went to get tools to free me. It took him three days. Mule showed up and brought me game, shared my fire, and protected me. When Grandpa got back, she hunted with him and flushed two elk. We ate well that winter."

"How old were you?" Elli said.

"Fifteen, sixteen? I don't remember exactly. She fishes too."

True to her form, Mule brought four rabbits for dinner that night. Emerson put the climate control system back on line and filled all the tanks from the cistern. There was unending hot water in minutes. After dinner, while he was cleaning up, he opened a blank document which he routed to the main room screen and listed the tasks he wanted to accomplish before they began preparing for winter. He told Quinn that he wanted to be ready at a moment's notice if the Enforcers showed up. He said, "They know where this place is. It's just a matter of time until they get here. We need to be ready."

The next day, they began taking the house apart. Quinn helped where she could. Ana spent her time cataloging the data storage. Chandler had several hellabytes in solid state drives. He had collected most books in print from the late twentieth century and thousands of other manuscripts in hundreds of languages, along with a wealth of movies and television shows, including educational, experimental, and surrealist films. One drive was a storehouse of videos on how to do just about anything that people did up to the year 2039.

Ana found the name of this drive funny and called Emerson over to his old bedroom where she and Elli had set up camp. "There's a bunch of weird videos on a drive called YouTube. From what I know about the history of data processing, we stopped using tubes when solid state semi-conductors were invented in the mid-1960s. And if we're talking about picture tubes, they went out with the advent of LCD in the later part of the same century. YouTube could not have been referring to screens when these short films began in the twenty-first. What in the hell were they talking about? These people were all zibs."

He called back, "That's how I learned to repair Chandler's tractor. It's an important compendium of empirical information about the technology and mechanics of that era. We find machines all over the place that require specific learning to operate or repair. Those files may be the only archive of that knowledge. I consider it more valuable than twenty seasons of *Gunsmoke*, but Chandler was an amateur archivist. He made no distinction between art and science. And I don't care what those people called it—his archive is like Alexander's library to us in this world. Remember, these were the people who murdered the world out of what my grandpa called malignant hubris."

Elli said, "Zibs?"

Ana said, "Idiots. Nincompoops!"

Quinn said, "Max knew all those old phrases. It's amazing how much of our lexicon includes references to things which are extinct and lost forever."

Emerson said, "Chandler was an archivist. He didn't know it, but his compulsive hoarding of what he termed The Useful Leftovers of a Doomed Race made him one."

◆

He packed the refrigeration unit, made crates to transport all the solar panels, boxed up the tools and pots. Chandler's 1901 Red Mountain wood-and-coal burning kitchen stove was far too big and heavy.

Elli went in search of weapons and ammunition which were not in the hunting locker. Chandler had them squirreled away all over the house. She found storage carts and crossbow cases, arrows with exchangeable points, a loaded .58-caliber pistol that looked big enough for a giant's hand, several boxes of bullets, a bullet press, and containers of gunpowder ingredients. She also found a matte-black box about a half-meter square. When she showed it to Emerson, he said, "Damn, Grandpa. I didn't know you had one of these."

"What is it?"

"A compact nuclear device. A unit like this can produce a huge amount of energy. But it can also be overloaded, which would cause it to implode on its plutonium core. I'd say this little thing is powerful enough to obliterate The City and everything in fifty surrounding miles." He paused for a moment, wondering why Chandler had such a thing. Emerson thought they had all been destroyed after the collapse. He said, "Everything would be incinerated, and the soil would be poisoned for 100 years."

When she asked what to do with it, he said, "It's disarmed now, but we can't leave it here or destroy it. Best we bring it along."

Ana raised an eyebrow but held her opinions.

She cataloged all of the data stores and removed the drives, the processors, and The Interface connections. Everything was wrapped in nonconductive plastic sheeting and crated. Quinn gathered up all the camping equipment along with bedding, pillows and extra clothing. She found Chandler's winter gear and came to Emerson wearing Chandler's coat, which was too big for her.

She told him, "These coats and mittens are amazing. They don't weigh hardly anything, but you can tell they are super-insulators as soon as you touch them."

Emerson said, "Find the small versions that I wore when I was six and eight. Marya will need them. Chandler also kept a bolt of the fabric. He adapted a military spec cloth he salvaged. The formula is in the files somewhere."

After dinner one night, Emerson brought out Chandler's Interface. Ana, Quinn, and Elli had chicory coffee in the main room, and Emerson activated it.

The room looked similar but was somehow different. Chandler sat on one of the wooden kitchen chairs, picking his teeth with a short wood stick. Emerson recognized the main room of the house from several years ago; he was probably around ten. It was before Chandler had installed the big west-facing window, the one he put in backward. The wall was still solid; there was a bookcase there in the simulation.

Emerson went to him, and they hugged. He said, "It's good to see you, Grandpa."

Chandler said, "Same, boy. So, who are these three pretty women you've brought to me? And wait, is that a baby..."

Emerson was completely absorbed in the experience. This was Chandler. He had never died. The simulation was so real that Chandler began to cry. He stood over baby Marya and said, "I can see where she is, but I can't hold her—she can't be implanted until she's five, and until then, she can't see me, nor can I touch her."

Emerson said, "Yes, Grandpa. That's your great-granddaughter. I named her Marya, after your mom's mom. Your grandma Marya came to see me during the birth."

Quinn extended her hand and said, "I'm glad to make your acquaintance. I've heard so much about you..."

Chandler ignored her hand and hugged her; her back cracked. He said, "C'mere, girl. Let me hold *you* at least." After a long moment, he said, "Wait, Quinn? Like Lord Quinn?"

Quinn said, "Yes, sir. That's my dad."

Chandler said, "And he's okay with you running off with my grandson, having babies and roaming around the woods with an orphan coder and a young commando?"

Elli said, "How do you know anything about me? I've never met you."

Ana said, "We are in a simulation, Elli. We are all with Chandler in the processor cube. Your Interface connects you with the construct—subsequently, it has complete knowledge of your memories. At least, most of them. If you are unaware of something, the construct can't see it."

They talked for hours, retelling stories about camping trips and embarrassing anecdotes about Emerson when he was a child. They laughed and cried. And when it was late and everyone was falling asleep, Chandler said, "You better get rested. The Enforcers will be here soon. Bring this cube with you and call me up whenever you need me. I will always be here for you." When the sim ended, the room went dark. They hadn't turned on the real lights. It was a shock at first, and then everyone laughed.

Quinn kissed Emerson and said, "Thank you. I feel like I know your grandfather now."

Ana said, "He was truly a genius. I have never been inside such a seamless sim before."

Elli said, "I felt his love. Is that even possible? I never had a grandfather…" Tears leaked from the corners of her eyes, but she didn't break down.

Emerson said, "Chandler was the wisest man I ever knew. Sometimes it seemed like he knew the future. If he thinks the Enforcers will be here soon, I'd believe him."

Quinn said, "I don't even know how that's possible. But I'm all for resting."

◆

In bed, right after turning out the light, Quinn said, "I should have killed the bastard. If I had killed him, we could have avoided the invasion."

Emerson said, "Not necessarily. The next lord in line would have probably done it anyway."

"Still. I should have killed him." She was silent for a while; Emerson thought she had gone to sleep and began drifting. She said, "I convinced Lucia to get involved. It's my fault she's dead."

Emerson turned the light back on and sat up. He looked into Quinn's face; her tears hadn't spilled over yet. He said, "Bullshit. She made her own decisions, Quinn. Your mother knew the consequences. You even told her it was too dangerous."

She kissed him; he shut off the light again. After a long minute, she said, "I still should have killed the bastard."

◆

Quinn, Marya, and Emerson slept in Chandler's king-sized bed. Mule joined them late by climbing into bed and falling asleep on Emerson's legs. He woke up around three and shoved the big cat off the bed. That night, there was a violent thunderstorm, a signal that summer was ending. Fall would rush in with little warning. Emerson knew what it meant. He was used to the weather at the homeplace; it was fairly random, but some cycles persisted. Lightning lit the room. Thunder rattled the glass and shelved items. The downpour started seconds after, rattling the metal roof.

Emerson drifted off. Thunder woke him again, and the next lightning flash revealed that Ana and Elli had joined them. When he woke the next morning, he was on the floor wrapped in Chandler's sheepskin rug. Mule slept on her back, huge paws in the air and head on Emerson's pillow.

A few days later, they finished stowing all the gear. All that was left was to winterize the house, lock up, and go.

◆ ◆ ◆

RUNNING NUMB

When it came, it came without warning, without hesitation, with a ferocity that was as surprising as it was terrifying. It looked like a rolling wave, which would have terrified Emerson normally, but this wave was a wall of fire, bearing down and threatening to engulf him. He woke up screaming, uncharacteristically long and loud.

Everyone in the house jumped to their feet without knowing how or why. Quinn was standing over him holding Marya, who was just waking to her state of shock; the babe would wail in a moment. Ana and Elli arrived. Mule was not in the house. Emerson's eyes were wide. He gripped his hands together. The house was dark, there was no moon, the silence was a physical thing between them.

Quinn whispered, "What did you dream?"

Emerson said, "It was real. It felt real. I died. We all died."

Elli said, "We have to go. Now!"

◆

The reactors whined. Everyone was strapped in. Emerson kept the door open, waiting for Mule. Ana yelled, "She's not coming. We have to go!" Wind whipped the tall grass.

The atmosphere was heavy, pressurized. Like the air before a massive electrical storm. Elli's hair felt statically charged, like it would stand up at any minute. And the pressure continued to rise. But there was another sound. If Emerson had ever heard one, he would have called it a freight train, but the books he read as a boy weren't animated. Besides, it wasn't a train at all. It was a tornado. And it was a monster.

When it appeared on the east horizon, Emerson thought it was a trick of the light. He had never been in the presence of one. And this one looked like a traveling wall. The sound grew louder. As it came closer, he could see the trees and debris it was throwing. It made thirteen-meter-tall oaks fly like broken sticks.

Quinn broke into his state of amazement by yelling in his ear. "Get this shit can in gear, Lloyde. We are out of time."

Just as he decided to close the door, Mule jumped in, skidding across the slick floor and slamming into the opposite wall. The shuttle was twenty meters off the ground before Emerson had strapped in with his helmet on. He yelled, "Hold tight!" And the ship shot off to the west at a slow angle. She punched through the clouds. The sun sat on the horizon behind them, beams streaming through the growing breaks.

Emerson trained the rear cameras on the tornado and projected the image on the shuttle wall. The clouds shredded away, revealing the land they had left. The view was amazing and horrifying. The tornado, a spinning 5,000-meter-tall demon, was consuming anything before it, leaving a five-kilometer-wide gash that wove behind it like a tail. The grey debris of pulverized trees and brush blanketed either side of the jagged brown wound in the earth.

They watched transfixed as the funnel, which had to be more powerful than a Fujita category 5, silently slid toward Chandler's cabin. Ana gasped when she realized what she was witnessing. When the tornado touched the house, the building simply disappeared in a puff of smoke. The twister continued on, leaving nothing in its wake but a ribbon of devastation. The spectacle grew smaller as they gained altitude.

Emerson turned the projection off and focused ahead toward the western horizon. Early light dusted the branches of the sparse forest with gold leaf.

◆ ◆ ◆

He switched control to autopilot, removed his helmet, and rubbed his eyes. He said, "I'm going to rest a bit. The Black will keep us safe." They let him sleep.

◆ ◆ ◆

"Dander Mitchel build several of these shacks all around the west woods near the Inland shore." Emerson had dropped down low enough to scan Dander's cabin. "We are close to Outpost 212. It's not what I'd call a town, but if we need any supplies, we might find them there. We can stay here. There's water and heat."

Ana said, "Heat?"

"We're above the fortieth parallel now. Blue Hole was near the thirty-fifth. Six degrees north is close to a month in season-time. There, we were just entering fall. Here, they are a month into it. You are going to need to wear coats."

Quinn said, "I got my hat."

He opened the door, and Mule jumped out, shook herself off, and sat licking her front paw. That was the last anyone saw of her until the next morning. Everyone else piled out and stretched. They needed to eat, and Emerson wanted to go remove Dander's snares. He called up the locations and copied them. He, Elli, and Quinn went for a hike.

After starting a fire, Ana checked over Dander's tool inventory and his data stores. When she found it, she copied his responder spoofing program, saying to herself, "Here's a tasty treat." He had a few more folders, but there was nothing much of value.

She checked out his food supplies but only found a portable replicator and half a jug of mushroom protein, which she took for emergencies. Emerson, Quinn and Elli returned at dusk with several squirrels and a fat bird neither Quinn or Emerson recognized. Elli claimed they were delicious, but she couldn't remember what they were called. Emerson also foraged some oyster mushrooms and a few bunches of wild onions. They made an earth oven by digging a shallow pit and filling it with hot coals. The trussed fowl was wrapped in metal foil and buried under more red-hot coals, then covered over with mud. Emerson said when the mud dried and cracked open, the bird would be done. He put on a pot of buckwheat groats and sat staring at the fire as the light faded.

◆ ◆ ◆

OUTPOST 212 REVISITED

Shuttles ran on concentrated hydrogen pellets. The process to make them required a large refinery. The City had a stockpile which could be recharged, but making pressurized hydrogen was dangerous. Emerson decided it was better to get a surplus from the outpost and worry about refilling them after they got to their new home, wherever that was.

Elli wanted to shop for weapons, and Ana heard that there was a Juice Hacker group there, and she wanted to see what they had to trade. Quinn just wanted to see what a foreign town looked like. Emerson said he'd save her the trouble. "It looks like a garbage dump in a sea of mud." But that just made her want to see it more. "Stinky mud," he added.

They flew The Black Mariah near the ground on stealth mode and hid her half a kilometer away from the outpost. Quinn wrapped Marya in a swathe of insulating material and tied it into a sling. When Ana asked if it was a custom in The City to wear children, she said, "Grendel showed me. I never saw a pod parent wearing a child. They are usually five before they go to a pod. Only the caretakers see the kids in the motherhood center."

"Pod? Motherhood center?"

Quinn explained the population controls and programming of Middles in The City. Ana was horrified. Elli said, "Sounds like any city run by men, to me."

293

Quinn said, "The Middles don't know any better. The whole system is designed to support the Elites' lavish lifestyle. People like my father spend their lives working out ways to stay in power. The Middles think they have everything they want and need, but they only know what they have been told. What they see of the world is limited by what the Lords want them to see."

They arrived at the outpost center, a monolithic two-story concrete block building, that was all glass on the side facing the town, if you could stretch the definition and actually call it a town. The three other walls looked more like a prison with their vertical slits every twenty meters. Occasionally, shuttles landed and took off from the roof.

Emerson and crew came around the building and entered the main street, which was mercifully cracked, dry earth. The rainy season would begin later. Each of the crew was armed with a visible short sword sheathed on their belts. Ana also had Chandler's nanocarbon fiber folding crossbow and a pack of short arrows in her pack. She and Quinn went in search of DP stalls. Quinn saw a vendor with brightly colored scarves and pulled Ana toward it.

Emerson and Elli found a metal shop and admired the craftsman's work. He was running a Bridgeport lathe; a hydrogen-powered generator puttered behind his shop. Elli fingered the milled stainless-steel tools and delicately threaded brass parts.

Emerson said, "Where can we find a knife shop? We need something sharp, if you catch my meaning."

The metal worker was a pale, paunchy man with a smoldering reed clamped between his teeth. Emerson smelled the opium before he was close enough to speak. The machinist had just finished polishing a perfectly round, ten-millimeter-wide ball of titanium. Emerson could see most of the street reflected in it behind him when the man held it up for inspection.

He shut off the buffing wheel, stubbed the reed out in a can of sand, and removed his glasses. When Emerson looked, he could see the broken blood vessels in the man's eye. The machinist noticed the attention and said, "I didn't always wear these glasses. Before this," he indicated his eye, "I could see out of both eyes. Tain't no way to remove that piece of steel.

Do more damage than good." He reached out toward Emerson and said, "I'm Rudy, but they call me Splinter." He shook Elli's hand too.

Splinter went on, "You're looking for The Australian. I warn you—he's a little unpredictable."

A woman entered the stall from the back wearing a leather apron and high boots and no shirt. The bib of the apron barely covered her large breasts which slid in and out from behind the apron, but the woman couldn't care less. Her face was smudged with soot, and her upper arms were streaked black and scarred above her rough goatskin gauntlets. She said, "He's fucking mad as a hatter."

Emerson said, "Where can we find this unpredictable Australian?"

Splinter said, "You don't. He finds you. Go tell Miss Magg over to the bar that you're looking to get your razor sharpened. She'll know what that means." He grinned. Elli thought it was more of a leer.

The woman said, "Anyways, Splint. Cluck and grunt's done." She left the way she arrived.

Splinter said, "Eggs and bacon."

Emerson nodded.

Splint added, "Tha's Mira. She's m'wife. A damn fine smithy too."

Elli said, "You have eggs?"

"Aaah, yeah, you can call em that. Chad tweaked the taste profiles, but it's still replicator slop."

Emerson said, "Where's Chad?"

"Oh, he's an Enforcer, not always around. Ask Magg 'bout him too. He's a regular of hers." He laughed, relit his reed, and sucked in a deep drag.

On the way to the bar, Emerson told Elli, "Hatters, people who made hats, used mercurous nitrate curing the felt. Mercury vapors are poison and slowly damaged their brains."

"So, all hatters were crazy?"

"It's hard to say. People say things for many reasons. But in this case, they really were poisoning themselves as late as the mid-twentieth century. The Mad Hatter is a character in the book *Alice in Wonderland*. It's in the files."

When they got to the bar, Elli tensed. The structure looked like other buildings on the street: a two-story wood house with windows facing the streets and a wide, sloping covered front porch, complete with double saloon doors. She recognized it as a flesh gallery where people with no choices offered themselves for a gain. It was a stark reminder of her old life and how helpless she had been, no matter how tough she made herself out to be. Naked women lounged on wooden chairs and benches, some openly masturbating, others moaning seductively. A dark-skinned woman with albino patches of vitiligo across her forehead and cheek hung over the railing, swinging her breasts at people walking past, calling out, "Hey, baby, want some sugar? I'm not particular."

Emerson took Elli's arm and said, "You're with me." For once she liked the idea of being claimed. It would shield her from unwanted advances. They walked past a crowd of gawkers and patrons on the porch. Inside, the stuffy room was dark and smelled of whiskey and mildew. Laughing patrons talked in little clots around the room. The music oozed from everywhere; Emerson felt the insistent bass in his bowels. Elli imagined that the room was dancing to this beat. It permeated everything like the smell of pee that lingered beneath the perfumes, alcohol, and sex.

The walls were covered by huge dark paintings in heavy ornate frames. A gaunt, bald-headed man towered above everyone in the center of the room. He wore an ill-fitting grey pinstriped suit and rubbed his palms together, smiling broadly. His long, pale feet contrasted starkly with the threadbare Persian rug that covered the floor.

Emerson approached him and said, "Magg?"

Without breaking his smile, the tall man said, "One moment," and snapped his long fingers. A boy rushed up. The tall man tipped his head, and the boy ran off toward the back of the building. A minute later, a girl strode toward them in what must have once been a white dress with a long, ratty train dragging on the ground behind her. It looked like an old-fashioned wedding dress, but Emerson couldn't understand why a child would have such a dress. The girl had a cigarette holder between her fingers. The cigarette was out.

She said, "I'm Magg. Speak." Her voice was gravelly. Emerson saw the wattle under her chin and the nest of wrinkles around her cold eyes and knew that she was no child. The top of her head came up to the center of his chest.

He said, "Is there somewhere we can go?"

She snapped back, "This is good for me. What?"

Clothed men and naked women walked between them, breaking Emerson's concentration. He stuttered, "S-s-sorry, I need a razor sharpened?"

She raised an eyebrow and said, "Looking to get your razor sharpened, you mean?"

"Ah, yes. Sorry. I need my razor sharpened?"

She rolled her eyes and turned to Elli, looked her body up and down, and said, "It this one available? She looks younger than she is—these pigs love that."

Emerson put his hand on Elli's arm as she opened her mouth. He said, "No. This one is mine." Elli knit her brows.

Magg said, "Aaah. Whatever." She whispered something to the boy who had retrieved her. He jogged out the front door. She went on, "Better get a drink. This may take some time."

They went to the bar. Emerson said, "I need to talk to Chad."

"That's lucky. He's here. I'll send him a message to meet us. How do you know Splinter?"

Emerson said, "Old family friend." Elli looked at him askance.

They sat on high barstools. Magg had to climb up, and her dress kept getting in the way. She looked at Emerson and said, "Are you going to help me?"

He lifted her up under the arms and placed her on the stool.

She said, "Trying to cop a feel from an old lady, eh? We have rooms for that, you know."

Emerson blushed. Elli laughed.

Magg whispered something to the bartender, and he set up four shot glasses, filling them with a thick green liquid. She took one and bid

Emerson and Elli to take theirs. She raised her glass and began to toast, but Emerson stopped her.

"Who's the fourth glass for?"

"The Domovoy, of course. We must give the Domovoy his share, or he would be offended."

"What are we toasting?"

"The Domovoy, of course." She turned to Elli and said, "Is he alright in the head? Seems a little slow."

They both smiled at Emerson. He blushed again.

Magg held up her glass and toasted: "To the Domovoy!"

Everyone at the bar joined the chorus and thundered, "TO THE DOMOVOY!" They stamped their feet in unison and broke into a boisterous cheer. They drank.

The liquid was warm and sweet. Soon after he'd swallowed it, he realized it was actually hot, so hot that he felt as though he was on fire from inside. Looking at Elli and Magg, he said, "What the hell was that?" His voice sounded higher, somehow squeaky and strained.

Elli burst out laughing.

Magg said, "We call it firefly fuel. You like?"

Emerson regained his voice and blinked. The room was no longer dark. Everything looked clean and new and bright. And the people were beautiful. All of them, Magg looked like a marble angel. He heard music; he felt like moving. It was amazing. His heart raced.

And as fast as it came, it went. The room dimmed down to the same flat darkness. The only sound was the low murmur of patrons and the squeaking and banging of beds in the floor above. The same redundant bass, off somewhere, everywhere, pumped and bumped in time with the sex. Magg said, "Want another?"

Emerson said, "No," at the same moment Elli said, "Yes."

Emerson said, "No." He raised his voice.

Elli said, "Fuck you. Yes."

Magg said, "Your father says no."

298

Elli spat back, "He's not my father."

Magg raised her finger, and the bartender poured three more, leaving the glass for the Domovoy. She said, "To health." They threw their drinks back into their mouths. Emerson poured his on the floor.

A man behind them said, "I saw that, pilgrim."

When Emerson and Elli turned around, the man stared at her, mouth open, eyes wide.

She said, "Michel."

He said, "Mew?"

Magg said, "Michel, come, drink with us."

Michel said, "I can't. But I will take my property." He reached out for Elli.

She pulled her arm out of his grip and said, "The fuck you will, Michel. You hurt me for the last time."

Michel moved fast. Emerson didn't anticipate how dangerous he was. But Elli bent his wrist back, knocking the knife to the floor. Michel produced a pistol and pointed it at Elli's face. He yelled, "YOU WERE ALWAYS MY PROPERTY, BITCH..."

Before Emerson could even stand, a short black crossbow arrow grew out of the side of his neck, spraying blood on several people at the bar. He was dead on the floor in a heartbeat. The crowd didn't notice; patrons just stepped over his body. Emerson never saw where it went.

Ana folded her weapon and reholstered it. She and Quinn crossed the rug and stood in front of Emerson and Elli. Ana said, "You looked like you needed a little help."

Elli said, "I had it under control, but thanks."

Magg looked from Elli to Ana and said, "Are any of you available? Red and black are our favorite colors." Quinn readjusted Marya's sling so she could nurse.

Magg jumped off her stool and ran to Quinn. "A baby? You have a baby?"

The entire room silenced. Men and women lined up to see her. Quinn lowered her so the dwarf could see too. Magg put her finger under Marya's chin and said, "I haven't seen a baby in decades."

One of the men introduced himself to Emerson. "Hi, I'm Chad. You're Emerson Lloyde. And this must be Elli Rattlesnake Quinn. We know all about you. How can I help?"

Emerson said, "I've heard you're the man to see for reactor pellets."

"How many you want?"

"How many can you get?"

"What are you trading?"

Emerson held up a shiny black cube similar to the one Chandler programmed himself into.

Chad said, "You can have as much as I've got for that. About 40,000, give or take."

Emerson shook his hand and said, "Deal."

They discussed delivery, and Chad left. Ten minutes later, a wild-eyed man in a broad, cowboy-style hat walked up to Magg and said, "Crikey, mate. Who's the buyer? A sheila, I hope."

Magg said, "Don't be an ass, Taylor. Talk like a normal human."

Taylor said, "Er um… yeah, sorry." He put out his hand. "I'm The Australian. Pleased."

Emerson noticed his fringe leather jacket. Most of the fringe had rotted away. He said, "We are going on a little expedition and need some difficult-to-find tools."

Magg said, "Speak freely. No one here cares what you do."

"Weapons, ammunition. We are going into the unknown."

Taylor grinned, slapped the bar, and called for whiskey. He said, "Why didn't you say so? We'll go have a look-see. Right after I finish me drink."

Quinn said, "Ana and I are going back. Marya needs a nap." Emerson kissed the baby's forehead, and they left.

Emerson, The Australian, and Elli left the brothel and crossed the cracked mud street. A legless old woman dressed in rags sat on a low, wheeled cart rattling a metal cup full of trinkets. She called to them, "Read your fortune for a bauble?"

Emerson and Turner ignored her, Elli bent and put the smooth stone she'd gotten from the Blue Hole baths in the cup. The crone had one milky eye that stared off onto the distance. The other was bright blue. She stared at Elli for a long moment and said, "The Western Seacoast. That's where you're heading. Keep your eyes open, girl. There's fortune and danger." She took Elli's hand and traced the lines in her palm. "And *love*. Dangerous love, I 'spect!" She cackled. She was still laughing as they walked away.

◆

The Australian's shack was dryer than most of the others Emerson had seen. It had an Interface lock on the door, and the only windows were short and near the high ceiling. Emerson was looking up at them when The Australian said, "One can't be too careful."

Elli found what looked to Emerson like a 1920s Tommy gun he'd seen in a black-and-white movie once, only it was thicker with a stubby barrel and some sort of coil in place of the ammo cartridge. She held the grip with her other hand under the fat short barrel. She said, "What does this run on?"

Taylor said, "That has a nuclear core."

"I need to fire it."

"Not possible now. Maybe later tonight after it's dark. That's a banned weapon."

Emerson said, "I need shells for a .38 and a .45."

Elli said, "I want this."

Emerson said, "What do you need that for?"

"I don't know. It just feels right."

Taylor returned with boxes of shells and said, "What else?"

"Plasma converter?"

He grinned. "I heard about that—The Authority is having a hemorrhage over those rifles. I can ask around, but everyone will know who wants it."

"See what you can quietly scare up by tonight when we come back to test the baby cannon."

Elli smiled and bent down to inspect a long-barreled pistol in a clear plastic case. Turner said, "You have a good eye for rare iron, girl." He opened the case and handed her the gun. "This is a .45 caliber Colt Single Action Army, Buntline Special."

Emerson said, "That's a ridiculously long barrel."

Elli said, "The name is pretty funny too. It's a gun. So what?"

"Sixteen inches. And this is a real one, assembled in 1876. You can shoot it if you want. It's loaded."

Elli hefted the big gun. "It's heavy," she said.

"Yeah, she takes a little getting used to, hell of a kick, too."

Outside, he set up a series of rusty cans and a few broken bottles along a rotting wood fence. Elli couldn't hold the massive pistol up with one arm; she had to use her other hand to support the barrel.

The Australian said, "The barrel gets hot after it's fired a few times. If you're gonna wield a Buntline, you gotta be strong."

Elli sighted down the barrel and fired four times. The first went wild; the second, third and fourth took two cans and the top of an antique amber longneck.

Turner said, "Damn, girl. You're some shot."

Emerson said, "She a natural."

Elli said, "I want it."

Emerson brought a small silver cylinder out of his pocket and held it up for Turner to see. He said, "You know what this is?"

"I do, and I'd call it a fair trade."

"It's a clean implant. You need a coder to make it function."

Turner grinned. "You let me worry about that."

They agreed to meet by the shoreline after dark. Emerson would fly over after he picked up the reactor pellets from Chad.

Elli said, "I need ammo."

"Yup. All included." He gave her an oak box for the pistol and two 100-round boxes of .45 ACP shells; he said, "They fire a standard lead bullet about 260 meters a second. These puppies will drop a grizzly."

Elli grinned.

◆

On the way back to the ship, Emerson asked, "What is your sudden infatuation with weapons, Elli?"

She didn't look at him. They continued walking. She said, "There's a war coming, Emerson. You feel it."

They continued on in silence. Emerson didn't know what was going to happen, but he was committed to crossing the Inland Sea and building a new life somewhere. He and those he loved would be pursued by a deadly hunter. He would always be looking over his shoulder. And still, he was more excited than he'd ever been. It dawned on him that Chandler knew he would always be opposed to the people in The City. It was as though he was fulfilling Chandler's dreams of independence and freedom. Chandler Estes wove those dreams into him; they were his dreams now. He was raised for this and happily accepted it.

The question was, now that he could see the costs of actually leaving, was this unknown freedom worth it? Was this the man he wanted to be? Was it too late to change that now? Boston Quinn had turned his eye on Emerson Lloyde. And though Lord Quinn had not found them yet, it was clear, Emerson felt it too. He was definitely coming.

◆

The transfer with Chad went smoothly. He met Ana in the woods a half mile from town. Emerson didn't want him to see The Black Mariah. Ana kept her crossbow out and nocked the whole time he unloaded the cases. When he was done, she gave him the cube. He said, "You're kinda cute, you know? How about a little…" He raised his eyebrows twice.

Ana cracked her neck and looked at her weapon. She looked back at him and sighed. "You are not that stupid, are you, Chad? Did I invite this behavior in some way? Or do you just imagine that because I have tits, I constantly want dick? Is there something magical about your specific dick, Chad? What in the ever-loving hell of this fucking fucked-up world ever gave you that idea, Chad?"

Chad backed away with his hands up.

Ana motioned with the crossbow. "Do you want somebody sniffing up your ass all the fucking time, thinking you're their property to do with as you wish? Nothing but a meat pocket? A goddammed fuck slave?"

"Whoa, whoa. It was just a suggestion. Don't get fucking hysterical, woman."

She said, "You should get going."

He walked away quickly, weaving between the trees, looking back. When he was out of sight, he shouted back, "Fucking bitch."

A short black arrow appeared in a tree next to his head. Chad began to run.

The Black Mariah landed a moment later. It took ten minutes to load the pellets. No one saw Chad hiding behind a stand of Douglas fir.

◆ ◆

The shore of the Inland Sea was rocky and rough. There was a sandy area about 100 meters from the water. White-capped waves as far as they could see in the moonlight slammed the coast, eroding the land. As they watched, large chunks of earth and rock fell into the churning foam.

The Australian was already there, sitting on a rock, the nuke gun in his lap. He said, "Nice shuttle. I hardly saw you until the door opened. Pretty snazzy, mate."

Emerson ignored him. He held a plasma rifle and watched the woods line. Turner gave the cannon to Elli and said to Emerson, "No-go on the converter. If you can get a hold of an 8,000 farad capacitor, you can make one..."

Elli interrupted him. "This is an Interface weapon, correct? So how do I adjust the power?"

"You don't; it's on, or it's off. This was a prototype. They never produced them in any quantity—too volatile. No, you just point, duck, and fire." He indicated the crashing shoreline. "Shoot that way, away from me."

The gun came alive when Elli touched it. She held it cradled in her arms, pointed at a pile of rock that had fallen into the churning water, and pulled the trigger. A red light lit on the top near the sight, and a low whine rose from inside. When the sound reached a nearly deafening pitch, a ball of silver matter shot out of the barrel with a FUMP noise. Static-like veins of electricity covered the rock, accompanied by a sizzling sound. The rock vanished. A few sparks remained, snapping in the air, swirling around like flies.

"Oh! We have to have this."

Emerson said, "I don't know what we have to trade for it."

Quinn stepped forward, removing her necklace, and held it out to The Australian. She said, "Will this be enough?"

He looked at the gem in his palm for a moment and said, "This is the biggest ruby I've ever seen."

Emerson said to Quinn, "Are you sure?"

Quinn said, "It was a gift from my father. I don't want it. Everything he touches is soaked in blood. Better to convert it to something useful."

Business concluded, Turner bid them a g'day and strode into the forest. The crew boarded the shuttle and flew to Dander's shack. Emerson wanted to leave the next morning. He slept under the stars. Mule was lying next to him when he woke. She'd brought two large rabbits. He butchered them and stored the meat in cold bags.

◆ ◆

The day was damp and cloudy, threatening rain. Leaves blew around their feet as they performed the final checks, and Emerson locked up the cabin. He got lost in thought remembering the first time he'd see Dander. The man connected him to Eggert, who gave him his ticket to fly. He said to himself, *I wonder if Chandler realized meeting an Enforcer pilot would be the beginning of the end*. He decided to ask the Cube. But that would have to be later. The rain and wind were increasing. He wanted to get above the clouds before the visibility dropped to zero; the temperature continued to fall. A dangerous storm was blowing in from the north.

The barometric alarm sounded, signaling plummeting pressure. He yelled, "Everybody in, now. The blizzard is here!"

The shuttle began to rise before Elli had buckled her harness. Emerson opened the windshield viewer. The snow was already thick. As they gained altitude, the size and ferocity of the storm filled the screen. Emerson hovered for a moment, turning a slow 360 to take in the forest of his youth; he might never see it again. Quinn sat next to him nursing Marya. When the reactors were fully charged, he shut down the stealth silencers, which didn't change the experience for the crew, but outside, the sound of The Black Mariah's powerful reactors at full power became a deafening high-pitched squeal that faded away as the craft picked up speed. He took one last look before the screen whited out and launched the craft out over the water.

◆ ◆ ◆

ADRIFT

"Fuel leak?" Emerson woke from a deep sleep; it was dark. Navigation showed: ERROR NO MAP. "How in hell is there a fuel leak and where the fuck are we?"

The cabin lights brightened slowly; the time was 3 a.m. City Standard. The ship's log registered a low fuel event and had automatically cut speed and power to nonessential systems, like lights for sleeping humans. Mule slept by Emerson's feet, unbothered by the fuel emergency.

Quinn was next to him. And said, "Marya's with Ana. What do we do? Can't we, like, put on suits and spacewalk?"

Emerson said, "You've been watching space operas, huh? No, we can't go outside the shuttle when it's flying. We are not in space."

Quinn thought about it for a moment and said, "The shuttle will float, right?"

Emerson didn't hear her. He was already imagining repairing a fuel leak on open water.

Quinn said, "Emerson. Do you hear me? Will the shuttle float?"

Ana arrived with Marya asleep in her arms. She said, "It should. Theoretically. At least the water won't get in."

Emerson said, "We are going to find out soon. We are below flight level. The shuttle will automatically set down now. I've never landed on water."

As the shuttle slowly descended, Emerson said, "I'm a little afraid of water."

Quinn said, "How afraid?"

"I become paralyzed. I used to just avoid it, but now the thought of anything bigger than a bathtub…"

Ana said, "But crossing this damn ocean is all you ever talked about. How can you be afraid of water?"

Elli said, "I get it. I never went in the water until Grendel took me to the baths. After that, I couldn't get enough. I'd live in the water if I could."

Ana said loudly, "Now you might die in the water."

Emerson yelled, "Quick! Strap Marya in her own seat. Make it as tight as you can. Put a pillow between her and the straps." They scrambled around strapping in. Emerson gripped his arm rests.

The shuttle touched the water, sinking several meters under the surface. The sudden deceleration was cushioned by the remaining power in the ship's inertial dampening system. That system was completely offline when the shuttle buoyed to the surface. Anything not contained was thrown up and into the bulkhead when the craft righted itself.

The people were strapped in and escaped injury. With the exception of a few cups and a sack of Marya's used nappies, everything stayed put. Except Mule. She was taken by surprise. Not completely; she was more aware than that. When Emerson initially woke up, she felt his anxiety. By the time everyone was near, she could tell it was serious. But she had no reference point in her experience to anticipate what happened. She found herself suddenly weightless and rushing up toward the ceiling, which she hit hard enough to knock her unconscious. No bones were broken, yet, but after The Black Mariah rushed to the surface, it rolled to the right. Mule, who was suspended four or five meters from the ceiling, met the port bulkhead on its way to balance. Emerson couldn't argue with the science; it was predictable. But he blamed himself immediately and irrevocably. He should have seen it; he should have known. Her injuries could have been prevented.

Mule fell to the floor; her hindquarters caught on a seat and flipped her body over for one last insult before hitting the floor. Blood trickled from her mouth. The sharp broken bone of her right foreleg stuck out of the mangled fur, gleaming white in the LED lights. The lights blinked once and then went out.

Quinn said, "Oh my Goddess, is she alright?" She bent to where she thought Mule was and felt around for her fur. "She's really banged up."

Emerson took a breath. He felt dizzy, but that might have been from lack of oxygen. The shuttle was floating. Luckily, the water was calm.

Quinn said, "Are we trapped? Don't fucking lie to me."

He said, "Power has failed and all systems stopped, but no, everything is manual now. We need to find a way to recharge. Grab a temporary light and see to Mule first."

He opened the outside cameras and fed them to the screens around the front half of the shuttle while Ana and Elli tended to Mule. It was dark outside. The power was at 0.5 percent; it would fail completely in a moment. The higher views showed endless water in every direction. There wasn't much more to see. The mid, lower, and bottom cameras were underwater and black besides a few green bubbles.

He checked the ship's vitals. He checked the people's vitals. He said, "Shit. I hate water." He was breathing too fast; he had to concentrate to keep from hyperventilating.

Elli turned on a portable handheld light and pointed it at Mule. She said, "Hold this," and Ana took it. Elli felt the big cat, pushing her fingers into her body, locating spots where heat or disrupted tissues would tell their story. Emerson had never seen her do this.

Ana smoothed the cat's whiskers and murmured calming words in her sleeping ear.

Elli said, "Doctor Pam taught me this. Apparently, I possess a rare sensitivity. Me. Do you believe it? But she was right. I got pretty good at diagnosis after the invasion."

They set and splinted Mule's fractured leg and bandaged her wounds. Emerson administered an anesthetic and an antibiot injection. They shaved patches of fur and rubbed a topical gel into her bruises. Without diagnostics, only time would show if there were internal injuries. At least her blood pressure was steady.

Emerson removed a mobile power supply from a storage bin, climbed on the backs of the center seats, and opened a panel in the ceiling. A moment later, the cool lake air flooded in, replacing the stale oxygen with a green watery smell. Emerson hoisted himself up and out to look around. He had to crouch. The water was close, too close to stand up in the wind. It had to be blowing eight to ten knots. There was no land in any direction. The sky was grey; the water was a deeper shade of the same color. He crawled on his hands and knees to the open port and called down, "Give me a scope, please." It took all his strength to crouch outside in the stiff wind.

He determined that the shuttle was drifting at about twelve knots, twenty-two kilometers per minute. They were moving south, toward the ocean. The water was only 100 meters deep, but it ran a chilly four degrees C. He found a single group of GPS satellites and copied the coordinates. They were 600 kilometers from the gulf. Before shutting the scope off, he gauged the sunrise to be about ten minutes away.

Back inside, he laid out a plan. He said, "We need to recharge the batteries. We can rig some solar panels together on top of the shuttle and let the sun do it for us. Then we need to assess our food stores."

Quinn and Elli did a food inventory while Ana and Emerson connected the solar cells together and ran a cable into the access panels. Black wires trailed on the floor between the seats. A mist had started. Emerson closed the door as far as he could, but rain was still coming through.

Elli and Quinn handed out jerky and juice. Quinn chewed on a licorice root to give to Marya once it was mashed and soggy; she was already teething. While they rested, Emerson said, "There is a way we could feed reactor pellets into the tanks at the bottom of the shuttle."

Ana said, "Do tell. I figured you'd find a way out of this."

Emerson said, "Well, I didn't." He went on to explain, "Someone needs to swim under the shuttle and attach a hose to the fuel door, and it's not going to be me. I don't swim. I can open it from inside, and we can put a vacuum on the hose to remove the water. Then the fuel intake pump will suck a packet of pellets into the tank. We seal the door and power up the reactors."

"What about the leak?" asked Ana.

"We'll have to wait until we are on dry land to fix it. Hopefully we'll make it."

Ana said, "Who's going to dive under the shuttle in this nasty green water?" She munched on a cracker and asked Quinn, "What are these? They're amazing."

Quinn said, "A doctor I know, or thought I knew, put them in Marya's baby sack before I left. I found them when we got to Blue Hole. A woman, Bette Craine, in The City's Birth Corps created them from an old family recipe stashed in a book. Morning crackers, they're called. I lived on them when I was pregnant."

Elli said, "Fuck it. I'll go. How hard can it be?"

◆

Emerson hooked a rope ladder from the hatch over the top of the shuttle to the water. The rain ended, and a blurry sun burned through the haze. The air was still damp and cold. He fit Elli with his helmet, saying, "This will extend your oxygen for a solid ten minutes—that should be plenty of time. Tie this rope around your waist so you don't get lost." They climbed through the hatch and onto the roof.

Elli said, "You don't need to hold my hand, *Daddy*. I know this is hard for you."

He said, "I want to hold your hand. I'm the closest thing to a father that you have."

She said, "I wasn't kidding," and smiled.

Once the helmet was sealed, they talked over the intercom.

Elli stripped off her clothes, grabbed the fill pipe—a twenty-millimeter-wide hose with a flared magnetic end—and tucked it under her arm. She said, "Wish me luck."

Emerson said, "There is a red indicator light next to the fuel door. Once it's open, you need to snap the hose in place as fast as possible. If there is too much water in it, I won't be able to purge it with the vacuum. Once it's attached, get out of there. I can do the rest through The Interface."

She jumped in and dove under. Emerson could see what she saw through the cam in the helmet, mostly dark green water. He asked if she was okay. Elli said, "It's fucking cold."

That was an understatement. It was freezing. When she hit the water, the shock actually made her lose consciousness for a moment. Her arms and legs threatened to cramp.

Emerson said, "Are you okay? Your heart rate went crazy."

Elli found her voice and said, "I'm fine. Now shut up."

She used the maintenance handles to pull her body down under the fuselage, but she had to hold the pipe in one arm, so she was handicapped. Plus, she couldn't feel her hands or feet. It was hard to navigate with one hand. The red light was dim, the water cloudy. Suspended algae drifted around her, sticking to the face shield. When she got close to the door, she saw one of the bottom cameras. Emerson said, "I see you. Get ready." He opened the door.

Elli pushed the flared end of the hose onto the opening, but it wouldn't catch. She had to use both hands and kick to get enough leverage. The flare slid around the opening but would not engage. Emerson said, "We may have to purge the pipe and try again."

Elli ignored him. She'd begun to perspire inside the helmet. The salty sweat ran into her eyes, blinding her. She grabbed a handle and, using her other arm, jockeyed the hose into position. She jerked her body sideways to try and leverage the mechanism to engage. Her helmet snagged on the fuel door. The hose attached with a snap.

Emerson said, "That's it—come on back!" He started the vacuum. Green water belched out onto the shuttle floor. The pipe was ready.

Elli said, "I can't move. I'm hooked on the fuel door."

"Shit, don't move. If that door breaks off, we're screwed. The reactor will not engage until it is sealed."

The oxygen alarm sounded. Emerson said, "You have thirty seconds of air left."

Elli said, "I'm taking it off." The transmission ended when she broke the seal.

Elli took a deep breath with the last of the air in the helmet and pulled the emergency release lever. Water flooded the inside. It was so cold she nearly gasped, sucking water into her lungs. She slipped out of the helmet and unhooked it from the door. She desperately needed air. She could not leave Emerson's helmet. Using the handles, she pulled herself out from under the shuttle and up with one hand. Emerson took the helmet from her when she surfaced near the ladder.

He helped her up and guided her to the hatch. The reactor was filled and the hose removed by the time Elli dropped down into the ship. Ana embraced her tightly.

She said, "Oh my god, I thought you were dead." They stayed in the embrace; Elli was still wet, soaking Ana's clothes. Nether seemed to notice. When Elli pulled away, Ana kissed her full on the mouth. They stayed locked together for a full minute.

Emerson closed the hatch and started the reactor. He said, "You might want to get strapped in."

Elli and Ana stayed locked together for a minute longer. Ana helped her get dressed and into a cot. She was asleep before the reactor was fully charged. The shuttle lifted out of the water and rose above the fog. When they were at about 2,000 meters, Emerson opened the windshield. Quinn and Ana cheered.

Near the western horizon, he could see the jagged peaks of a mountain range. They glowed pink in the misty light. He set a course for it and said, "Land ho!"

◆ ◆ ◆

Perr Sullivan and his assistant, Cam, had been scouring the countryside since the erasure of Blue Hole. The Lord, Boston Quinn, commissioned them personally, and they answered only to him. Neither could fly a shuttle, so a pilot had been assigned, sworn to secrecy upon pain of death.

They had unrestricted access to any resources they wanted. Beginning at the farthest outposts first, they interviewed most of the indigents and all of the Enforcers. Boston had no reason to believe that his daughter survived, but he had a feeling. Perr and Cam were sent to confirm it one way or the other.

After traveling to Chandler Estes's homeplace and finding nothing left but a five-kilometer-wide dirt trench where the house was supposed to be, they began at outpost number one and had been doing nonstop interviews since. The weekly reports were always the same: no news. Until they arrived at Outpost 212 two days after The Black Mariah embarked on her Inland Sea passage. Splinter feigned ignorance, as did Magg and The Australian. They were all nomads and drifters, experts at deflecting questions and misleading interrogators. Lying was like drinking water for them, somewhat distasteful but often necessary.

Chad was a different story. He'd been stealing Enforcer supplies and trading them in town for personal gain for nearly five years. His opium habit wasn't nearly as costly as his tab at The Fly Saloon. And of course, Sullivan and Cam's reputation preceded them, leaving Chad in a constant state of anxiety. This required more frequent indulgence in his vices, costing more. He was caught in a whirlpool, spiraling down a dark hole. The gossip was thick with rumors. They could see into your soul, they possessed a second sense, if they suspected anything they could torture you with truth serum, they could kill you on the authority of Lord Quinn. But all they really did was ask questions and send the answers to Quinn.

By the time of his interview, Chad was blubbering like an idiot. He told them everything: how he met with Emerson Lloyde and his crew and that Elli Rattlesnake was among them. He told them Ana tried to shoot him in the head. He admitted to punching a hole in their fuel tank.

When the news reached Boston later that day, he ordered Perr and Cal to bring Chad to The City. When the shuttle set down in the courtyard of Founder's Quarter, five Elite Guard shackled Chad and dragged him, in chains, to kneel before Lord Quinn.

Lord Quinn had begun cultivating his image as royalty. If the Middles believed that he was retaliating against his daughter's kidnappers, he would be praised. If it turned out she was dead, he'd make her a martyr. He sat on a raised dais in an intricately carved chair painted with gold leaf. He gave up the hairpiece, proudly displaying his polished, bald pate and had taken to wearing fur-collared robes. A brass scepter with a massive jewel mounted at the head rested against the chair arm. He rapped it on the stone floor, and the room went silent.

He said, "Tell me, Chad, why would you want to kill my daughter and my heir?"

Chad's mind raced. He'd known it was Elli Rattlesnake, and he knew the enforcers were looking for her. He was angry at that other bitch, Ana. She shot a fucking arrow at his head. All he was looking for was a little coochie.

Quinn banged his brass pole on the stone and yelled, "Answer me!"

Chad stuttered, "I didn't think, sir, lord. I—I was mad at the other one. I just wanted a kiss and—and…"

Quinn stood and dropped the scepter. It rattled on the floor. He pulled the Luger from his belt and said, "You were mad? You got your dick bent out of shape, and so you drained the fuel out of my daughter's aircraft so she would crash into the water out in the middle of the Inland Sea. Right? You murdered my only fucking daughter, a lord, your future queen, because some twat from the nonexistent village of Blue Hole refused to spread her legs for your ham-handed advances."

Chad looked at the floor and said, "Yes," so quietly that Quinn could hardly hear. But Chad raised his head and took a breath. And looking directly at Lord Quinn, he said, "But I would never willingly hurt your daughter, sir. You must know I have always been a loyal Enforcer. I took the oath and…"

Quinn said, "Oh fuck me!" and shot Chad in his face.

◆ ◆

Emerson monitored the fuel level. After an hour, the levels were just below half. He thought, *The hole must be getting bigger.* A sighting through the scope estimated four hours until they reached the mountains, but he assumed the shore was several kilometers closer. Any way he looked at it, they only had another hour of reserves before the ship began to shut down again.

◆ ◆ ◆

THE WEST

"Water, water everywhere." Quinn was looking out the windshield with Marya sitting in her lap, leaning back against her mother's chest.

Emerson said, "And not a drop to drink."

She said, "You know Coleridge?"

"Chandler was eclectic."

"I received what my father thought was a *classical education.*"

"Grandpa believed that 'The Rime of the Ancient Mariner' was essential to a complete education. But I never got to talk to him about his childhood."

"You could, you know. Let's conjure him up and ask him."

Emerson set The Interface cube on the shuttle's dashboard and activated it. Their surroundings instantly changed. The three of them were sitting in front of the fire at Chandler's cabin. Before he had a chance to speak, Ana and Elli appeared.

Elli said, "Holy shit." She grabbed a chair back for balance.

Ana said, "It took a moment to figure out what happened. You're still flying the shuttle, right?"

Chandler said, "You're flying? Damn, boy, you did it!"

Emerson said, "This is the weirdest thing. Yes, I am still in control of The Black Mariah though my implant. I don't know exactly how to

317

explain it. The shuttle is on autopilot, but I am monitoring everything. Meanwhile, instead of being in the cockpit, I'm with my dead grandfather in a house that we just watched a tornado obliterate. I feel like I'm two people in one body."

Chandler said, "That's diabolical! So, you're saying that my house is gone? Hmm. I guess we're lucky I made a copy in here." He laughed. "Where ya headed?"

"We are seeking others in the West."

"So, you crossed the Inland Sea, eh? Good deal. What do you think you'll find?"

"What you told me was there: a society of people who live in accord with nature, thriving on the abundance of the planet, practicing kindness and cooperation."

Chandler said, "You won't find them. They're long gone."

"What do you mean? You told me stories about them my whole life. I thought that everything you taught me came from them. You always called them *our people.*"

"I know, son. They will be."

"Who were our real people, then?"

Chandler sat forward in his chair and looked into Emerson's face. He shook his head and said, "I guess it's time you know."

"Know? Know what?"

"The whole story, Emmer."

◆

"I told you about becoming an Enforcer when I first came to the City, right?"

Emerson nodded; the others settled in. Chandler looked somehow greyer, faded. He wasn't older; if anything, he was years younger than when

Emerson last saw him alive. But this was a side of Chandler Emmer had never seen, not the confident grandfather he'd relied on.

Chandler sighed. Emerson stepped back from the simulation. He briefly contemplated ending the sim and avoiding whatever it was that made Chandler look like that. It was a passing impulse.

Chandler said, "When the world collapsed and I came to The City with my mom and dad, I was conscripted into the Enforcers. I was a new recruit, but I was anything but green. By that point in my life, I had become a competent hunter. The people I had grown up among were self-sufficient. I knew how to take care of myself.

"I found a lifelong friendship with another new cadet, Eric Eggert."

Emerson drew breath but hesitated to interrupt his grandfather. It was an old habit. Quinn didn't know anything about that. She blurted, "Eggert? Our Eggert? He was an Enforcer with you?"

Chandler was unperturbed, Emerson thought, *Maybe things aren't so much the way I remembered them.* He continued, "He was younger than me, sixteen then. I was twenty-five. Your grandmother was eighteen, but we hadn't met yet.

"Yeah, Emerson. Eggert was the Enforcer who flew me up to get you."

"He recruited me."

"I figured. He had his eye on you; we'd spoken."

"Wait, Grandpa. You were in contact with people in The City? How come I never knew?"

"Well, damn, boy. What kind of an old man would I be if couldn't keep a few secrets from a child?

"Maybe too many secrets. But I did what I thought was best. I won't apologize for that." He stretched and said, "Anyway, we're getting ahead of our story. I worked with the Enforcers for a few years, but my heart was never in it. They closed the gates and made us into thugs for the Lords. It was hardly tolerable. That's when they began playing with behavior modification. Before experimenting on the Middles, they tried it out on us.

"I met your grandmother at the annual Enforcers' dinner in Founder's

Quarter. Ciara Coke. She was having a heated argument with an older man. I learned later he was her father, Jules, one of the original Founders. They seldom agreed when he was coherent, and by the time I met him, he was hardly ever understandable.

"I must have had my mouth open. After all these years, I must admit that woman was captivating. I believe I fell in love with her that night. You have her eyes, Emerson. We drank and talked and ate and danced…"

"You dance?" Emerson was shocked. Quinn laughed.

Chandler smiled. "I did back then. We talked till late…"

Quinn interjected, "I don't recognize the name Coke."

"Oh, that's 'cause your father rewrote the history so he could take credit for their contributions. Which justified erasing them. It's an old game."

"Yes, that sounds like Boston."

He went on, "Ciara'd been educated before the collapse and was doing advanced Interface programming design. Real cutting-edge stuff. I wanted to be a machinist. I loved sculpting metal, forging forms out of function. Together, we designed toolsets for Interfaces and connected them together. But I guess you get the picture. We became inseparable. And since her mom was gone and her dad was feeble, I just moved into their apartment. Jules died soon after.

"The other Lords didn't think much of me. She took my last name, Estes, to try and help me fit in some. They never accepted us, and frankly, we didn't think much of them either. While I lived there, I started the archive for books, films, and music. Ciara designed a cleaner, smaller implant. But it was always tense. They wanted her working in governance. She didn't agree with how they were constructing the society. They wanted me gone.

"We decided it was time to leave. The Lords couldn't do anything to Ciara; she was a born Elite. I was only tolerated because of her. When we announced our departure, they banished me. Eggert helped scout the location for the homeplace and brought salvage to construct buildings. We spent twenty years there."

Chandler's sim looked off into the distance, his eyes unfocused.

Emerson took a moment to check vitals on the Black. They were still over the ocean. Fuel was getting low.

Chandler said, "Your grandmother didn't think she could have children anymore. But when she was forty-nine, we became pregnant with your mom. That same summer, Ciara developed a weird bullseye rash. Before the first snows that year, she was hardly able to get out of bed. We decided it must have been some sort of insect bite. I never liked any one of those flying stinging things.

"We were scared she'd lose the baby. Eggert brought her back to The City. She planned to come back to the homeplace after the birth, once she was healed. But that day never arrived. Oh, we tried to reconnect, but her health was always in a state of flux. Eric snuck me back in after she died, when your mom was only six. She'd been living with the Serlings. Another Elite family. I thought they poisoned her against me. But she didn't know me. And even after she moved back in, we were like oil and water. After living together for years, we still couldn't get along. She wouldn't consider coming back to the homeplace; her friends were in The City. Barbarians lived outside the wall. She was young. I ignored her. I was a shitty parent.

"When she was sixteen, she ran. We searched but never found a trace. Being a founder's child, her implant was locked. If she wanted to stay missing, she would. I didn't hear from her again.

"Eggert discovered that she and Marc escaped to a tiny Juice Hacker community in the north. She and your dad dug out their implants to escape The City. But living, let alone raising a child in the northern suburbs, was rough. They lived in squalor. After Marc was beat up pretty badly, Deborah Soo decided they should move back and take their chances.

"From what we can piece together, Marc patched a fiberglass fishing boat and entered The City by rowing up the center of the reservoir. Of course, nobody knew anything about boats, and Marc's makeshift oars broke in the middle of the water, leaving them to drift aimlessly for hours. They didn't anticipate the drones that guarded the shoreline. After demanding authorization codes, the drones perceived them as a threat and riddled the craft with rockets, killing Soo and Marc, but leaving you alive in the half sunken boat."

Ana said, "Oh my God, that must have been horrible, Em."

He said, "It's not like I remember. I was only five."

Chandler said, "It was just dumb luck that Eric was doing patrols that night. He rescued you and brought you to the Founders' hospital. You were in shock with hypothermia, and they stabilized you. He came and got me, and well, the rest is your memory."

Quinn said, "So many things make sense now. You were always an Elite."

"By matrilineal bloodline. But if it weren't for Doctor Sailor's help, we'd have never have gotten you out."

Emerson said, "She locked my implant when she gave it to me."

Elli said, "I guess we're all orphans."

Ana passed Marya to Quinn and gave Emerson a hug. She said, "I'm sorry about your mom. I know you never knew her, but still…"

Emerson said, "Why did you keep this from me my whole life, Chandler? Wasn't I entitled to know who I was?"

Chandler looked at the floor and said, "I can't apologize for my past, boy. I did my best. I thought it was too terrible for a boy. Hell, it was too terrible for an old man. By the time you were older, I—I could never find the right time."

Emerson stood and said, "Damn. I thought there was some place to go home to, that we had people, that we came *from* somewhere."

Chandler said, "Ah, son. You know you can never go home. The home we remember is gone."

Ana said, "Besides, Emerson, you *do* come from somewhere. You come from *us*." She patted her heart. "You are already where you belong."

The shuttle alarm began to ring. Emerson checked and said, "Land. 150 kilometers. We should be there in a half hour."

Ana said, "How much fuel is left?"

"It will be close."

Quinn said, "We should pick up stuff laying around the ship. Strap Mule in and tie down anything that could become a projectile."

Emerson was conflicted. He said, "We have to go, Grandpa, but what are you saying?"

Chandler stood and hugged Emerson. He said over the boy's shoulder, "There is no society in the West except a handful of old men and women like me, living alone and as far away from each other as possible. You are the future, Emerson. You will be the beginning of the people I told you stories about. You are my hope for the future."

Emerson looked his grandfather in the eye, said, "We're not done," and ended the simulation. They were back in the shuttle, cruising 300 kilometers an hour at an altitude of 5,000 kilometers. The vertigo was momentary. He opened the windshield shutters. The vista before them glowed. The image began with the shore of the Inland Sea. It was much calmer on this side; the water lapped lazily on a gradually sloping shoreline. Grasses began after the sand ended and covered a band about a kilometer wide, bordering the shore as far as they could see in both directions.

A white birch forest began at the edge of the grass. From their decreasing altitude, they could see the foothills to the mountains rising like the humps of green-backed behemoths from the ground. The snowcapped peaks loomed behind them.

Emerson said, "Let's hope it's solid under the grass. It could be marshy, which would be worse than open water. We'd sink down too far to get at the fuel door."

Quinn said, "What did your grandfather mean by that?"

Emerson said, "I don't know. I think he believes we are supposed to start a civilization, but I need to talk to him some more. He taught me to take things slow."

The shuttle was at about 2,000 meters when they crossed over the beach. Emerson routed the front cameras to a screen and tipped them down to project the grass rushing under them. He said, "I want to get as close to the woods as possible where the ground will likely be dry."

He slowed down. Fuel was nearly zero; a low altitude notification flashed at him.

Within a few moments, the craft set down. After scanning for infrared signatures, he opened the side door. Elli brought her rifle. Quinn held

Marya. When Ana and Emerson stepped down, Mule howled behind them. Emerson called, "We'll be right back."

The grasslands stretched to the water and as far as they could see to the north and south. The sea filled the rest of the space to the eastern horizon in an icy grey-green. Ana said, "This is amazing." The sky was cloudless and azure. The air was warmer than they expected; a quick check verified that they had drifted nearly 100 kilometers south. The autumn here hadn't even begun yet.

Elli was entranced by the mountains. She pointed and said, "Are we going there?"

Emerson said, "That was the plan before I found out that we're probably alone."

Quinn said, "I don't want to disrespect Chandler, but I doubt he knew *all* the people in the West. I mean, we can ask the sim, but really, how would that be possible?"

He said, "It's all speculation. You know what's not? Repairing the fuel tank and getting out of here. I feel vulnerable in this much open."

The leak was an easy fix. All shuttles had wielders, sealants, and cutters to repair metal tears, breaks, and punctures. Emerson patched Chad's sabotage in less than thirty minutes. Ana and Elli explored the edge of the forest. The floor was cool, dark, and bare; the canopy blocked most of the sunlight. Elli saw a small animal move in the shadows and aimed her rifle but didn't fire.

Emerson had the fuel topped off and the reactor purged and ready before they returned. He and Quinn had written a list of necessities, which included washing clothes and making diapers. Marya was growing; she would want more than milk soon. It was the first time they'd actually considered life outside of a support society, and the list was huge. Everything was essential. And the prospect of satisfying all their needs was daunting.

He moved the shuttle just inside the shade of the woods. They made a fire and roasted the rabbits Mule had brought them at Dander's camp. Ana set the onboard computer to make a rudimentary map out of the new geological data they'd gathered while crossing the 1500-kilometer wide

Inland Sea. She displayed the map on the main screen. The blank areas were filled in by old remnant maps archived in Chandler's data.

Elli said, "That fortuneteller told me I was going to The Western Seacoast. Is that it on the map up there? She said it was dangerous and that I'd find love."

Ana looked at her but said nothing. Emerson said, "That's about a five-hour flight. But I would guess that the coastline looks pretty different now."

Quinn said, "We need to make a camp somewhere. Elli's the only one who's washed in days."

Elli said, "That water was gross. My entire body is covered with dried green slime."

Emerson said, "I've gotten used to the way we smell, but I am sure it's rank. We need to find a sheltered spot. Ana, can you set up a scanner routine to search for structures?" After they finished the meal, Ana and Elli helped Mule get outside. The big cat didn't like the splint and began chewing it. Elli gave her a half-sedative injection and fed her some rabbit before she fell back to sleep. They packed up and began searching for a place to camp.

The ship was hovering at 1,000 meters, creeping over the trees. For the first hour, they saw nothing. It was as if the past fifty years had erased all traces of people out here. They saw plenty of wildlife. Emerson proposed that the majority of farms were to the east; there was much less soil degradation here before the collapse.

Quinn said, "But it was dry here before. When the Inland Sea formed, probably from sea-level rise, the desert was transformed."

Emerson said, "Except that the Inland Sea isn't saltwater. But yeah, the land was rehydrated and given a fifty-year rest."

Ana said, "It doesn't look anything like the pictures I've seen of this area."

The search program pinged and showed a crosshair on a building fifty kilometers to the north. Emerson changed course. A minute later, a four-story tall cement block structure with a tin roof appeared. They landed in a clear area beside a series of garage-type openings. The doors themselves were missing, and the interior, a maintenance building of some sort, was empty except for piles of dry leaves and a thick layer of dirt. Elli and Ana went to explore the upper levels. Quinn and Emerson located a spring and tested the water, which was clean. Quinn said, "Hey, do you hear that?"

It was the sound of falling water. A short walk through the trees led them to the bank of a stream. It opened up into a shallow pond before continuing on toward the Inland Sea. Emerson tested this water and found it clean as well.

When they met back at the building, Ana said, "The roof is in good shape. There's grass and bushes growing on it, but it seems secure, and I found no obvious leaks."

Mule hobbled out of the shuttle and stretched in a beam of sunlight. Emerson scratched her behind the ears. He told the others about the creek and the pond. Within five minutes, everyone, except Emerson, was naked and in the water. He brought a bar of soap and a couple towels. But he stood no closer than five meters from the edge.

Quinn teased him, "Come on in, baby. I can smell you from here. "

Ana said, "It's no deeper than the baby pools at the Blue Hole Baths."

Emerson reluctantly pulled off his shirt and pants, socks, and boots. He stepped to the edge and put his toe in the water. He shivered and pulled it out. "Nope. Not interested."

Quinn said, "Don't be afraid, baby. It's okay. We got you." She reached up and took his hands. He stepped carefully into the shallow and stood ankle deep.

He said, "This is good. I'm in."

Elli said, "Bullshit, Lloyde. C'mere!" She grabbed his foot and pulled him into the water; he thrashed helplessly.

Ana yelled, "Stand the hell up, Emerson!"

He got to his feet and stood. The water came up to his waist. The others stood too. He began to laugh. Everyone joined him. He laughed harder. His laugh transformed into tears. The others gathered close and hugged him. He cried on Ana and Elli's shoulder. Marya reached out and grabbed his ear. He cried and cried and cried. And he remembered.

◆

Emerson sat in his mother's lap. They were on the water. The sky was black, scattered over by blue and silver glass-chip stars. She was agitated, and he tried to calm her by pressing his face into her breast. She hugged him tighter. He watched the band of the Milky Way turn in space like a cosmic clock, and he slipped in and out of dreams.

His father cursed; the stick he was using to move the water snapped off. Marc said, "We're adrift."

A moment later, his mom said, "What's that?" Her heart beat faster; she hugged him tighter.

Marc said, "Drones. We must have drifted too close to shore." He stood and raised his hands, yelling, "We surrender. Don't shoot."

The night exploded into orange flashes and fireballs. His father was struck several times by the guard drone's rockets. Marc looked at his young son, opened his mouth, and collapsed face down into the boat. Water already filled around his body. Deborah Soo jumped up, shoving Emerson against the bulkhead, and ran to Marc, covering him with her body. A second volley of rockets killed her where she lay. Water flooded. Within moments, the boat was half submerged. A few boxes floated alongside his parents' dead bodies in the greasy black water.

The sound of the drones receded. Emerson climbed up on the seat and crouched, shivering in the cool night air. The entire interchange took less than a minute. The boy squeezed his eyes shut and shivered, numb in the endless blackness.

A long time later, a light shone on him; he opened his eyes. The screaming whistle of the shuttle made him cover his ears; his hands and clothes were wet with bloody water. His teeth chattered. The reactor went silent as the craft hovered above the water next to the half-sunken boat. A doorway traced itself in blue on the hull and opened into a staircase. A balding man in a green uniform reached both hands toward him, lifting him into the warm blue glow of the cabin. The man sucked his teeth and said, "Well, hello, Emerson Lloyde, glad to finally meet you."

◆ ◆ ◆

327

BEGIN AGAIN

After a few weeks, the nights got colder. They woke to frosted dew in the mornings; it melted off by ten. They calculated the differences between when the sun rose in The City and where they were and adjusted the shuttle's clocks. The quality of light seemed different, but nobody could articulate precisely what had changed.

Emerson and Quinn spent most of their waking time together. She often accompanied him while he built things or did tasks. They talked about their respective upbringings and the hypocrisy of the Lords running The City. When she got going, her rants became eloquent and impassioned. Emerson would stop what he was doing and often clapped when she was done.

He confided in Quinn that as a child, he worried about his grandfather dying and leaving him alone in the woods. "The scars of that trauma make me hyper-protective. Being a smart kid, I was always calculating possibilities in advance to protect my fragile young self in case I was abandoned. The more angles I could see, the safer I felt. But since I moved to Blue Hole, I've recognized that there really is unconditional love in this world. And you and Elli and Anna have saved me more times than I can count. It made me see that life and love are transitory. Life without the love of others is a cold and hollow existence."

Quinn kissed him suddenly, distracting him from the controls for a second. When she broke away, she said, "I knew I had a reason to love you, Emerson Lloyde."

Ana worked on the interior structure. They decided to spend the last warm months at the block building, which was what they had come to call it without discussing the name. Each of them had a private space that Ana called their cubbies, though Elli often slept with Ana. Quinn stayed with Marya until the baby was deep asleep, and then she'd get into Emerson's bedroll. More often than not, he would sleep outside with a fire burning.

They hunted the small game surrounding the camp. Mule recovered enough to bring fish back regularly. The days got shorter and the nights colder. Emerson cut up an old tank to fabricate a wood stove for indoors. The ship's calendar said it was late November, but the leaves were still on the trees, and days were hot enough to swim when the sun was out. They spent time together in the little pond. On any afternoon, they could lay out on a smooth rock in the sun to dry.

Emerson told Quinn that he realized that he was actually happy. She hugged him. Their relationship was more like close friends than a couple. On one of their exploration flights together, he said, "I've always had a feeling that I am supposed to do something special. Chandler hinted at it all the time. But I got to tell you, Quinn, I have no idea what I'm doing."

She waited until he had talked himself out on the subject.

"I mean, Chandler gave me this vision of freedom, and now I'm stuck with it. Problem is I can't tell whose vision it is anymore."

When she was sure he had finished, she gave him a side hug with one arm and said, "We've made a beautiful, exceptionally healthy child. I think that makes you pretty special."

He and Ana were also close. She invited him over to her cubby for the night occasionally. He told her he'd had way more sex with Quinn before the baby. "I'm not complaining," he said. "Somehow, it seems right."

Ana told him she loved Elli, but she was still in love with him. She said, "It's a slow simmering kind of love, with high and low cycles." That night, it was particularly high.

The days got colder. One morning, the ground was snow-dusted. The temperature didn't go over ten degrees all day, and the next morning, the pond had a scrim of ice. Emerson announced that it was probably time to leave.

Quinn ribbed him. "You are such a confident leader! Probably?"

He ignored her. She turned to Ana and said, "He loves it."

Camp was cleaned up and the shuttle packed by sundown. Emerson and Elli made a huge fire and ate Mule's latest catch of rainbow trout and bass. Emerson brought out a quart jar of hooch he'd been saving, and they drank it all. The fire burned all night.

Quinn held out her hand. The nuggets in her open palm flickered in the firelight. She said, "I've been saving these for the right moment." They each ate several. By the time the moon was directly overhead, they were whirling and dancing, shedding clothes and spinning around the fire. The tension of the past few months poured into the obsidian sky as they spun, rising in sparks and ash, swirling orange and red.

The frenetic dancers sang and stepped wildly. Mule, still not fully healed, rested on her haunches a safe distance away, lashing her tail in the fine dirt behind her.

The next morning, Emerson woke up from a startling and disjointed dream to find himself under a blanket with Quinn and Ana. Mule was at their feet, snoring. He eased himself out and realized he was naked. Everyone else was unclothed as well except Marya, who was wrapped in a loincloth made from someone's t-shirt.

Ana was awake next. And since Quinn slept when Marya slept, they let her. She was often up when everyone else was down. Emerson reheated a cup of tea and put on pants. He sat in a swivel chair near the makeshift bed and blew on his tea.

He said, "I had the damnedest dream. We were dancing around a huge bonfire, and we were zozzled. The air was moist. Drums rumbled from somewhere; the beat was intense. The next thing I know, you and I are kissing. And we're all naked, and then Quinn was there kissing me and—and, well…"

He stopped. Ana smiled at him. He looked back and said, "It wasn't a dream, was it."

Ana shook her head. "No." Quinn came up behind him and hugged him around the neck.

Elli arrived from the pond, drying her hair. The air was brisk. She said, "I hope you guys had fun. I did. While you were getting busy under the covers, I went down to the clearing and watched the stars cross the sky until the sun came up. I did a cold plunge. It was glorious!"

◆ ◆

The flight over the mountains was breathtaking. They decided to head directly to the coast. Following the premonitions of the fortuneteller could wait. They landed on a beach with a deep blue ocean breaking on the white sand shore. The cove was a protected spot surrounded by high cliffs. The only approach, other than by sea or air, was a sheer drop over the deadly-looking rocks that lined the shoreline past the cove to the north, east and south. A small stream trickled from between the rocks and ran a snaking line through the sand to the ocean.

They set up camp. This would be home for a while. Emerson and Ana went on reconnaissance trips to collect useful artifacts and get a better idea of the surrounding land. They built a shelter to the side of the shuttle. It eventually grew into a house with many rooms. The recon trips became a regular habit even after everything was set up. They went together one day each week. Besides collecting cool stuff, the two learned about each other's pasts and dreams. Emerson brought snacks, jerky, and iced tea. Ana finished eating a strip and suddenly turned pale. She ran to the head and threw up.

"Damn," she said, "No more jerky for me. Once I yak something up, I'm done with it."

Emerson looked at her slyly. "You still drink hooch. I clearly remember you getting sick on it."

"That was another life."

"You sure you're not getting sick?"

"Who would I catch something from, huh? We haven't seen another human in months."

"You do have a certain glow to you."

"Fuck you, Emerson. I'm not pregnant. I can't be pregnant. Christ. I've never had a period."

"Dr. Pam didn't have the kind of diagnostics she would need to determine a woman's sterility. She just supposed that you were sterile because so many other women are."

"I'm twenty-seven, Emerson. Believe me, I'm not fucking pregnant."

"The Black has a medical diagnostic system that would detect pregnancy—I've been thinking we should all get a blood scan anyway, make sure we haven't contracted some manufactured illness from zombie mosquitos." She laughed. He said, "I'm serious. They're real."

◆

Everyone got a finger jab. The results were pages long and highlighted potential abnormalities. Emerson's blood sugar was a little high. Quinn's calcium and estrogen were depleted. Elli was a little anemic, and Ana was pregnant.

Ana said, "What the ever-loving fuck is this? I'm sterile."

Elli said, "Apparently not."

Quinn laughed. "Maybe it's you, Emerson. Maybe your superior DNA produces mega-sperm." Elli laughed with her.

Eventually, Emerson laughed too. "Probably has more to do with the fact that I didn't eat that crap they call food in The City for most of my life." Mule slept near the fire on the beach in the fading light. The sunsets were always glorious on the beach, and it hadn't rained since they got there. Emerson thought, *Not a bad place to spark a different kind of civilization.*

END OF BOOK ONE: CONNECTION

ACKNOWLEDGMENTS

We can never thank all those beings who have had a positive effect on our lives and our projects. Those who have brought us to this place. You know who you are. We thank the living earth on which we live and breathe together.

That said, this project would never have happened without the expert assistance of Paper Raven Books. They are professional and personable, knowledgeable, and attentive. We thank our advisors and colleagues at Goddard College, Prescott College, and Portland State University, who ushered us toward becoming our best selves. If only every relationship in life were as satisfying.

High thanks go to our immediate family—the folks living with us day to day through two years of COVID. We know the difficulties. We could not have done this without your support.

Thank you to our first readers. Your feedback went into smoothing the rough corners of the Interface story. We appreciate every word, even when we could not always take your advice. We appreciate the time you took out of your busy lives, especially when the work was in its unfinished raw phases. Your input has been valued and deeply appreciated. We are grateful for your friendship and are glad you enjoyed the story.

The next installment of *Interface* will be along shortly.

Contact the author and learn more at **rkhillhouse.com**.
1280 Lexington Ave Front 2 #1288 New York, NY 10028

Made in United States
Orlando, FL
24 November 2024